CHARLES DICKENS

BARNABY RUDGE

A TALE OF THE RIOTS OF 'EIGHTY

I

Introduction by
Kathleen Tillotson

HERON BOOKS

*The introduction to this book
was originally published for the
Oxford Illustrated Dickens,
published by
the Oxford University Press*

I.S.B.N. for this volume:
0 86225 104 4

*Illustrations by
George Cattermole and Hablot K. Browne ('Phiz')*

*Printed in England by
Hazell Watson & Viney Limited
Aylesbury, Bucks*

CHARLES DICKENS

COMPLETE
WORKS

CENTENNIAL EDITION

Charles Dickens

INTRODUCTION

Barnaby Rudge *was the fifth of Dickens's novels to be publish-ed, but had nothing interfered with his original plan it would have been the first. Instead of coming out in the threepenny numbers of* Master Humphrey's Clock *in 1841, it would have appeared in all the traditional dignity of 'three compact individual wollumes' at the end of 1836, when Mr. Pickwick had progressed no farther than Ipswich. That, at least, was the agreement made in May with* Macrone, *publisher of* Sketches by Boz. *What interfered was the soaring circulation of* Pickwick; *by July a contract for an outright payment of £ 200 and an edition of a thousand copies, welcome enough for the young beginner, could only seem derisory. The agreement was cancelled and the projected novel (its title changed from* Gabriel Vardon, the Locksmith of London *to* Barnaby Rudge, a tale of the Riots of '80*) transferred to Bentley. In Sep-tember 1837 its delivery was promised by October 1838; but this was soon found incompatible with the claims of serial writing, and the next project, to run* Barnaby *as a monthly serial in* Bentley's Miscellany *in 1839–40, also broke down. It was postponed again to January 1840 ('as a novel, and not in portions'); in the follow-*

in July transferred to Chapman and Hall as a novel 'sufficient for ten monthly numbers', and finally appeared weekly in the Clock[1] from February to November 1841. This complicated and harassing history has a more than biographical interest; the novel was affected by the change of form, and still more by its exceptionally long period of incubation. Dickens's persistence in his plan for 'a tale of the Riots of' 80' is evidence of his tenacity of purpose and the grip of the original idea on his imagination; not, as has been suggested, of the grudging performance of a task. There were difficulties; being committed to the Clock, he had to begin with all his 'thoughts and interest hanging about' the just-concluded Old Curiosity Shop; and to the last he was, as he told his readers, 'often cramped and confined in a very irksome degree' by the short weekly instalments: 'I have wanted you to know more at once than I could tell you; and it has frequently been of the greatest importance to my cherished intention, that you should do so.'[2] But after 'warming up' in the middle chapters, he could write to Forster: 'I was always sure I could make a good thing of Barnaby, and I think you'll find it comes out strong to the last vord. . . . I am in great heart and spirits with the story.'

What was the original idea? We know from the Preface that Dickens began with the object of writing about the Gordon Riots, which he saw as new material for fiction,[3] 'presenting many very extraordinary and remarkable features'. This means that in 1836 Dickens set out to write a serious historical novel, and by his choice of subject challenged comparison with Scott – not, as is sometimes suggested, with his friend Ainsworth, whose Jack Sheppard did not appear till 1839–40. The storming of the Tolbooth in the opening chapters of The Heart of Mid-Lothian is the literary inspiration of his central scene, and Madge Wildfire of his central figure – who also recalls (especially in appearance) Davie Gellatley, the daft servant in Waverley.

All this, however, is secondary to the direct inspiration of Newgate itself, both as place and symbol. Its exterior was a familiar

[1] Nos. 46–87.

[2] 'To the Readers', October 1841; never reprinted.

[3] Thomas Gaspey's The Mystery (3 vols., 1820) was evidently not known to him.

INTRODUCTION

and awesome sight to Dickens as a schoolboy.[1] *In 1835 he visited it, in order to write a description for the collected* Sketches by Boz[2], *and was struck by the aspect and the imagined suffering of three condemned men, of whom two, he learnt, were afterwards executed, and one respited during his majesty's pleasure. There is the germ of chapters 76–77 of* Barnaby. *His essay also emphasized the massiveness of the walls and gates, the hopelessness of escape; a perception closely connected with his triumphant letter of September 1841: 'I have just burnt into Newgate, and am going in the next number to tear the prisoners out by the hair of their heads.' It was this incident in the Riots which, I believe, first fired his interest in the subject. In contemporary accounts, the burning of Newgate appears more terrifying than all the attacks upon Catholic chapels and property in its expression of the lawlessness of the mob; and to the next generation it carried the shadow of a greater historic event, the fall of the Bastille. Dickens's imagination was also stirred by a rumoured scheme of violence still more terrifying – the release of the lunatics from Bedlam. This, along with the mad streak in Gordon's own character, contributed to his conception of Barnaby; at one time he had even thought of making good the rumour, and showing three Bedlamites as the unsuspected leaders of the rioters. Forster's sober counsels deterred him, and indeed the ironic social point is better made by his actual choice of leaders – Hugh, the bastard of a fine gentleman and a gipsy hanged at Tyburn; Barnaby, the imbecile son of a murderer; and Dennis, the public hangman.*

Dickens went to see Bedlam in 1836 and this, with his second visit to Newgate and the two titles of the projected novel, suggest that the outline of his main design was already formed. The writing, however, is not known to have begun until the autumn of 1839; by February 1840 two chapters were written, substantially chapters 1–3 of the published novel, and providing clear evidence of an elaborated plan for the whole. In January 1841 he revised and redivided the two opening chapters. Thereafter he wrote mainly from week to week.

The five years' delay between design and publication had in-

[1] Sketches by Boz, *ch. 24.*
[2] *Ibid., ch. 25.*

creased the novel's topicality. At any time in the 30s and 40s, it would have suggested (as most historical novels did) 'new foes with old faces', for the revolution that never happened seemed always imminent. But the events of 1836–41 made the novel almost journalistically apt. The Poor Law riots, the Chartist risings at Devizes, Birmingham, and Sheffield, the mass meetings on Kersal Moor and Kennington Common, and most pointed of all, the Newport rising of 1839 with its attempt to release Chartist prisoners – all these, with their aftermath of trials, convictions, and petitions against the punishment of death, gave special point in 1841 to 'a tale of the Riots of '80'. The imperfections of the historical parallel, the vital difference between agitation directed to limited and specific ends, and the madness of the underworld let loose, were less obvious then than now. What most often repeats itself in history is the fear that history will do so. Dickens was responding not to enlightened historical analysis, but to the average man's horror of looted chapels and distilleries, armed robbery in the streets, prisons and mansions ablaze – sights imprinted ineffaceably upon the memories of many living individuals, and the family memories of thousands more.

There were other topical parallels. 'It is a common but dangerous error', wrote Thomas Hood[1], rebuking Dickens for a too charitable view of Gordon, 'to attribute all moral to mental obliquities.' The question of criminal responsibility and degrees of insanity had been newly raised by the 1840 trial of Edward Oxford, who shot at the Queen and was found guilty but insane. (Three years later the McNaghten rules were framed.) Dickens recognized that in the popular mind madness, crime, and revolutionary agitation ran into and coloured each other; but he saw the need for discrimination, and suggests it by his emphasis on Gordon's abnormality and the reprieve of Barnaby. These questions are also related to the growing pressure of capital punishment, and especially of public executions, upon the conscience of the thoughtful; Courvoisier's execution and Thackeray's harrowing account of it in 'Going to See a Man Hanged'[2] are also part of the contemporary context of Barnaby.

[1] Athenaeum, *22 January 1842.*

[2] Fraser's Magazine, *1840.*

INTRODUCTION

Dickens gives most emphasis to the dangers of the unscrupulous exploiting of Protestant bigotry, and the timely relevance of this warning is less likely to be grasped by modern readers. But his contemporaries were well aware of the Protestant Association, newly founded in 1839, with local branches for 'operatives', great meetings in Exeter Hall, and petitions to the government against favours supposedly shown to Catholics, especially in education. Though violent only in language, and dissociating itself emphatically from social agitation, it gave grounds, not least by its defence of the Association of 1779–80[1], for fears of another 'false religious cry'. The unexpected religious animus in the novel also expresses Dickens's general dislike of puritanism, whether in Little Bethel or the 'Protestant Manual'; as a defender of the humble, he strikes a blow for the domestic happiness of Mrs. Nubbles and of Gabriel Varden. In Mrs. Varden (and Mr. Chester) he must have had his eye especially on the Evangelicals; Crabb Robinson noted in his diary that 'Dickens will lose popularity with the saints, for he too faithfully exposes cant'. Thomas Hood, in his review, comparing 1841 with 1780, saw 'the same – nay, a worse fanatical demon abroad ... a Zeal-of-the-Land Busy' attacking 'Art, Science, Literature, the Drama and all other public amusements'; which alone would explain Dickens's bias in making all his 'Protestants' objectionable. Ten years later he would have had other axes to grind, and would hardly have drawn the Catholics Langdale and Haredale sympathetically: indeed, 1841 was only just in time. During that year the waves from Oxford (Tract 90 was published in March) were to reach London; early in 1842 Dickens's friends in Punch were attacking the 'Pussyites'.[2]

Barnaby, then, is related to the events and mood of the exact years of its writing and publication. Further, as a novel of recent history, history at the ideal distance of 'sixty years since'[3], it drew support from the memories, oral and written, of men living or recently dead. One passage (at the end of ch. 65) suggests that Dickens had talked to eyewitnesses, and he is likely to have read many recently published reminiscences – those, for instance, of

[1] Protestant Magazine, *January 1840.*

[2] *'Punch's Pencillings', no. xxxii (vol. ii, p. 109).*

[3] *See the defence in* Waverley, *ch. 1.*

*Frederick Reynolds the actor (1827; d. 1841) and Henry Angelo
(1828; d. 1839). He would read too the published letters of Dr.
Johnson, Horace Walpole, and Crabbe; and if he wanted general
inspiration for description of mob violence, there was Carlyle's*
French Revolution *(1837), 'that wonderful book'. But his main
sources were undoubtedly the brilliantly written* Narrative of
'William Vincent' *(Thomas Holcroft)[1], and the reports in the
newspapers.[2]*

*Dickens's use of his historical sources, which has never received
the detailed consideration it deserves, can only be summarized here.
What is most remarkable in his powerful narrative of the riots
(chs. 36–73) is the way he combines fidelity to fact with the doings
of his fictitious characters. He adds, but never falsifies. The main
events of eight days (2 June to 9 June) are all brought in, with
accurate particulars of time and place; almost every action as-
cribed to the mob in London or to unnamed individuals is factual,
down to such telling anecdotes as the burning of the canary-birds
and the young man hanged in Bishopsgate. The* Thunderer *and*
England in Blood *really existed, some released Newgate convicts
did return voluntarily to the jail, and the attack on the Bank was
led by a man on 'a brewer's horse ... caparisoned with fetters'. The
break into Newgate and the burning of Langdale's distillery are
described often in the very words of contemporary accounts. No
rioters are known to have gone as far as Chigwell, but several
country mansions were threatened, and the mob's attempt 'to burn
the Warren' (i.e. the Woolwich Arsenal) probably gave Mr. Haredale's house its name. General Conway, Sir John Fielding, Lord
Mansfield, Akerman the keeper of Newgate, and the Lord Mayor
acted or suffered just as Dickens describes. The appearance, manner, and after-history of Gordon, and some of his words (as in the
warrant of protection conveyed to Gabriel Varden) are faithfully
given, and Dickens's interpretation of his character and actions,
coloured by Robert Watson's* Life *(1795), represents at least a
legitimate reading of the evidence.*

For the actions and motives of other characters, fact and fiction

---

[1] *See the Bibliography in J.P. de Castro,* The Gordon Riots *(1926), for
this and other contemporary pamphlets.*
[2] *They are named in ch. 39.*

are mingled in varying proportions. At one end of the scale is Mr. Langdale, historic except for his dealings with the invented characters; at the other, Gabriel Varden, whose valiant refusal to break the lock of Newgate is based on the resistance of a Moravian blacksmith, urged under threats to strike off the prisoners' irons. Dickens may have noticed that idiots, gipsies, apprentices, and a 'one-armed-man' were among the rioters; and he surely caught hints for Miggs and Sim from a description of 'debating societies' with 'female orators' and the 'apprentice' who spent the night 'in rehearsing harangues' and 'wasted the day (the property of his master)' in dreams of political power.[1] In two characters, Gashford and Dennis, the interweaving of fact and fiction is especially curious, and in the former case still a matter of conjecture. Something is borrowed from the career of the secretary Robert Watson (whose suicide was fully reported in 1838) and the treachery of James Fisher; but Gashford exists mainly as an ingenious means of connecting Dickens's sympathetic interpretation of Gordon with his view of the riots. His plot and his picture alike require a cold-blooded villain manœuvring in the dark, and the presence of such an agent is a plausible reading of events. With Dennis he worked more imaginatively. The presence of 'Edward Dennis, the public hangman' among the rioters convicted of helping to burn a private house, was sufficient basis: Dickens's sense of ironic fitness extended Dennis's activities to Newgate, had him hanged instead of respited, and elaborated his craftsman's pride in his calling in a way both diverting and horrible. In him Dickens continues the studies of evil begun in Sikes and Quilp. But Dennis, though a grotesque, is less of a bogy-man than Quilp, and more closely related to the themes of the novel. He embodies Dickens's open concern with the social horror of hanging and his less conscious obsession with the man about to be hanged; and he also derives something from literary tradition – from the first chapter of Charles Whitehead's Autobiography of Jack Ketch, *and, more generally, from the irony of* Jonathan Wild.

Dickens's complex intentions are fulfilled in the almost allegorical juxtaposition of Dennis, Hugh, and Barnaby, and their dis-

---

[1] Fanaticism and Treason *(anon.; new edition, 1780), p. 22.*

criminated attitudes to violence and death. Through Hugh and
Barnaby the fictitious and historical parts of the novel are firmly
related; and they, perhaps alone of the invented characters, gain in
interest under the pressure of public events. Dickens's slow approach to his historical subject, though it has many advantages,
brings certain difficulties. The first third of the novel is all fiction:
the Haredale-Rudge murder mystery and Mr. Chester's intrigues,
diversified with the domestic comedy of the Willet and Varden
households, are set out in a leisurely way without much 'period'
colouring and with hardly a hint of history to come. Then, after a
silent lapse of five years, the tide of history advances, slowly at first,
then with increasing force, involving all the characters; as it re-
cedes, the mystery is resolved, and the nemesis, tragic and comic,
fulfilled. Although the mystery-plot could be detached (as was done
in two dramatic versions, presented before publication was complete), it loses thereby much of its interest, for Dickens's integra-
tion of the two main lines of narrative, which, as we realize later,
he is quietly preparing throughout the early chapters, is excellently
managed. By reserving the history till later he conveys the irony of
the common assumption that private lives are immune from public
events, an irony pointed by his presentation of the same scene
under two different lights; the snugness of the Maypole makes us
share John Willet's sense of its devastation as an almost personal
insult, while we also enjoy the nicely contrived nemesis by which
'history' converts the innkeeper from invincible stupidity to imbecile stupor, and from petty tyranny to submissiveness. But the
change in tempo in the middle chapters is exacting, and the rush of
events in what Dickens called 'the thick of the story' made him
chafe at his 'want' of 'elbow-room'. Whether he realized it or not,
he also missed the elbow-room needed by such superb comic in-
ventions as Sim Tappertit and Miggs. They continue to appear,
but something of their vital essence is lost. For their native country
is the happy Alsatia of comic speech, in perpetual anticipation of
violent action; and Sim grinding Varden's tools with 'Something
will come of this. I hope it mayn't be human gore' or contemplating
his own legs – 'If they're a dream, let sculptures have such visions' – is preferable even to Sim displaying a Bishop's tooth as
his trophy from Westminster.

XIV

This apart, the novel has a remarkable unity of feeling; though it would have gained, as Poe[1] saw, from more unity of place and time. And Poe was surely right in feeling 'disappointed' with Barnaby himself. He noted 'opportunities missed' in the raven (which was to inspire his poem) and in Barnaby's 'horror of blood' which he called 'inconsequential'. Dickens is up against the difficulty of displaying inborn insanity in a major character. Barnaby is generally either too coherent (like the hero of 'The Madman's Manuscript' in Pickwick) or else recalls the theatrical stereotypes of lunacy. In his relation to his mother there is a hint of Wordsworthian pathos; for the rest, we admire the conception (as in his lonely patrol at the Boot and his light-hearted facing of death) but find the details implausible because over-picturesque. Not by feathers in the hair and pet ravens did Dickens achieve the psychological and poetic truth of Mr. Dick and Mr. F.'s Aunt. Barnaby must finally be accepted less as a study of individual character than as an expression of the Dickensian compassion for the helpless and exploited.

The manuscript of the novel (in the Forster collection), which is marked up by the printer, shows at times considerable differences from the printed text; the proof-sheets are missing. Each serial-part consisted of 16½ 'slips', which, allowing for illustrations, made a 12-page weekly number. The serial-divisions can easily be traced in a modern edition, since with two exceptions (no. 46 = ch. 1, no. 52 = ch. 12) each number contained two chapters.

Dickens wrote a new Preface for the edition of 1849, quoting part of the original Preface of November 1841, and further revised this in 1858 and 1868.

1953   Kathleen Tillotson

---

[1] Works *(1871 ed.), iii; reprinted from* Graham's Magazine, *February 1842.*

PREFACE

The late Mr. Waterton having, some time ago, expressed his opinion that ravens are gradually becoming extinct in England, I offered the few following words about my experience of these birds.

The raven in this story is a compound of two great originals, of whom I was, at different times, the proud possessor. The first was in the bloom of his youth, when he was discovered in a modest retirement in London, by a friend of mine, and given to me. He had from the first, as Sir Hugh Evans says of Anne Page, " good gifts," which he improved by study and attention in a most exemplary manner. He slept in a stable —generally on horseback—and so terrified a Newfoundland dog by his preternatural sagacity, that he has been known, by the mere superiority of his genius, to walk off unmolested with the dog's dinner, from before his face. He was rapidly rising in acquirements and virtues, when, in an evil hour, his stable was newly painted. He observed the workmen closely, saw that they were careful of the paint, and immediately burned to possess it. On their going to dinner, he ate up all they had left behind, consisting of a pound or two of white lead; and this youthful indiscretion terminated in death.

PREFACE

While I was yet inconsolable for his loss, another friend of mine in Yorkshire discovered an older and more gifted raven at a village public-house, which he prevailed upon the landlord to part with for a consideration, and sent up to me. The first act of this Sage, was, to administer to the effects of his predecessor, by disinterring all the cheese and halfpence he had buried in the garden—a work of immense labour and research, to which he devoted all the energies of his mind. When he had achieved his task, he applied himself to the acquisition of stable language, in which he soon became such an adept, that he would perch outside my window and drive imaginary horses with great skill, all day. Perhaps even I never saw him at his best, for his former master sent his duty with him, "and if I wished the bird to come out very strong, would I be so good as to show him a drunken man" —which I never did, having (unfortunately) none but sober people at hand. But I could hardly have respected him more, whatever the stimulating influences of this sight might have been. He had not the least respect, I am sorry to say, for me in return, or for anybody but the cook; to whom he was attached—but only, I fear, as a Policeman might have been. Once, I met him unexpectedly, about half-a-mile from my house, walking down the middle of a public street, attended by a pretty large crowd, and spontaneously exhibiting the whole of his accomplishments. His gravity under those trying circumstances, I can never forget, nor the extraordinary gallantry with which, refusing to be brought home, he defended himself behind a pump, until overpowered by numbers. It may have been that he was too bright a genius to live long, or it may have been that he took some pernicious substance into his bill, and thence into his maw— which is not improbable, seeing that he new-pointed the greater part of the garden-wall by digging out the mortar, broke countless squares of glass by scraping away the putty all round the frames, and tore up and swallowed, in splinters, the greater part of a wooden staircase of six steps and a landing—but after some three years he too was taken ill, and died before the kitchen fire. He kept his eye to the last upon the meat as it roasted, and suddenly turned over on his back with a sepulchral cry of "Cuckoo!" Since then I have been ravenless.

No account of the Gordon Riots having been to my knowledge introduced into any Work of Fiction, and the subject presenting very extraordinary and remarkable features, I was led to project this Tale.

It is unnecessary to say, that those shameful tumults, while they reflect indelible disgrace upon the time in which they occurred, and all who had act or part in them, teach a good lesson. That what we falsely call a religious cry is easily raised by men who have no religion, and who in their daily practice set at nought the commonest principles of right and wrong; that it is begotten of intolerance and persecution; that it is senseless, besotted, inveterate and unmerciful; all History teaches us. But perhaps we do not know it in our hearts too well, to profit by even so humble an example as the "No Popery" riots of Seventeen Hundred and Eighty.

However imperfectly those disturbances are set forth in the following pages, they are impartially painted by one who has no sympathy with the Romish Church, though he acknowledges as most men do, some esteemed friends among the followers of its creed.

In the description of the principal outrages, reference has been had to the best authorities of that time, such as they

PREFACE.

are; the account given in this Tale, of all the main features of the Riots, is substantially correct.

Mr. Dennis's allusions to the flourishing condition of his trade in those days, have their foundation in Truth, and not in the Author's fancy. Any file of old Newspapers, or odd volume of the Annual Register, will prove this with terrible ease.

Even the case of Mary Jones, dwelt upon with so much pleasure by the same character, is no effort of invention. The facts were stated, exactly as they are stated here, in the House of Commons. Whether they afforded as much entertainment to the merry gentlemen assembled there, as some other most affecting circumstances of a similar nature mentioned by Sir Samuel Romilly, is not recorded.

That the case of Mary Jones may speak the more emphatically for itself, I subjoin it, as related by Sir William Meredith in a speech in Parliament, "on Frequent Executions," made in 1777.

"Under this act," the Shop-lifting Act, "one Mary Jones was executed, whose case I shall just mention; it was at the time when press warrants were issued, on the alarm about Falkland Islands. The woman's husband was pressed, their goods seized for some debts of his, and she, with two small children, turned into the streets a-begging. It is a circumstance not to be forgotten, that she was very young (under nineteen), and most remarkably handsome. She went to a linen-draper's shop, took some coarse linen off the counter, and slipped it under her cloak; the shopman saw her, and she laid it down: for this she was hanged. Her defence was (I have the trial in my pocket), 'that she had lived in credit, and wanted for nothing, till a press-gang came and stole her husband from her; but since then, she had no bed to lie on;

nothing to give her children to eat ; and they were almost
naked ; and perhaps she might have done something wrong,
for she hardly knew what she did.' The parish officers testified
the truth of this story ; but it seems, there had been a good
deal of shop-lifting about Ludgate ; an example was thought
necessary ; and this woman was hanged for the comfort and
satisfaction of shopkeepers in Ludgate Street. When brought
to receive sentence, she behaved in such a frantic manner, as
proved her mind to be in a distracted and desponding state ;
and the child was suckling at her breast when she set out for
Tyburn."

CHAPTER I

In the year 1775, there stood upon the borders of Epping Forest, at a distance of about twelve miles from London—measuring from the Standard in Cornhill, or rather from the spot on or near to which the Standard used to be in days of yore—a house of public entertainment called the Maypole; which fact was demonstrated to all such travellers as could neither read nor write (and at that time a vast number both of travellers and stay-at-homes were in this condition) by the emblem reared on the roadside over against the house, which, if not of those goodly proportions that Maypoles were wont to present in olden times, was a fair young ash, thirty feet in height, and straight as any arrow that ever English yeoman drew.

BARNABY RUDGE

The Maypole—by which term from henceforth is meant the house, and not its sign—the Maypole was an old building, with more gable ends than a lazy man would care to count on a sunny day; huge zig-zag chimneys, out of which it seemed as though even smoke could not choose but come in more than naturally fantastic shapes, imparted to it in its tortuous progress; and vast stables, gloomy, ruinous, and empty. The place was said to have been built in the days of King Henry the Eighth; and there was a legend, not only that Queen Elizabeth had slept there one night while upon a hunting excursion, to wit, in a certain oak-panelled room with a deep bay window, but that next morning, while standing on a mounting block before the door with one foot in the stirrup, the virgin monarch had then and there boxed and cuffed an unlucky page for some neglect of duty. The matter-of-fact and doubtful folks, of whom there were a few among the Maypole customers, as unluckily there always are in every little community, were inclined to look upon this tradition as rather apocryphal; but, whenever the landlord of that ancient hostelry appealed to the mounting block itself as evidence, and triumphantly pointed out that there it stood in the same place to that very day, the doubters never failed to be put down by a large majority, and all true believers exulted as in a victory.

Whether these, and many other stories of the like nature, were true or untrue, the Maypole was really an old house, a very old house, perhaps as old as it claimed to be, and perhaps older, which will sometimes happen with houses of an uncertain, as with ladies of a certain, age. Its windows were old diamond-pane lattices, its floors were sunken and uneven, its ceilings blackened by the hand of time, and heavy with massive beams. Over the doorway was an ancient porch, quaintly and grotesquely carved; and here on summer evenings the more favoured customers smoked and drank—ay, and sang many a good song too, sometimes—reposing on two grim-looking high-backed settles, which, like the twin dragons of some fairy tale, guarded the entrance to the mansion.

In the chimneys of the disused rooms, swallows had built their nests for many a long year, and from earliest spring to latest autumn whole colonies of sparrows chirped and twittered in the eaves. There were more pigeons about the dreary stable yard and out-buildings than anybody but the landlord could reckon up. The wheeling and circling flights of runts, fantails, tumblers, and pouters, were perhaps not quite consistent with the grave and sober character of the building, but the monotonous cooing, which never ceased to be raised by some among them all day long, suited it exactly, and seemed to lull it to rest. With its overhanging stories, drowsy little panes of glass, and front bulging out and projecting over the pathway, the old house looked as if it were nodding in its sleep. Indeed, it needed no very great stretch of fancy to detect in it other resemblances to humanity. The bricks of which it was built had originally been a deep dark red, but had grown yellow and discoloured like an old man's skin; the sturdy timbers had decayed like teeth; and here and there the ivy, like a warm garment to comfort it in its age, wrapt its green leaves closely round the time-worn walls.

It was a hale and hearty age though, still: and in the summer or autumn evenings, when the glow of the setting sun fell upon the oak and chestnut trees of the adjacent forest, the old house, partaking of its lustre, seemed their fit companion, and to have many good years of life in him yet.

The evening with which we have to do, was neither a summer nor an autumn one, but the twilight of a day in March, when the wind howled dismally among the bare branches of the trees, and rumbling in the wide chimneys and driving the rain against the windows of the Maypole Inn, gave such of its frequenters as chanced to be there at the moment an undeniable reason for prolonging their stay, and caused the landlord to prophesy that the night would

3

certainly clear at eleven o'clock precisely,—which by a remarkable coincidence was the hour at which he always closed his house.

The name of him upon whom the spirit of prophecy thus descended was John Willet, a burly, large-headed man with a fat face, which betokened profound obstinacy and slowness of apprehension, combined with a very strong reliance upon his own merits. It was John Willet's ordinary boast in his more placid moods that if he were slow he was sure ; which assertion could, in one sense at least, be by no means gainsaid, seeing that he was in everything unquestionably the reverse of fast, and withal one of the most dogged and positive fellows in existence—always sure that what he thought or said or did was right, and holding it as a thing quite settled and ordained by the laws of nature and Providence, that anybody who said or did or thought otherwise must be inevitably and of necessity wrong.

Mr. Willet walked slowly up to the window, flattened his fat nose against the cold glass, and shading his eyes that his sight might not be affected by the ruddy glow of the fire, looked abroad. Then he walked slowly back to his old seat in the chimney corner, and, composing himself in it with a slight shiver, such as a man might give way to and so acquire an additional relish for the warm blaze, said, looking round upon his guests :

"It'll clear at eleven o'clock. No sooner and no later. Not before and not arterwards."

"How do you make out that?" said a little man in the opposite corner. "The moon is past the full, and she rises at nine."

John looked sedately and solemnly at his questioner until he had brought his mind to bear upon the whole of his observation, and then made answer, in a tone which seemed to imply that the moon was peculiarly his business and nobody else's :

"Never you mind about the moon. Don't you trouble

yourself about her. You let the moon alone, and I'll let you alone."

"No offence I hope?" said the little man.

Again John waited leisurely until the observation had thoroughly penetrated to his brain, and then replying, "No offence *as yet*," applied a light to his pipe and smoked in placid silence; now and then casting a sidelong look at a man wrapped in a loose riding-coat with huge cuffs ornamented with tarnished silver lace and large metal buttons, who sat apart from the regular frequenters of the house, and wearing a hat flapped over his face, which was still further shaded by the hand on which his forehead rested, looked unsociable enough.

There was another guest, who sat, booted and spurred, at some distance from the fire also, and whose thoughts—to judge from his folded arms and knitted brows, and from the untasted liquor before him—were occupied with other matters than the topics under discussion or the persons who discussed them. This was a young man of about eight-and-twenty, rather above the middle height, and though of a somewhat slight figure, gracefully and strongly made. He wore his own dark hair, and was accoutred in a riding-dress, which together with his large boots (resembling in shape and fashion those worn by our Life Guardsmen at the present day), showed indisputable traces of the bad condition of the roads. But travel-stained though he was, he was well and even richly attired, and without being over-dressed looked a gallant gentleman.

Lying upon the table beside him, as he had carelessly thrown them down, were a heavy riding-whip and a slouched hat, the latter worn no doubt as being best suited to the inclemency of the weather. There, too, were a pair of pistols in a holster-case, and a short riding-cloak. Little of his face was visible, except the long dark lashes which concealed his downcast eyes, but an air of careless ease and natural gracefulness of demeanour pervaded the figure, and seemed to

5

comprehend even those slight accessories, which were all handsome, and in good keeping.

Towards this young gentleman the eyes of Mr. Willet wandered but once, and then as if in mute inquiry whether he had observed his silent neighbour. It was plain that John and the young gentleman had often met before. Finding that his look was not returned, or indeed observed by the person to whom it was addressed, John gradually concentrated the whole power of his eyes into one focus, and brought it to bear upon the man in the flapped hat, at whom he came to stare in course of time with an intensity so remarkable, that it affected his fireside cronies, who all, as with one accord, took their pipes from their lips, and stared with open mouths at the stranger likewise.

The sturdy landlord had a large pair of dull fish-like eyes, and the little man who had hazarded the remark about the moon (and who was the parish-clerk and bell-ringer of Chigwell; a village hard by) had little round black shiny eyes like beads; moreover this little man wore at the knees of his rusty black breeches, and on his rusty black coat, and all down his long flapped waistcoat, little queer buttons like nothing except his eyes; but so like them, that as they twinkled and glistened in the light of the fire, which shone too in his bright shoe-buckles, he seemed all eyes from head to foot, and to be gazing with every one of them at the unknown customer. No wonder that a man should grow restless under such an inspection as this, to say nothing of the eyes belonging to short Tom Cobb the general chandler and post-office keeper, and long Phil Parkes the ranger, both of whom, infected by the example of their companions, regarded him of the flapped hat no less attentively.

The stranger became restless; perhaps from being exposed to this raking fire of eyes, perhaps from the nature of his previous meditations—most probably from the latter cause, for as he changed his position and looked hastily round, he started to find himself the object of such keen regard, and

6

darted an angry and suspicious glance at the fireside group. It had the effect of immediately diverting all eyes to the chimney, except those of John Willet, who finding himself,

as it were, caught in the fact, and not being (as has been already observed) of a very ready nature, remained staring at his guest in a particularly awkward and disconcerted manner.

"Well?" said the stranger.

Well. There was not much in well. It was not a long speech. "I thought you gave an order," said the landlord, after a pause of two or three minutes for consideration.

The stranger took off his hat, and disclosed the hard features of a man of sixty or thereabouts, much weather-beaten and worn by time, and the naturally harsh expression of which was not improved by a dark handkerchief which was bound tightly round his head, and, while it served the purpose of a wig, shaded his forehead, and almost hid his eyebrows. If it were intended to conceal or divert attention from a deep gash, now healed into an ugly seam, which when it was first inflicted must have laid bare his cheekbone, the object was but indifferently attained, for it could scarcely fail to be noted at a glance. His complexion was of a cadaverous hue, and he had a grizzly jagged beard of some three weeks' date. Such was the figure (very meanly and poorly clad) that now rose from the seat, and stalking across the room sat down in a corner of the chimney, which the politeness or fears of the little clerk very readily assigned to him.

"A highwayman!" whispered Tom Cobb to Parkes the ranger.

"Do you suppose highwaymen don't dress handsomer than that?" replied Parkes. "It's a better business than you think for, Tom, and highwaymen don't need or use to be shabby, take my word for it."

Meanwhile the subject of their speculations had done due honour to the house by calling for some drink, which was promptly supplied by the landlord's son Joe, a broad-shouldered strapping young fellow of twenty, whom it pleased his father still to consider a little boy, and to treat accordingly. Stretching out his hands to warm them by the blazing fire, the man turned his head towards the company, and after running his eye sharply over them, said in a voice well suited to his appearance:

8

"What house is that which stands a mile or so from here?"

"Public-house?" said the landlord, with his usual deliberation.

"Public-house, father!" exclaimed Joe, "where's the public-house within a mile or so of the Maypole? He means the great house—the Warren—naturally and of course. The old red brick house, sir, that stands in its own grounds—?"

"Aye," said the stranger.

"And that fifteen or twenty years ago stood in a park five times as broad, which with other and richer property has bit by bit changed hands and dwindled away—more's the pity!" pursued the young man.

"Maybe," was the reply. "But my question related to the owner. What it has been I don't care to know, and what it is I can see for myself."

The heir-apparent to the Maypole pressed his finger on his lips, and glancing at the young gentleman already noticed, who had changed his attitude when the house was first mentioned, replied in a lower tone,

"The owner's name is Haredale, Mr. Geoffrey Haredale, and"—again he glanced in the same direction as before—"and a worthy gentleman too—hem!"

Paying as little regard to this admonitory cough, as to the significant gesture that had preceded it, the stranger pursued his questioning.

"I turned out of my way coming here, and took the foot-path that crosses the grounds. Who was the young lady that I saw entering a carriage? His daughter?"

"Why, how should I know, honest man?" replied Joe, contriving in the course of some arrangements about the hearth, to advance close to his questioner and pluck him by the sleeve, "*I* didn't see the young lady you know. Whew! There's the wind again—*and* rain—well it *is* a night!"

"Rough weather indeed!" observed the strange man.

"You're used to it?" said Joe, catching at anything which seemed to promise a diversion of the subject.

"Pretty well," returned the other. "About the young lady—has Mr. Haredale a daughter?"

"No, no," said the young fellow fretfully, "he's a single gentleman—he's—be quiet, can't you, man? Don't you see this talk is not relished yonder?"

Regardless of this whispered remonstrance, and affecting not to hear it, his tormentor provokingly continued:

"Single men have had daughters before now. Perhaps she may be his daughter, though he is not married."

"What do you mean?" said Joe, adding in an under tone as he approached him again, "You'll come in for it presently, I know you will!"

"I mean no harm"—returned the traveller boldly, "and have said none that I know of. I ask a few questions—as any stranger may, and not unnaturally—about the inmates of a remarkable house in a neighbourhood which is new to me, and you are as aghast and disturbed as if I were talking treason against King George. Perhaps you can tell me why, sir, for (as I say) I am a stranger, and this is Greek to me?"

The latter observation was addressed to the obvious cause of Joe Willet's discomposure, who had risen and was adjusting his riding-cloak preparatory to sallying abroad. Briefly replying that he could give him no information, the young man beckoned to Joe, and handing him a piece of money in payment of his reckoning, hurried out attended by young Willet himself, who taking up a candle followed to light him to the house door.

While Joe was absent on this errand, the elder Willet and his three companions continued to smoke with profound gravity, and in a deep silence, each having his eyes fixed on a huge copper boiler that was suspended over the fire. After some time John Willet slowly shook his head, and thereupon his friends slowly shook theirs; but no man withdrew his

10

eyes from the boiler, or altered the solemn expression of his countenance in the slightest degree.

At length Joe returned—very talkative and conciliatory, as though with a strong presentiment that he was going to be found fault with.

"Such a thing as love is!" he said, drawing a chair near the fire, and looking round for sympathy. "He has set off to walk to London,—all the way to London. His nag gone lame in riding out here this blessed afternoon, and comfortably littered down in our stable at this minute; and he giving up a good hot supper and our best bed, because Miss Haredale has gone to a masquerade up in town, and he has set his heart upon seeing her! I don't think I could persuade myself to do that, beautiful as she is,—but then I'm not in love, (at least I don't think I am,) and that's the whole difference."

"He is in love then?" said the stranger.

"Rather," replied Joe. "He'll never be more in love, and may very easily be less."

"Silence, sir!" cried his father.

"What a chap you are, Joe!" said Long Parkes.

"Such a inconsiderate lad!" murmured Tom Cobb.

"Putting himself forward and wringing the very nose off his own father's face!" exclaimed the parish-clerk, metaphorically.

"What *have* I done?" reasoned poor Joe.

"Silence, sir!" returned his father, "what do you mean by talking, when you see people that are more than two or three times your age, sitting still and silent and not dreaming of saying a word?"

"Why that's the proper time for me to talk, isn't it?" said Joe rebelliously.

"The proper time, sir!" retorted his father, "the proper time's no time."

"Ah to be sure!" muttered Parkes, nodding gravely to the other two who nodded likewise, observing under their breaths that that was the point.

11

"The proper time's no time, sir," repeated John Willet; "when I was your age I never talked, I never wanted to talk. I listened and improved myself, that's what *I* did."

"And you'd find your father rather a tough customer in argeyment, Joe, if anybody was to try and tackle him," said Parkes.

"For the matter o' that, Phil!" observed Mr. Willet, blowing a long, thin, spiral cloud of smoke out of the corner of his mouth, and staring at it abstractedly as it floated away; "For the matter o' that, Phil, argeyment is a gift of Natur. If Natur has gifted a man with powers of argeyment, a man has a right to make the best of 'em, and has not a right to stand on false delicacy, and deny that he is so gifted; for that is a turning of his back on Natur, a flouting of her, a slighting of her precious caskets, and a proving of one's self to be a swine that isn't worth her scattering pearls before."

The landlord pausing here for a very long time, Mr. Parkes' naturally concluded that he had brought his discourse to an end; and therefore, turning to the young man with some austerity, exclaimed:

"You hear what your father says, Joe? You wouldn't much like to tackle him in argeyment, I'm thinking, sir."

"IF," said John Willet, turning his eyes from the ceiling to the face of his interrupter, and uttering the monosyllable in capitals, to apprise him that he had put in his oar, as the vulgar say, with unbecoming and irreverent haste; "IF, sir, Natur has fixed upon me the gift of argeyment, why should I not own to it, and rather glory in the same? Yes, sir, I *am* a tough customer that way. You are right, sir. My toughness has been proved, sir, in this room many and many a time, as I think you know; and if you don't know," added John, putting his pipe in his mouth again, "so much the better, for I an't proud and am not going to tell you."

A general murmur from his three cronies, and a general shaking of heads at the copper boiler, assured John Willet that they had had good experience of his powers and needed no further evidence to assure them of his superiority. John smoked with a little more dignity and surveyed them in silence.

"It's all very fine talking," muttered Joe, who had been fidgeting in his chair with divers uneasy gestures. "But if you mean to tell me that I'm never to open my lips—"

"Silence, sir!" roared his father. "No, you never are. When your opinion's wanted, you give it. When you're spoke to, you speak. When your opinion's not wanted and you're not spoke to, don't give an opinion and don't you speak. The world's undergone a nice alteration since my time, certainly. My belief is that there an't any boys left —that there isn't such a thing as a boy—that there's nothing now between a male baby and a man—and that all the boys went out with his blessed Majesty King George the Second."

"That's a very true observation, always excepting the young princes," said the parish-clerk, who, as the representative of church and state in that company, held himself bound to the nicest loyalty. "If it's godly and righteous for boys, being of the ages of boys, to behave themselves like boys, then the young princes must be boys and cannot be otherwise."

"Did you ever hear tell of mermaids, sir?" said Mr. Willet.

"Certainly I have," replied the clerk.

"Very good," said Mr. Willet. "According to the constitution of mermaids, so much of a mermaid as is not a woman must be a fish. According to the constitution of young princes, so much of a young prince (if anything) as is not actually an angel, must be godly and righteous. Therefore if it's becoming and godly and righteous in the young princes (as it is at their ages) that they should be boys, they are and must be boys, and cannot by possibility be anything else."

BARNABY RUDGE

This elucidation of a knotty point being received with such marks of approval as to put John Willet into a good humour, he contented himself with repeating to his son his command of silence, and addressing the stranger, said :

" If you had asked your questions of a grown-up person— of me or any of these gentlemen—you'd have had some satis- faction, and wouldn't have wasted breath. Miss Haredale is Mr. Geoffrey Haredale's niece."

" Is her father alive ? " said the man, carelessly.

" No," rejoined the landlord, " he is not alive, and he is not dead— "

" Not dead ! " cried the other.

" Not dead in a common sort of way," said the landlord.

The cronies nodded to each other, and Mr. Parkes remarked in an under tone, shaking his head meanwhile as who should say, " let no man contradict me, for I won't believe him," that John Willet was in amazing force to-night, and fit to tackle a Chief Justice.

The stranger suffered a short pause to elapse, and then asked abruptly, " What do you mean ? "

" More than you think for, friend," returned John Willet. " Perhaps there's more meaning in them words than you suspect."

" Perhaps there is," said the strange man, gruffly; " but what the devil do you speak in such mysteries for ? You tell me, first, that a man is not alive, nor yet dead—then, that he's not dead in a common sort of way—then, that you mean a great deal more than I think for. To tell you the truth, you may do that easily ; for so far as I can make out, you mean nothing. What *do* you mean, I ask again ? "

" That," returned the landlord, a little brought down from his dignity by the stranger's surliness, " is a Maypole story, and has been any time these four-and-twenty years. That story is Solomon Daisy's story. It belongs to the house ; and nobody but Solomon Daisy has ever told it under this roof, or ever shall—that's more."

14

THE MAYPOLE STORY

The man glanced at the parish-clerk, whose air of consciousness and importance plainly betokened him to be the person referred to, and, observing that he had taken his pipe from his lips, after a very long whiff to keep it alight, and was evidently about to tell his story without further solicitation, gathered his large coat about him, and shrinking further back was almost lost in the gloom of the spacious chimney corner, except when the flame, struggling from under a great faggot, whose weight almost crushed it for the time, shot upward with a strong and sudden glare, and illumining his figure for a moment, seemed afterwards to cast it into deeper obscurity than before.

By this flickering light, which made the old room, with its heavy timbers and panelled walls, look as if it were built of polished ebony—the wind roaring and howling without, now rattling the latch and creaking the hinges of the stout oaken door, and now driving at the casement as though it would beat it in—by this light, and under circumstances so auspicious, Solomon Daisy began his tale:

"It was Mr. Reuben Haredale, Mr. Geoffrey's elder brother—"

Here he came to a dead stop, and made so long a pause that even John Willet grew impatient and asked why he did not proceed.

"Cobb," said Solomon Daisy, dropping his voice and appealing to the post-office keeper; "what day of the month is this?"

"The nineteenth."

"Of March," said the clerk, bending forward, "the nineteenth of March; that's very strange."

In a low voice they all acquiesced, and Solomon went on:

"It was Mr. Reuben Haredale, Mr. Geoffrey's elder brother, that twenty-two years ago was the owner of the Warren, which, as Joe has said—not that you remember it, Joe, for a boy like you can't do that, but because you have often heard me say so—was then a much larger and better

15

place, and a much more valuable property than it is now. His lady was lately dead, and he was left with one child—the Miss Haredale you have been inquiring about—who was then scarcely a year old."

Although the speaker addressed himself to the man who had shown so much curiosity about this same family, and made a pause here as if expecting some exclamation of surprise or encouragement, the latter made no remark, nor gave any indication that he heard or was interested in what was said. Solomon therefore turned to his old companions, whose noses were brightly illuminated by the deep red glow from the bowls of their pipes; assured, by long experience, of their attention, and resolved to show his sense of such indecent behaviour.

"Mr. Haredale," said Solomon, turning his back upon the strange man, "left this place when his lady died, feeling it lonely like, and went up to London, where he stopped some months; but finding that place as lonely as this—as I suppose and have always heard say—he suddenly came back again with his little girl to the Warren, bringing with him besides, that day, only two women servants, and his steward, and a gardener."

Mr. Daisy stopped to take a whiff at his pipe, which was going out, and then proceeded—at first in a snuffling tone, occasioned by keen enjoyment of the tobacco and strong pulling at the pipe, and afterwards with increasing distinctness:

"—Bringing with him two women servants, and his steward, and a gardener. The rest stopped behind up in London, and were to follow next day. It happened that that night, an old gentleman who lived at Chigwell-row, and had long been poorly, deceased, and an order came to me at half after twelve o'clock at night to go and toll the passing-bell."

There was a movement in the little group of listeners, sufficiently indicative of the strong repugnance any one of them would have felt to have turned out at such a time upon such an errand. The clerk felt and understood it, and pursued his theme accordingly.

"It *was* a dreary thing, especially as the grave-digger was laid up in his bed, from long working in a damp soil and sitting down to take his dinner on cold tombstones, and I was consequently under obligation to go alone, for it was too late to hope to get any other companion. However, I wasn't unprepared for it; as the old gentleman had often made it a request that the bell should be tolled as soon as possible after the breath was out of his body, and he had been expected to go for some days. I put as good a face upon it as I could, and muffling myself up (for it was mortal cold), started out with a lighted lantern in one hand and the key of the church in the other."

At this point of the narrative, the dress of the strange man rustled as if he had turned himself to hear more distinctly. Slightly pointing over his shoulder, Solomon elevated his eyebrows and nodded a silent inquiry to Joe whether this was the case. Joe shaded his eyes with his hand and peered into the corner, but could make out nothing, and so shook his head.

"It was just such a night as this; blowing a hurricane, raining heavily, and very dark—I often think now, darker than I ever saw it before or since; that may be my fancy, but the houses were all close shut and the folks in doors, and perhaps there is only one other man who knows how dark it really was. I got into the church, chained the door back so that it should keep ajar—for, to tell the truth, I didn't like to be shut in there alone—and putting my lantern on the stone seat in the little corner where the bell-rope is, sat down beside it to trim the candle.

"I sat down to trim the candle, and when I had done so I could not persuade myself to get up again, and go about my work. I don't know how it was, but I thought of all the ghost stories I had ever heard, even those that I had

17

heard when I was a boy at school, and had forgotten long ago; and they didn't come into my head one after another, but all crowding at once, like. I recollected one story there was in the village, how that on a certain night in the year (it might be that very night for anything I knew), all the dead people came out of the ground and sat at the heads of their own graves till morning. This made me think how many people I had known, were buried between the church door and the churchyard gate, and what a dreadful thing it would be to have to pass among them and know them again, so earthy and unlike themselves. I had known all the niches and arches in the church from a child; still, I couldn't persuade myself that those were their natural shadows which I saw on the pavement, but felt sure there were some ugly figures hiding among 'em and peeping out. Thinking on in this way, I began to think of the old gentleman who was just dead, and I could have sworn, as I looked up the dark chancel, that I saw him in his usual place, wrapping his shroud about him and shivering as if he felt it cold. All this time I sat listening and listening, and hardly dared to breathe. At length I started up and took the bell-rope in my hands. At that minute there rang—not that bell, for I had hardly touched the rope—but another!

"I heard the ringing of another bell, and a deep bell too, plainly. It was only for an instant, and even then the wind carried the sound away, but I heard it. I listened for a long time, but it rang no more. I had heard of corpse candles, and at last I persuaded myself that this must be a corpse bell tolling of itself at midnight for the dead. I tolled my bell—how, or how long, I don't know—and ran home to bed as fast as I could touch the ground.

"I was up early next morning after a restless night, and told the story to my neighbours. Some were serious and some made light of it; I don't think anybody believed it real. But, that morning, Mr. Reuben Haredale was found murdered in his bed-chamber; and in his hand was a piece of the cord attached to an alarm-bell outside the roof, which hung in his room and had been cut asunder, no doubt by the murderer, when he seized it.

"That was the bell I heard.

"A bureau was found opened, and a cash-box, which Mr. Haredale had brought down that day, and was supposed to contain a large sum of money, was gone. The steward and gardener were both missing and both suspected for a long time, but they were never found, though hunted far and wide. And far enough they might have looked for poor Mr. Rudge the steward, whose body—scarcely to be recognised by his clothes and the watch and ring he wore—was found, months afterwards, at the bottom of a piece of water in the grounds, with a deep gash in the breast where he had been stabbed with a knife. He was only partly dressed; and people all agreed that he had been sitting up reading in his own room, where there were many traces of blood, and was suddenly fallen upon and killed before his master.

"Everybody now knew that the gardener must be the murderer, and though he has never been heard of from that day to this, he will be, mark my words. The crime was committed this day two-and-twenty years—on the nineteenth of March, one thousand seven hundred and fifty-three. On the nineteenth of March in some year—no matter when—I know it, I am sure of it, for we have always, in some strange way or other, been brought back to the subject on that day ever since—on the nineteenth of March in some year, sooner or later, that man will be discovered."

CHAPTER II

" A strange story !" said the man who had been the cause
of the narration.—" Stranger still if it comes about as you
predict. Is that all ?"

A question so unexpected, nettled Solomon Daisy not a
little. By dint of relating the story very often, and orna-
menting it (according to village report) with a few flourishes
suggested by the various hearers from time to time, he had
come by degrees to tell it with great effect; and " is that
all ?" after the climax, was not what he was accustomed to.

" Is that all ?" he repeated, " yes, that's all, sir. And
enough too, I think."

" I think so too. My horse, young man ! He is but a
hack hired from a roadside posting house, but he must carry
me to London to-night."

" To-night !" said Joe.

" To-night," returned the other. " What do you stare at ?
This tavern would seem to be a house of call for all the
gaping idlers of the neighbourhood !"

At this remark, which evidently had reference to the
scrutiny he had undergone, as mentioned in the foregoing
chapter, the eyes of John Willet and his friends were diverted
with marvellous rapidity to the copper boiler again. Not
so with Joe, who, being a mettlesome fellow, returned the
stranger's angry glance with a steady look, and rejoined :

" It is not a very bold thing to wonder at your going on

to-night. Surely you have been asked such a harmless question in an inn before, and in better weather than this. I thought you mightn't know the way, as you seem strange to this part."

"The way——" repeated the other, irritably.

"Yes. *Do* you know it?"

"I'll—humph!—I'll find it," replied the man, waving his hand and turning on his heel. "Landlord, take the reckoning here."

John Willet did as he was desired; for on that point he was seldom slow, except in the particulars of giving change, and testing the goodness of any piece of coin that was proffered to him, by the application of his teeth or his tongue, or some other test, or in doubtful cases, by a long series of tests terminating in its rejection. The guest then wrapped his garments about him so as to shelter himself as effectually as he could from the rough weather, and without any word or sign of farewell betook himself to the stable-yard. Here Joe (who had left the room on the conclusion of their short dialogue) was protecting himself and the horse from the rain under the shelter of an old pent-house roof.

"He's pretty much of my opinion," said Joe, patting the horse upon the neck. "I'll wager that your stopping here to-night would please him better than it would please me."

"He and I are of different opinions, as we have been more than once on our way here," was the short reply.

"So I was thinking before you came out, for he has felt your spurs, poor beast."

The stranger adjusted his coat-collar about his face, and made no answer.

"You'll know me again, I see," he said, marking the young fellow's earnest gaze, when he had sprung into the saddle.

"The man's worth knowing, master, who travels a road he don't know, mounted on a jaded horse, and leaves good quarters to do it on such a night as this."

"You have sharp eyes and a sharp tongue I find."

"Both I hope by nature, but the last grows rusty sometimes for want of using."

"Use the first less too, and keep their sharpness for your sweethearts, boy," said the man.

So saying he shook his hand from the bridle, struck him roughly on the head with the butt end of his whip, and galloped away; dashing through the mud and darkness with a headlong speed, which few badly mounted horsemen would have cared to venture, even had they been thoroughly acquainted with the country; and which, to one who knew nothing of the way he rode, was attended at every step with great hazard and danger.

The roads, even within twelve miles of London, were at that time ill paved, seldom repaired, and very badly made. The way this rider traversed had been ploughed up by the wheels of heavy waggons, and rendered rotten by the frosts and thaws of the preceding winter, or possibly of many winters. Great holes and gaps had been worn into the soil, which, being now filled with water from the late rains, were not easily distinguishable even by day; and a plunge into any one of them might have brought down a surer-footed horse than the poor beast now urged forward to the utmost extent of his powers. Sharp flints and stones rolled from under his hoofs continually; the rider could scarcely see beyond the animal's head, or farther on either side than his own arm would have extended. At that time, too, all the roads in the neighbourhood of the metropolis were infested by footpads or highwaymen, and it was a night, of all others, in which any evil-disposed person of this class might have pursued his unlawful calling with little fear of detection.

Still, the traveller dashed forward at the same reckless pace, regardless alike of the dirt and wet which flew about his head, the profound darkness of the night, and the probability of encountering some desperate characters abroad. At every turn and angle, even where a deviation from the direct course might have been least expected, and could not possibly be seen until he was close upon it, he guided the bridle with an unerring hand, and kept the middle of the road. Thus he sped onward, raising himself in the stirrups, leaning his body forward until it almost touched the horse's neck, and flourishing his heavy whip above his head with the fervour of a madman.

There are times when, the elements being in unusual commotion, those who are bent on daring enterprises, or agitated by great thoughts, whether of good or evil, feel a mysterious sympathy with the tumult of nature, and are roused into corresponding violence. In the midst of thunder, lightning, and storm, many tremendous deeds have been committed; men, self-possessed before, have given a sudden loose to passions they could no longer control. The demons of wrath and despair have striven to emulate those who ride the whirlwind and direct the storm; and man, lashed into madness with the roaring winds and boiling waters, has become for the time as wild and merciless as the elements themselves.

Whether the traveller was possessed by thoughts which the fury of the night had heated and stimulated into a quicker current, or was merely impelled by some strong motive to reach his journey's end, on he swept more like a hunted phantom than a man, nor checked his pace until, arriving at some cross roads, one of which led by a longer route to the place whence he had lately started, he bore down so suddenly upon a vehicle which was coming towards him, that in the effort to avoid it he well-nigh pulled his horse upon his haunches, and narrowly escaped being thrown.

"Yoho!" cried the voice of a man. "What's that? who goes there?"

"A friend!" replied the traveller.

"A friend!" repeated the voice. "Who calls himself a friend and rides like that, abusing Heaven's gifts in the shape of horseflesh, and endangering, not only his own neck (which might be no great matter) but the necks of other people?"

"You have a lantern there, I see," said the traveller dismounting, "lend it me for a moment. You have wounded my horse, I think, with your shaft or wheel."

"Wounded him!" cried the other, "if I haven't killed him, it's no fault of yours. What do you mean by galloping along the king's highway like that, eh?"

A SLIGHT ENCOUNTER

"Give me the light," returned the traveller, snatching it from his hand, "and don't ask idle questions of a man who is in no mood for talking."

"If you had said you were in no mood for talking before, I should perhaps have been in no mood for lighting," said the voice. "Hows'ever as it's the poor horse that's damaged and not you, one of you is welcome to the light at all events—but it's not the crusty one."

The traveller returned no answer to this speech, but holding the light near to his panting and reeking breast, examined him in limb and carcass. Meanwhile, the other man sat very composedly in his vehicle, which was a kind of chaise with a depository for a large bag of tools, and watched his proceedings with a careful eye.

The looker-on was a round, red-faced, sturdy yeoman, with a double chin, and a voice husky with good living, good sleeping, good humour, and good health. He was past the prime of life, but Father Time is not always a hard parent, and, though he tarries for none of his children, often lays his hand lightly upon those who have used him well; making them old men and women inexorably enough, but leaving their hearts and spirits young and in full vigour. With such people the grey head is but the impression of the old fellow's hand in giving them his blessing, and every wrinkle but a notch in the quiet calendar of a well-spent life.

The person whom the traveller had so abruptly encountered was of this kind: bluff, hale, hearty, and in a green old age: at peace with himself, and evidently disposed to be so with all the world. Although muffled up in divers coats and handkerchiefs—one of which, passed over his crown, and tied in a convenient crease of his double chin, secured his three-cornered hat and bob-wig from blowing off his head—there was no disguising his plump and comfortable figure; neither did certain dirty finger-marks upon his face give it any other than an odd and comical expression, through which its natural good humour shone with undiminished lustre.

25

"He is not hurt," said the traveller at length, raising his head and the lantern together.

"You have found that out at last, have you?" rejoined the old man. "My eyes have seen more light than yours, but I wouldn't change with you."

"What do you mean?"

"Mean! I could have told you he wasn't hurt, five minutes ago. Give me the light, friend; ride forward at a gentler pace; and good night."

In handing up the lantern, the man necessarily cast its rays full on the speaker's face. Their eyes met at the instant. He suddenly dropped it and crushed it with his foot.

"Did you never see a locksmith before, that you start as if you had come upon a ghost?" cried the old man in the chaise, "or is this," he added hastily, thrusting his hand into the tool basket and drawing out a hammer, "a scheme for robbing me? I know these roads, friend. When I travel them, I carry nothing but a few shillings, and not a crown's worth of them. I tell you plainly, to save us both trouble, that there's nothing to be got from me but a pretty stout arm considering my years, and this tool, which, mayhap from long acquaintance with, I can use pretty briskly. You shall not have it all your own way, I promise you, if you play at that game." With these words he stood upon the defensive.

"I am not what you take me for, Gabriel Varden," replied the other.

"Then what and who are you?" returned the locksmith. "You know my name it seems. Let me know yours."

"I have not gained the information from any confidence of yours, but from the inscription on your cart which tells it to all the town," replied the traveller.

"You have better eyes for that than you had for your horse, then," said Varden, descending nimbly from his chaise; "who are you? Let me see your face."

While the locksmith alighted, the traveller had regained his saddle, from which he now confronted the old man, who, moving as the horse moved in chafing under the tightened rein, kept close beside him.

"Let me see your face, I say."

"Stand off!"

"No masquerading tricks," said the locksmith, "and tales at the club to-morrow, how Gabriel Varden was frightened by a surly voice and a dark night. Stand—let me see your face."

Finding that further resistance would only involve him in a personal struggle with an antagonist by no means to be despised, the traveller threw back his coat, and stooping down looked steadily at the locksmith.

Perhaps two men more powerfully contrasted, never opposed each other face to face. The ruddy features of the locksmith so set off and heightened the excessive paleness of the man on horseback, that he looked like a bloodless ghost, while the moisture, which hard riding had brought out upon his skin, hung there in dark and heavy drops, like dews of agony and death. The countenance of the old locksmith lighted up with the smile of one expecting to detect in this unpromising stranger some latent roguery of eye or lip, which should reveal a familiar person in that arch disguise, and spoil his jest. The face of the other, sullen and fierce, but shrinking too, was that of a man who stood at bay; while his firmly closed jaws, his puckered mouth, and more than all a certain stealthy motion of the hand within his breast, seemed to announce a desperate purpose very foreign to acting, or child's play.

Thus they regarded each other for some time, in silence.

"Humph!" he said when he had scanned his features; "I don't know you."

"Don't desire to?"—returned the other, muffling himself as before.

"I don't," said Gabriel; "to be plain with you, friend, you don't carry in your countenance a letter of recommendation."

"It's not my wish," said the traveller. "My humour is to be avoided."

"Well," said the locksmith bluntly, "I think you'll have your humour."

"I will, at any cost," rejoined the traveller. "In proof of it, lay this to heart—that you were never in such peril of your life as you have been within these few moments; when you are within five minutes of breathing your last, you will not be nearer death than you have been to-night!"

"Aye!" said the sturdy locksmith.

"Aye! and a violent death."

"From whose hand?"

"From mine," replied the traveller.

With that he put spurs to his horse, and rode away; at first plashing heavily through the mire at a smart trot, but gradually increasing in speed until the last sound of his horse's hoofs died away upon the wind; when he was again hurrying on at the same furious gallop, which had been his pace when the locksmith first encountered him.

Gabriel Varden remained standing in the road with the broken lantern in his hand, listening in stupefied silence until no sound reached his ear but the moaning of the wind, and the fast-falling rain; when he struck himself one or two smart blows in the breast by way of rousing himself, and broke into an exclamation of surprise.

"What in the name of wonder can this fellow be! a madman? a highwayman? a cut-throat? If he had not scoured off so fast, we'd have seen who was in most danger, he or I. I never nearer death than I have been to-night! I hope I may be no nearer to it for a score of years to come—if so, I'll be content to be no farther from it. My stars!—a pretty brag this to a stout man—pooh, pooh!"

Gabriel resumed his seat, and looked wistfully up the road by which the traveller had come; murmuring in a half whisper:

"The Maypole—two miles to the Maypole. I came the

other road from the Warren after a long day's work at locks
and bells, on purpose that I should not come by the Maypole
and break my promise to Martha by looking in—there's
resolution! It would be dangerous to go on to London
without a light; and it's four miles, and a good half-mile
besides, to the Halfway-House; and between this and that is
the very place where one needs a light most. Two miles to
the Maypole! I told Martha I wouldn't; I said I wouldn't,
and I didn't—there's resolution!"

Repeating these two last words very often, as if to com-
pensate for the little resolution he was going to show by
piquing himself on the great resolution he had shown,
Gabriel Varden quietly turned back, determining to get a
light at the Maypole, and to take nothing but a light.

When he got to the Maypole, however, and Joe, responding
to his well-known hail, came running out to the horse's head,
leaving the door open behind him, and disclosing a delicious
perspective of warmth and brightness—when the ruddy gleam
of the fire, streaming through the old red curtains of the
common room, seemed to bring with it, as part of itself, a
pleasant hum of voices, and a fragrant odour of steaming
grog and rare tobacco, all steeped as it were in the cheerful
glow—when the shadows, flitting across the curtain, showed
that those inside had risen from their snug seats, and were
making room in the snuggest corner (how well he knew that
corner!) for the honest locksmith, and a broad glare, suddenly
streaming up, bespoke the goodness of the crackling log from
which a brilliant train of sparks was doubtless at that
moment whirling up the chimney in honour of his coming—
when, superadded to these enticements, there stole upon him
from the distant kitchen a gentle sound of frying, with a
musical clatter of plates and dishes, and a savoury smell that
made even the boisterous wind a perfume—Gabriel felt his
firmness oozing rapidly away. He tried to look stoically
at the tavern, but his features would relax into a look of
fondness. He turned his head the other way, and the cold

black country seemed to frown him off, and drive him for a refuge into its hospitable arms.

"The merciful man, Joe," said the locksmith, "is merciful to his beast. I'll get out for a little while."

And how natural it was to get out! And how unnatural it seemed for a sober man to be plodding wearily along through miry roads, encountering the rude buffets of the wind and pelting of the rain, when there was a clean floor covered with crisp white sand, a well-swept hearth, a blazing fire, a table decorated with white cloth, bright pewter flagons, and other tempting preparations for a well-cooked meal—when there were these things, and company disposed to make the most of them, all ready to his hand, and entreating him to enjoyment!

CHAPTER III

Such were the locksmith's thoughts when first seated in the snug corner, and slowly recovering from a pleasant defect of vision—pleasant, because occasioned by the wind blowing in his eyes—which made it a matter of sound policy and duty to himself, that he should take refuge from the weather, and tempted him, for the same reason, to aggravate a slight cough, and declare he felt but poorly. Such were still his thoughts more than a full hour afterwards, when, supper over, he still sat with shining jovial face in the same warm nook, listening to the cricket-like chirrup of little Solomon Daisy, and bearing no unimportant or slightly respected part in the social gossip round the Maypole fire.

"I wish he may be an honest man, that's all," said Solomon, winding up a variety of speculations relative to the stranger, concerning whom Gabriel had compared notes with the company, and so raised a grave discussion; "*I* wish he may be an honest man."

"So we all do, I suppose, don't we?" observed the locksmith.

"I don't," said Joe.

"No!" cried Gabriel.

"No. He struck me with his whip, the coward, when he was mounted and I afoot, and I should be better pleased that he turned out what I think him."

"And what may that be, Joe?"

"No good, Mr. Varden. You may shake your head, father,

but I say no good, and will say no good, and I would say
no good a hundred times over, if that would bring him back
to have the drubbing he deserves."

"Hold your tongue, sir," said John Willet.

"I won't, father. It's all along of you that he ventured
to do what he did. Seeing me treated like a child, and put
down like a fool, *he* plucks up a heart and has a fling at a
fellow that he thinks—and may well think too—hasn't a
grain of spirit. But he's mistaken, as I'll show him, and as
I'll show all of you before long."

"Does the boy know what he's a saying of!" cried the
astonished John Willet.

"Father," returned Joe, "I know what I say and mean,
well—better than you do when you hear me. I can bear
with you, but I cannot bear the contempt that your treating
me in the way you do, brings upon me from others every
day. Look at other young men of my age. Have they no
liberty, no will, no right to speak? Are they obliged to
sit mum-chance, and to be ordered about till they are the
laughing-stock of young and old? I am a bye-word all over
Chigwell, and I say—and it's fairer my saying so now, than
waiting till you are dead, and I have got your money—I
say, that before long I shall be driven to break such bounds,
and that when I do, it won't be me that you'll have to blame,
but your own self, and no other."

John Willet was so amazed by the exasperation and boldness of his hopeful son, that he sat as one bewildered, staring
in a ludicrous manner at the boiler, and endeavouring, but
quite ineffectually, to collect his tardy thoughts, and invent
an answer. The guests, scarcely less disturbed, were equally
at a loss; and at length, with a variety of muttered, half-
expressed condolences, and pieces of advice, rose to depart;
being at the same time slightly muddled with liquor.

The honest locksmith alone addressed a few words of
coherent and sensible advice to both parties, urging John
Willet to remember that Joe was nearly arrived at man's

estate, and should not be ruled with too tight a hand, and exhorting Joe himself to bear with his father's caprices, and rather endeavour to turn them aside by temperate remonstrance than by ill-timed rebellion. This advice was received as such advice usually is. On John Willet it made almost as much impression as on the sign outside the door, while Joe, who took it in the best part, avowed himself more obliged than he could well express, but politely intimated his intention nevertheless of taking his own course uninfluenced by anybody.

"You have always been a very good friend to me, Mr. Varden," he said, as they stood without, in the porch, and the locksmith was equipping himself for his journey home; "I take it very kind of you to say all this, but the time's nearly come when the Maypole and I must part company."

"Roving stones gather no moss, Joe," said Gabriel.

"Nor mile-stones much," replied Joe. "I'm little better than one here, and see as much of the world."

"Then, what would you do, Joe?" pursued the locksmith, stroking his chin reflectively. "What could you be? where could you go, you see?"

"I must trust to chance, Mr. Varden."

"A bad thing to trust to, Joe. I don't like it. I always tell my girl when we talk about a husband for her, never to trust to chance, but to make sure beforehand that she has a good man and true, and then chance will neither make her nor break her. What are you fidgeting about there, Joe? Nothing gone in the harness I hope?"

"No, no," said Joe—finding, however, something very engrossing to do in the way of strapping and buckling—"Miss Dolly quite well?"

"Hearty, thankye. She looks pretty enough to be well, and good too."

"She's always both, sir—"

"So she is, thank God!"

"I hope," said Joe after some hesitation, "that you won't

tell this story against me—this of my having been beat like the boy they'd make of me—at all events, till I have met this man again and settled the account. It'll be a better story then."

"Why who should I tell it to?" returned Gabriel. "They know it here, and I'm not likely to come across anybody else who would care about it."

"That's true enough," said the young fellow with a sigh. "I quite forgot that. Yes, that's true!"

So saying, he raised his face, which was very red,—no doubt from the exertion of strapping and buckling as aforesaid,—and giving the reins to the old man, who had by this time taken his seat, sighed again and bade him good night.

"Good night!" cried Gabriel. "Now think better of what we have just been speaking of, and don't be rash, there's a good fellow! I have an interest in you, and wouldn't have you cast yourself away. Good night!"

Returning his cheery farewell with cordial good-will, Joe Willet lingered until the sound of wheels ceased to vibrate in his ears, and then, shaking his head mournfully, re-entered the house.

Gabriel Varden went his way towards London, thinking of a great many things, and most of all of flaming terms in which to relate his adventure, and so account satisfactorily to Mrs. Varden for visiting the Maypole, despite certain solemn covenants between himself and that lady. Thinking begets, not only thought, but drowsiness occasionally, and the more the locksmith thought, the more sleepy he became.

A man may be very sober—or at least firmly set upon his legs on that neutral ground which lies between the confines of perfect sobriety and slight tipsiness—and yet feel a strong tendency to mingle up present circumstances with others which have no manner of connection with them; to confound all consideration of persons, things, times, and places; and to jumble his disjointed thoughts together in a kind of mental kaleidoscope, producing combinations as unexpected as they are transitory. This was Gabriel Varden's state, as, nodding in his dog sleep, and leaving his horse to pursue a road with which he was well acquainted, he got over the ground unconsciously, and drew nearer and nearer home. He had roused himself once, when the horse stopped until the turnpike gate was opened, and had cried a lusty "good night!" to the toll-keeper; but then he awoke out of a dream about picking a lock in the stomach of the Great Mogul, and even when he did wake, mixed up the turnpike man with his mother-in-law who had been dead twenty years. It is not surprising, therefore, that he soon relapsed, and jogged heavily along, quite insensible to his progress.

And, now, he approached the great city, which lay out-stretched before him like a dark shadow on the ground, reddening the sluggish air with a deep dull light, that told of labyrinths of public ways and shops, and swarms of busy people. Approaching nearer and nearer yet, this halo began to fade, and the causes which produced it slowly to develop themselves. Long lines of poorly lighted streets might be faintly traced, with here and there a lighter spot, where lamps were clustered round a square or market, or round some great building; after a time these grew more distinct, and the lamps themselves were visible; slight yellow specks, that seemed to be rapidly snuffed out, one by one, as intervening obstacles hid them from the sight. Then, sounds arose—the striking of church clocks, the distant bark of dogs, the hum of traffic in the streets; then outlines might be traced—tall steeples looming in the air, and piles of un-equal roofs oppressed by chimneys; then, the noise swelled into a louder sound, and forms grew more distinct and numerous still, and London—visible in the darkness by its own faint light, and not by that of Heaven—was at hand.

The locksmith, however, all unconscious of its near vicinity, still jogged on, half sleeping and half waking, when a loud cry at no great distance ahead, roused him with a start.

For a moment or two he looked about him like a man

35

who had been transported to some strange country in his sleep, but soon recognising familiar objects, rubbed his eyes lazily and might have relapsed again, but that the cry was repeated—not once or twice or thrice, but many times, and each time, if possible, with increased vehemence. Thoroughly aroused, Gabriel, who was a bold man and not easily daunted, made straight to the spot, urging on his stout little horse as if for life or death.

The matter indeed looked sufficiently serious, for, coming to the place whence the cries had proceeded, he descried the figure of a man extended in an apparently lifeless state upon the pathway, and, hovering round him, another person with a torch in his hand, which he waved in the air with a wild impatience, redoubling meanwhile those cries for help which had brought the locksmith to the spot.

"What's here to do?" said the old man, alighting. "How's this—what—Barnaby?"

The bearer of the torch shook his long loose hair back from his eyes, and thrusting his face eagerly into that of the locksmith, fixed upon him a look which told his history at once.

"You know me, Barnaby?" said Varden.

He nodded—not once or twice, but a score of times, and that with a fantastic exaggeration which would have kept his head in motion for an hour, but that the locksmith held up his finger, and fixing his eye sternly upon him caused him to desist; then pointed to the body with an inquiring look.

"There's blood upon him," said Barnaby with a shudder. "It makes me sick!"

"How came it there?" demanded Varden.

"Steel, steel, steel!" he replied fiercely, imitating with his hand the thrust of a sword.

"Is he robbed?" said the locksmith.

Barnaby caught him by the arm, and nodded "Yes;" then pointed towards the city.

A WOUNDED MAN

"Oh!" said the old man, bending over the body and looking round as he spoke into Barnaby's pale face, strangely lighted up by something that was *not* intellect. "The robber made off that way, did he? Well, well, never mind that just now. Hold your torch this way—a little farther off—so. Now stand quiet, while I try to see what harm is done."

With these words, he applied himself to a closer examination of the prostrate form, while Barnaby, holding the torch as he had been directed, looked on in silence, fascinated by interest or curiosity, but repelled nevertheless by some strong and secret horror which convulsed him in every nerve.

As he stood, at that moment, half shrinking back and half bending forward, both his face and figure were full in the strong glare of the link, and as distinctly revealed as though it had been broad day. He was about three-and-twenty years old, and though rather spare, of a fair height and strong make. His hair, of which he had a great profusion, was red, and hanging in disorder about his face and shoulders, gave to his restless looks an expression quite unearthly—enhanced by the paleness of his complexion, and the glassy lustre of his large protruding eyes. Startling as his aspect was, the features were good, and there was something even plaintive in his wan and haggard aspect. But, the absence of the soul is far more terrible in a living man than in a dead one; and in this unfortunate being its noblest powers were wanting.

His dress was of green, clumsily trimmed here and there —apparently by his own hands—with gaudy lace; brightest where the cloth was most worn and soiled, and poorest where it was at the best. A pair of tawdry ruffles dangled at his wrists, while his throat was nearly bare. He had ornamented his hat with a cluster of peacock's feathers, but they were limp and broken, and now trailed negligently down his back. Girt to his side was the steel hilt of an old sword without blade or scabbard; and some parti-coloured ends of ribands and poor glass toys completed the ornamental portion of his attire. The fluttered and confused disposition of all the motley scraps that formed his dress, bespoke, in a scarcely less degree than his eager and unsettled manner, the disorder of his mind, and by a grotesque contrast set off and heightened the more impressive wildness of his face.

"Barnaby," said the locksmith, after a hasty but careful inspection, "this man is not dead, but he has a wound in his side, and is in a fainting-fit."

"I know him, I know him!" cried Barnaby, clapping his hands.

"Know him?" repeated the locksmith.

"Hush!" said Barnaby, laying his fingers upon his lips. "He went out to-day a wooing. I wouldn't for a light guinea that he should never go a wooing again, for, if he did, some eyes would grow dim that are now as bright as —see, when I talk of eyes, the stars come out! Whose eyes are they? If they are angels' eyes, why do they look down here and see good men hurt, and only wink and sparkle all the night?"

"Now Heaven help this silly fellow," murmured the perplexed locksmith; "can he know this gentleman? His mother's house is not far off; I had better see if she can tell me who he is. Barnaby, my man, help me to put him in the chaise, and we'll ride home together."

"I can't touch him!" cried the idiot falling back, and shuddering as with a strong spasm; "he's bloody!"

"It's in his nature I know," muttered the locksmith, "it's cruel to ask him, but I must have help. Barnaby—good Barnaby—dear Barnaby—if you know this gentleman, for the sake of his life and everybody's life that loves him, help me to raise him and lay him down."

"Cover him then, wrap him close—don't let me see it— smell it—hear the word. Don't speak the word—don't!"

"No, no, I'll not. There, you see he's covered now. Gently. Well done, well done!"

They placed him in the carriage with great ease, for

Barnaby was strong and active, but all the time they were so occupied he shivered from head to foot, and evidently experienced an ecstasy of terror.

This accomplished, and the wounded man being covered with Varden's own great-coat which he took off for the purpose, they proceeded onward at a brisk pace: Barnaby gaily counting the stars upon his fingers, and Gabriel inwardly congratulating himself upon having an adventure now, which would silence Mrs. Varden on the subject of the Maypole, for that night, or there was no faith in woman.

CHAPTER IV

In the venerable suburb—it was a suburb once—of Clerkenwell, towards that part of its confines which is nearest to
the Charter House, and in one of those cool, shady streets,
of which a few, widely scattered and dispersed, yet remain
in such old parts of the metropolis,—each tenement quietly
vegetating like an ancient citizen who long ago retired from
business, and dozing on in its infirmity until in course of
time it tumbles down, and is replaced by some extravagant
young heir, flaunting in stucco and ornamental work, and all
the vanities of modern days,—in this quarter, and in a street
of this description, the business of the present chapter lies.

At the time of which it treats, though only six-and-sixty
years ago, a very large part of what is London now had no
existence. Even in the brains of the wildest speculators,
there had sprung up no long rows of streets connecting
Highgate with Whitechapel, no assemblages of palaces in
the swampy levels, nor little cities in the open fields.
Although this part of town was then, as now, parcelled
out in streets, and plentifully peopled, it wore a different
aspect. There were gardens to many of the houses, and trees
by the pavement side; with an air of freshness breathing
up and down, which in these days would be sought in vain.
Fields were nigh at hand, through which the New River
took its winding course, and where there was merry hay-
making in the summer time. Nature was not so far removed,
or hard to get at, as in these days; and although there were

busy trades in Clerkenwell, and working jewellers by scores, it was a purer place, with farmhouses nearer to it than many modern Londoners would readily believe, and lovers' walks at no great distance, which turned into squalid courts, long before the lovers of this age were born, or, as the phrase goes, thought of.

In one of these streets, the cleanest of them all, and on the shady side of the way—for good housewives know that sunlight damages their cherished furniture, and so choose the shade rather than its intrusive glare—there stood the house with which we have to deal. It was a modest building, not very straight, not large, not tall; not bold-faced, with great staring windows, but a shy, blinking house, with a conical roof going up into a peak over its garret window of four small panes of glass, like a cocked hat on the head of an elderly gentleman with one eye. It was not built of brick or lofty stone, but of wood and plaster; it was not planned with a dull and wearisome regard to regularity, for no one window matched the other, or seemed to have the slightest reference to anything besides itself.

The shop—for it had a shop—was, with reference to the first floor, where shops usually are; and there all resemblance between it and any other shop stopped short and ceased. People who went in and out didn't go up a flight of steps to it, or walk easily in upon a level with the street, but dived down three steep stairs, as into a cellar. Its floor was paved with stone and brick, as that of any other cellar might be; and in lieu of window framed and glazed it had a great black wooden flap or shutter, nearly breast high from the ground, which turned back in the day-time, admitting as much cold air as light, and very often more. Behind this shop was a wainscoted parlour, looking first into a paved yard, and beyond that again into a little terrace garden, raised some feet above it. Any stranger would have supposed that this wainscoted parlour, saving for the door of communication by which he had entered, was cut off and detached from all the world; and indeed most strangers on their first entrance were observed to grow extremely thoughtful, as weighing and pondering in their minds whether the upper rooms were only approachable by ladders from without; never suspecting that two of the most unassuming and unlikely doors in existence, which the most ingenious mechanician on earth must of necessity have supposed to be the doors of closets, opened out of this room—each without the smallest preparation, or so much as a quarter of an inch of passage—upon two dark winding flights of stairs, the one upward, the other downward, which were the sole means of communication between that chamber and the other portions of the house.

With all these oddities, there was not a neater, more scrupulously tidy, or more punctiliously ordered house, in Clerkenwell, in London, in all England. There were not cleaner windows, or whiter floors, or brighter stoves, or more highly shining articles of furniture in old mahogany; there was not more rubbing, scrubbing, burnishing and polishing, in the whole street put together. Nor was this excellence attained without some cost and trouble and great expenditure of voice, as the neighbours were frequently reminded when the good lady of the house overlooked and assisted in its being put to rights on cleaning days—which were usually from Monday morning till Saturday night, both days inclusive.

Leaning against the door-post of this, his dwelling, the locksmith stood early on the morning after he had met with the wounded man, gazing disconsolately at a great wooden emblem of a key, painted in vivid yellow to resemble gold, which dangled from the house-front, and swung to and fro with a mournful creaking noise, as if complaining that it had nothing to unlock. Sometimes, he looked over his shoulder into the shop, which was so dark and dingy with numerous tokens of his trade, and so blackened by the smoke of a little forge, near which his 'prentice was at work, that

42

it would have been difficult for one unused to such espials to have distinguished anything but various tools of uncouth make and shape, great bunches of rusty keys, fragments of iron, half-finished locks, and such-like things, which garnished the walls and hung in clusters from the ceiling.

After a long and patient contemplation of the golden key, and many such backward glances, Gabriel stepped into the road, and stole a look at the upper windows. One of them chanced to be thrown open at the moment, and a roguish face met his; a face lighted up by the loveliest pair of sparkling eyes that ever locksmith looked upon; the face of a pretty, laughing, girl; dimpled and fresh, and healthful —the very impersonation of good-humour and blooming beauty.

"Hush!" she whispered, bending forward and pointing archly to the window underneath. "Mother is still asleep."

"Still, my dear," returned the locksmith in the same tone. "You talk as if she had been asleep all night, instead of little more than half an hour. But I'm very thankful. Sleep's a blessing—no doubt about it." The last few words he muttered to himself.

"How cruel of you to keep us up so late this morning, and never tell us where you were, or send us word!" said the girl.

"Ah, Dolly, Dolly!" returned the locksmith, shaking his head, and smiling, "how cruel of you to run up-stairs to bed! Come down to breakfast, madcap, and come down lightly, or you'll wake your mother. She must be tired, I am sure—*I* am."

Keeping these latter words to himself, and returning his daughter's nod, he was passing into the workshop, with the smile she had awakened still beaming on his face, when he just caught sight of his 'prentice's brown paper cap ducking down to avoid observation, and shrinking from the window back to its former place, which the wearer no sooner reached than he began to hammer lustily.

"Listening again, Simon!" said Gabriel to himself.

43

"That's bad. What in the name of wonder does he expect the girl to say, that I always catch him listening when *she* speaks, and never at any other time! A bad habit, Sim, a sneaking, underhanded way. Ah! you may hammer, but you won't beat that out of me, if you work at it till your time's up!"

So saying, and shaking his head gravely, he re-entered the workshop, and confronted the subject of these remarks.

"There's enough of that just now," said the locksmith. "You needn't make any more of that confounded clatter. Breakfast's ready."

"Sir," said Sim, looking up with amazing politeness, and a peculiar little bow cut short off at the neck. "I shall attend you immediately."

"I suppose," muttered Gabriel, "that's out of the 'Prentice's Garland, or the 'Prentice's Delight, or the 'Prentice's Warbler, or the 'Prentice's Guide to the Gallows, or some such improving text-book. Now he's going to beautify himself—here's a precious locksmith!"

Quite unconscious that his master was looking on from the dark corner by the parlour door, Sim threw off the paper cap, sprang from his seat, and in two extraordinary steps, something between skating and minuet dancing, bounded to a washing place at the other end of the shop, and there removed from his face and hands all traces of his previous work—practising the same step all the time with the utmost gravity. This done, he drew from some concealed place a little scrap of looking-glass, and with its assistance arranged his hair, and ascertained the exact state of a little carbuncle on his nose. Having now completed his toilet, he placed the fragment of mirror on a low bench, and looked over his shoulder at so much of his legs as could be reflected in that small compass, with the greatest possible complacency and satisfaction.

Sim, as he was called in the locksmith's family, or Mr. Simon Tappertit, as he called himself, and required all men

44

to style him out of doors, on holidays, and Sundays out,—
was an old-fashioned, thin-faced, sleek-haired, sharp-nosed,
small-eyed little fellow, very little more than five feet high,
and thoroughly convinced in his own mind that he was above
the middle size; rather tall, in fact, than otherwise. Of his
figure, which was well enough formed, though somewhat of
the leanest, he entertained the highest admiration; and with
his legs, which, in knee-breeches, were perfect curiosities of
littleness, he was enraptured to a degree amounting to
enthusiasm. He also had some majestic, shadowy ideas,
which had never been quite fathomed by his intimate friends,
concerning the power of his eye. Indeed he had been known
to go so far as to boast that he could utterly quell and
subdue the haughtiest beauty by a simple process, which he
termed "eyeing her over;" but it must be added, that
neither of this faculty, nor of the power he claimed to have,
through the same gift, of vanquishing and heaving down
dumb animals, even in a rabid state, had he ever furnished
evidence which could be deemed quite satisfactory and
conclusive.

It may be inferred from these premises, that in the small
body of Mr. Tappertit there was locked up an ambitious
and aspiring soul. As certain liquors, confined in casks too
cramped in their dimensions, will ferment, and fret, and
chafe in their imprisonment, so the spiritual essence or
soul of Mr. Tappertit would sometimes fume within that
precious cask, his body, until, with great foam and froth
and splutter, it would force a vent, and carry all before it.
It was his custom to remark, in reference to any one of these
occasions, that his soul had got into his head; and in this
novel kind of intoxication many scrapes and mishaps befell
him which he had frequently concealed with no small
difficulty from his worthy master.

Sim Tappertit, among the other fancies upon which his
before-mentioned soul was for ever feasting and regaling
itself (and which fancies, like the liver of Prometheus, grew

45

as they were fed upon), had a mighty notion of his order; and had been heard by the servant-maid openly expressing his regret that the 'prentices no longer carried clubs wherewith to mace the citizens : that was his strong expression. He was likewise reported to have said that in former times a stigma had been cast upon the body by the execution of George Barnwell, to which they should not have basely submitted, but should have demanded him of the legislature —temperately at first; then by an appeal to arms, if necessary—to be dealt with as they in their wisdom might think fit. These thoughts always led him to consider what a glorious engine the 'prentices might yet become if they had but a master spirit at their head ; and then he would darkly, and to the terror of his hearers, hint at certain reckless fellows that he knew of, and at a certain Lion Heart ready to become their captain, who, once afoot, would make the Lord Mayor tremble on his throne.

In respect of dress and personal decoration, Sim Tappertit was no less of an adventurous and enterprising character. He had been seen, beyond dispute, to pull off ruffles of the finest quality at the corner of the street on Sunday nights, and to put them carefully in his pocket before returning home; and it was quite notorious that on all great holiday occasions it was his habit to exchange his plain steel knee-buckles for a pair of glittering paste, under cover of a friendly post, planted most conveniently in that same spot. Add to this that he was in years just twenty, in his looks much older, and in conceit at least two hundred; that he had no objection to be jested with, touching his admiration of his master's daughter; and had even, when called upon at a certain obscure tavern to pledge the lady whom he honoured with his love, toasted, with many winks and leers, a fair creature whose Christian name, he said, began with a D—;—and as much is known of Sim Tappertit, who has by this time followed the locksmith in to breakfast, as is necessary to be known in making his acquaintance.

ABOUT YOUNG MR. CHESTER

It was a substantial meal; for, over and above the ordinary tea equipage, the board creaked beneath the weight of a jolly round of beef, a ham of the first magnitude, and sundry towers of buttered Yorkshire cake, piled slice upon slice in most alluring order. There was also a goodly jug of well-browned clay, fashioned into the form of an old gentleman, not by any means unlike the locksmith, atop of whose bald head was a fine white froth answering to his wig, indicative, beyond dispute, of sparkling home-brewed ale. But, better far than fair home-brewed, or Yorkshire cake, or ham, or beef, or anything to eat or drink that earth or air or water can supply, there sat, presiding over all, the locksmith's rosy daughter, before whose dark eyes even beef grew insignificant, and malt became as nothing.

Fathers should never kiss their daughters when young men are by. It's too much. There are bounds to human endurance. So thought Sim Tappertit when Gabriel drew those rosy lips to his—those lips within Sim's reach from day to day, and yet so far off. He had a respect for his master, but he wished the Yorkshire cake might choke him.

"Father," said the locksmith's daughter, when this salute was over, and they took their seats at table, "what is this I hear about last night?"

"All true, my dear; true as the Gospel, Doll."

"Young Mr. Chester robbed, and lying wounded in the road, when you came up!"

"Ay—Mr. Edward. And beside him, Barnaby, calling for help with all his might. It was well it happened as it did; for the road's a lonely one, the hour was late, and, the night being cold, and poor Barnaby even less sensible than usual from surprise and fright, the young gentleman might have met his death in a very short time."

"I dread to think of it!" cried his daughter with a shudder. "How did you know him?"

"Know him!" returned the locksmith. "I didn't know him—how could I? I had never seen him, often as I had

47

heard and spoken of him. I took him to Mrs. Rudge's; and she no sooner saw him than the truth came out."

"Miss Emma, father—If this news should reach her, enlarged upon as it is sure to be, she will go distracted."

"Why, lookye there again, how a man suffers for being good-natured," said the locksmith. "Miss Emma was with her uncle at the masquerade at Carlisle House, where she had gone, as the people at the Warren told me, sorely against her will. What does your blockhead father when he and Mrs. Rudge have laid their heads together, but goes there when he ought to be abed, makes interest with his friend the doorkeeper, slips him on a mask and domino, and mixes with the masquers."

"And like himself to do so!" cried the girl, putting her fair arm round his neck, and giving him a most enthusiastic kiss.

"Like himself!" repeated Gabriel, affecting to grumble, but evidently delighted with the part he had taken, and with her praise. "Very like himself—so your mother said. However, he mingled with the crowd, and prettily worried and badgered he was, I warrant you, with people squeaking, 'Don't you know me?' and 'I've found you out,' and all that kind of nonsense in his ears. He might have wandered on till now, but in a little room there was a young lady who had taken off her mask, on account of the place being very warm, and was sitting there alone."

"And that was she?" said his daughter hastily.

"And that was she," replied the locksmith; "and I no sooner whispered to her what the matter was—as softly, Doll, and with nearly as much art as you could have used yourself—than she gives a kind of scream and faints away."

"What did you do—what happened next?" asked his daughter.

"Why, the masks came flocking round, with a general noise and hubbub, and I thought myself in luck to get clear off, that's all," rejoined the locksmith. "What happened

48

when I reached home you may guess, if you didn't hear it. Ah! Well, it's a poor heart that never rejoices.—Put Toby this way, my dear."

This Toby was the brown jug of which previous mention has been made. Applying his lips to the worthy old gentleman's benevolent forehead, the locksmith, who had all this time been ravaging among the eatables, kept them there so long, at the same time raising the vessel slowly in the air, that at length Toby stood on his head upon his nose, when he smacked his lips, and set him on the table again with fond reluctance.

Although Sim Tappertit had taken no share in this conversation, no part of it being addressed to him, he had not been wanting in such silent manifestations of astonishment, as he deemed most compatible with the favourable display of his eyes. Regarding the pause which now ensued, as a particularly advantageous opportunity for doing great execution with them upon the locksmith's daughter (who he had no doubt was looking at him in mute admiration), he began to screw and twist his face, and especially those features, into such extraordinary, hideous, and unparalleled contortions, that Gabriel, who happened to look towards him, was stricken with amazement.

"Why, what the devil's the matter with the lad?" cried the locksmith. "Is he choking?"

"Who?" demanded Sim, with some disdain.

"Who? why, you," returned his master. "What do you mean by making those horrible faces over your breakfast?"

"Faces are matters of taste, sir," said Mr. Tappertit, rather discomfited; not the less so because he saw the locksmith's daughter smiling.

"Sim," rejoined Gabriel, laughing heartily. "Don't be a fool, for I'd rather see you in your senses. These young fellows," he added, turning to his daughter, "are always committing some folly or another. There was a quarrel between Joe Willet and old John last night—though I can't say Joe was much in fault either. He'll be missing one of these mornings, and will have gone away upon some wild-goose errand, seeking his fortune.—Why, what's the matter,

Doll? *You* are making faces now. The girls are as bad as the boys every bit!"

"It's the tea," said Dolly, turning alternately very red and very white, which is no doubt the effect of a slight scald— "so very hot."

A MESSAGE FROM MRS. VARDEN

Mr. Tappertit looked immensely big at a quartern loaf on the table, and breathed hard.

"Is that all?" returned the locksmith. "Put some more milk in it.—Yes, I am sorry for Joe, because he is a likely young fellow, and gains upon one every time one sees him. But he'll start off, you'll find. Indeed he told me as much himself!"

"Indeed!" cried Dolly in a faint voice. "In—deed!"

"Is the tea tickling your throat still, my dear?" said the locksmith.

But, before his daughter could make him any answer, she was taken with a troublesome cough, and it was such a very unpleasant cough, that, when she left off, the tears were starting in her bright eyes. The good-natured locksmith was still patting her on the back and applying such gentle restoratives, when a message arrived from Mrs. Varden, making known to all whom it might concern, that she felt too much indisposed to rise after her great agitation and anxiety of the previous night; and therefore desired to be immediately accommodated with the little black tea-pot of strong mixed tea, a couple of rounds of buttered toast, a middling-sized dish of beef and ham cut thin, and the Protestant Manual in two volumes post octavo. Like some other ladies who in remote ages flourished upon this globe, Mrs. Varden was most devout when most ill-tempered. Whenever she and her husband were at unusual variance, then the Protestant Manual was in high feather.

Knowing from experience what these requests portended, the triumvirate broke up; Dolly, to see the orders executed with all despatch; Gabriel, to some out-of-door work in his little chaise; and Sim, to his daily duty in the workshop, to which retreat he carried the big look, although the loaf remained behind.

Indeed the big look increased immensely, and when he had tied his apron on, became quite gigantic. It was not until he had several times walked up and down with folded arms,

51

and the longest strides he could take, and had kicked a
great many small articles out of his way, that his lip began
to curl. At length, a gloomy derision came upon his features,

and he smiled; uttering meanwhile with supreme contempt
the monosyllable "Joe!"

"I eyed her over, while he talked about the fellow," he

said, "and that was of course the reason of her being confused. Joe!"

He walked up and down again much quicker than before, and if possible with longer strides; sometimes stopping to take a glance at his legs, and sometimes to jerk out, and cast from him, another "Joe!" In the course of a quarter of an hour or so he again assumed the paper cap and tried to work. No. It could not be done.

"I'll do nothing to-day," said Mr. Tappertit, dashing it down again, "but grind. I'll grind up all the tools. Grinding will suit my present humour well. Joe!"

Whirr-r-r-r. The grindstone was soon in motion; the sparks were flying off in showers. This was the occupation for his heated spirit.

Whirr-r-r-r-r-r.

"Something will come of this!" said Mr. Tappertit, pausing as if in triumph, and wiping his heated face upon his sleeve. "Something will come of this. I hope it mayn't be human gore!"

Whirr-r-r-r-r-r-r.

CHAPTER V

As soon as the business of the day was over, the locksmith sallied forth, alone, to visit the wounded gentleman and ascertain the progress of his recovery. The house where he had left him was in a by-street in Southwark, not far from London Bridge; and thither he hied with all speed, bent upon returning with as little delay as might be, and getting to bed betimes.

The evening was boisterous—scarcely better than the previous night had been. It was not easy for a stout man like Gabriel to keep his legs at the street corners, or to make head against the high wind, which often fairly got the better of him, and drove him back some paces, or, in defiance of all his energy, forced him to take shelter in an arch or doorway until the fury of the gust was spent. Occasionally a hat or wig, or both, came spinning and trundling past him, like a mad thing; while the more serious spectacle of falling tiles and slates, or of masses of brick and mortar or fragments of stone-coping rattling upon the pavement near at hand, and splitting into fragments, did not increase the pleasure of the journey, or make the way less dreary.

"A trying night for a man like me to walk in!" said the locksmith, as he knocked softly at the widow's door. "I'd rather be in old John's chimney-corner, faith!"

"Who's there?" demanded a woman's voice from within. Being answered, it added a hasty word of welcome, and the door was quickly opened.

BARNABY'S MOTHER

She was about forty—perhaps two or three years older—with a cheerful aspect, and a face that had once been pretty. It bore traces of affliction and care, but they were of an old date, and Time had smoothed them. Any one who had bestowed but a casual glance on Barnaby might have known that this was his mother, from the strong resemblance between them; but where in his face there was wildness and vacancy, in hers there was the patient composure of long effort and quiet resignation.

One thing about this face was very strange and startling. You could not look upon it in its most cheerful mood without feeling that it had some extraordinary capacity of expressing terror. It was not on the surface. It was in no one feature that it lingered. You could not take the eyes or mouth, or lines upon the cheek, and say, if this or that were otherwise, it would not be so. Yet there it always lurked—something for ever dimly seen, but ever there, and never absent for a moment. It was the faintest, palest shadow of some look, to which an instant of intense and most unutterable horror only could have given birth; but indistinct and feeble as it was, it did suggest what that look must have been, and fixed it in the mind as if it had had existence in a dream.

More faintly imaged, and wanting force and purpose, as it were, because of his darkened intellect, there was this same stamp upon the son. Seen in a picture, it must have had some legend with it, and would have haunted those who looked upon the canvas. They who knew the Maypole story, and could remember what the widow was, before her husband's and his master's murder, understood it well. They recollected how the change had come, and could call to mind that when her son was born, upon the very day the deed was known, he bore upon his wrist what seemed a smear of blood but half washed out.

"God save you, neighbour!" said the locksmith, as he followed her, with the air of an old friend, into a little parlour where a cheerful fire was burning.

"And you," she answered smiling. "Your kind heart has brought you here again. Nothing will keep you at home, I know of old, if there are friends to serve or comfort, out of doors."

"Tut, tut," returned the locksmith, rubbing his hands and warming them. "You women are such talkers. What of the patient, neighbour?"

"He is sleeping now. He was very restless towards daylight, and for some hours tossed and tumbled sadly. But the fever has left him, and the doctor says he will soon mend. He must not be removed until to-morrow."

"He has had visitors to-day—humph?" said Gabriel, slyly.

"Yes. Old Mr. Chester has been here ever since we sent for him, and had not been gone many minutes when you knocked."

"No ladies?" said Gabriel, elevating his eyebrows and looking disappointed.

"A letter," replied the widow.

"Come. That's better than nothing!" replied the locksmith. "Who was the bearer?"

"Barnaby, of course."

"Barnaby's a jewel!" said Varden; "and comes and goes with ease where we who think ourselves much wiser would make but a poor hand of it. He is not out wandering, again, I hope?"

"Thank Heaven he is in his bed; having been up all night, as you know, and on his feet all day. He was quite tired out. Ah, neighbour, if I could but see him oftener so—if I could but tame down that terrible restlessness——"

"In good time," said the locksmith, kindly, "in good time—don't be down-hearted. To my mind he grows wiser every day."

The widow shook her head. And yet, though she knew the locksmith sought to cheer her, and spoke from no conviction of his own, she was glad to hear even this praise of her poor benighted son.

"He will be a 'cute man yet," resumed the locksmith. "Take care, when we are growing old and foolish, Barnaby doesn't put us to the blush, that's all. But our other friend," he added, looking under the table and about the floor— "sharpest and cunningest of all the sharp and cunning ones —where's he?"

"In Barnaby's room," rejoined the widow, with a faint smile.

"Ah! He's a knowing blade!" said Varden, shaking his head. "I should be sorry to talk secrets before him. Oh! He's a deep customer. I've no doubt he can read, and write, and cast accounts if he chooses. What was that? Him tapping at the door?"

"No," returned the widow. "It was in the street, I think. Hark! Yes. There again! 'Tis some one knocking softly at the shutter. Who can it be!"

They had been speaking in a low tone, for the invalid lay overhead, and the walls and ceilings being thin and poorly built, the sound of their voices might otherwise have disturbed his slumber. The party without, whoever it was, could have stood close to the shutter without hearing anything spoken; and, seeing the light through the chinks and finding all so quiet, might have been persuaded that only one person was there.

"Some thief or ruffian maybe," said the locksmith. "Give me the light."

"No, no," she returned hastily. "Such visitors have never come to this poor dwelling. Do you stay here. You're within call, at the worst. I would rather go myself—alone."

"Why?" said the locksmith, unwillingly relinquishing the candle he had caught up from the table.

"Because—I don't know why—because the wish is so strong upon me," she rejoined. "There again—do not detain me, I beg of you!"

Gabriel looked at her, in great surprise to see one who was usually so mild and quiet thus agitated, and with so little cause. She left the room and closed the door behind her. She stood for a moment as if hesitating, with her hand upon the lock. In this short interval the knocking came again, and a voice close to the window—a voice the locksmith seemed to recollect, and to have some disagreeable association with—whispered " Make haste."

The words were uttered in that low distinct voice which finds its way so readily to sleepers' ears, and wakes them in a fright. For a moment it startled even the locksmith; who involuntarily drew back from the window, and listened.

The wind rumbling in the chimney made it difficult to hear what passed, but he could tell that the door was opened, that there was the tread of a man upon the creaking boards, and then a moment's silence—broken by a suppressed something which was not a shriek, or groan, or cry for help, and yet might have been either or all three; and the words " My God!" uttered in a voice it chilled him to hear.

He rushed out upon the instant. There, at last, was that dreadful look—the very one he seemed to know so well and yet had never seen before—upon her face. There she stood, frozen to the ground, gazing with starting eyes, and livid cheeks, and every feature fixed and ghastly, upon the man he had encountered in the dark last night. His eyes met those of the locksmith. It was but a flash, an instant, a breath upon the polished glass, and he was gone.

The locksmith was upon him—had the skirts of his streaming garment almost in his grasp—when his arms were tightly clutched, and the widow flung herself upon the ground before him.

"The other way—the other way," she cried. " He went the other way. Turn—turn!"

"The other way! I see him now," rejoined the locksmith, pointing—" yonder—there—there is his shadow passing by that light. What—who is this? Let me go."

" Come back, come back!" exclaimed the woman, clasping him. "Do not touch him on your life. I charge you, come back. He carries other lives besides his own. Come back!"

"What does this mean?" cried the locksmith.

"No matter what it means, don't ask, don't speak, don't think about it. He is not to be followed, checked, or stopped. Come back!"

The old man looked at her in wonder, as she writhed and clung about him; and, borne down by her passion, suffered her to drag him into the house. It was not until she had chained and double-locked the door, fastened every bolt and bar with the heat and fury of a maniac, and drawn him back into the room, that she turned upon him, once again, that stony look of horror, and, sinking down into a chair, covered her face, and shuddered, as though the hand of death were on her.

CHAPTER VI

BEYOND all measure astonished by the strange occurrences which had passed with so much violence and rapidity, the locksmith gazed upon the shuddering figure in the chair like one half stupefied, and would have gazed much longer, had not his tongue been loosened by compassion and humanity.

"You are ill," said Gabriel. "Let me call some neighbour in."

"Not for the world," she rejoined, motioning to him with her trembling hand, and holding her face averted. "It is enough that you have been by, to see this."

"Nay, more than enough—or less," said Gabriel.

"Be it so," she returned. "As you like. Ask me no questions, I entreat you."

"Neighbour," said the locksmith, after a pause. "Is this fair, or reasonable, or just to yourself? Is it like you, who have known me so long and sought my advice in all matters —like you, who from a girl have had a strong mind and a staunch heart?"

"I have need of them," she replied. "I am growing old, both in years and care. Perhaps that, and too much trial, have made them weaker than they used to be. Do not speak to me."

"How can I see what I have seen, and hold my peace!" returned the locksmith. "Who was that man, and why has his coming made this change in you?"

She was silent, but held to the chair as though to save herself from falling on the ground.

"I take the licence of an old acquaintance, Mary," said the locksmith, "who has ever had a warm regard for you, and maybe has tried to prove it when he could. Who is this ill-favoured man, and what has he to do with you? Who is this ghost, that is only seen in the black nights and bad weather? How does he know, and why does he haunt, this house, whispering through chinks and crevices, as if there was that between him and you, which neither durst so much as speak aloud of. Who is he?"

"You do well to say he haunts this house," returned the widow, faintly. "His shadow has been upon it and me, in light and darkness, at noonday and midnight. And now, at last, he has come in the body!"

"But he wouldn't have gone in the body," returned the locksmith with some irritation, "if you had left my arms and legs at liberty. What riddle is it?"

"It is one," she answered, rising as she spoke, "that must remain for ever as it is. I dare not say more than that."

"Dare not!" repeated the wondering locksmith.

"Do not press me," she replied. "I am sick and faint, and every faculty of life seems dead within me.—No!—Do not touch me, either."

Gabriel, who had stepped forward to render her assistance, fell back as she made this hasty exclamation, and regarded her in silent wonder.

"Let me go my way alone," she said in a low voice, "and let the hands of no honest man touch mine to-night." When

61

she had tottered to the door, she turned, and added with a stronger effort, " This is a secret, which, of necessity, I trust to you. You are a true man. As you have ever been good and kind to me,—keep it. If any noise was heard above, make some excuse—say anything but what you really saw, and never let a word or look between us, recall this circumstance. I trust to you. Mind, I trust to you. How much I trust, you never can conceive."

Casting her eyes upon him for an instant, she withdrew, and left him there alone.

Gabriel, not knowing what to think, stood staring at the door with a countenance full of surprise and dismay. The more he pondered on what had passed, the less able he was to give it any favourable interpretation. To find this widow woman, whose life for so many years had been supposed to be one of solitude and retirement, and who, in her quiet suffering character, had gained the good opinion and respect of all who knew her—to find her linked mysteriously with an ill-omened man, alarmed at his appearance, and yet favouring his escape, was a discovery that pained as much as startled him. Her reliance on his secrecy, and his tacit acquiescence, increased his distress of mind. If he had spoken boldly, persisted in questioning her, detained her when she rose to leave the room, made any kind of protest, instead of silently compromising himself, as he felt he had done, he would have been more at ease.

" Why did I let her say it was a secret, and she trusted it to me ! " said Gabriel, putting his wig on one side to scratch his head with greater ease, and looking ruefully at the fire. "I have no more readiness than old John himself. Why didn't I say firmly, ' You have no right to such secrets, and I demand of you to tell me what this means,' instead of standing gaping at her, like an old mooncalf as I am ! But there's my weakness. I can be obstinate enough with men if need be, but women may twist me round their fingers at their pleasure."

BARNABY'S SHADOW

He took his wig off outright as he made this reflection, and, warming his handkerchief at the fire, began to rub and polish his bald head with it, until it glistened again.

"And yet," said the locksmith, softening under this soothing process, and stopping to smile, "it *may* be nothing. Any drunken brawler trying to make his way into the house, would have alarmed a quiet soul like her. But then"—and here was the vexation—"how came it to be that man; how comes he to have this influence over her; how came she to favour his getting away from me; and, more than all, how came she not to say it was a sudden fright, and nothing more? It's a sad thing to have, in one minute, reason to mistrust a person I have known so long, and an old sweetheart into the bargain; but what else can I do, with all this upon my mind!—Is that Barnaby outside there?"

"Ay!" he cried, looking in and nodding. "Sure enough it's Barnaby—how did you guess?"

"By your shadow," said the locksmith.

"Oho!" cried Barnaby, glancing over his shoulder. "He's a merry fellow, that shadow, and keeps close to me, though I *am* silly. We have such pranks, such walks, such runs, such gambols on the grass! Sometimes he'll be half as tall as a church steeple, and sometimes no bigger than a dwarf. Now, he goes on before, and now behind, and anon he'll be stealing on, on this side, or on that, stopping whenever I stop, and thinking I can't see him, though I have my eye on him sharp enough. Oh! he's a merry fellow. Tell me—is he silly too! I think he is."

"Why?" asked Gabriel.

"Because he never tires of mocking me, but does it all day long.—Why don't you come?"

"Where?"

"Up-stairs. He wants you. Stay—where's *his* shadow? Come. You're a wise man; tell me that."

"Beside him, Barnaby; beside him, I suppose," returned the locksmith.

" No ! " he replied, shaking his head. " Guess again."

" Gone out a walking, maybe ? "

" He has changed shadows with a woman," the idiot whispered in his ear, and then fell back with a look of triumph. " Her shadow's always with him, and his with her. That's sport I think, eh ? "

" Barnaby," said the locksmith, with a grave look ; " come hither, lad."

" I know what you want to say. I know ! " he replied, keeping away from him. " But I'm cunning, I'm silent. I only say so much to you—are you ready ? " As he spoke, he caught up the light, and waved it with a wild laugh above his head.

" Softly—gently," said the locksmith, exerting all his influence to keep him calm and quiet. " I thought you had been asleep."

" So I *have* been asleep," he rejoined, with widely-opened eyes. " There have been great faces coming and going—close to my face, and then a mile away—low places to creep through, whether I would or no—high churches to fall down from—strange creatures crowded up together neck and heels, to sit upon the bed—that's sleep, eh ? "

" Dreams, Barnaby, dreams," said the locksmith.

" Dreams ! " he echoed softly, drawing closer to him. " Those are not dreams."

" What are," replied the locksmith, " if they are not ? "

" I dreamed," said Barnaby, passing his arm through Varden's, and peering close into his face as he answered in a whisper, " I dreamed just now that something—it was in the shape of a man—followed me—came softly after me—wouldn't let me be—but was always hiding and crouching, like a cat in dark corners, waiting till I should pass ; when it crept out and came softly after me.—Did you ever see me run ? "

" Many a time, you know."

" You never saw me run as I did in this dream. Still it came creeping on to worry me. Nearer, nearer, nearer—I

64

ran faster—leaped—sprung out of bed, and to the window—
and there, in the street below—but he is waiting for us.
Are you coming?"

"What in the street below, Barnaby?" said Varden,
imagining that he traced some connection between this
vision and what had actually occurred.

Barnaby looked into his face, muttered incoherently, waved
the light above his head again, laughed, and drawing the
locksmith's arm more tightly through his own, led him up
the stairs in silence.

They entered a homely bedchamber, garnished in a scanty
way with chairs, whose spindle-shanks bespoke their age, and
other furniture of very little worth; but clean and neatly
kept. Reclining in an easy-chair before the fire, pale and
weak from waste of blood, was Edward Chester, the young
gentleman who had been the first to quit the Maypole on
the previous night, and who, extending his hand to the
locksmith, welcomed him as his preserver and friend.

"Say no more, sir, say no more," said Gabriel. "I hope
I would have done at least as much for any man in such a
strait, and most of all for you, sir. A certain young lady,"
he added, with some hesitation, "has done us many a kind
turn, and we naturally feel—I hope I give you no offence in
saying this, sir?"

The young man smiled and shook his head; at the same
time moving in his chair as if in pain.

"It's no great matter," he said, in answer to the locksmith's sympathising look, "a mere uneasiness arising at least
as much from being cooped up here, as from the slight wound
I have, or from the loss of blood. Be seated, Mr. Varden."

"If I may make so bold, Mr. Edward, as to lean upon
your chair," returned the locksmith, accommodating his
action to his speech, and bending over him, "I'll stand here
for the convenience of speaking low. Barnaby is not in his
quietest humour to-night, and at such times talking never
does him good."

They both glanced at the subject of this remark, who had taken a seat on the other side of the fire, and, smiling vacantly, was making puzzles on his fingers with a skein of string.

" Pray, tell me, sir," said Varden, dropping his voice still lower, " exactly what happened last night. I have my reason for inquiring. You left the Maypole, alone?"

" And walked homeward alone, until I had nearly reached the place where you found me, when I heard the gallop of a horse."

" Behind you?" said the locksmith.

" Indeed, yes—behind me. It was a single rider, who soon overtook me, and checking his horse, inquired the way to London."

" You were on the alert, sir, knowing how many highwaymen there are, scouring the roads in all directions?" said Varden.

" I was, but I had only a stick, having imprudently left my pistols in their holster-case with the landlord's son. I directed him as he desired. Before the words had passed my lips, he rode upon me furiously, as if bent on trampling me down beneath his horse's hoofs. In starting aside, I slipped and fell. You found me with this stab. and an ugly bruise or two, and without my purse—in which he found little enough for his pains. And now, Mr. Varden," he added, shaking the locksmith by the hand, " saving the extent of my gratitude to you, you know as much as I."

" Except," said Gabriel, bending down yet more, and looking cautiously towards their silent neighbour, " except in respect of the robber himself. What like was he, sir? Speak low, if you please. Barnaby means no harm, but I have watched him oftener than you, and I know, little as you would think it, that he's listening now."

It required a strong confidence in the locksmith's veracity to lead any one to this belief, for every sense and faculty that Barnaby possessed, seemed to be fixed upon his game, to the exclusion of all other things. Something in the young man's face expressed this opinion, for Gabriel repeated what he had just said, more earnestly than before, and with another glance towards Barnaby, again asked what like the man was.

"The night was so dark," said Edward, "the attack so sudden, and he so wrapped and muffled up, that I can hardly say. It seems that—"

"Don't mention his name, sir," returned the locksmith, following his look towards Barnaby; "I know *he* saw him. I want to know what *you* saw."

"All I remember is," said Edward, "that as he checked his horse his hat was blown off. He caught it, and replaced it on his head, which I observed was bound with a dark handkerchief. A stranger entered the Maypole while I was there, whom I had not seen—for I had sat apart for reasons of my own—and when I rose to leave the room and glanced round, he was in the shadow of the chimney and hidden from my sight. But, if he and the robber were two different persons, their voices were strangely and most remarkably alike; for directly the man addressed me in the road, I recognised his speech again."

"It is as I feared. The very man was here to-night," thought the locksmith, changing colour. "What dark history is this!"

"Halloa!" cried a hoarse voice in his ear. "Halloa, halloa, halloa! Bow wow wow. What's the matter here! Hal-loa!"

The speaker—who made the locksmith start as if he had seen some supernatural agent—was a large raven, who had perched upon the top of the easy-chair, unseen by him and Edward, and listened with a polite attention and a most extraordinary appearance of comprehending every word, to all they had said up to this point; turning his head from one to the other, as if his office were to judge between them, and it were of the very last importance that he should not lose a word.

"Look at him!" said Varden, divided between admiration of the bird and a kind of fear of him. "Was there ever such a knowing imp as that! Oh he's a dreadful fellow!"

The raven, with his head very much on one side, and his bright eye shining like a diamond, preserved a thoughtful silence for a few seconds, and then replied in a voice so hoarse and distant, that it seemed to come through his thick feathers rather than out of his mouth.

"Halloa, halloa, halloa! What's the matter here! Keep up your spirits. Never say die. Bow wow wow. I'm a devil, I'm a devil, I'm a devil. Hurrah!"—And then, as if exulting in his infernal character, he began to whistle.

"I more than half believe he speaks the truth. Upon my word I do," said Varden. "Do you see how he looks at me, as if he knew what I was saying?"

To which the bird, balancing himself on tiptoe, as it were, and moving his body up and down in a sort of grave dance, rejoined, "I'm a devil, I'm a devil, I'm a devil," and flapped his wings against his sides as if he were bursting with laughter. Barnaby clapped his hands, and fairly rolled upon the ground in an ecstasy of delight.

"Strange companions, sir," said the locksmith, shaking his head, and looking from one to the other. "The bird has all the wit."

"Strange indeed!" said Edward, holding out his forefinger to the raven, who, in acknowledgment of the attention, made a dive at it immediately with his iron bill. "Is he old?"

"A mere boy, sir," replied the locksmith. "A hundred and twenty, or thereabouts. Call him down, Barnaby, my man."

"Call him!" echoed Barnaby, sitting upright upon the floor, and staring vacantly at Gabriel, as he thrust his hair back from his face. "But who can make him come! He calls me, and makes me go where he will. He goes on before, and I follow. He's the master, and I'm the man. Is that the truth, Grip?"

A KNOWING BIRD

The raven gave a short, comfortable, confidential kind of croak;—a most expressive croak, which seemed to say, "You needn't let these fellows into our secrets. We understand each other. It's all right."

"*I* make *him* come?" cried Barnaby, pointing to the bird. "Him, who never goes to sleep, or so much as winks!—Why, any time of night, you may see his eyes in my dark room, shining like two sparks. And every night, and all night too, he's broad awake, talking to himself, thinking what he shall do to-morrow, where we shall go, and what he shall steal, and hide, and bury. *I* make *him* come. Ha ha ha!"

On second thoughts, the bird appeared disposed to come of himself. After a short survey of the ground, and a few sidelong looks at the ceiling and at everybody present in turn, he fluttered to the floor, and went to Barnaby—not in a hop, or walk, or run, but in a pace like that of a very particular gentleman with exceedingly tight boots on, trying to walk fast over loose pebbles. Then, stepping into his extended hand, and condescending to be held out at arm's length, he gave vent to a succession of sounds, not unlike the drawing of some eight or ten dozen of long corks, and again asserted his brimstone birth and parentage with great distinctness.

The locksmith shook his head—perhaps in some doubt of the creature's being really nothing but a bird—perhaps in pity for Barnaby, who by this time had him in his arms, and was rolling about, with him, on the ground. As he raised his eyes from the poor fellow he encountered those of his mother, who had entered the room, and was looking on in silence.

She was quite white in the face, even to her lips, but had wholly subdued her emotion, and wore her usual quiet look. Varden fancied as he glanced at her that she shrunk from his eye; and that she busied herself about the wounded gentleman to avoid him the better.

It was time he went to bed, she said. He was to be

removed to his own home on the morrow, and he had already exceeded his time for sitting up, by a full hour. Acting on this hint, the locksmith prepared to take his leave.

"By the bye," said Edward, as he shook him by the hand, and looked from him to Mrs. Rudge and back again, "what noise was that below? I heard your voice in the midst of it, and should have inquired before, but our other conversation drove it from my memory. What was it?"

The locksmith looked towards her, and bit his lip. She leant against the chair, and bent her eyes upon the ground. Barnaby too—he was listening.

—"Some mad or drunken fellow, sir," Varden at length made answer, looking steadily at the widow as he spoke. "He mistook the house, and tried to force an entrance."

She breathed more freely, but stood quite motionless. As the locksmith said "Good night," and Barnaby caught up the candle to light him down the stairs, she took it from him, and charged him—with more haste and earnestness than so slight an occasion appeared to warrant—not to stir. The raven followed them to satisfy himself that all was right below, and when they reached the street-door, stood on the bottom stair drawing corks out of number.

With a trembling hand she unfastened the chain and bolts, and turned the key. As she had her hand upon the latch, the locksmith said in a low voice,

"I have told a lie to-night, for your sake, Mary, and for the sake of bygone times and old acquaintance, when I would scorn to do so for my own. I hope I may have done no harm, or led to none. I can't help the suspicions you have forced upon me, and I am loth, I tell you plainly, to leave Mr. Edward here. Take care he comes to no hurt. I doubt the safety of this roof, and am glad he leaves it so soon. Now, let me go."

For a moment she hid her face in her hands and wept; but resisting the strong impulse which evidently moved her to reply, opened the door—no wider than was sufficient for the passage of his body—and motioned him away. As the locksmith stood upon the step, it was chained and locked behind him, and the raven, in furtherance of these precautions, barked like a lusty house-dog.

"In league with that ill-looking figure that might have fallen from a gibbet—he listening and hiding here—Barnaby first upon the spot last night—can she who has always borne so fair a name be guilty of such crimes in secret!" said the locksmith, musing. "Heaven forgive me if I am wrong, and send me just thoughts; but she is poor, the temptation may be great, and we daily hear of things as strange.—Ay, bark away, my friend. If there's any wickedness going on, that raven's in it, I'll be sworn."

CHAPTER VII

Mrs. Varden was a lady of what is commonly called an uncertain temper—a phrase which being interpreted signifies a temper tolerably certain to make everybody more or less uncomfortable. Thus it generally happened, that when other people were merry, Mrs. Varden was dull; and that when other people were dull, Mrs. Varden was disposed to be amazingly cheerful. Indeed the worthy housewife was of such a capricious nature, that she not only attained a higher pitch of genius than Macbeth, in respect of her ability to be wise, amazed, temperate and furious, loyal and neutral in an instant, but would sometimes ring the changes backwards and· forwards on all possible moods and flights in one short quarter of an hour; performing, as it were, a kind of triple bob major on the peal of instruments in the female belfry, with a skilfulness and rapidity of execution that astonished all who heard her.

It had been observed in this good lady (who did not want for personal attractions, being plump and buxom to look at, though like her fair daughter, somewhat short in stature) that this uncertainty of disposition strengthened and increased with her temporal prosperity; and divers wise men and matrons, on friendly terms with the locksmith and his family, even went so far as to assert, that a tumble down some half-dozen rounds in the world's ladder—such as the breaking of the bank in which her husband kept his money, or some little fall of that kind—would be the making of her, and could hardly fail to render her one of the most agreeable companions in existence. Whether they were right or wrong in this conjecture, certain it is that minds, like bodies, will often fall into a pimpled ill-conditioned state from mere excess of comfort, and like them, are often successfully cured by remedies in themselves very nauseous and unpalatable.

Mrs. Varden's chief aider and abettor, and at the same time her principal victim and object of wrath, was her single domestic servant, one Miss Miggs; or as she was called, in conformity with those prejudices of society which lop and top from poor handmaidens all such genteel excrescences— Miggs. This Miggs was a tall young lady, very much addicted to pattens in private life; slender and shrewish, of a rather uncomfortable figure, and though not absolutely ill-looking, of a sharp and acid visage. As a general principle and abstract proposition, Miggs held the male sex to be utterly contemptible and unworthy of notice; to be fickle, false, base, sottish, inclined to perjury, and wholly undeserving. When particularly exasperated against them (which, scandal said, was when Sim Tappertit slighted her most) she was accustomed to wish with great emphasis that the whole race of women could but die off, in order that the men might be brought to know the real value of the blessings by which they set so little store; nay, her feeling for her order ran so high, that she sometimes declared, if she could only have good security for a fair, round number—say ten thousand—of young virgins following her example, she would, to spite mankind, hang, drown, stab, or poison herself, with a joy past all expression.

It was the voice of Miggs that greeted the locksmith, when he knocked at his own house, with a shrill cry of "Who's there?"

"Me, girl, me," returned Gabriel.

"What, already, sir!" said Miggs, opening the door with a look of surprise. "We were just getting on our nightcaps to sit up,—me and mistress. Oh, she has been *so* bad!"

Miggs said this with an air of uncommon candour and concern; but the parlour-door was standing open, and as Gabriel very well knew for whose ears it was designed, he regarded her with anything but an approving look as he passed in.

"Master's come home, mim," cried Miggs, running before him into the parlour. "You was wrong, mim, and I was right. I thought he wouldn't keep us up so late, two nights running, mim. Master's always considerate so far. I'm so glad, mim, on your account. I'm a little "—here Miggs simpered—"a little sleepy myself; I'll own it now, mim, though I said I wasn't when you asked me. It ain't of no consequence, mim, of course."

"You had better," said the locksmith, who most devoutly wished that Barnaby's raven was at Miggs's ankles, "you had better get to bed at once then."

"Thanking you kindly, sir," returned Miggs, "I couldn't take my rest in peace, nor fix my thoughts upon my prayers, otherways than that I knew mistress was comfortable in her bed this night; by rights she ought to have been there, hours ago."

"You're talkative, mistress," said Varden, pulling off his great-coat, and looking at her askew.

"Taking the hint, sir," cried Miggs, with a flushed face, "and thanking you for it most kindly, I will make bold to say, that if I give offence by having consideration for my mistress, I do not ask your pardon, but am content to get myself into trouble and to be in suffering."

Here Mrs. Varden, who, with her countenance shrouded in a large nightcap, had been all this time intent upon the Protestant Manual, looked round, and acknowledged Miggs's championship by commanding her to hold her tongue.

Every little bone in Miggs's throat and neck developed itself with a spitefulness quite alarming, as she replied, "Yes, mim, I will."

"How do you find yourself now, my dear?" said the

locksmith, taking a chair near his wife (who had resumed her book), and rubbing his knees hard as he made the inquiry.

"You're very anxious to know, an't you?" returned Mrs. Varden, with her eyes upon the print. "You, that have not been near me all day, and wouldn't have been if I was dying!"

"My dear Martha—" said Gabriel.

Mrs. Varden turned over to the next page; then went back again to the bottom line over leaf to be quite sure of the last words; and then went on reading with an appearance of the deepest interest and study.

"My dear Martha," said the locksmith, "how can you say such things, when you know you don't mean them? If you were dying! Why, if there was anything serious the matter with you, Martha, shouldn't I be in constant attendance upon you?"

"Yes!" cried Mrs. Varden, bursting into tears, "yes, you would. I don't doubt it, Varden. Certainly you would. That's as much as to tell me that you would be hovering round me like a vulture, waiting till the breath was out of my body, that you might go and marry somebody else."

Miggs groaned in sympathy—a little short groan, checked in its birth, and changed into a cough. It seemed to say, "I can't help it. It's wrung from me by the dreadful brutality of that monster master."

"But you'll break my heart one of these days," added Mrs. Varden, with more resignation, "and then we shall both be happy. My only desire is to see Dolly comfortably settled, and when she is, you may settle *me* as soon as you like."

"Ah!" cried Miggs—and coughed again.

Poor Gabriel twisted his wig about in silence for a long time, and then said mildly, "Has Dolly gone to bed?"

"Your master speaks to you," said Mrs. Varden, looking sternly over her shoulder at Miss Miggs in waiting.

"No, my dear, I spoke to you," suggested the locksmith.

"Did you hear me, Miggs?" cried the obdurate lady,

75

stamping her foot upon the ground. "*You* are beginning to despise me now, are you? But this is example!"

At this cruel rebuke, Miggs, whose tears were always ready, for large or small parties, on the shortest notice and the most reasonable terms, fell a crying violently; holding both her hands tight upon her heart meanwhile, as if nothing less would prevent its splitting into small fragments. Mrs. Varden, who likewise possessed that faculty in high perfection, wept too, against Miggs; and with such effect that Miggs gave in after a time, and, except for an occasional sob, which seemed to threaten some remote intention of breaking out again, left her mistress in possession of the field. Her superiority being thoroughly asserted, that lady soon desisted likewise, and fell into a quiet melancholy.

The relief was so great, and the fatiguing occurrences of last night so completely overpowered the locksmith, that he nodded in his chair, and would doubtless have slept there all night, but for the voice of Mrs. Varden, which, after a pause of some five minutes, awoke him with a start.

"If I am ever," said Mrs. V.—not scolding, but in a sort of monotonous remonstrance—"in spirits, if I am ever cheerful, if I am ever more than usually disposed to be talkative and comfortable, this is the way I am treated."

"Such spirits as you was in too, mim, but half an hour ago!" cried Miggs. "I never see such company!"

"Because," said Mrs. Varden, "because I never interfere or interrupt; because I never question where anybody comes or goes; because my whole mind and soul is bent on saving where I can save, and labouring in this house;—therefore, they try me as they do."

"Martha," urged the locksmith, endeavouring to look as wakeful as possible, "what is it you complain of? I really came home with every wish and desire to be happy. I did, indeed."

"What do I complain of!" retorted his wife. "Is it a chilling thing to have one's husband sulking and falling asleep directly he comes home—to have him freezing all one's warm-heartedness, and throwing cold water over the fireside? Is it natural, when I know he went out upon a matter in which I am as much interested as anybody can be, that I should wish to know all that has happened, or that he should tell me without my begging and praying him to do it? Is that natural, or is it not?"

"I am very sorry, Martha," said the good-natured locksmith. "I was really afraid you were not disposed to talk pleasantly; I'll tell you everything; I shall only be too glad, my dear."

"No, Varden," returned his wife, rising with dignity. "I dare say—thank you! I'm not a child to be corrected one minute and petted the next—I'm a little too old for that, Varden. Miggs, carry the light. *You* can be cheerful, Miggs, at least."

Miggs, who, to this moment, had been in the very depths of compassionate despondency, passed instantly into the liveliest state conceivable, and tossing her head as she glanced towards the locksmith, bore off her mistress and the light together.

"Now, who would think," thought Varden, shrugging his shoulders and drawing his chair nearer to the fire, "that that woman could ever be pleasant and agreeable? And yet she can be. Well, well, all of us have our faults. I'll not be hard upon hers. We have been man and wife too long for that."

He dozed again—not the less pleasantly, perhaps, for his hearty temper. While his eyes were closed, the door leading to the upper stairs was partially opened; and a head appeared, which, at sight of him, hastily drew back again.

"I wish," murmured Gabriel, waking at the noise, and looking round the room, "I wish somebody would marry Miggs. But that's impossible! I wonder whether there's any madman alive, who would marry Miggs!"

This was such a vast speculation that he fell into a doze

again, and slept until the fire was quite burnt out. At last he roused himself; and having double-locked the street-door according to custom, and put the key in his pocket, went off to bed.

He had not left the room in darkness many minutes, when the head again appeared, and Sim Tappertit entered, bearing in his hand a little lamp.

"What the devil business has he to stop up so late!" muttered Sim, passing into the workshop, and setting it down upon the forge. "Here's half the night gone already. There's only one good that has ever come to me out of this cursed old rusty mechanical trade, and that's this piece of ironmongery, upon my soul!"

As he spoke, he drew from the right hand, or rather right leg pocket of his smalls, a clumsy large-sized key, which he inserted cautiously in the lock his master had secured, and softly opened the door. That done, he replaced his piece of secret workmanship in his pocket; and leaving the lamp burning, and closing the door carefully and without noise, stole out into the street—as little suspected by the locksmith in his sound deep sleep, as by Barnaby himself in his phantom-haunted dreams.

CHAPTER VIII

CLEAR of the locksmith's house, Sim Tappertit laid aside his cautious manner, and assuming in its stead that of a ruffling, swaggering, roving blade, who would rather kill a man than otherwise, and eat him too if needful, made the best of his way along the darkened streets.

Half pausing for an instant now and then to smite his pocket and assure himself of the safety of his master key, he hurried on to Barbican, and turning into one of the narrowest of the narrow streets which diverged from that centre, slackened his pace and wiped his heated brow, as if the termination of his walk were near at hand.

It was not a very choice spot for midnight expeditions, being in truth one of more than questionable character, and of an appearance by no means inviting. From the main street he had entered, itself little better than an alley, a low-browed doorway led into a blind court, or yard, profoundly dark, unpaved, and reeking with stagnant odours. Into this ill-favoured pit, the locksmith's vagrant 'prentice groped his way; and stopping at a house from whose defaced and rotten front the rude effigy of a bottle swung to and fro like some gibbeted malefactor, struck thrice upon an iron grating with his foot. After listening in vain for some response to his signal, Mr. Tappertit became impatient, and struck the grating thrice again.

A further delay ensued, but it was not of long duration.

The ground seemed to open at his feet, and a ragged head appeared.

"Is that the captain?" said a voice as ragged as the head.

"Yes," replied Mr. Tappertit haughtily, descending as he spoke, "who should it be?"

"It's so late, we gave you up," returned the voice, as its owner stopped to shut and fasten the grating. "You're late, sir."

"Lead on," said Mr. Tappertit, with a gloomy majesty, "and make remarks when I require you. Forward!"

This latter word of command was perhaps somewhat theatrical and unnecessary, inasmuch as the descent was by a very narrow, steep, and slippery flight of steps, and any rashness or departure from the beaten track must have ended in a yawning water-butt. But Mr. Tappertit being, like some other great commanders, favourable to strong effects, and personal display, cried "Forward!" again, in the hoarsest voice he could assume; and led the way, with folded arms and knitted brows, to the cellar down below, where there was a small copper fixed in one corner, a chair or two, a form and table, a glimmering fire, and a truckle-bed, covered with a ragged patchwork rug.

"Welcome, noble captain!" cried a lanky figure, rising as from a nap.

The captain nodded. Then, throwing off his outer coat, he stood composed in all his dignity, and eyed his follower over.

"What news to-night?" he asked, when he had looked into his very soul.

"Nothing particular," replied the other, stretching himself —and he was so long already that it was quite alarming to see him do it—"how come you to be so late?"

"No matter," was all the captain deigned to say in answer. "Is the room prepared?"

"It is," replied the follower.

"The comrade—is he here?"

"Yes. And a sprinkling of the others—you hear 'em?"

"Playing skittles!" said the captain moodily. "Light-hearted revellers!"

There was no doubt respecting the particular amusement in which these heedless spirits were indulging, for even in the close and stifling atmosphere of the vault, the noise sounded like distant thunder. It certainly appeared, at first sight, a singular spot to choose, for that or any other purpose of relaxation, if the other cellars answered to the one in which this brief colloquy took place; for the floors were of sodden earth, the walls and roof of damp bare brick tapestried with the tracks of snails and slugs; the air was sickening, tainted, and offensive. It seemed, from one strong flavour which was uppermost among the various odours of the place, that it had, at no very distant period, been used as a storehouse for cheeses; a circumstance which, while it accounted for the greasy moisture that hung about it, was agreeably suggestive of rats. It was naturally damp besides, and little trees of fungus sprung from every mouldering corner.

The proprietor of this charming retreat, and owner of the ragged head before mentioned—for he wore an old tie-wig as bare and frouzy as a stunted hearth-broom—had by this time joined them; and stood a little apart, rubbing his hands, wagging his hoary bristled chin, and smiling in silence. His eyes were closed; but had they been wide open, it would have been easy to tell, from the attentive expression of the face he turned towards them—pale and unwholesome as might be expected in one of his under-ground existence—and from a certain anxious raising and quivering of the lids, that he was blind.

"Even Stagg hath been asleep," said the long comrade, nodding towards this person.

"Sound, captain, sound!" cried the blind man; "what does my noble captain drink—is it brandy, rum, usquebaugh? Is it soaked gunpowder, or blazing oil? Give it a name, heart of oak, and we'd get it for you, if it was wine from a bishop's cellar, or melted gold from King George's mint."

"See," said Mr. Tappertit haughtily, "that it's something strong, and comes quick; and so long as you take care of that, you may bring it from the devil's cellar, if you like."

"Boldly said, noble captain!" rejoined the blind man. "Spoken like the 'Prentices' Glory. Ha, ha! From the devil's cellar! A brave joke! The captain joketh. Ha, ha, ha!"

"I'll tell you what, my fine feller," said Mr. Tappertit, eyeing the host over as he walked to a closet, and took out a bottle and glass as carelessly as if he had been in full possession of his sight, "if you make that row, you'll find that the captain's very far from joking, and so I tell you."

"He's got his eyes on me!" cried Stagg, stopping short on his way back, and affecting to screen his face with the bottle. "I feel 'em though I can't see 'em. Take 'em off, noble captain. Remove 'em, for they pierce like gimlets."

Mr. Tappertit smiled grimly at his comrade; and twisting out one more look—a kind of ocular screw—under the influence of which the blind man feigned to undergo great anguish and torture, bade him, in a softened tone, approach, and hold his peace.

"I obey you, captain," cried Stagg, drawing close to him and filling out a bumper without spilling a drop, by reason that he held his little finger at the brim of the glass, and stopped at the instant the liquor touched it, "drink, noble governor. Death to all masters, life to all 'prentices, and love to all fair damsels. Drink, brave general, and warm your gallant heart!"

Mr. Tappertit condescended to take the glass from his outstretched hand. Stagg then dropped on one knee, and gently smoothed the calves of his legs, with an air of humble admiration.

"That I had but eyes!" he cried, "to behold my captain's

symmetrical proportions! That I had but eyes, to look upon these twin invaders of domestic peace!"

"Get out!" said Mr. Tappertit, glancing downward at his favourite limbs. "Go along, will you, Stagg!"

"When I touch my own afterwards," cried the host, smiting them reproachfully, "I hate 'em. Comparatively speaking, they've no more shape than wooden legs, beside these models of my noble captain's."

"Yours!" exclaimed Mr. Tappertit. "No, I should think not. Don't talk about those precious old toothpicks in the same breath with mine; that's rather too much. Here. Take the glass. Benjamin. Lead on. To business!"

With these words, he folded his arms again; and frowning with a sullen majesty, passed with his companion through a little door at the upper end of the cellar, and disappeared; leaving Stagg to his private meditations.

The vault they entered, strewn with sawdust and dimly lighted, was between the outer one from which they had just come, and that in which the skittle-players were diverting themselves; as was manifested by the increased noise and clamour of tongues, which was suddenly stopped, however, and replaced by a dead silence, at a signal from the long comrade. Then, this young gentleman, going to a little cupboard, returned with a thigh-bone, which in former times must have been part and parcel of some individual at least as long as himself, and placed the same in the hands of Mr. Tappertit; who, receiving it as a sceptre and staff of authority, cocked his three-cornered hat fiercely on the top of his head, and mounted a large table, whereon a chair of state, cheerfully ornamented with a couple of skulls, was placed ready for his reception.

He had no sooner assumed this position, than another young gentleman appeared, bearing in his arms a huge clasped book, who made him a profound obeisance, and delivering it to the long comrade, advanced to the table, and turning his back upon it, stood there Atlas-wise. Then, the long comrade got upon the table too; and seating himself in a lower chair than Mr. Tappertit's, with much state and ceremony, placed the large book on the shoulders of their mute companion as deliberately as if he had been a wooden desk, and prepared to make entries therein with a pen of corresponding size.

When the long comrade had made these preparations, he looked towards Mr. Tappertit; and Mr. Tappertit, flourishing the bone, knocked nine times therewith upon one of the skulls. At the ninth stroke, a third young gentleman emerged from the door leading to the skittle-ground, and bowing low, awaited his commands.

"'Prentice!" said the mighty captain, "who waits without?"

The 'prentice made answer that a stranger was in attendance, who claimed admission into that secret society of 'Prentice Knights, and a free participation in their rights, privileges, and immunities. Thereupon Mr. Tappertit flourished the bone again, and giving the other skull a prodigious rap on the nose, exclaimed "Admit him!" At these dread words the 'prentice bowed once more, and so withdrew as he had come.

There soon appeared at the same door, two other 'prentices, having between them a third, whose eyes were bandaged, and who was attired in a bag-wig, and a broad-skirted coat, trimmed with tarnished lace; and who was girded with a sword, in compliance with the laws of the Institution regulating the introduction of candidates, which required them to assume this courtly dress, and kept it constantly in lavender, for their convenience. One of the conductors of this novice held a rusty blunderbuss pointed towards his ear, and the other a very ancient sabre, with which he carved imaginary offenders as he came along in a sanguinary and anatomical manner.

As this silent group advanced, Mr. Tappertit fixed his hat upon his head. The novice then laid his hand upon his breast and bent before him. When he had humbled himself sufficiently, the captain ordered the bandage to be removed, and proceeded to eye him over.

"Ha!" said the captain, thoughtfully, when he had concluded this ordeal. "Proceed."

The long comrade read aloud as follows:—"Mark Gilbert. Age, nineteen. Bound to Thomas Curzon, hosier, Golden

Fleece, Aldgate. Loves Curzon's daughter. Cannot say
that Curzon's daughter loves him. Should think it probable.
Curzon pulled his ears last Tuesday week."

"How!" cried the captain, starting.

"For looking at his daughter, please you," said the novice.

"Write Curzon down, Denounced," said the captain. "Put
a black cross against the name of Curzon."

"So please you," said the novice, "that's not the worst—
he calls his 'prentice idle dog, and stops his beer unless he
works to his liking. He gives Dutch cheese, too, eating
Cheshire, sir, himself; and Sundays out, are only once a
month."

"This," said Mr. Tappertit gravely, "is a flagrant case.
Put two black crosses to the name of Curzon."

"If the society," said the novice, who was an ill-looking,
one-sided, shambling lad, with sunken eyes set close together
in his head—"if the society would burn his house down—
for he's not insured—or beat him as he comes home from
his club at night, or help me to carry off his daughter, and
marry her at the Fleet, whether she gave consent or no—"

Mr. Tappertit waved his grizzly truncheon as an admonition to him not to interrupt, and ordered three black crosses
to the name of Curzon.

"Which means," he said in gracious explanation, "vengeance, complete and terrible. 'Prentice, do you love the
Constitution?"

To which the novice (being to that end instructed by his
attendant sponsors) replied "I do!"

"The Church, the State, and everything established—but
the masters?" quoth the captain.

Again the novice said "I do."

Having said it, he listened meekly to the captain, who in
an address prepared for such occasions, told him how that
under that same Constitution (which was kept in a strong
box somewhere, but where exactly he could not find out,
or he would have endeavoured to procure a copy of it), the

'prentices had, in times gone by, had frequent holidays of right, broken people's heads by scores, defied their masters, nay, even achieved some glorious murders in the streets, which privileges had gradually been wrested from them, and in all which noble aspirations they were now restrained; how the degrading checks imposed upon them were unquestionably attributable to the innovating spirit of the times, and how they united therefore to resist all change, except such change as would restore those good old English customs, by which they would stand or fall. After illustrating the wisdom of going backward, by reference to that sagacious fish, the crab, and the not unfrequent practice of the mule and donkey, he described their general objects; which were briefly vengeance on their Tyrant Masters (of whose grievous and insupportable oppression no 'prentice could entertain a moment's doubt) and the restoration, as aforesaid, of their ancient rights and holidays; for neither of which objects were they now quite ripe, being barely twenty strong, but which they pledged themselves to pursue with fire and sword when needful. Then he described the oath which every member of that small remnant of a noble body took, and which was of a dreadful and impressive kind; binding him, at the bidding of his chief, to resist and obstruct the Lord Mayor, sword-bearer, and chaplain; to despise the authority of the sheriffs; and to hold the court of aldermen as nought; but not on any account, in case the fulness of time should bring a general rising of 'prentices, to damage or in any way disfigure Temple Bar, which was strictly constitutional and always to be approached with reverence. Having gone over these several heads with great eloquence and force, and having further informed the novice that this society had its origin in his own teeming brain, stimulated by a swelling sense of wrong and outrage, Mr. Tappertit demanded whether he had strength of heart to take the mighty pledge required, or whether he would withdraw while retreat was yet in his power.

To this the novice made rejoinder, that he would take the

vow, though it should choke him; and it was accordingly administered with many impressive circumstances, among which the lighting up of the two skulls with a candle-end inside of each, and a great many flourishes with the bone, were chiefly conspicuous; not to mention a variety of grave exercises with the blunderbuss and sabre, and some dismal groaning by unseen 'prentices without. All these dark and direful cere-monies being at length completed, the table was put aside, the chair of state removed, the sceptre locked up in its usual cupboard, the doors of communication between the three cellars thrown freely open, and the 'Prentice Knights resigned them-selves to merriment.

But Mr. Tappertit, who had a soul above the vulgar herd, and who, on account of his greatness, could only afford to be merry now and then, threw himself on a bench with the air of a man who was faint with dignity. He looked with an indifferent eye, alike on skittles, cards, and dice, thinking only of the locksmith's daughter, and the base degenerate days on which he had fallen.

"My noble captain neither games, nor sings, nor dances," said his host, taking a seat beside him. "Drink, gallant general!"

Mr. Tappertit drained the proffered goblet to the dregs; then thrust his hands into his pockets, and with a lowering visage walked among the skittles, while his followers (such is the influence of superior genius) restrained the ardent ball, and held his little shins in dumb respect.

"If I had been born a corsair or a pirate, a brigand, gen-teel highwayman or patriot—and they're the same thing," thought Mr. Tappertit, musing among the nine-pins, "I should have been all right. But to drag out a ignoble existence unbeknown to mankind in general—patience! I will be famous yet. A voice within me keeps on whispering Greatness. I shall burst out one of these days, and when I do, what power can keep me down? I feel my soul getting into my head at the idea. More drink there!"

THE CAPTAIN AND THE NEW KNIGHT

"The novice," pursued Mr. Tappertit, not exactly in a voice of thunder, for his tones, to say the truth, were rather cracked and shrill—but very impressively, notwithstanding— "where is he?"

"Here, noble captain!" cried Stagg. "One stands beside me who I feel is a stranger."

"Have you," said Mr. Tappertit, letting his gaze fall on the party indicated, who was indeed the new knight, by this time restored to his own apparel; "have you the impression of your street-door key in wax?"

The long comrade anticipated the reply, by producing it from the shelf on which it had been deposited.

"Good," said Mr. Tappertit, scrutinising it attentively, while a breathless silence reigned around; for he had constructed secret door-keys for the whole society, and perhaps owed something of his influence to that mean and trivial circumstance—on such slight accidents do even men of mind depend!—"This is easily made. Come hither, friend."

With that, he beckoned the new knight apart, and putting the pattern in his pocket, motioned to him to walk by his side.

"And so," he said, when they had taken a few turns up and down, "you—you love your master's daughter?"

"I do," said the 'prentice. "Honour bright. No chaff, you know."

"Have you," rejoined Mr. Tappertit, catching him by the wrist, and giving him a look which would have been expressive of the most deadly malevolence, but for an accidental hiccup that rather interfered with it; "have you a—a rival?"

"Not as I know on," replied the 'prentice.

"If you had now—" said Mr. Tappertit—"what would you—eh?—"

The 'prentice looked fierce and clenched his fists.

"It is enough," cried Mr. Tappertit hastily, "we understand each other. We are observed. I thank you."

So saying, he cast him off again; and calling the long

comrade aside after taking a few hasty turns by himself, bade
him immediately write and post against the wall, a notice,
proscribing one Joseph Willet (commonly known as Joe)
of Chigwell; forbidding all 'Prentice Knights to succour,
comfort, or hold communion with him; and requiring them,
on pain of excommunication, to molest, hurt, wrong, annoy,
and pick quarrels with the said Joseph, whensoever and wheresoever they, or any of them, should happen to encounter him.

Having relieved his mind by this energetic proceeding, he
condescended to approach the festive board, and warming by
degrees, at length deigned to preside, and even to enchant the
company with a song. After this, he rose to such a pitch
as to consent to regale the society with a hornpipe, which he
actually performed to the music of a fiddle (played by an
ingenious member) with such surpassing agility and brilliancy
of execution, that the spectators could not be sufficiently
enthusiastic in their admiration; and their host protested,
with tears in his eyes, that he had never truly felt his blind-
ness until that moment.

But the host withdrawing—probably to weep in secret—
soon returned with the information that it wanted little
more than an hour of day, and that all the cocks in Barbican
had already begun to crow, as if their lives depended on it.
At this intelligence, the 'Prentice Knights arose in haste,
and marshalling into a line, filed off one by one and dispersed with all speed to their several homes, leaving their
leader to pass the grating last.

"Good night, noble captain," whispered the blind man as
he held it open for his passage out. "Farewell, brave general.
Bye, bye, illustrious commander. Good luck go with you
for a—conceited, bragging, empty-headed, duck-legged idiot."

With which parting words, coolly added as he listened to
his receding footsteps and locked the grate upon himself,
he descended the steps, and lighting the fire below the little
copper, prepared, without any assistance, for his daily occupation; which was to retail at the area-head above pennyworths

of broth and soup, and savoury puddings, compounded of such scraps as were to be bought in the heap for the least money at Fleet Market in the evening time; and for the sale of which he had need to have depended chiefly on his private connection, for the court had no thoroughfare, and was not that kind of place in which many people were likely to take the air, or to frequent as an agreeable promenade.

CHAPTER IX

CHRONICLERS are privileged to enter where they list, to come and go through keyholes, to ride upon the wind, to overcome, in their soarings up and down, all obstacles of distance, time, and place. Thrice blessed be this last consideration, since it enables us to follow the disdainful Miggs even into the sanctity of her chamber, and to hold her in sweet companionship through the dreary watches of the night!

Miss Miggs, having undone her mistress, as she phrased it (which means, assisted to undress her), and having seen her comfortably to bed in the back room on the first floor, withdrew to her own apartment, in the attic story. Notwithstanding her declaration in the locksmith's presence, she was in no mood for sleep; so, putting her light upon the table and withdrawing the little window curtain, she gazed out pensively at the wild night sky.

Perhaps she wondered what star was destined for her habitation when she had run her little course below; perhaps speculated which of those glimmering spheres might be the natal orb of Mr. Tappertit; perhaps marvelled how they could gaze down on that perfidious creature, man, and not sicken and turn green as chemists' lamps; perhaps thought of nothing in particular. Whatever she thought about, there she sat, until her attention, alive to anything connected with the insinuating 'prentice, was attracted by a noise in the next room to her own—his room; the room in which he slept, and dreamed—it might be, sometimes dreamed of her.

MYSTERIES!

That he was not dreaming now, unless he was taking a walk in his sleep, was clear, for every now and then there came a shuffling noise, as though he were engaged in polishing the whitewashed wall; then a gentle creaking of his door; then the faintest indication of his stealthy footsteps on the landing-place outside. Noting this latter circumstance, Miss Miggs turned pale and shuddered, as mistrusting his intentions; and more than once exclaimed, below her breath, "Oh! what a Providence it is, as I am bolted in!"—which, owing doubtless to her alarm, was a confusion of ideas on her part between a bolt and its use; for though there was one on the door, it was not fastened.

Miss Miggs's sense of hearing, however, having as sharp an edge as her temper, and being of the same snappish and suspicious kind, very soon informed her that the footsteps passed her door, and appeared to have some object quite separate and disconnected from herself. At this discovery she became more alarmed than ever, and was about to give utterance to those cries of "Thieves!" and "Murder!" which she had hitherto restrained, when it occurred to her to look softly out, and see that her fears had some good palpable foundation.

Looking out accordingly, and stretching her neck over the handrail, she descried, to her great amazement, Mr. Tappertit completely dressed, stealing down-stairs, one step at a time, with his shoes in one hand and a lamp in the other. Following him with her eyes, and going down a little way herself to get the better of an intervening angle, she beheld him thrust his head in at the parlour-door, draw it back again with great swiftness, and immediately begin a retreat up-stairs with all possible expedition.

"Here's mysteries!" said the damsel, when she was safe in her own room again, quite out of breath. "Oh gracious, here's mysteries!"

The prospect of finding anybody out in anything, would have kept Miss Miggs awake under the influence of henbane.

Presently, she heard the step again, as she would have done if it had been that of a feather endowed with motion and walking down on tiptoe. Then gliding out as before, she again beheld the retreating figure of the 'prentice; again he looked cautiously in at the parlour-door, but this time instead of retreating, he passed in and disappeared.

Miggs was back in her room, and had her head out of the window, before an elderly gentleman could have winked and recovered from it. Out he came at the street-door, shut it carefully behind him, tried it with his knee, and swaggered off, putting something in his pocket as he went along. At this spectacle Miggs cried "Gracious!" again, and then "Goodness gracious!" and then "Goodness gracious me!" and then, candle in hand, went down-stairs as he had done. Coming to the workshop, she saw the lamp burning on the forge, and everything as Sim had left it.

"Why I wish I may only have a walking funeral, and never be buried decent with a mourning-coach and feathers, if the boy hasn't been and made a key for his own self!" cried Miggs. "Oh the little villain!"

This conclusion was not arrived at without consideration, and much peeping and peering about; nor was it unassisted by the recollection that she had on several occasions come upon the 'prentice suddenly, and found him busy at some mysterious occupation. Lest the fact of Miss Miggs calling him, on whom she stooped to cast a favourable eye, a boy, should create surprise in any breast, it may be observed that she invariably affected to regard all male bipeds under thirty as mere chits and infants; which phenomenon is not unusual in ladies of Miss Miggs's temper, and is indeed generally found to be the associate of such indomitable and savage virtue.

Miss Miggs deliberated within herself for some little time, looking hard at the shop-door while she did so, as though her eyes and thoughts were both upon it; and then, taking a sheet of paper from a drawer, twisted it into a long thin

spiral tube. Having filled this instrument with a quantity
of small coal-dust from the forge, she approached the door,
and dropping on one knee before it, dexterously blew into
the keyhole as much of these fine ashes as the lock would
hold. When she had filled it to the brim in a very work-
manlike and skilful manner, she crept up-stairs again, and
chuckled as she went.

"There!" cried Miggs, rubbing her hands, "now let's see
whether you won't be glad to take some notice of me, mister.
He, he, he! You'll have eyes for somebody besides Miss
Dolly now, I think. A fat-faced puss she is, as ever *I*
come across!"

As she uttered this criticism, she glanced approvingly at
her small mirror, as who should say, I thank my stars that
can't be said of me!—as it certainly could not; for Miss
Miggs's style of beauty was of that kind which Mr.
Tappertit himself had not inaptly termed, in private,
"scraggy."

"I don't go to bed this night!" said Miggs, wrapping
herself in a shawl, and drawing a couple of chairs near the
window, flouncing down upon one, and putting her feet upon
the other, "till you come home, my lad. I wouldn't," said
Miggs viciously, "no, not for five-and-forty pound!"

With that, and with an expression of face in which a
great number of opposite ingredients, such as mischief,
cunning, malice, triumph, and patient expectation, were all
mixed up together in a kind of physiognomical punch, Miss
Miggs composed herself to wait and listen, like some fair
ogress who had set a trap and was watching for a nibble
from a plump young traveller.

She sat there, with perfect composure, all night. At
length, just upon <u>break</u> of day, there was a footstep in the
street, and presently she could hear Mr. Tappertit stop at
the door. Then she could make out that he tried his key
—that he was blowing into it—that he knocked it on the
nearest post to beat the dust out—that he took it under a

lamp to look at it—that he poked bits of stick into the lock to clear it—that he peeped into the keyhole, first with one eye, and then with the other—that he tried the key again—that he couldn't turn it, and what was worse, couldn't

get it out—that he bent it—that then it was much less disposed to come out than before—that he gave it a mighty twist and a great pull, and then it came out so suddenly that he staggered backwards—that he kicked the door—that he shook it—finally, that he smote his forehead, and sat down on the step in despair.

When this crisis had arrived, Miss Miggs, affecting to be exhausted with terror, and to cling to the window-sill for support, put out her nightcap, and demanded in a faint voice who was there.

Mr. Tappertit cried "Hush!" and, backing into the road, exhorted her in frenzied pantomime to secrecy and silence.

"Tell me one thing," said Miggs. "Is it thieves?"

"No—no—no!" cried Mr. Tappertit.

"Then," said Miggs, more faintly than before, "it's fire. Where is it, sir? It's near this room, I know. I've a good conscience, sir, and would much rather die than go down a ladder. All I wish is, respecting my love to my married sister, Golden Lion Court, number twenty-sivin, second bell-handle on the right-hand door-post."

"Miggs!" cried Mr. Tappertit, "don't you know me? Sim, you know—Sim—"

"Oh! what about him!" cried Miggs, clasping her hands. "Is he in any danger? Is he in the midst of flames and blazes! Oh gracious, gracious!"

"Why I'm here, an't I?" rejoined Mr. Tappertit, knocking himself on the breast. "Don't you see me? What a fool you are, Miggs!"

"There!" cried Miggs, unmindful of this compliment. "Why—so it—Goodness, what is the meaning of—If you please, mim, here's—"

"No, no!" cried Mr. Tappertit, standing on tiptoe, as if by that means he, in the street, were any nearer being able to stop the mouth of Miggs in the garret. "Don't!—I've been out without leave, and something or another's the matter with the lock. Come down, and undo the shop window, that I may get in that way."

"I dursn't do it, Simmun," cried Miggs—for that was her pronunciation of his Christian name. "I dursn't do it, indeed. You know as well as anybody, how particular I

am. And to come down in the dead of night, when the
house is wrapped in slumbers and weiled in obscurity."
And there she stopped and shivered, for her modesty caught
cold at the very thought.

"But, Miggs," cried Mr. Tappertit, getting under the
lamp, that she might see his eyes. "My darling Miggs—"

Miggs screamed slightly.

" —That I love so much, and never can help thinking of,"
and it is impossible to describe the use he made of his eyes
when he said this—"do—for my sake, do."

"Oh Simmun," cried Miggs, "this is worse than all. I
know if I come down, you'll go, and—"

"And what, my precious!" said Mr. Tappertit.

"And try," said Miggs, hysterically, "to kiss me, or some
such dreadfulness; I know you will!"

"I swear I won't," said Mr. Tappertit, with remarkable
earnestness. "Upon my soul I won't. It's getting broad
day, and the watchman's waking up. Angelic Miggs! If
you'll only come and let me in, I promise you faithfully and
truly I won't."

Miss Miggs, whose gentle heart was touched, did not wait
for the oath (knowing how strong the temptation was, and
fearing he might forswear himself), but tripped lightly down
the stairs, and with her own fair hands drew back the rough
fastenings of the workshop window. Having helped the
wayward 'prentice in, she faintly articulated the words
"Simmun is safe!" and yielding to her woman's nature,
immediately became insensible.

"I knew I should quench her," said Sim, rather embarrassed by this circumstance. "Of course I was certain
it would come to this, but there was nothing else to be
done—if I hadn't eyed her over, she wouldn't have come
down. Here. Keep up a minute, Miggs. What a slippery
figure she is! There's no holding her, comfortably. Do
keep up a minute, Miggs, will you?"

As Miggs, however, was deaf to all entreaties, Mr.

MISS MIGGS EXULTANT

Tappertit leant her against the wall as one might dispose of a walking-stick or umbrella, until he had secured the window, when he took her in his arms again, and, in short stages and with great difficulty—arising from her being tall, and his being short, and perhaps in some degree from that peculiar physical conformation on which he had already remarked—carried her up-stairs, and planting her in the same umbrella and walking-stick fashion, just inside her own door, left her to her repose.

"He may be as cool as he likes," said Miss Miggs, recovering as soon as she was left alone; "but I'm in his confidence and he can't help himself, nor couldn't if he was twenty Simmunses!"

CHAPTER X

It was on one of those mornings, common in early spring, when the year, fickle and changeable in its youth like all other created things, is undecided whether to step backward into winter or forward into summer, and in its uncertainty inclines now to the one and now to the other, and now to both at once—wooing summer in the sunshine, and lingering still with winter in the shade—it was, in short, on one of those mornings, when it is hot and cold, wet and dry, bright and lowering, sad and cheerful, withering and genial, in the compass of one short hour, that old John Willet, who was dropping asleep over the copper boiler, was roused by the sound of a horse's feet, and glancing out at window, beheld a traveller of goodly promise, checking his bridle at the Maypole door.

He was none of your flippant young fellows, who would call for a tankard of mulled ale, and make themselves as much at home as if they had ordered a hogshead of wine; none of your audacious young swaggerers, who would even penetrate into the bar—that solemn sanctuary—and, smiting old John upon the back, inquire if there was never a pretty girl in the house, and where he hid his little chambermaids, with a hundred other impertinences of that nature; none of your free-and-easy companions, who would scrape their boots upon the fire-dogs in the common room, and be not at all particular on the subject of spittoons; none of your unconscionable blades, requiring impossible chops, and taking unheard-of pickles for granted. He was a staid, grave, placid gentleman, something past the prime of life, yet upright in his carriage, for all that, and slim as a greyhound. He was well mounted upon a sturdy chestnut cob, and had the graceful seat of an experienced horseman ; while his riding gear, though free from such fopperies as were then in vogue, was handsome and well chosen. He wore a riding-coat of a somewhat brighter green than might have been expected to suit the taste of a gentleman of his years, with a short, black velvet cape, and laced pocket-holes and cuffs, all of a jaunty fashion ; his linen, too, was of the finest kind, worked in a rich pattern at the wrists and throat, and scrupulously white. Although he seemed, judging from the mud he had picked up on the way, to have come from London, his horse was as smooth and cool as his own iron-grey periwig and pigtail. Neither man nor beast had turned a single hair ; and saving for his soiled skirts and spatterdashes, this gentleman, with his blooming face, white teeth, exactly-ordered dress, and perfect calmness, might have come from making an elaborate and leisurely toilet, to sit for an equestrian portrait at old John Willet's gate.

It must not be supposed that John observed these several characteristics by other than very slow degrees, or that he took in more than half a one at a time, or that he even made up his mind upon that, without a great deal of very serious consideration. Indeed, if he had been distracted in the first instance by questionings and orders, it would have taken him at the least a fortnight to have noted what is here set down ; but it happened that the gentleman, being struck with the old house, or with the plump pigeons which were skimming and curtseying about it, or with the tall maypole, on the top of which a weathercock, which had been out of order for fifteen years, performed a perpetual walk to the music of its own creaking, sat for some little time looking round in silence. Hence John, standing with his hand upon the horse's bridle, and his great eyes on the rider, and with nothing passing to divert his thoughts, had really got some of these little circumstances into his brain by the time he was called upon to speak.

"A quaint place this," said the gentleman—and his voice was as rich as his dress. "Are you the landlord?"

"At your service, sir," replied John Willet.

"You can give my horse good stabling, can you, and me an early dinner (I am not particular what, so that it be cleanly served), and a decent room—of which there seems to be no lack in this great mansion," said the stranger, again running his eyes over the exterior.

"You can have, sir," returned John with a readiness quite surprising, "anything you please."

"It's well I am easily satisfied," returned the other with a smile, "or that might prove a hardy pledge, my friend." And saying so, he dismounted, with the aid of the block before the door, in a twinkling.

"Halloa there! Hugh!" roared John. "I ask your pardon, sir, for keeping you standing in the porch; but my son has gone to town on business, and the boy being, as I may say, of a kind of use to me, I'm rather put out when he's away. Hugh!—a dreadful idle vagrant fellow, sir, half a gipsy, as I think—always sleeping in the sun in summer, and in the straw in winter time, sir—Hugh! Dear Lord, to keep a gentleman a waiting here through him!—Hugh! I wish that chap was dead, I do indeed."

"Possibly he is," returned the other. "I should think if he were living, he would have heard you by this time."

"In his fits of laziness, he sleeps so desperate hard," said the distracted host, "that if you were to fire off cannon-balls into his ears, it wouldn't wake him, sir."

The guest made no remark upon this novel cure for drowsiness, and recipe for making people lively, but, with his hands clasped behind him, stood in the porch very much amused to see old John, with the bridle in his hand, wavering between a strong impulse to abandon the animal to his fate, and a half disposition to lead him into the house, and shut him up in the parlour, while he waited on his master.

"Pillory the fellow, here he is at last!" cried John, in the very height and zenith of his distress. "Did you hear me a calling, villain?"

The figure he addressed made no answer, but putting his hand upon the saddle, sprung into it at a bound, turned the horse's head towards the stable, and was gone in an instant.

"Brisk enough when he is awake," said the guest.

"Brisk enough, sir!" replied John, looking at the place where the horse had been, as if not yet understanding quite, what had become of him. "He melts, I think. He goes like a drop of froth. You look at him, and there he is. You look at him again, and—there he isn't."

Having, in the absence of any more words, put this sudden climax to what he had faintly intended should be a long explanation of the whole life and character of his man, the oracular John Willet led the gentleman up his wide dismantled staircase into the Maypole's best apartment.

It was spacious enough in all conscience, occupying the whole depth of the house, and having at either end a great bay window, as large as many modern rooms; in which some few panes of stained glass, emblazoned with fragments of armorial bearings, though cracked, and patched, and shattered, yet remained; attesting, by their presence, that the former owner had made the very light subservient to his state, and pressed the sun itself into his list of flatterers; bidding it, when it shone into his chamber, reflect the badges of his ancient family, and take new hues and colours from their pride.

But those were old days, and now every little ray came and went as it would; telling the plain, bare, searching truth. Although the best room of the inn, it had the melancholy aspect of grandeur in decay, and was much too vast for comfort. Rich rustling hangings, waving on the walls; and, better far, the rustling of youth and beauty's dress; the light

of women's eyes, outshining the tapers and their own rich
jewels; the sound of gentle tongues, and music, and the
tread of maiden feet, had once been there, and filled it with

delight. But they were gone, and with them all its gladness.
It was no longer a home; children were never born and bred
there; the fireside had become mercenary—a something to
be bought and sold—a very courtezan: let who would die,

or sit beside, or leave it, it was still the same—it missed nobody, cared for nobody, had equal warmth and smiles for all. God help the man whose heart ever changes with the world, as an old mansion when it becomes an inn!

No effort had been made to furnish this chilly waste, but before the broad chimney a colony of chairs and tables had been planted on a square of carpet, flanked by a ghostly screen, enriched with figures, grinning and grotesque. After lighting with his own hands the faggots which were heaped upon the hearth, old John withdrew to hold grave council with his cook, touching the stranger's entertainment; while the guest himself, seeing small comfort in the yet unkindled wood, opened a lattice in the distant window, and basked in a sickly gleam of cold March sun.

Leaving the window now and then, to rake the crackling logs together, or pace the echoing room from end to end, he closed it when the fire was quite burnt up, and having wheeled the easiest chair into the warmest corner, summoned John Willet.

"Sir," said John.

He wanted pen, ink, and paper. There was an old standish on the high mantel-shelf containing a dusty apology for all three. Having set this before him, the landlord was retiring, when he motioned him to stay.

"There's a house not far from here," said the guest when he had written a few lines, "which you call the Warren, I believe?"

As this was said in the tone of one who knew the fact, and asked the question as a thing of course, John contented himself with nodding his head in the affirmative; at the same time taking one hand out of his pockets to cough behind, and then putting it in again.

"I want this note"—said the guest, glancing on what he had written, and folding it, "conveyed there without loss of time, and an answer brought back here. Have you a messenger at hand?"

John was thoughtful for a minute or thereabouts, and then said Yes.

"Let me see him," said the guest.

This was disconcerting; for Joe being out, and Hugh engaged in rubbing down the chestnut cob, he designed sending on the errand, Barnaby, who had just then arrived in one of his rambles, and who, so that he thought himself employed on a grave and serious business, would go anywhere.

"Why the truth is," said John after a long pause, "that the person who'd go quickest, is a sort of natural, as one may say, sir; and though quick of foot, and as much to be trusted as the post itself, he's not good at talking, being touched and flighty, sir."

"You don't," said the guest, raising his eyes to John's fat face, "you don't mean—what's the fellow's name—you don't mean Barnaby?"

"Yes, I do," returned the landlord, his features turning quite expressive with surprise.

"How comes he to be here?" inquired the guest, leaning back in his chair; speaking in the bland, even tone, from which he never varied; and with the same soft, courteous, never-changing smile upon his face. "I saw him in London last night."

"He's, for ever, here one hour, and there the next," returned old John, after the usual pause to get the question in his mind. "Sometimes he walks, and sometimes runs. He's known along the road by everybody, and sometimes comes here in a cart or chaise, and sometimes riding double. He comes and goes, through wind, rain, snow, and hail, and on the darkest nights. Nothing hurts *him.*"

"He goes often to the Warren, does he not?" said the guest carelessly. "I seem to remember his mother telling me something to that effect yesterday. But I was not attending to the good woman much."

"You're right, sir," John made answer, "he does. His father, sir, was murdered in that house."

"So I have heard," returned the guest, taking a gold toothpick from his pocket with the same sweet smile. "A very disagreeable circumstance for the family."

"Very," said John with a puzzled look, as if it occurred to him, dimly and afar off, that this might by possibility be a cool way of treating the subject.

"All the circumstances after a murder," said the guest soliloquising, "must be dreadfully unpleasant—so much bustle and disturbance—no repose—a constant dwelling upon one subject—and the running in and out, and up and down stairs, intolerable. I wouldn't have such a thing happen to anybody I was nearly interested in, on any account. 'Twould be enough to wear one's life out.—You were going to say, friend—" he added, turning to John again.

"Only that Mrs. Rudge lives on a little pension from the family, and that Barnaby's as free of the house as any cat or dog about it," answered John. "Shall he do your errand, sir?"

"Oh yes," replied the guest. "Oh certainly. Let him do it by all means. Please to bring him here that I may charge him to be quick. If he objects to come you may tell him it's Mr. Chester. He will remember my name, I dare say."

John was so very much astonished to find who his visitor was, that he could express no astonishment at all, by looks or otherwise, but left the room as if he were in the most placid and imperturbable of all possible conditions. It has been reported that when he got down-stairs, he looked steadily at the boiler for ten minutes by the clock, and all that time never once left off shaking his head; for which statement there would seem to be some ground of truth and feasibility, inasmuch as that interval of time did certainly elapse, before he returned with Barnaby to the guest's apartment.

"Come hither, lad," said Mr. Chester. "You know Mr. Geoffrey Haredale?"

Barnaby laughed, and looked at the landlord as though he

107

would say, "You hear him?" John, who was greatly shocked at this breach of decorum, clapped his finger to his nose, and shook his head in mute remonstrance.

"He knows him, sir," said John, frowning aside at Barnaby, "as well as you or I do."

"I haven't the pleasure of much acquaintance with the gentleman," returned his guest. "*You* may have. Limit the comparison to yourself, my friend."

Although this was said with the same easy affability, and the same smile, John felt himself put down, and laying the indignity at Barnaby's door, determined to kick his raven, on the very first opportunity.

"Give that," said the guest, who had by this time sealed the note, and who beckoned his messenger towards him as he spoke, "into Mr. Haredale's own hands. Wait for an answer, and bring it back to me—here. If you should find that Mr. Haredale is engaged just now, tell him—can he remember a message, landlord?"

"When he chooses, sir," replied John. "He won't forget this one."

"How are you sure of that?"

John merely pointed to him as he stood with his head bent forward, and his earnest gaze fixed closely on his questioner's face; and nodded sagely.

"Tell him then, Barnaby, should he be engaged," said Mr. Chester, "that I shall be glad to wait his convenience here, and to see him (if he will call) at any time this evening.— At the worst I can have a bed here, Willet, I suppose?"

Old John, immensely flattered by the personal notoriety implied in this familiar form of address, answered, with something like a knowing look, "I should believe you could, sir," and was turning over in his mind various forms of eulogium, with the view of selecting one appropriate to the qualities of his best bed, when his ideas were put to flight by Mr. Chester giving Barnaby the letter, and bidding him make all speed away.

"Speed!" said Barnaby, folding the little packet in his breast. "Speed! If you want to see hurry and mystery, come here. Here!"

With that, he put his hand, very much to John Willet's horror, on the guest's fine broadcloth sleeve, and led him stealthily to the back window.

"Look down there," he said softly; "do you mark how they whisper in each other's ears; then dance and leap, to make believe they are in sport? Do you see how they stop for a moment, when they think there is no one looking, and mutter among themselves again; and then how they roll and gambol, delighted with the mischief they've been plotting? Look at 'em now. See how they whirl and plunge. And now they stop again, and whisper, cautiously together—little thinking, mind, how often I have lain upon the grass and watched them. I say—what is it that they plot and hatch? Do you know?"

"They are only clothes," returned the guest, "such as we wear; hanging on those lines to dry, and fluttering in the wind."

"Clothes!" echoed Barnaby, looking close into his face, and falling quickly back. "Ha ha! Why, how much better to be silly, than as wise as you! You don't see shadowy people there, like those that live in sleep—not you. Nor eyes in the knotted panes of glass, nor swift ghosts when it blows hard, nor do you hear voices in the air, nor see men stalking in the sky—not you! I lead a merrier life than you, with all your cleverness. You're the dull men. We're the bright ones. Ha! ha! I'll not change with you, clever as you are,—not I!"

With that, he waved his hat above his head, and darted off.

"A strange creature, upon my word!" said the guest, pulling out a handsome box, and taking a pinch of snuff.

"He wants imagination," said Mr. Willet, very slowly, and after a long silence; "that's what he wants. I've tried to instil it into him, many and many's the time; but"—

John added this in confidence—"he an't made for it; that's the fact."

To record that Mr. Chester smiled at John's remark would be little to the purpose, for he preserved the same conciliatory and pleasant look at all times. He drew his chair nearer to the fire though, as a kind of hint that he would prefer to be alone, and John, having no reasonable excuse for remaining, left him to himself.

Very thoughtful old John Willet was, while the dinner was preparing; and if his brain were ever less clear at one time than another, it is but reasonable to suppose that he addled it in no slight degree by shaking his head so much that day. That Mr. Chester, between whom and Mr. Haredale, it was notorious to all the neighbourhood, a deep and bitter animosity existed, should come down there for the sole purpose, as it seemed, of seeing him, and should choose the Maypole for their place of meeting, and should send to him express, were stumbling-blocks John could not overcome. The only resource he had, was to consult the boiler, and wait impatiently for Barnaby's return.

But Barnaby delayed beyond all precedent. The visitor's dinner was served, removed, his wine was set, the fire replenished, the hearth clean swept; the light waned without, it grew dusk, became quite dark, and still no Barnaby appeared. Yet, though John Willet was full of wonder and misgiving, his guest sat cross-legged in the easy-chair, to all appearance as little ruffled in his thoughts as in his dress—the same calm, easy, cool gentleman, without a care or thought beyond his golden toothpick.

"Barnaby's late," John ventured to observe, as he placed a pair of tarnished candlesticks, some three feet high, upon the table, and snuffed the lights they held.

"He is rather so," replied the guest, sipping his wine. "He will not be much longer, I dare say."

John coughed and raked the fire together.

"As your roads bear no very good character, if I may

judge from my son's mishap, though," said Mr. Chester, "and as I have no fancy to be knocked on the head—which is not only disconcerting at the moment, but places one, besides, in a ridiculous position with respect to the people who chance to pick one up—I shall stop here to-night. I think you said you had a bed to spare."

"Such a bed, sir," returned John Willet; "ay, such a bed as few, even of the gentry's houses, own. A fixter here, sir. I've heard say that bedstead is nigh two hundred years of age. Your noble son—a fine young gentleman—slept in it last, sir, half a year ago."

"Upon my life, a recommendation!" said the guest, shrugging his shoulders and wheeling his chair nearer to the fire. "See that it be well aired, Mr. Willet, and let a blazing fire be lighted there at once. This house is something damp and chilly."

John raked the faggots up again, more from habit than presence of mind, or any reference to this remark, and was about to withdraw, when a bounding step was heard upon the stair, and Barnaby came panting in.

"He'll have his foot in the stirrup in an hour's time," he cried, advancing. "He has been riding hard all day—has just come home—but will be in the saddle again as soon as he has eat and drank, to meet his loving friend."

"Was that his message?" asked the visitor, looking up, but without the smallest discomposure—or at least without the show of any.

"All but the last words," Barnaby rejoined. "He meant those. I saw that, in his face."

"This for your pains," said the other, putting money in his hand, and glancing at him steadfastly. "This for your pains, sharp Barnaby."

"For Grip, and me, and Hugh, to share among us," he rejoined, putting it up, and nodding, as he counted it on his fingers. "Grip one, me two, Hugh three; the dog, the goat, the cats—well, we shall spend it pretty soon, I warn you. Stay.—Look. Do you wise men see nothing there, now?"

He bent eagerly down on one knee, and gazed intently at the smoke, which was rolling up the chimney in a thick black cloud. John Willet, who appeared to consider himself particularly and chiefly referred to under the term wise men, looked that way likewise, and with great solidity of feature.

"Now, where do they go to, when they spring so fast up there," asked Barnaby; "eh? Why do they tread so closely on each other's heels, and why are they always in a hurry—which is what you blame me for, when I only take pattern by these busy folk about me. More of 'em! catching to each other's skirts; and as fast as they go, others come! What a merry dance it is! I would that Grip and I could frisk like that!"

"What has he in that basket at his back?" asked the guest after a few moments, during which Barnaby was still bending down to look higher up the chimney, and earnestly watching the smoke.

"In this?" he answered, jumping up, before John Willet could reply—shaking it as he spoke, and stooping his head to listen. "In this? What is there here? Tell him!"

"A devil, a devil, a devil!" cried a hoarse voice.

"Here's money?" said Barnaby, chinking it in his hand, "money for a treat, Grip!"

"Hurrah! Hurrah! Hurrah!" replied the raven, "keep up your spirits. Never say die. Bow, wow, wow!"

Mr. Willet, who appeared to entertain strong doubts whether a customer in a laced coat and fine linen could be supposed to have any acquaintance even with the existence of such unpolite gentry as the bird claimed to belong to, took Barnaby off at this juncture, with the view of preventing any other improper declarations, and quitted the room with his very best bow.

CHAPTER XI

THERE was great news that night for the regular Maypole customers, to each of whom, as he straggled in to occupy his allotted seat in the chimney-corner, John, with a most impressive slowness of delivery, and in an apoplectic whisper, communicated the fact that Mr. Chester was alone in the large room up-stairs, and was waiting the arrival of Mr. Geoffrey Haredale, to whom he had sent a letter (doubtless of a threatening nature) by the hands of Barnaby, then and there present.

For a little knot of smokers and solemn gossips, who had seldom any new topics of discussion, this was a perfect God-send. Here was a good, dark-looking mystery progressing under that very roof—brought home to the fireside, as it were, and enjoyable without the smallest pains or trouble. It is extraordinary what a zest and relish it gave to the drink, and how it heightened the flavour of the tobacco. Every man smoked his pipe with a face of grave and serious delight, and looked at his neighbour with a sort of quiet congratulation. Nay, it was felt to be such a holiday and special night, that, on the motion of little Solomon Daisy, every man (including John himself) put down his sixpence for a can of flip, which grateful beverage was brewed with all despatch, and set down in the midst of them on the brick floor; both that it might simmer and stew before the fire, and that its fragrant steam, rising up among them, and mixing with the wreaths of vapour from their pipes, might shroud them in a delicious atmosphere of their own, and shut out all the world. The very furniture of the room seemed to mellow and deepen in its tone; the ceiling and walls looked blacker and more highly polished, the curtains of a ruddier red; the fire burnt clear and high, and the crickets in the hearth-stone chirped with a more than wonted satisfaction.

There were present two, however, who showed but little interest in the general contentment. Of these, one was Barnaby himself, who slept, or, to avoid being beset with questions, feigned to sleep, in the chimney-corner; the other, Hugh, who, sleeping too, lay stretched upon the bench on the opposite side, in the full glare of the blazing fire.

The light that fell upon this slumbering form, showed it in all its muscular and handsome proportions. It was that of a young man, of a hale athletic figure, and a giant's strength, whose sunburnt face and swarthy throat, overgrown with jet black hair, might have served a painter for a model. Loosely attired, in the coarsest and roughest garb, with scraps of straw and hay—his usual bed—clinging here and there, and mingling with his uncombed locks, he had fallen asleep in a posture as careless as his dress. The negligence and disorder of the whole man, with something fierce and sullen in his features, gave him a picturesque appearance, that attracted the regards even of the Maypole customers who knew him well, and caused Long Parkes to say that Hugh looked more like a poaching rascal to-night than ever he had seen him yet.

"He's waiting here, I suppose," said Solomon, "to take Mr. Haredale's horse."

"That's it, sir," replied John Willet. "He's not often in the house, you know. He's more at his ease among horses than men. I look upon him as a animal himself."

Following up this opinion with a shrug that seemed meant to say, "we can't expect everybody to be like us," John put his pipe into his mouth again, and smoked like one who felt his superiority over the general run of mankind.

"That chap, sir," said John, taking it out again after a

time, and pointing at him with the stem, "though he's got all his faculties about him—bottled up and corked down, if I may say so, somewheres or another—"

"Very good!" said Parkes, nodding his head. "A very

good expression, Johnny. You'll be a tackling somebody presently. You're in twig to-night, I see."

"Take care," said Mr. Willet, not at all grateful for the compliment, "that I don't tackle you, sir, which I shall certainly endeavour to do, if you interrupt me when I'm making observations.—That chap, I was a saying, though he has all his faculties about him, somewheres or another, bottled up and corked down, has no more imagination than Barnaby has. And why hasn't he?"

The three friends shook their heads at each other; saying by that action, without the trouble of opening their lips, "Do you observe what a philosophical mind our friend has?"

"Why hasn't he?" said John, gently striking the table with his open hand. "Because they was never drawed out of him when he was a boy. That's why. What would any of us have been, if our fathers hadn't drawed our faculties out of us? What would my boy Joe have been, if I hadn't drawed his faculties out of him?—Do you mind what I'm a saying of, gentlemen?"

"Ah! we mind you," cried Parkes. "Go on improving of us, Johnny."

"Consequently, then," said Mr. Willet, "that chap, whose mother was hung when he was a little boy, along with six others, for passing bad notes—and it's a blessed thing to think how many people are hung in batches every six weeks for that, and such-like offences, as showing how wide awake our government is—that chap was then turned loose, and had to mind cows, and frighten birds away, and what not, for a few pence to live on, and so got on by degrees to mind horses, and to sleep in course of time in lofts and litter, instead of under haystacks and hedges, till at last he come to be hostler at the Maypole for his board and lodging and a annual trifle—that chap that can't read nor write, and has never had much to do with anything but animals, and has never lived in any way but like the animals he has lived among, *is* a animal. And," said Mr. Willet, arriving at his logical conclusion, "is to be treated accordingly."

"Willet," said Solomon Daisy, who had exhibited some impatience at the intrusion of so unworthy a subject on their more interesting theme, "when Mr. Chester come this morning, did he order the large room?"

"He signified, sir," said John, "that he wanted a large apartment. Yes. Certainly."

"Why then, I'll tell you what," said Solomon, speaking softly and with an earnest look. "He and Mr. Haredale are going to fight a duel in it."

Everybody looked at Mr. Willet, after this alarming suggestion. Mr. Willet looked at the fire, weighing in his own mind the effect which such an occurrence would be likely to have on the establishment.

"Well," said John, "I don't know—I am sure—I remember that when I went up last, he *had* put the lights upon the mantel-shelf."

"It's as plain," returned Solomon, "as the nose on Parkes's face"—Mr. Parkes, who had a large nose, rubbed it, and looked as if he considered this a personal allusion—"they'll fight in that room. You know by the newspapers what a common thing it is for gentlemen to fight in coffee-houses without seconds. One of 'em will be wounded or perhaps killed in this house."

"That was a challenge that Barnaby took then, eh?" said John.

"—Inclosing a slip of paper with the measure of his sword upon it, I'll bet a guinea," answered the little man. "We know what sort of gentleman Mr. Haredale is. You have told us what Barnaby said about his looks, when he came back. Depend upon it, I'm right. Now, mind."

The flip had had no flavour till now. The tobacco had been of mere English growth, compared with its present taste. A duel in that great old rambling room up-stairs, and the best bed ordered already for the wounded man!

"Would it be swords or pistols, now?" said John.

"Heaven knows. Perhaps both," returned Solomon. "The gentlemen wear swords, and may easily have pistols in their pockets—most likely have, indeed. If they fire at each other without effect, then they'll draw, and go to work in earnest."

A shade passed over Mr. Willet's face as he thought of broken windows and disabled furniture, but bethinking himself that one of the parties would probably be left alive to pay the damage, he brightened up again.

"And then," said Solomon, looking from face to face, "then we shall have one of those stains upon the floor that never come out. If Mr. Haredale wins, depend upon it, it'll be a deep one; or if he loses, it will perhaps be deeper still, for he'll never give in unless he's beaten down. We know him better, eh?"

"Better indeed!" they whispered all together.

"As to its ever being got out again," said Solomon, "I tell you it never will, or can be. Why, do you know that it has been tried, at a certain house we are acquainted with?"

"The Warren!" cried John. "No, sure!"

"Yes, sure—yes. It's only known by very few. It has been whispered about though for all that. They planed the board away, but there it was. They went deep, but it went deeper. They put new boards down, but there was one great spot that came through still, and showed itself in the old place. And—harkye—draw nearer—Mr. Geoffrey made that room his study, and sits there, always, with his foot (as I have heard) upon it; and he believes, through thinking of it long and very much, that it will never fade until he finds the man who did the deed."

As this recital ended, and they all drew closer round the fire, the tramp of a horse was heard without.

"The very man!" cried John, starting up. "Hugh! Hugh!"

The sleeper staggered to his feet, and hurried after him.

118

John quickly returned, ushering in with great attention and deference (for Mr. Haredale was his landlord) the long-expected visitor, who strode into the room clanking his heavy boots upon the floor; and looking keenly round upon the bowing group, raised his hat in acknowledgment of their profound respect.

"You have a stranger here, Willet, who sent to me," he said, in a voice which sounded naturally stern and deep. "Where is he?"

"In the great room up-stairs, sir," answered John.

"Show the way. Your staircase is dark, I know. Gentlemen, good night."

With that, he signed to the landlord to go on before; and went clanking out, and up the stairs; old John, in his agitation, ingeniously lighting everything but the way, and making a stumble at every second step.

"Stop!" he said, when they reached the landing. "I can announce myself. Don't wait."

He laid his hand upon the door, entered, and shut it heavily. Mr. Willet was by no means disposed to stand there listening by himself, especially as the walls were very thick; so descended, with much greater alacrity than he had come up, and joined his friends below.

CHAPTER XII

THERE was a brief pause in the state-room of the Maypole, as Mr. Haredale tried the lock to satisfy himself that he had shut the door securely, and, striding up the dark chamber to where the screen inclosed a little patch of light and warmth, presented himself, abruptly and in silence, before the smiling guest.

If the two had no greater sympathy in their inward thoughts than in their outward bearing and appearance, the meeting did not seem likely to prove a very calm or pleasant one. With no great disparity between them in point of years, they were, in every other respect, as unlike and far removed from each other as two men could well be. The one was soft-spoken, delicately made, precise, and elegant; the other, a burly square-built man, negligently dressed, rough and abrupt in manner, stern, and, in his present mood, forbidding both in look and speech. The one preserved a calm and placid smile; the other, a distrustful frown. The new-comer, indeed, appeared bent on showing by his every tone and gesture his determined opposition and hostility to the man he had come to meet. The guest who received him, on the other hand, seemed to feel that the contrast between them was all in his favour, and to derive a quiet exultation from it which put him more at his ease than ever.

" Haredale," said this gentleman, without the least appearance of embarrassment or reserve, " I am very glad to see you."

120

"Let us dispense with compliments. They are misplaced between us," returned the other, waving his hand, "and say plainly what we have to say. You have asked me to meet you. I am here. Why do we stand face to face again?"

"Still the same frank and sturdy character, I see!"

"Good or bad, sir, I am," returned the other, leaning his arm upon the chimney-piece, and turning a haughty look upon the occupant of the easy-chair, "the man I used to be. I have lost no old likings or dislikings; my memory has not failed me by a hair's-breadth. You ask me to give you a meeting. I say, I am here."

"Our meeting, Haredale," said Mr. Chester, tapping his snuff-box, and following with a smile the impatient gesture he had made—perhaps unconsciously—towards his sword, "is one of conference and peace, I hope?"

"I have come here," returned the other, "at your desire, holding myself bound to meet you, when and where you would. I have not come to bandy pleasant speeches, or hollow professions. You are a smooth man of the world, sir, and at such play have me at a disadvantage. The very last man on this earth with whom I would enter the lists to combat with gentle compliments and masked faces, is Mr. Chester, I do assure you. I am not his match at such weapons, and have reason to believe that few men are."

"You do me a great deal of honour, Haredale," returned the other, most composedly, "and I thank you. I will be frank with you— "

"I beg your pardon—will be what?"

"Frank—open—perfectly candid.'

"Hah!" cried Mr. Haredale, drawing his breath. "But don't let me interrupt you."

"So resolved am I to hold this course," returned the other, tasting his wine with great deliberation, "that I have determined not to quarrel with you, and not to be betrayed into a warm expression or a hasty word."

"There again," said Mr. Haredale, "you have me at a great advantage. Your self-command——"

"Is not to be disturbed, when it will serve my purpose, you would say"—rejoined the other, interrupting him with the same complacency. "Granted. I allow it. And I have a purpose to serve now. So have you. I am sure our object is the same. Let us attain it like sensible men, who have ceased to be boys some time.—Do you drink?"

"With my friends," returned the other.

"At least," said Mr. Chester, "you will be seated?"

"I will stand," returned Mr. Haredale impatiently, "on this dismantled beggared hearth, and not pollute it, fallen as it is, with mockeries. Go on."

"You are wrong, Haredale," said the other, crossing his legs, and smiling as he held his glass up in the bright glow of the fire. "You are really very wrong. The world is a lively place enough, in which we must accommodate ourselves to circumstances, sail with the stream as glibly as we can, be content to take froth for substance, the surface for the depth, the counterfeit for the real coin. I wonder no philosopher has ever established that our globe itself is hollow. It should be, if Nature is consistent in her works."

"*You* think it is, perhaps?"

"I should say," he returned, sipping his wine, "there could be no doubt about it. Well; we, in trifling with this jingling toy, have had the ill-luck to jostle and fall out. We are not what the world calls friends; but we are as good and true and loving friends for all that, as nine out of every ten of those on whom it bestows the title. You have a niece, and I a son—a fine lad, Haredale, but foolish. They fall in love with each other, and form what this same world calls an attachment; meaning a something fanciful and false like the rest, which, if it took its own free time, would break like any other bubble. But it may not have its own free time—will not, if they are left alone—and the question is, shall we two, because society calls us enemies, stand aloof, and let them rush into each other's arms, when, by approaching each other sensibly, as we do now, we can prevent it, and part them?"

"I love my niece," said Mr. Haredale, after a short silence. "It may sound strangely in your ears; but I love her."

"Strangely, my good fellow!" cried Mr. Chester, lazily filling his glass again, and pulling out his toothpick. "Not at all. I like Ned too—or, as you say, love him—that's the word among such near relations. I'm very fond of Ned. He's an amazingly good fellow, and a handsome fellow—foolish and weak as yet; that's all. But the thing is, Haredale —for I'll be very frank, as I told you I would at first— independently of any dislike that you and I might have to being related to each other, and independently of the religious differences between us—and damn it, that's important—I couldn't afford a match of this description. Ned and I couldn't do it. It's impossible."

"Curb your tongue, in God's name, if this conversation is to last," retorted Mr. Haredale fiercely. "I have said I love my niece. Do you think that, loving her, I would have her fling her heart away on any man who had your blood in his veins?"

"You see," said the other, not at all disturbed, "the advantage of being so frank and open. Just what I was about to add, upon my honour! I am amazingly attached to Ned—quite doat upon him, indeed—and even if we could afford to throw ourselves away, that very objection would be quite insuperable.—I wish you'd take some wine?"

"Mark me," said Mr. Haredale, striding to the table, and laying his hand upon it heavily. "If any man believes— presumes to think—that I, in word or deed, or in the wildest dream, ever entertained remotely the idea of Emma Haredale's favouring the suit of any one who was akin to you—in any way—I care not what—he lies. He lies, and does me grievous wrong, in the mere thought."

"Haredale," returned the other, rocking himself to and fro

as in assent, and nodding at the fire, " it's extremely manly, and really very generous in you, to meet me in this unreserved and handsome way. Upon my word, those are exactly my sentiments, only expressed with much more force and power than I could use—you know my sluggish nature, and will forgive me, I am sure."

" While I would restrain her from all correspondence with your son, and sever their intercourse here, though it should cause her death," said Mr. Haredale, who had been pacing to and fro, " I would do it kindly and tenderly if I can. I have a trust to discharge, which my nature is not formed to understand, and, for this reason, the bare fact of there being any love between them comes upon me to-night, almost for the first time."

" I am more delighted than I can possibly tell you," rejoined Mr. Chester with the utmost blandness, " to find my own impression so confirmed. You see the advantage of our having met. We understand each other. We quite agree. We have a most complete and thorough explanation, and we know what course to take.—Why don't you taste your tenant's wine? It's really very good."

" Pray who," said Mr. Haredale, " have aided Emma, or your son? Who are their go-betweens, and agents—do you know?"

" All the good people hereabouts—the neighbourhood in general, I think," returned the other, with his most affable smile. " The messenger I sent to you to-day, foremost among them all."

" The idiot? Barnaby?"

" You are surprised? I am glad of that, for I was rather so myself. Yes. I wrung that from his mother—a very decent sort of woman—from whom, indeed, I chiefly learnt how serious the matter had become, and so determined to ride out here to-day, and hold a parley with you on this neutral ground.—You're stouter than you used to be, Haredale, but you look extremely well."

124

QUITE A GOOD UNDERSTANDING

"Our business, I presume, is nearly at an end," said Mr. Haredale, with an expression of impatience he was at no pains to conceal. "Trust me, Mr. Chester, my niece shall change from this time. I will appeal," he added in a lower tone, "to her woman's heart, her dignity, her pride, her duty—"

"I shall do the same by Ned," said Mr. Chester, restoring some errant faggots to their places in the grate with the toe of his boot. "If there is anything real in this world, it is those amazingly fine feelings and those natural obligations which must subsist between father and son. I shall put it to him on every ground of moral and religious feeling. I shall represent to him that we cannot possibly afford it—that I have always looked forward to his marrying well, for a genteel provision for myself in the autumn of life—that there are a great many clamorous dogs to pay, whose claims are perfectly just and right, and who must be paid out of his wife's fortune. In short, that the very highest and most honourable feelings of our nature, with every consideration of filial duty and affection, and all that sort of thing, imperatively demand that he should run away with an heiress."

"And break her heart as speedily as possible?" said Mr. Haredale, drawing on his glove.

"There Ned will act exactly as he pleases," returned the other, sipping his wine; "that's entirely his affair. I wouldn't for the world interfere with my son, Haredale, beyond a certain point. The relationship between father and son, you know, is positively quite a holy kind of bond.—*Won't* you let me persuade you to take one glass of wine? Well! as you please, as you please," he added, helping himself again.

"Chester," said Mr. Haredale, after a short silence, during which he had eyed his smiling face from time to time intently, "you have the head and heart of an evil spirit in all matters of deception."

"Your health!" said the other, with a nod. "But I have interrupted you—"

"If now," pursued Mr. Haredale, "we should find it difficult to separate these young people, and break off their intercourse—if, for instance, you find it difficult on your side, what course do you intend to take?"

"Nothing plainer, my good fellow, nothing easier," returned the other, shrugging his shoulders and stretching himself more comfortably before the fire. "I shall then exert those powers on which you flatter me so highly—though, upon my word, I don't deserve your compliments to their full extent—and resort to a few little trivial subterfuges for rousing jealousy and resentment. You see?"

"In short, justifying the means by the end, we are, as a last resource for tearing them asunder, to resort to treachery and—and lying," said Mr. Haredale.

"Oh dear no. Fie, fie!" returned the other, relishing a pinch of snuff extremely. "Not lying. Only a little management, a little diplomacy, a little—intriguing, that's the word."

"I wish," said Mr. Haredale, moving to and fro, and stopping, and moving on again, like one who was ill at ease, "that this could have been foreseen or prevented. But as it has gone so far, and it is necessary for us to act, it is of no use shrinking or regretting. Well! I shall second your endeavours to the utmost of my power. There is one topic in the whole wide range of human thoughts on which we both agree. We shall act in concert, but apart. There will be no need, I hope, for us to meet again."

"Are you going?" said Mr. Chester, rising with a graceful indolence. "Let me light you down the stairs."

"Pray keep your seat," returned the other drily, "I know the way." So, waving his hand slightly, and putting on his hat as he turned upon his heel, he went clanking out as he had come, shut the door behind him, and tramped down the echoing stairs.

A STRICT SCRUTINY

"Pah! A very coarse animal, indeed!" said Mr. Chester, composing himself in the easy-chair again. "A rough brute. Quite a human badger!"

John Willet and his friends, who had been listening intently for the clash of swords, or firing of pistols in the great room, and had indeed settled the order in which they should rush in when summoned—in which procession old John had carefully arranged that he should bring up the rear—were very much astonished to see Mr. Haredale come down without a scratch, call for his horse, and ride away thoughtfully at a foot-pace. After some consideration, it was decided that he had left the gentleman above, for dead, and had adopted this stratagem to divert suspicion or pursuit.

As this conclusion involved the necessity of their going up-stairs forthwith, they were about to ascend in the order they had agreed upon, when a smart ringing at the guest's bell, as if he had pulled it vigorously, overthrew all their speculations, and involved them in great uncertainty and doubt. At length Mr. Willet agreed to go up-stairs himself, escorted by Hugh and Barnaby, as the strongest and stoutest fellows on the premises, who were to make their appearance under pretence of clearing away the glasses.

Under this protection, the brave and broad-faced John boldly entered the room, half a foot in advance, and received an order for a boot-jack without trembling. But when it was brought, and he leant his sturdy shoulder to the guest, Mr. Willet was observed to look very hard into his boots as he pulled them off, and, by opening his eyes much wider than usual, to appear to express some surprise and disappointment at not finding them full of blood. He took occasion, too, to examine the gentleman as closely as he could, expecting to discover sundry loopholes in his person, pierced by his adversary's sword. Finding none, however, and observing in course of time that his guest was as cool and unruffled, both in his dress and temper, as he had been all day, old John at last heaved a deep sigh, and began to think no duel had been fought that night.

"And now, Willet," said Mr. Chester, "if the room's well aired, I'll try the merits of that famous bed."

"The room, sir," returned John, taking up a candle, and nudging Barnaby and Hugh to accompany them, in case the gentleman should unexpectedly drop down faint or dead from some internal wound, "the room's as warm as any toast in a tankard. Barnaby, take you that other candle, and go on before. Hugh! Follow up, sir, with the easy-chair."

In this order—and still, in his earnest inspection, holding his candle very close to the guest; now making him feel extremely warm about the legs, now threatening to set his wig on fire, and constantly begging his pardon with great awkwardness and embarrassment—John led the party to the best bedroom, which was nearly as large as the chamber from which they had come, and held, drawn out near the fire for warmth, a great old spectral bedstead, hung with faded brocade, and ornamented, at the top of each carved post, with a plume of feathers that had once been white, but with dust and age had now grown hearse-like and funereal.

"Good night, my friends," said Mr. Chester with a sweet smile, seating himself, when he had surveyed the room from end to end, in the easy-chair which his attendants wheeled before the fire. "Good night! Barnaby, my good fellow, you say some prayers before you go to bed, I hope?"

Barnaby nodded. "He has some nonsense that he calls his prayers, sir," returned old John, officiously. "I'm afraid there an't much good in 'em."

"And Hugh?" said Mr. Chester, turning to him.

"Not I," he answered. "I know his"—pointing to Barnaby—"they're well enough. He sings 'em sometimes in the straw. I listen."

"He's quite a animal, sir," John whispered in his ear with dignity. "You'll excuse him, I'm sure. If he has any soul at all, sir, it must be such a very small one that it don't signify what he does or doesn't in that way. Good night, sir!"

The guest rejoined "God bless you!" with a fervour that was quite affecting; and John, beckoning his guards to go before, bowed himself out of the room, and left him to his rest in the Maypole's ancient bed.

CHAPTER XIII

IF Joseph Willet, the denounced and proscribed of 'prentices,
had happened to be at home when his father's courtly guest
presented himself before the Maypole door—that is, if it had
not perversely chanced to be one of the half-dozen days in
the whole year on which he was at liberty to absent himself
for as many hours without question or reproach—he would
have contrived, by hook or crook, to dive to the very bottom
of Mr. Chester's mystery, and to come at his purpose with
as much certainty as though he had been his confidential
adviser. In that fortunate case, the lovers would have had
quick warning of the ills that threatened them, and the aid
of various timely and wise suggestions to boot; for all Joe's
readiness of thought and action, and all his sympathies and
good wishes, were enlisted in favour of the young people, and
were staunch in devotion to their cause. Whether this disposition arose out of his old prepossessions in favour of the

young lady, whose history had surrounded her in his mind, almost from his cradle, with circumstances of unusual interest; or from his attachment towards the young gentleman, into whose confidence he had, through his shrewdness and alacrity, and the rendering of sundry important services as a spy and messenger, almost imperceptibly glided; whether they had their origin in either of these sources, or in the habit natural to youth, or in the constant badgering and worrying of his venerable parent, or in any hidden little love affair of his own which gave him something of a fellow-feeling in the matter, it is needless to inquire—especially as Joe was out of the way, and had no opportunity on that particular occasion of testifying to his sentiments either on one side or the other.

It was, in fact, the twenty-fifth of March, which, as most people know to their cost, is, and has been time out of mind, one of those unpleasant epochs termed quarter-days. On this twenty-fifth of March, it was John Willet's pride annually to settle, in hard cash, his account with a certain vintner and distiller in the city of London; to give into whose hands a canvas bag containing its exact amount, and not a penny more or less, was the end and object of a journey for Joe, so surely as the year and day came round.

This journey was performed upon an old grey mare, concerning whom John had an indistinct set of ideas hovering about him, to the effect that she could win a plate or cup if she tried. She never had tried, and probably never would now, being some fourteen or fifteen years of age, short in wind, long in body, and rather the worse for wear in respect of her mane and tail. Notwithstanding these slight defects, John perfectly gloried in the animal; and when she was brought round to the door by Hugh, actually retired into the bar, and there, in a secret grove of lemons, laughed with pride.

"There's a bit of horseflesh, Hugh!" said John, when he had recovered enough self-command to appear at the door again. "There's a comely creature! There's high mettle! There's bone!"

There was bone enough beyond all doubt; and so Hugh seemed to think, as he sat sideways in the saddle, lazily doubled up with his chin nearly touching his knees; and heedless of the dangling stirrups and loose bridle-rein, sauntered up and down on the little green before the door.

"Mind you take good care of her, sir," said John, appealing from this insensible person to his son and heir, who now appeared, fully equipped and ready. "Don't you ride hard."

"I should be puzzled to do that, I think, father," Joe replied, casting a disconsolate look at the animal.

"None of your impudence, sir, if you please," retorted old John. "What would you ride, sir? A wild ass or zebra would be too tame for you, wouldn't he, eh, sir? You'd like to ride a roaring lion, wouldn't you, sir, eh, sir? Hold your tongue, sir." When Mr. Willet, in his differences with his son, had exhausted all the questions that occurred to him, and Joe had said nothing at all in answer, he generally wound up by bidding him hold his tongue.

"And what does the boy mean," added Mr. Willet, after he had stared at him for a little time, in a species of stupefaction, "by cocking his hat, to such an extent! Are you going to kill the wintner, sir?"

"No," said Joe, tartly; "I'm not. Now your mind's at ease, father."

"With a milintary air, too!" said Mr. Willet, surveying him from top to toe; "with a swaggering, fire-eating, biling-water drinking sort of way with him! And what do you mean by pulling up the crocuses and snowdrops, eh, sir?"

"It's only a little nosegay," said Joe, reddening. "There's no harm in that, I hope?"

"You're a boy of business, you are, sir!" said Mr. Willet, disdainfully, "to go supposing that wintners care for nosegays."

"I don't suppose anything of the kind," returned Joe.

"Let them keep their red noses for bottles and tankards. These are going to Mr. Varden's house."

"And do you suppose *he* minds such things as crocuses?" demanded John.

"I don't know, and to say the truth, I don't care," said Joe. "Come, father, give me the money, and in the name of patience let me go."

"There it is, sir," replied John; "and take care of it; and mind you don't make too much haste back, but give the mare a long rest.—Do you mind?"

"Ay, I mind," returned Joe. "She'll need it, Heaven knows."

"And don't you score up too much at the Black Lion," said John. "Mind that too."

"Then why don't you let me have some money of my own?" retorted Joe, sorrowfully; "why don't you, father? What do you send me into London for, giving me only the right to call for my dinner at the Black Lion, which you're to pay for next time you go, as if I was not to be trusted with a few shillings? Why do you use me like this? It's not right of you. You can't expect me to be quiet under it."

"Let him have money!" cried John, in a drowsy reverie. "What does he call money—guineas? Hasn't he got money? Over and above the tolls, hasn't he one and sixpence?"

"One and sixpence!" repeated his son contemptuously.

"Yes, sir," returned John, "one and sixpence. When I was your age, I had never seen so much money, in a heap. A shilling of it is in case of accidents—the mare casting a shoe, or the like of that. The other sixpence is to spend in the diversions of London; and the diversion I recommend is to go to the top of the Monument, and sitting there. There's no temptation there, sir—no drink—no young women—no bad characters of any sort—nothing but imagination. That's the way I enjoyed myself when I was your age, sir."

To this, Joe made no answer, but beckoning Hugh, leaped

into the saddle and rode away ; and a very stalwart, manly horseman he looked, deserving a better charger than it was his fortune to bestride. John stood staring after him, or rather after the grey mare (for he had no eyes for her rider), until man and beast had been out of sight some twenty minutes, when he began to think they were gone, and slowly re-entering the house, fell into a gentle doze.

The unfortunate grey mare, who was the agony of Joe's life, floundered along at her own will and pleasure until the Maypole was no longer visible, and then contracting her legs into what in a puppet would have been looked upon as a clumsy and awkward imitation of a canter, mended her pace all at once, and did it of her own accord. The acquaintance with her rider's usual mode of proceeding, which suggested this improvement in hers, impelled her likewise to turn up a bye-way, leading—not to London, but through lanes running parallel with the road they had come, and passing within a few hundred yards of the Maypole, which led finally to an inclosure surrounding a large, old, red-brick mansion—the same of which mention was made as the Warren in the first chapter of this history. Coming to a dead stop in a little copse thereabout, she suffered her rider to dismount with right good-will, and to tie her to the trunk of a tree.

"Stay there, old girl," said Joe, "and let us see whether there's any little commission for me to-day." So saying, he left her to browse upon such stunted grass and weeds as happened to grow within the length of her tether, and passing through a wicket gate, entered the grounds on foot.

The pathway, after a very few minutes' walking, brought him close to the house, towards which, and especially towards one particular window, he directed many covert glances. It was a dreary, silent building, with echoing courtyards, desolated turret-chambers, and whole suites of rooms shut up and mouldering to ruin.

The terrace-garden, dark with the shade of overhanging trees, had an air of melancholy that was quite oppressive.

THE WARREN

Great iron gates, disused for many years, and red with rust, drooping on their hinges and overgrown with long rank grass, seemed as though they tried to sink into the ground, and hide their fallen state among the friendly weeds. The fantastic monsters on the walls, green with age and damp, and covered here and there with moss, looked grim and desolate. There was a sombre aspect even on that part of the mansion which was inhabited and kept in good repair, that struck the beholder with a sense of sadness; of something forlorn and failing, whence cheerfulness was banished. It would have been difficult to imagine a bright fire blazing in the dull and darkened rooms, or to picture any gaiety of heart or revelry that the frowning walls shut in. It seemed a place where such things had been, but could be no more —the very ghost of a house, haunting the old spot in its old outward form, and that was all.

Much of this decayed and sombre look was attributable, no doubt, to the death of its former master, and the temper of its present occupant; but remembering the tale connected with the mansion, it seemed the very place for such a deed, and one that might have been its predestined theatre years upon years ago. Viewed with reference to this legend, the sheet of water where the steward's body had been found appeared to wear a black and sullen character, such as no other pool might own; the bell upon the roof that had told the tale of murder to the midnight wind, became a very phantom whose voice would raise the listener's hair on end; and every leafless bough that nodded to another, had its stealthy whispering of the crime.

Joe paced up and down the path, sometimes stopping in affected contemplation of the building or the prospect, sometimes leaning against a tree with an assumed air of idleness and indifference, but always keeping an eye upon the window he had singled out at first. After some quarter of an hour's delay, a small white hand was waved to him for an instant from this casement, and the young man, with a respectful

135

bow, departed; saying under his breath as he crossed his horse again, "No errand for me to-day!"

But the air of smartness, the cock of the hat to which John Willet had objected, and the spring nosegay, all betokened some little errand of his own, having a more interesting object than a vintner or even a locksmith. So, indeed, it turned out; for when he had settled with the vintner—whose place of business was down in some deep cellars hard by Thames-street, and who was as purple-faced an old gentleman as if he had all his life supported their arched roof on his head—when he had settled the account, and taken the receipt, and declined tasting more than three glasses of old sherry, to the unbounded astonishment of the purple-faced vintner, who, gimlet in hand, had projected an attack upon at least a score of dusty casks, and who stood transfixed, or morally gimleted as it were, to his own wall —when he had done all this, and disposed besides of a frugal dinner at the Black Lion in Whitechapel; spurning the Monument and John's advice, he turned his steps towards the locksmith's house, attracted by the eyes of blooming Dolly Varden.

Joe was by no means a sheepish fellow, but, for all that, when he got to the corner of the street in which the locksmith lived, he could by no means make up his mind to walk straight to the house. First, he resolved to stroll up another street for five minutes, then up another street for five minutes more, and so on until he had lost full half an hour, when he made a bold plunge and found himself with a red face and a beating heart in the smoky workshop.

"Joe Willet, or his ghost?" said Varden, rising from the desk at which he was busy with his books, and looking at him under his spectacles. "Which is it? Joe in the flesh, eh? That's hearty. And how are all the Chigwell company, Joe?"

"Much as usual, sir—they and I agree as well as ever."

"Well, well!" said the locksmith. "We must be patient,

Joe, and bear with old folks' foibles. How's the mare, Joe? Does she do the four miles an hour as easily as ever? Ha, ha, ha! Does she, Joe? Eh!—What have we there, Joe— a nosegay!"

"A very poor one, sir—I thought Miss Dolly—"

"No, no," said Gabriel, dropping his voice, and shaking his head, "not Dolly. Give 'em to her mother, Joe. A great deal better give 'em to her mother. Would you mind giving 'em to Mrs. Varden, Joe?"

"Oh no, sir," Joe replied, and endeavouring, but not with the greatest possible success, to hide his disappointment. "I shall be very glad, I'm sure."

"That's right," said the locksmith, patting him on the back. "It don't matter who has 'em, Joe?"

"Not a bit, sir."—Dear heart, how the words stuck in his throat!

"Come in," said Gabriel. "I have just been called to tea. She's in the parlour."

"She," thought Joe. "Which of 'em I wonder—Mrs. or Miss?" The locksmith settled the doubt as neatly as if it had been expressed aloud, by leading him to the door, and saying, "Martha, my dear, here's young Mr. Willet."

Now, Mrs. Varden, regarding the Maypole as a sort of human man-trap, or decoy for husbands; viewing its proprietor, and all who aided and abetted him, in the light of so many poachers among Christian men; and believing, moreover, that the publicans coupled with sinners in Holy Writ were veritable licensed victuallers; was far from being favourably disposed towards her visitor. Wherefore she was taken faint directly; and being duly presented with the crocuses and snowdrops, divined on further consideration that they were the occasion of the languor which had seized upon her spirits. "I'm afraid I couldn't bear the room another minute," said the good lady, "if they remain here. *Would* you excuse my putting them out of window?"

Joe begged she wouldn't mention it on any account, and

smiled feebly as he saw them deposited on the sill outside. If anybody could have known the pains he had taken to make up that despised and misused bunch of flowers!—

"I feel it quite a relief to get rid of them, I assure you," said Mrs. Varden. "I'm better already." And indeed she did appear to have plucked up her spirits.

Joe expressed his gratitude to Providence for this favourable dispensation, and tried to look as if he didn't wonder where Dolly was.

"You're sad people at Chigwell, Mr. Joseph," said Mrs. V.

"I hope not, ma'am," returned Joe.

"You're the cruellest and most inconsiderate people in the world," said Mrs. Varden, bridling. "I wonder old Mr. Willet, having been a married man himself, doesn't know better than to conduct himself as he does. His doing it for profit is no excuse. I would rather pay the money twenty times over, and have Varden come home like a respectable and sober tradesman. If there is one character," said Mrs. Varden with great emphasis, "that offends and disgusts me more than another, it is a sot."

"Come, Martha, my dear," said the locksmith cheerily, "let us have tea, and don't let us talk about sots. There are none here, and Joe don't want to hear about them, I dare say."

At this crisis, Miggs appeared with toast.

"I dare say he does not," said Mrs. Varden; "and I dare say you do not, Varden. It's a very unpleasant subject I have no doubt, though I won't say it's personal"—Miggs coughed—"whatever I may be forced to think," Miggs sneezed expressively. "You never will know, Varden, and nobody at young Mr. Willet's age—you'll excuse me, sir— can be expected to know what a woman suffers when she is waiting at home under such circumstances. If you don't believe me, as I know you don't, here's Miggs, who is only too often a witness of it—ask her.'

"Oh! she were very bad the other night, sir, indeed she

were," said Miggs. "If you hadn't the sweetness of an angel in you, mim, I don't think you could abear it, I raly don't."

"Miggs," said Mrs. Varden, "you're profane."

"Begging your pardon, mim," returned Miggs, with shrill rapidity, "such was not my intentions, and such I hope is not my character, though I am but a servant."

"Answering me, Miggs, and providing yourself," retorted her mistress, looking round with dignity, "is one and the same thing. How dare you speak of angels in connection with your sinful fellow-beings—mere"—said Mrs. Varden, glancing at herself in a neighbouring mirror, and arranging the ribbon of her cap in a more becoming fashion—"mere worms and grovellers as we are!"

"I did not intend, mim, if you please, to give offence," said Miggs, confident in the strength of her compliment, and developing strongly in the throat as usual, "and I did not expect it would be took as such. I hope I know my own unworthiness, and that I hate and despise myself and all my fellow-creatures as every practicable Christian should."

"You'll have the goodness, if you please," said Mrs. Varden, loftily, "to step up-stairs and see if Dolly has finished dressing, and to tell her that the chair that was ordered for her will be here in a minute, and that if she keeps it waiting, I shall send it away that instant.—I'm sorry to see that you don't take your tea, Varden, and that you don't take yours, Mr. Joseph; though of course it would be foolish of me to expect that anything that can be had at home, and in the company of females, would please *you*."

This pronoun was understood in the plural sense, and included both gentlemen, upon both of whom it was rather hard and undeserved, for Gabriel had applied himself to the meal with a very promising appetite, until it was spoilt by Mrs. Varden herself, and Joe had as great a liking for the female society of the locksmith's house—or for a part of it at all events—as man could well entertain.

But he had no opportunity to say anything in his own defence, for at that moment Dolly herself appeared, and struck him quite dumb with her beauty. Never had Dolly looked so handsome as she did then, in all the glow and grace of youth, with all her charms increased a hundredfold by a most becoming dress, by a thousand little coquettish ways which nobody could assume with a better grace, and all the sparkling expectation of that accursed party. It is impossible to tell how Joe hated that party wherever it was, and all the other people who were going to it, whoever they were.

And she hardly looked at him—no, hardly looked at him. And when the chair was seen through the open door coming blundering into the workshop, she actually clapped her hands and seemed glad to go. But Joe gave her his arm—there was some comfort in that—and handed her into it. To see her seat herself inside, with her laughing eyes brighter than diamonds, and her hand—surely she had the prettiest hand in the world—on the ledge of the open window, and her little finger provokingly and pertly tilted up, as if it wondered why Joe didn't squeeze or kiss it! To think how well one or two of the modest snowdrops would have become that delicate bodice, and how they were lying neglected outside the parlour window! To see how Miggs looked on with a face expressive of knowing how all this loveliness was got up, and of being in the secret of every string and pin and hook and eye, and of saying it ain't half as real as you think, and I could look quite as well myself if I took the pains! To hear that provoking precious little scream when the chair was hoisted on its poles, and to catch that transient but not-to-be-forgotten vision of the happy face within— what torments and aggravations, and yet what delights were these! The very chairmen seemed favoured rivals as they bore her down the street.

There never was such an alteration in a small room in a small time as in that parlour when they went back to finish tea. So dark, so deserted, so perfectly disenchanted. It seemed such sheer nonsense to be sitting tamely there, when she was at a dance with more lovers than man could calculate fluttering about her—with the whole party doting on and adoring her, and wanting to marry her. Miggs was hovering about too; and the fact of her existence, the mere circumstance of her ever having been born, appeared, after Dolly, such an unaccountable practical joke. It was impossible to talk. It couldn't be done. He had nothing left for it but to stir his tea round, and round, and round, and ruminate on all the fascinations of the locksmith's lovely daughter.

Gabriel was dull too. It was a part of the certain uncertainty of Mrs. Varden's temper, that when they were in this condition, she should be gay and sprightly.

"I need have a cheerful disposition, I am sure," said the smiling housewife, "to preserve any spirits at all; and how I do it I can scarcely tell."

"Ah, mim," sighed Miggs, "begging your pardon for the interruption, there an't a many like you."

"Take away, Miggs," said Mrs. Varden, rising, "take away, pray. I know I'm a restraint here, and as I wish everybody to enjoy themselves as they best can, I feel I had better go."

"No, no, Martha," cried the locksmith. "Stop here. I'm sure we shall be very sorry to lose you, eh, Joe!" Joe started, and said "Certainly."

"Thank you, Varden, my dear," returned his wife; "but I know your wishes better. Tobacco and beer, or spirits, have much greater attractions than any *I* can boast of, and therefore I shall go and sit up-stairs and look out of window, my love. Good night, Mr. Joseph, I'm very glad to have seen you, and I only wish I could have provided something more suitable to your taste. Remember me very kindly if you please to old Mr. Willet, and tell him that whenever he comes here I have a crow to pluck with him. Good night!"

Having uttered these words with great sweetness of manner, the good lady dropped a curtsey remarkable for its condescension, and serenely withdrew.

And it was for this Joe had looked forward to the twenty-fifth of March for weeks and weeks, and had gathered the flowers with so much care, and had cocked his hat, and made himself so smart! This was the end of all his bold determination, resolved upon for the hundredth time, to speak out to Dolly and tell her how he loved her! To see her for a minute—for but a minute—to find her going out to a party and glad to go; to be looked upon as a common pipe-smoker, beer-bibber, spirit-guzzler, and tosspot! He bade farewell to his friend the locksmith, and hastened to take horse at the Black Lion, thinking as he turned towards home, as many another Joe has thought before and since, that here was an end to all his hopes—that the thing was impossible and never could be—that she didn't care for him—that he was wretched for life—and that the only congenial prospect left him, was to go for a soldier or a sailor, and get some obliging enemy to knock his brains out as soon as possible.

CHAPTER XIV

JOE WILLET rode leisurely along in his desponding mood, picturing the locksmith's daughter going down long country-dances, and poussetting dreadfully with bold strangers—which was almost too much to bear—when he heard the tramp of a horse's feet behind him, and looking back, saw a well-mounted gentleman advancing at a smart canter. As this rider passed, he checked his steed, and called him of the Maypole by his name. Joe set spurs to the grey mare, and was at his side directly.

"I thought it was you, sir," he said, touching his hat. "A fair evening, sir. Glad to see you out of doors again."

The gentleman smiled and nodded. "What gay doings have been going on to-day, Joe? Is she as pretty as ever? Nay, don't blush, man."

"If I coloured at all, Mr. Edward," said Joe, "which I didn't know I did, it was to think I should have been such a fool as ever to have any hope of her. She's as far out of my reach as—as Heaven is."

"Well, Joe, I hope that's not altogether beyond it," said Edward, good-humouredly. "Eh?"

"Ah!" sighed Joe. "It's all very fine talking, sir. Proverbs are easily made in cold blood. But it can't be helped. Are you bound for our house, sir?"

"Yes. As I am not quite strong yet, I shall stay there to-night, and ride home coolly in the morning."

"If you're in no particular hurry," said Joe after a short silence, "and will bear with the pace of this poor jade, I shall be glad to ride on with you to the Warren, sir, and hold your horse when you dismount. It'll save you having to walk from the Maypole, there and back again. I can spare the time well, sir, for I am too soon."

"And so am I," returned Edward, "though I was unconsciously riding fast just now, in compliment I suppose to the pace of my thoughts, which were travelling post. We will keep together, Joe, willingly, and be as good company as may be. And cheer up, cheer up, think of the locksmith's daughter with a stout heart, and you shall win her yet."

Joe shook his head; but there was something so cheery in the buoyant hopeful manner of this speech, that his spirits rose under its influence, and communicated as it would seem some new impulse even to the grey mare, who, breaking from her sober amble into a gentle trot, emulated the pace of Edward Chester's horse, and appeared to flatter herself that he was doing his very best.

It was a fine dry night, and the light of a young moon, which was then just rising, shed around that peace and tranquillity which gives to evening time its most delicious charm. The lengthened shadows of the trees, softened as if reflected in still water, threw their carpet on the path the travellers pursued, and the light wind stirred yet more softly than before, as though it were soothing Nature in her sleep. By little and little they ceased talking, and rode on side by side in a pleasant silence.

"The Maypole lights are brilliant to-night," said Edward, as they rode along the lane from which, while the intervening trees were bare of leaves, that hostelry was visible.

"Brilliant indeed, sir," returned Joe, rising in his stirrups to get a better view. "Lights in the large room, and a fire glimmering in the best bed-chamber? Why, what company can this be for, I wonder!"

"Some benighted horseman wending towards London, and

deterred from going on to-night by the marvellous tales of my friend the highwayman, I suppose," said Edward.

"He must be a horseman of good quality to have such accommodations. Your bed too, sir—!"

"No matter, Joe. Any other room will do for me. But come—there's nine striking. We may push on."

They cantered forward at as brisk a pace as Joe's charger could attain, and presently stopped in the little copse where he had left her in the morning. Edward dismounted, gave his bridle to his companion, and walked with a light step towards the house.

A female servant was waiting at a side gate in the garden-wall, and admitted him without delay. He hurried along the terrace-walk, and darted up a flight of broad steps leading into an old and gloomy hall, whose walls were ornamented with rusty suits of armour, antlers, weapons of the chase, and such-like garniture. Here he paused, but not long; for as he looked round, as if expecting the attendant to have followed, and wondering she had not done so, a lovely girl appeared, whose dark hair next moment rested on his breast. Almost at the same instant a heavy hand was laid upon her arm, Edward felt himself thrust away, and Mr. Haredale stood between them.

He regarded the young man sternly without removing his hat; with one hand clasped his niece, and with the other, in which he held his riding-whip, motioned him towards the door. The young man drew himself up, and returned his gaze.

"'This is well done of you, sir, to corrupt my servants, and enter my house unbidden and in secret, like a thief!" said Mr. Haredale. "Leave it, sir, and return no more."

"Miss Haredale's presence," returned the young man, "and your relationship to her, give you a licence which, if you are a brave man, you will not abuse. You have compelled me to this course, and the fault is yours—not mine."

"It is neither generous, nor honourable, nor the act of a true man, sir," retorted the other, "to tamper with the affections of a weak, trusting girl, while you shrink, in your unworthiness, from her guardian and protector, and dare not meet the light of day. More than this I will not say to

you, save that I forbid you this house, and require you to be gone."

"It is neither generous, nor honourable, nor the act of a true man to play the spy," said Edward. "Your words imply dishonour, and I reject them with the scorn they merit."

"You will find," said Mr. Haredale, calmly, "your trusty go-between in waiting at the gate by which you entered. I have played no spy's part, sir. I chanced to see you pass the gate, and followed. You might have heard me knocking for admission, had you been less swift of foot, or lingered in the garden. Please to withdraw. Your presence here is offensive to me and distressful to my niece." As he said these words, he passed his arm about the waist of the terrified and weeping girl, and drew her closer to him; and though the habitual severity of his manner was scarcely changed, there was yet apparent in the action an air of kindness and sympathy for her distress.

"Mr. Haredale," said Edward, "your arm encircles her on whom I have set my every hope and thought, and to purchase one minute's happiness for whom I would gladly lay down my life; this house is the casket that holds the precious jewel of my existence. Your niece has plighted her faith to me, and I have plighted mine to her. What have I done that you should hold me in this light esteem, and give me these discourteous words?"

"You have done that, sir," answered Mr. Haredale, "which must be undone. You have tied a lover's-knot here which must be cut asunder. Take good heed of what I say. Must. I cancel the bond between ye. I reject you, and all of your kith and kin—all the false, hollow, heartless stock."

"High words, sir," said Edward, scornfully.

"Words of purpose and meaning, as you will find," replied the other. "Lay them to heart."

"Lay you then, these," said Edward. "Your cold and sullen temper, which chills every breast about you, which turns affection into fear, and changes duty into dread, has forced us on this secret course, repugnant to our nature and our wish, and far more foreign, sir, to us than you. I am not a false, a hollow, or a heartless man; the character is

147

yours, who poorly venture on these injurious terms, against
the truth, and under the shelter whereof I reminded you just
now. You shall not cancel the bond between us. I will not
abandon this pursuit. I rely upon your niece's truth and
honour, and set your influence at nought. I leave her with
a confidence in her pure faith, which you will never weaken,
and with no concern but that I do not leave her in some
gentler care."

With that, he pressed her cold hand to his lips, and once
more encountering and returning Mr. Haredale's steady look,
withdrew.

A few words to Joe as he mounted his horse sufficiently
explained what had passed, and renewed all that young
gentleman's despondency with tenfold aggravation. They
rode back to the Maypole without exchanging a syllable,
and arrived at the door with heavy hearts.

Old John, who had peeped from behind the red curtain as
they rode up shouting for Hugh, was out directly, and said
with great importance as he held the young man's stirrup,

"He's comfortable in bed—the best bed. A thorough
gentleman; the smilingest, affablest gentleman I ever had
to do with."

"Who, Willet?" said Edward carelessly, as he dismounted.

"Your worthy father, sir," replied John. "Your honourable, venerable father."

"What does he mean?" said Edward, looking with a
mixture of alarm and doubt, at Joe.

"What *do* you mean?" said Joe. "Don't you see Mr.
Edward doesn't understand, father?"

"Why, didn't you know of it, sir?" said John, opening
his eyes wide. "How very singular! Bless you, he's been
here ever since noon to-day, and Mr. Haredale has been
having a long talk with him, and hasn't been gone an hour."

"My father, Willet!"

"Yes, sir, he told me so—a handsome, slim, upright
gentleman, in green-and-gold. In your old room up yonder,

sir. No doubt you can go in, sir," said John, walking backwards into the road and looking up at the window. " He hasn't put out his candles yet, I see."

Edward glanced at the window also, and hastily murmuring that he had changed his mind—forgotten something—and must return to London, mounted his horse again and rode away; leaving the Willets, father and son, looking at each other in mute astonishment.

CHAPTER XV

At noon next day, John Willet's guest sat lingering over his breakfast in his own home, surrounded by a variety of comforts, which left the Maypole's highest flight and utmost stretch of accommodation at an infinite distance behind, and suggested comparisons very much to the disadvantage and disfavour of that venerable tavern.

In the broad old-fashioned window-seat—as capacious as many modern sofas, and cushioned to serve the purpose of a luxurious settee—in the broad old-fashioned window-seat of a roomy chamber, Mr. Chester lounged, very much at his ease, over a well-furnished breakfast-table. He had exchanged his riding-coat for a handsome morning-gown, his boots for slippers; had been at great pains to atone for the having been obliged to make his toilet when he rose without the aid of dressing-case and tiring equipage; and, having gradually forgotten through these means the discomforts of an indifferent night and an early ride, was in a state of perfect complacency, indolence, and satisfaction.

The situation in which he found himself, indeed, was particularly favourable to the growth of these feelings; for, not to mention the lazy influence of a late and lonely breakfast, with the additional sedative of a newspaper, there was an air of repose about his place of residence peculiar to itself, and which hangs about it, even in these times, when it is more bustling and busy than it was in days of yore.

PAPER BUILDINGS

There are, still, worse places than the Temple, on a sultry day, for basking in the sun, or resting idly in the shade. There is yet a drowsiness in its courts, and a dreamy dulness in its trees and gardens; those who pace its lanes and squares may yet hear the echoes of their footsteps on the sounding stones, and read upon its gates, in passing from the tumult of the Strand or Fleet Street, "Who enters here leaves noise behind." There is still the plash of falling water in fair Fountain Court, and there are yet nooks and corners where dun-haunted students may look down from their dusty garrets, on a vagrant ray of sunlight patching the shade of the tall houses, and seldom troubled to reflect a passing stranger's form. There is yet, in the Temple, something of a clerkly monkish atmosphere, which public offices of law have not disturbed, and even legal firms have failed to scare away. In summer time, its pumps suggest to thirsty idlers, springs cooler, and more sparkling, and deeper than other wells; and as they trace the spillings of full pitchers on the heated ground, they snuff the freshness, and, sighing, cast sad looks towards the Thames, and think of baths and boats, and saunter on, despondent.

It was in a room in Paper Buildings—a row of goodly tenements, shaded in front by ancient trees, and looking, at the back, upon the Temple Gardens—that this, our idler, lounged; now taking up again the paper he had laid down a hundred times; now trifling with the fragments of his meal; now pulling forth his golden toothpick, and glancing leisurely about the room, or out at window into the trim garden walks, where a few early loiterers were already pacing to and fro. Here a pair of lovers met to quarrel and ke up; there a dark-eyed nursery-maid had better eyes for Templars than her charge; on this hand an ancient spinster, with her lapdog in a string, regarded both enormities with scornful sidelong looks; on that a weazen old gentleman, ogling the nursery-maid, looked with like scorn upon the spinster, and wondered she didn't know she was no longer young. Apart from all these, on the river's margin two or three couple of business-talkers walked slowly up and down in earnest conversation; and one young man sat thoughtfully on a bench, alone.

"Ned is amazingly patient!" said Mr. Chester, glancing at this last-named person as he set down his tea-cup and plied the golden toothpick, "immensely patient! He was sitting yonder when I began to dress, and has scarcely changed his posture since. A most eccentric dog!"

FATHER AND SON

As he spoke, the figure rose, and came towards him with a rapid pace.

"Really, as if he had heard me," said the father, resuming his newspaper with a yawn. "Dear Ned!"

Presently the room-door opened, and the young man entered; to whom his father gently waved his hand, and smiled.

"Are you at leisure for a little conversation, sir?" said Edward.

"Surely, Ned. I am always at leisure. You know my constitution.—Have you breakfasted?"

"Three hours ago."

"What a very early dog!" cried his father, contemplating him from behind the toothpick, with a languid smile.

"The truth is," said Edward, bringing a chair forward, and seating himself near the table, "that I slept but ill last night, and was glad to rise. The cause of my uneasiness cannot but be known to you, sir; and it is upon that I wish to speak."

"My dear boy," returned his father, "confide in me, I beg. But you know my constitution—don't be prosy, Ned."

"I will be plain, and brief," said Edward.

"Don't say you will, my good fellow," returned his father, crossing his legs, "or you certainly will not. You are going to tell me—"

"Plainly this, then," said the son, with an air of great concern, "that I know where you were last night—from being on the spot, indeed—and whom you saw, and what your purpose was."

"You don't say so!" cried his father. "I am delighted to hear it. It saves us the worry, and terrible wear and tear of a long explanation, and is a great relief for both. At the very house! Why didn't you come up? I should have been charmed to see you."

"I knew that what I had to say would be better said after a night's reflection, when both of us were cool," returned the son.

153

"'Fore Gad, Ned," rejoined the father, "I was cool enough last night. That detestable Maypole! By some infernal contrivance of the builder, it holds the wind, and keeps it fresh. You remember the sharp east wind that blew so hard five weeks ago? I give you my honour it was rampant in that old house last night, though out of doors there was a dead calm. But you were saying—"

"I was about to say, Heaven knows how seriously and earnestly, that you have made me wretched, sir. Will you hear me gravely for a moment?"

"My dear Ned," said his father, "I will hear you with the patience of an anchorite. Oblige me with the milk."

"I saw Miss Haredale last night," Edward resumed, when he had complied with this request; "her uncle, in her presence, immediately after your interview, and, as of course I know, in consequence of it, forbade me the house, and, with circumstances of indignity which are of your creation I am sure, commanded me to leave it on the instant."

"For his manner of doing so, I give you my honour, Ned, I am not accountable," said his father. "That you must excuse. He is a mere boor, a log, a brute, with no address in life.—Positively a fly in the jug. The first I have seen this year."

Edward rose, and paced the room. His imperturbable parent sipped his tea.

"Father," said the young man, stopping at length before him, "we must not trifle in this matter. We must not deceive each other, or ourselves. Let me pursue the manly open part I wish to take, and do not repel me by this unkind indifference."

"Whether I am indifferent or no," returned the other, "I leave you, my dear boy, to judge. A ride of twenty-five or thirty miles, through miry roads—a Maypole dinner—a tête-à-tête with Haredale, which, vanity apart, was quite a Valentine and Orson business—a Maypole bed—a Maypole landlord, and a Maypole retinue of idiots and centaurs;—

whether the voluntary endurance of these things looks like indifference, dear Ned, or like the excessive anxiety, and devotion, and all that sort of thing, of a parent, you shall determine for yourself."

"I wish you to consider, sir," said Edward, "in what a cruel situation I am placed. Loving Miss Haredale as I do— "

"My dear fellow," interrupted his father with a compassionate smile, "you do nothing of the kind. You don't know anything about it. There's no such thing, I assure you. Now, do take my word for it. You have good sense, Ned,—great good sense. I wonder you should be guilty of such amazing absurdities. You really surprise me."

"I repeat," said his son firmly, "that I love her. You have interposed to part us, and have, to the extent I have just now told you of, succeeded. May I induce you, sir, in time, to think more favourably of our attachment, or is it your intention and your fixed design to hold us asunder if you can?"

"My dear Ned," returned his father, taking a pinch of snuff and pushing his box towards him, "that *is* my purpose most undoubtedly."

"The time that has elapsed," rejoined his son, "since I began to know her worth, has flown in such a dream that until now I have hardly once paused to reflect upon my true position. What is it? From my childhood I have been accustomed to luxury and idleness, and have been bred as though my fortune were large, and my expectations almost without a limit. The idea of wealth has been familiarised to me from my cradle. I have been taught to look upon those means, by which men raise themselves to riches and distinction, as being beyond my breeding, and beneath my care. I have been, as the phrase is, liberally educated, and am fit for nothing. I find myself at last wholly dependent upon you, with no resource but in your favour. In this momentous question of my life we do not, and it would seem we never can, agree. I have shrunk instinctively alike from

155

those to whom you have urged me to pay court, and from
the motives of interest and gain which have rendered them
in your eyes visible objects for my suit. If there never has
been thus much plain-speaking between us before, sir, the
fault has not been mine, indeed. If I seem to speak too
plainly now, it is, believe me, father, in the hope that there
may be a franker spirit, a worthier reliance, and a kinder
confidence between us in time to come."

"My good fellow," said his smiling father, "you quite
affect me. Go on, my dear Edward, I beg. But remember
your promise. There is great earnestness, vast candour, a
manifest sincerity in all you say, but I fear I observe the
faintest indications of a tendency to prose."

"I am very sorry, sir."

"I am very sorry, too, Ned, but you know that I cannot
fix my mind for any long period upon one subject. If you'll
come to the point at once, I'll imagine all that ought to go
before, and conclude it said. Oblige me with the milk again.
Listening invariably makes me feverish."

"What I would say then, tends to this," said Edward.
"I cannot bear this absolute dependence, sir, even upon you.
Time has been lost and opportunity thrown away, but I am
yet a young man, and may retrieve it. Will you give me
the means of devoting such abilities and energies as I possess,
to some worthy pursuit? Will you let me try to make for
myself an honourable path in life? For any term you please
to name—say for five years if you will—I will pledge myself
to move no further in the matter of our difference without
your full concurrence. During that period, I will endeavour
earnestly and patiently, if ever man did, to open some
prospect for myself, and free you from the burden you fear
I should become if I married one whose worth and beauty
are her chief endowments. Will you do this, sir? At the
expiration of the term we agree upon, let us discuss this
subject again. Till then, unless it is revived by you, let it
never be renewed between us."

FAMILY AFFAIRS

"My dear Ned," returned his father, laying down the newspaper at which he had been glancing carelessly, and throwing himself back in the window-seat, "I believe you know how very much I dislike what are called family affairs, which are only fit for plebeian Christmas days, and have no manner of business with people of our condition. But as you are proceeding upon a mistake, Ned—altogether upon a mistake—I will conquer my repugnance to entering on such matters, and give you a perfectly plain and candid answer, if you will do me the favour to shut the door."

Edward having obeyed him, he took an elegant little knife from his pocket, and paring his nails, continued:

"You have to thank me, Ned, for being of good family; for your mother, charming person as she was, and almost broken-hearted, and so forth, as she left me, when she was prematurely compelled to become immortal—had nothing to boast of in that respect."

"Her father was at least an eminent lawyer, sir," said Edward.

"Quite right, Ned; perfectly so. He stood high at the bar, had a great name and great wealth, but having risen from nothing—I have always closed my eyes to the circumstance and steadily resisted its contemplation, but I fear his father dealt in pork, and that his business did once involve cow-heel and sausages—he wished to marry his daughter into a good family. He had his heart's desire, Ned. I was a younger son's younger son, and I married her. We each had our object, and gained it. She stepped at once into the politest and best circles, and I stepped into a fortune which I assure you was very necessary to my comfort— quite indispensable. Now, my good fellow, that fortune is among the things that have been. It is gone, Ned, and has been gone—how old are you? I always forget."

"Seven-and-twenty, sir."

"Are you indeed?" cried his father, raising his eyelids in a languishing surprise. "So much! Then I should say,

157

Ned, that as nearly as I remember, its skirts vanished from human knowledge, about eighteen or nineteen years ago. It was about that time when I came to live in these chambers (once your grandfather's, and bequeathed by that extremely respectable person to me), and commenced to live upon an inconsiderable annuity and my past reputation."

"You are jesting with me, sir," said Edward.

"Not in the slightest degree, I assure you," returned his father with great composure. "These family topics are so extremely dry, that I am sorry to say they don't admit of any such relief. It is for that reason, and because they have an appearance of business, that I dislike them so very much. Well! You know the rest. A son, Ned, unless he is old enough to be a companion—that is to say, unless he is some two or three and twenty—is not the kind of thing to have about one. He is a restraint upon his father, his father is a restraint upon him, and they make each other mutually uncomfortable. Therefore, until within the last four years or so—I have a poor memory for dates, and if I mistake, you will correct me in your own mind—you pursued your studies at a distance, and picked up a great variety of accomplishments. Occasionally we passed a week or two together here, and disconcerted each other as only such near relations can. At last you came home. I candidly tell you, my dear boy, that if you had been awkward and overgrown, I should have exported you to some distant part of the world."

"I wish with all my soul you had, sir," said Edward.

"No you don't, Ned," said his father coolly; "you are mistaken, I assure you. I found you a handsome, prepossessing, elegant fellow, and I threw you into the society I can still command. Having done that, my dear fellow, I consider that I have provided for you in life, and rely upon your doing something to provide for me in return."

"I do not understand your meaning, sir."

"My meaning, Ned, is obvious—I observe another fly in

the cream-jug, but have the goodness not to take it out as you did the first, for their walk when their legs are milky, is extremely ungraceful and disagreeable—my meaning is, that you must do as I did; that you must marry well and make the most of yourself."

"A mere fortune-hunter!" cried the son, indignantly.

"What in the devil's name, Ned, would you be!" returned the father. "All men are fortune-hunters, are they not? The law, the church, the court, the camp—see how they are all crowded with fortune-hunters, jostling each other in the pursuit. The Stock-exchange, the pulpit, the counting-house, the royal drawing-room, the senate,—what but fortune-hunters are they filled with? A fortune-hunter! Yes. You *are* one; and you would be nothing else, my dear Ned, if you were the greatest courtier, lawyer, legislator, prelate, or merchant, in existence. If you are squeamish and moral, Ned, console yourself with the reflection that at the very worst your fortune-hunting can make but one person miserable or unhappy. How many people do you suppose these other kinds of huntsmen crush in following their sport—hundreds at a step? Or thousands?"

The young man leant his head upon his hand, and made no answer.

"I am quite charmed," said the father rising, and walking slowly to and fro—stopping now and then to glance at himself in the mirror, or survey a picture through his glass, with the air of a connoisseur, "that we have had this conversation, Ned, unpromising as it was. It establishes a confidence between us which is quite delightful, and was certainly necessary, though how you can ever have mistaken our positions and designs, I confess I cannot understand. I conceived, until I found your fancy for this girl, that all these points were tacitly agreed upon between us."

"I knew you were embarrassed, sir," returned the son, raising his head for a moment, and then falling into his former attitude, "but I had no idea we were the beggared

159

wretches you describe. How could I suppose it, bred as I have been; witnessing the life you have always led; and the appearance you have always made?"

" My dear child," said the father—" for you really talk so like a child that I must call you one—you were bred upon a careful principle; the very manner of your education, I assure you, maintained my credit surprisingly. As to the life I lead, I must lead it, Ned. I must have these little refinements about me. I have always been used to them, and I cannot exist without them. They must surround me, you observe, and therefore they are here. With regard to our circumstances, Ned, you may set your mind at rest upon that score. They are desperate. Your own appearance is by no means despicable, and our joint pocket-money alone devours our income. That's the truth."

" Why have I never known this before? Why have you encouraged me, sir, to an expenditure and mode of life to which we have no right or title?"

" My good fellow," returned his father more compassionately than ever, " if you made no appearance, how could you possibly succeed in the pursuit for which I destined you? As to our mode of life, every man has a right to live in the best way he can; and to make himself as comfortable as he can, or he is an unnatural scoundrel. Our debts, I grant, are very great, and therefore it the more behoves you, as a young man of principle and honour, to pay them off as speedily as possible."

" The villain's part," muttered Edward, " that I have unconsciously played! I to win the heart of Emma Haredale! I would, for her sake, I had died first!"

" I am glad you see, Ned," returned his father, " how perfectly self-evident it is, that nothing can be done in that quarter. But apart from this, and the necessity of your speedily bestowing yourself on another (as you know you could to-morrow, if you chose), I wish you'd look upon it pleasantly. In a religious point of view alone, how could you ever think of uniting yourself to a Catholic, unless she was amazingly rich? You ought to be so very Protestant, coming of such a Protestant family as you do. Let us be moral, Ned, or we are nothing. Even if one could set that objection aside, which is impossible, we come to another which is quite conclusive. The very idea of marrying a girl whose father was killed, like meat! Good God, Ned, how disagreeable! Consider the impossibility of having any respect for your father-in-law under such unpleasant circumstances—think of his having been 'viewed' by jurors, and 'sat upon' by coroners, and of his very doubtful position in the family ever afterwards. It seems to me such an indelicate sort of thing that I really think the girl ought to have been put to death by the state to prevent its happening. But I tease you perhaps. You would rather be alone? My dear Ned, most willingly. God bless you. I shall be going out presently, but we shall meet to-night, or if not to-night, certainly to-morrow. Take care of yourself in the mean time, for both our sakes. You are a person of great consequence to me, Ned—of vast consequence indeed. God bless you!"

With these words, the father, who had been arranging his cravat in the glass, while he uttered them in a disconnected careless manner, withdrew, humming a tune as he went. The son, who had appeared so lost in thought as not to hear or understand them, remained quite still and silent. After the lapse of half an hour or so, the elder Chester, gaily dressed, went out. The younger still sat with his head resting on his hands, in what appeared to be a kind of stupor.

CHAPTER XVI

A SERIES of pictures representing the streets of London in the night, even at the comparatively recent date of this tale, would present to the eye something so very different in character from the reality which is witnessed in these times, that it would be difficult for the beholder to recognise his most familiar walks in the altered aspect of little more than half a century ago.

They were, one and all, from the broadest and best to the narrowest and least frequented, very dark. The oil and cotton lamps, though regularly trimmed twice or thrice in the long winter nights, burnt feebly at the best; and at a late hour, when they were unassisted by the lamps and candles in the shops, cast but a narrow track of doubtful light upon the footway, leaving the projecting doors and house-fronts in the deepest gloom. Many of the courts and lanes were left in total darkness; those of the meaner sort, where one glimmering light twinkled for a score of houses, being favoured in no slight degree. Even in these places, the inhabitants had often good reason for extinguishing their lamp as soon as it was lighted; and the watch being utterly inefficient and powerless to prevent them, they did so at their pleasure. Thus, in the lightest thoroughfares, there was at every turn some obscure and dangerous spot whither a thief might fly for shelter, and few would care to follow; and the city being belted round by fields, green lanes, waste grounds, and lonely roads, dividing it at that time from the suburbs that have joined it since, escape, even where the pursuit was hot, was rendered easy.

It is no wonder that with these favouring circumstances in full and constant operation, street robberies, often accompanied by cruel wounds, and not unfrequently by loss of life, should have been of nightly occurrence in the very heart of London, or that quiet folks should have had great dread of traversing its streets after the shops were closed. It was not unusual for those who wended home alone at midnight, to keep the middle of the road, the better to guard against surprise from lurking footpads; few would venture to repair at a late hour to Kentish Town or Hampstead, or even to Kensington or Chelsea, unarmed and unattended; while he who had been loudest and most valiant at the supper-table or the tavern, and had but a mile or so to go, was glad to fee a link-boy to escort him home.

There were many other characteristics—not quite so disagreeable—about the thoroughfares of London then, with which they had been long familiar. Some of the shops, especially those to the eastward of Temple Bar, still adhered to the old practice of hanging out a sign; and the creaking and swinging of these boards in their iron frames on windy nights, formed a strange and mournful concert for the ears of those who lay awake in bed or hurried through the streets. Long stands of hackney-chairs and groups of chairmen, compared with whom the coachmen of our day are gentle and polite, obstructed the way and filled the air with clamour; night-cellars, indicated by a little stream of light crossing the pavement, and stretching out half-way into the road, and by the stifled roar of voices from below, yawned for the reception and entertainment of the most abandoned of both sexes; under every shed and bulk small groups of link-boys gamed away the earnings of the day; or one more weary than the rest, gave way to sleep, and let the fragment of his torch fall hissing on the puddled ground.

Then there was the watch with staff and lantern crying

the hour, and the kind of weather; and those who woke up
at his voice and turned them round in bed, were glad to
hear it rained, or snowed, or blew, or froze, for very comfort's
sake. The solitary passenger was startled by the chairmen's
cry of "By your leave there!" as two came trotting past

him with their empty vehicle—carried backwards to show its
being disengaged and hurried to the nearest stand. Many
a private chair, too, inclosing some fine lady, monstrously
hooped and furbelowed, and preceded by running-footmen
bearing flambeaux—for which extinguishers are yet suspended
before the doors of a few houses of the better sort—made

the way gay and light as it danced along, and darker and
more dismal when it had passed. It was not unusual for
these running gentry, who carried it with a very high hand,
to quarrel in the servants' hall while waiting for their
masters and mistresses; and, falling to blows either there or
in the street without, to strew the place of skirmish with
hair-powder, fragments of bag-wigs, and scattered nosegays.
Gaming, the vice which ran so high among all classes (the
fashion being of course set by the upper), was generally the
cause of these disputes; for cards and dice were as openly
used, and worked as much mischief, and yielded as much
excitement below stairs, as above. While incidents like
these, arising out of drums and masquerades and parties at
quadrille, were passing at the west end of the town, heavy
stage-coaches and scarce heavier waggons were lumbering
slowly towards the city, the coachmen, guard, and passengers,
armed to the teeth, and the coach—a day or so perhaps
behind its time, but that was nothing—despoiled by highwaymen; who made no scruple to attack, alone and single-
handed, a whole caravan of goods and men, and sometimes
shot a passenger or two, and were sometimes shot themselves,
as the case might be. On the morrow, rumours of this new
act of daring on the road yielded matter for a few hours'
conversation through the town, and a Public Progress of
some fine gentleman (half drunk) to Tyburn, dressed in the
newest fashion, and damning the ordinary with unspeakable
gallantry and grace, furnished to the populace, at once a
pleasant excitement and a wholesome and profound example.

Among all the dangerous characters who, in such a state
of society, prowled and skulked in the metropolis at night,
there was one man from whom many as uncouth and fierce as
he, shrunk with an involuntary dread. Who he was, or whence
he came, was a question often asked, but which none could
answer. His name was unknown, he had never been seen
until within about eight days or thereabouts, and was equally
a stranger to the old ruffians, upon whose haunts he ventured

fearlessly, as to the young. He could be no spy, for he never removed his slouched hat to look about him, entered into conversation with no man, heeded nothing that passed, listened to no discourse, regarded nobody that came or went. But so surely as the dead of night set in, so surely this man was in the midst of the loose concourse in the night-cellar where outcasts of every grade resorted; and there he sat till morning.

He was not only a spectre at their licentious feasts; a something in the midst of their revelry and riot that chilled and haunted them; but out of doors he was the same. Directly it was dark, he was abroad—never in company with any one, but always alone; never lingering or loitering, but always walking swiftly; and looking (so they said who had seen him) over his shoulder from time to time, and as he did so quickening his pace. In the fields, the lanes, the roads, in all quarters of the town—east, west, north, and south—that man was seen gliding on like a shadow. He was always hurrying away. Those who encountered him, saw him steal past, caught sight of the backward glance, and so lost him in the darkness.

This constant restlessness, and flitting to and fro, gave rise to strange stories. He was seen in such distant and remote places, at times so nearly tallying with each other, that some doubted whether there were not two of them, or more—some, whether he had not unearthly means of travelling from spot to spot. The footpad hiding in a ditch had marked him passing like a ghost along its brink; the vagrant had met him on the dark high-road; the beggar had seen him pause upon the bridge to look down at the water, and then sweep on again; they who dealt in bodies with the surgeons could swear he slept in churchyards, and that they had beheld him glide away among the tombs on their approach. And as they told these stories to each other, one who had looked about him would pull his neighbour by the sleeve, and there he would be among them.

IN A THREATENING ATTITUDE

At last, one man—he was one of those whose commerce lay among the graves—resolved to question this strange companion. Next night, when he had eat his poor meal voraciously (he was accustomed to do that, they had observed, as though he had no other in the day), this fellow sat down at his elbow.

"A black night, master!"

"It is a black night."

"Blacker than last, though that was pitchy too. Didn't I pass you near the turnpike in the Oxford-road?"

"It's like you may. I don't know."

"Come, come, master," cried the fellow, urged on by the looks of his comrades, and slapping him on the shoulder; "be more companionable and communicative. Be more the gentleman in this good company. There are tales among us that you have sold yourself to the devil, and I know not what."

"We all have, have we not?" returned the stranger, looking up. "If we were fewer in number, perhaps he would give better wages."

"It goes rather hard with you, indeed," said the fellow, as the stranger disclosed his haggard unwashed face, and torn clothes. "What of that? Be merry, master. A stave of a roaring song now—"

"Sing you, if you desire to hear one," replied the other, shaking him roughly off; "and don't touch me if you're a prudent man; I carry arms which go off easily—they have done so, before now—and make it dangerous for strangers who don't know the trick of them, to lay hands upon me."

"Do you threaten?" said the fellow.

"Yes," returned the other, rising and turning upon him, and looking fiercely round as if in apprehension of a general attack.

His voice, and look, and bearing—all expressive of the wildest recklessness and desperation—daunted while they repelled the bystanders. Although in a very different sphere

167

of action now, they were not without much of the effect they had wrought at the Maypole Inn.

"I am what you all are, and live as you all do," said the man sternly, after a short silence. "I am in hiding here like the rest, and if we were surprised would perhaps do my part with the best of ye. If it's my humour to be left to myself, let me have it. Otherwise,"—and here he swore a tremendous oath—"there'll be mischief done in this place, though there *are* odds of a score against me."

A low murmur, having its origin perhaps in a dread of the man and the mystery that surrounded him, or perhaps in a sincere opinion on the part of some of those present, that it would be an inconvenient precedent to meddle too curiously with a gentleman's private affairs if he saw reason to conceal them, warned the fellow who had occasioned this discussion that he had best pursue it no further. After a short time the strange man lay down upon a bench to sleep, and when they thought of him again, they found he was gone.

Next night, as soon as it was dark, he was abroad again and traversing the streets; he was before the locksmith's house more than once, but the family were out, and it was close shut. This night he crossed London Bridge and passed into Southwark. As he glided down a bye-street, a woman with a little basket on her arm, turned into it at the other end. Directly he observed her, he sought the shelter of an archway, and stood aside until she had passed. Then he emerged cautiously from his hiding-place, and followed.

She went into several shops to purchase various kinds of household necessaries, and round every place at which she stopped he hovered like her evil spirit; following her when she reappeared. It was nigh eleven o'clock, and the passengers in the streets were thinning fast, when she turned, doubtless to go home. The phantom still followed her.

She turned into the same bye-street in which he had seen her first, which, being free from shops, and narrow, was extremely dark. She quickened her pace here, as though

168

distrustful of being stopped, and robbed of such trifling property as she carried with her. He crept along on the other side of the road. Had she been gifted with the speed of wind, it seemed as if his terrible shadow would have tracked her down.

At length the widow—for she it was—reached her own door, and, panting for breath, paused to take the key from her basket. In a flush and glow, with the haste she had made, and the pleasure of being safe at home, she stooped to draw it out, when, raising her head, she saw him standing silently beside her: the apparition of a dream.

His hand was on her mouth, but that was needless, for her tongue clove to its roof, and her power of utterance was gone. " I have been looking for you many nights. Is the house empty? Answer me. Is any one inside ? "

She could only answer by a rattle in her throat.

" Make me a sign."

She seemed to indicate that there was no one there. He took the key, unlocked the door, carried her in, and secured it carefully behind them.

CHAPTER XVII

It was a chilly night, and the fire in the widow's parlour had burnt low. Her strange companion placed her in a chair, and stooping down before the half-extinguished ashes, raked them together and fanned them with his hat. From time to time he glanced at her over his shoulder, as though to assure himself of her remaining quiet and making no effort to depart; and that done, busied himself about the fire again.

It was not without reason that he took these pains, for his dress was dank and drenched with wet, his jaws rattled with cold, and he shivered from head to foot. It had rained hard during the previous night and for some hours in the morning, but since noon it had been fine. Wheresoever he had passed the hours of darkness, his condition sufficiently betokened that many of them had been spent beneath the open sky. Besmeared with mire; his saturated clothes clinging with a damp embrace about his limbs; his beard unshaven, his face unwashed, his meagre cheeks worn into deep hollows, —a more miserable wretch could hardly be, than this man who now cowered down upon the widow's hearth, and watched the struggling flame with bloodshot eyes.

She had covered her face with her hands, fearing, as it seemed, to look towards him. So they remained for some short time in silence. Glancing round again, he asked at length:

AGAIN, WHO IS IT?

" Is this your house ? "

" It is. Why, in the name of Heaven, do you darken it ? "

" Give me meat and drink," he answered sullenly, " or I dare do more than that. The very marrow in my bones is cold with wet and hunger. I must have warmth and food, and I will have them here."

" You were the robber on the Chigwell-road."

" I was."

" And nearly a murderer then."

" The will was not wanting. There was one came upon me and raised the hue-and-cry, that it would have gone hard with, but for his nimbleness. I made a thrust at him."

" You thrust your sword at *him!*" cried the widow, looking upwards. " You hear this man! you hear and saw!"

He looked at her, as, with her head thrown back, and her hands tight clenched together, she uttered these words in an agony of appeal. Then, starting to his feet as she had done, he advanced towards her.

" Beware!" she cried in a suppressed voice, whose firmness stopped him midway. " Do not so much as touch me with a finger, or you are lost; body and soul, you are lost."

" Hear me," he replied, menacing her with his hand. " I, that in the form of a man live the life of a hunted beast! that in the body am a spirit, a ghost upon the earth, a thing from which all creatures shrink, save those curst beings of another world, who will not leave me;—I am, in my desperation of this night, past all fear but that of the hell in which I exist from day to day. Give the alarm, cry out, refuse to shelter me. I will not hurt you. But I will not be taken alive; and so surely as you threaten me above your breath, I fall a dead man on this floor. The blood with which I sprinkle it, be on you and yours, in the name of the Evil Spirit that tempts men to their ruin!"

As he spoke, he took a pistol from his breast, and firmly clutched it in his hand.

" Remove this man from me, good Heaven!" cried the

171

widow. " In thy grace and mercy, give him one minute's penitence, and strike him dead ! "

" It has no such purpose," he said, confronting her. " It is deaf. Give me to eat and drink, lest I do that it cannot help my doing, and will not do for you."

" Will you leave me, if I do thus much? Will you leave me and return no more ? "

" I will promise nothing," he rejoined, seating himself at the table, " nothing but this—I will execute my threat if you betray me."

She rose at length, and going to a closet or pantry in the room, brought out some fragments of cold meat and bread and put them on the table. He asked for brandy, and for water. These she produced likewise; and he ate and drank with the voracity of a famished hound. All the time he was so engaged she kept at the uttermost distance of the chamber, and sat there shuddering, but with her face towards him. She never turned her back upon him once ; and although when she passed him (as she was obliged to do in going to and from the cupboard) she gathered the skirts of her garment about her, as if even its touching his by chance were horrible to think of, still, in the midst of all this dread and terror, she kept her face towards his own, and watched his every movement.

His repast ended—if that can be called one, which was a mere ravenous satisfying of the calls of hunger—he moved his chair towards the fire again, and warming himself before the blaze which had now sprung brightly up, accosted her once more.

" I am an outcast, to whom a roof above his head is often an uncommon luxury, and the food a beggar would reject is delicate fare. You live here at your ease. Do you live alone?"

" I do not," she made answer with an effort.

" Who dwells here besides ? "

" One—it is no matter who. You had best begone, or he may find you here. Why do you linger ? "

172

"For warmth," he replied, spreading out his hands before the fire. "For warmth. You are rich, perhaps?"

"Very," she said faintly. "Very rich. No doubt I am very rich."

"At least you are not penniless. You have some money. You were making purchases to-night."

"I have a little left. It is but a few shillings."

"Give me your purse. You had it in your hand at the door. Give it to me!"

She stepped to the table and laid it down. He reached across, took it up, and told the contents into his hand. As he was counting them, she listened for a moment, and sprung towards him.

"Take what there is, take all, take more if more were there, but go before it is too late. I have heard a wayward step without, I know full well. It will return directly. Begone."

"What do you mean?"

"Do not stop to ask. I will not answer. Much as I dread to touch you, I would drag you to the door if I possessed the strength, rather than you should lose an instant. Miserable wretch! fly from this place."

"If there are spies without, I am safer here," replied the man, standing aghast. "I will remain here, and will not fly till the danger is past."

"It is too late!" cried the widow, who had listened for the step, and not to him. "Hark to that foot upon the ground. Do you tremble to hear it! It is my son, my idiot son!"

As she said this wildly, there came a heavy knocking at the door. He looked at her, and she at him.

"Let him come in," said the man, hoarsely. "I fear him less than the dark, houseless night. He 'mocks again. Let him come in!"

"The dread of this hour," returned the widow, "has been upon me all my life, and I will not. Evil will fall upon him, if you stand eye to eye. My blighted boy! Oh! all good angels who know the truth—hear a poor mother's prayer, and spare my boy from knowledge of this man!"

"He rattles at the shutters!" cried the man. "He calls you. That voice and cry! It was he who grappled with me in the road. Was it he?"

She had sunk upon her knees, and so knelt down, moving her lips, but uttering no sound. As he gazed upon her, uncertain what to do or where to turn, the shutters flew open. He had barely time to catch a knife from the table, sheathe it in the loose sleeve of his coat, hide in the closet, and do all with the lightning's speed, when Barnaby tapped at the bare glass, and raised the sash exultingly.

"Why, who can keep out Grip and me!" he cried, thrusting in his head, and staring round the room. "Are you there, mother? How long you keep us from the fire and light!"

She stammered some excuse and tendered him her hand. But Barnaby sprung lightly in without assistance, and putting his arms about her neck, kissed her a hundred times.

"We have been afield, mother—leaping ditches, scrambling through hedges, running down steep banks, up and away, and hurrying on. The wind has been blowing, and the rushes and young plants bowing and bending to it, lest it should do them harm, the cowards—and Grip—ha ha ha!—brave Grip, who cares for nothing, and when the wind rolls him over in the dust, turns manfully to bite it—Grip, bold Grip, has quarrelled with every little bowing twig—thinking, he told me, that it mocked him—and has worried it like a bull-dog. Ha ha ha!"

The raven, in his little basket at his master's back, hearing this frequent mention of his name in a tone of exultation, expressed his sympathy by crowing like a cock, and afterwards running over his various phrases of speech with such rapidity, and in so many varieties of hoarseness, that they sounded like the murmurs of a crowd of people.

174

"He takes such care of me besides!" said Barnaby. "Such care, mother! He watches all the time I sleep, and when I shut my eyes and make-believe to slumber, he practises new learning softly; but he keeps his eye on me the while, and if he sees me laugh, though never so little, stops directly. He won't surprise me till he's perfect."

The raven crowed again in a rapturous manner which plainly said, "Those are certainly some of my characteristics, and I glory in them." In the meantime, Barnaby closed the window and secured it, and coming to the fireplace, prepared to sit down with his face to the closet. But his mother prevented this, by hastily taking that side herself, and motioning him towards the other.

"How pale you are to-night!" said Barnaby, leaning on his stick. "We have been cruel, Grip, and made her anxious!"

Anxious in good truth, and sick at heart! The listener held the door of his hiding-place open with his hand, and closely watched her son. Grip—alive to everything his master was unconscious of—had his head out of the basket, and in return was watching him intently with his glistening eye.

"He flaps his wings," said Barnaby, turning almost quickly enough to catch the retreating form and closing door, "as if there were strangers here, but Grip is wiser than to fancy that. Jump then!"

Accepting this invitation with a dignity peculiar to himself, the bird hopped up on his master's shoulder, from that to his extended hand, and so to the ground. Barnaby unstrapping the basket and putting it down in a corner with the lid open, Grip's first care was to shut it down with all possible despatch, and then to stand upon it. Believing, no doubt, that he had now rendered it utterly impossible, and beyond the power of mortal man, to shut him up in it any more, he drew a great many corks in triumph, and uttered a corresponding number of hurrahs.

"Mother!" said Barnaby, laying aside his hat and stick,

BARNABY RUDGE

and returning to the chair from which he had risen, "I'll tell you where we have been to-day, and what we have been doing,—shall I?"

She took his hand in hers, and holding it, nodded the word she could not speak.

"You mustn't tell," said Barnaby, holding up his finger, "for it's a secret, mind, and only known to me, and Grip, and Hugh. We had the dog with us, but he's not like Grip, clever as he is, and doesn't guess it yet, I'll wager.—Why do you look behind me so?"

"Did I?" she answered faintly. "I didn't know I did. Come nearer me."

"You are frightened!" said Barnaby, changing colour. "Mother—you don't see—"

"See what?"

"There's—there's none of this about, is there?" he answered in a whisper, drawing closer to her and clasping the mark upon his wrist. "I am afraid there is, somewhere. You make my hair stand on end, and my flesh creep. Why do you look like that? Is it in the room as I have seen it in my dreams, dashing the ceiling and the walls with red? Tell me. Is it?"

He fell into a shivering fit as he put the question, and shutting out the light with his hands, sat shaking in every limb until it had passed away. After a time, he raised his head and looked about him.

"Is it gone?"

"There has been nothing here," rejoined his mother, soothing him. "Nothing indeed, dear Barnaby. Look! You see there are but you and me."

He gazed at her vacantly, and, becoming reassured by degrees, burst into a wild laugh.

"But let us see," he said, thoughtfully. "We were talking? Was it you and me? Where have we been?"

"Nowhere but here."

"Aye, but Hugh, and I," said Barnaby,—"that's it. Maypole Hugh, and I, you know, and Grip—we have been lying in the forest, and among the trees by the roadside, with a dark lantern after night came on, and the dog in a noose ready to slip him when the man came by."

"What man?"

"The robber; him that the stars winked at. We have waited for him after dark these many nights, and we shall have him. I'd know him in a thousand. Mother, see here! This is the man. Look!"

He twisted his handkerchief round his head, pulled his hat upon his brow, wrapped his coat about him, and stood up before her: so like the original he counterfeited, that the dark figure peering out behind him might have passed for his own shadow.

"Ha ha ha! We shall have him," he cried, ridding himself of the semblance as hastily as he had assumed it. "You shall see him, mother, bound hand and foot, and brought to London at a saddle-girth; and you shall hear of him at Tyburn Tree if we have luck. So Hugh says. You're pale again, and trembling. And why *do* you look behind me so?"

"It is nothing," she answered. "I am not quite well. Go you to bed, dear, and leave me here."

"To bed!" he answered. "I don't like bed. I like to lie before the fire, watching the prospects in the burning coals—the rivers, hills, and dells, in the deep, red sunset, and the wild faces. I am hungry too, and Grip has eaten nothing since broad noon. Let us to supper. Grip! To supper, lad!"

The raven flapped his wings, and, croaking his satisfaction, hopped to the feet of his master, and there held his bill open, ready for snapping up such lumps of meat as he should throw him. Of these he received about a score in rapid succession, without the smallest discomposure.

"That's all," said Barnaby.

"More!" cried Grip. "More!"

But it appearing for a certainty that no more was to be had, he retreated with his store; and disgorging the morsels one by one from his pouch, hid them in various corners—taking particular care, however, to avoid the closet, as being doubtful of the hidden man's propensities and power of resisting temptation. When he had concluded these arrangements, he took a turn or two across the room with an elaborate assumption of having nothing on his mind (but with one eye hard upon his treasure all the time), and then, and not till then, began to drag it out, piece by piece, and eat it with the utmost relish.

Barnaby, for his part, having pressed his mother to eat, in vain, made a hearty supper too. Once during the progress of his meal, he wanted more bread from the closet and rose to get it. She hurriedly interposed to prevent him, and summoning her utmost fortitude, passed into the recess, and brought it out herself.

"Mother," said Barnaby, looking at her steadfastly as she sat down beside him after doing so; "is to-day my birthday?"

"To-day!" she answered. "Don't you recollect it was but a week or so ago, and that summer, autumn, and winter have to pass before it comes again?"

"I remember that it has been so till now," said Barnaby. "But I think to-day must be my birthday too, for all that."

She asked him why? "I'll tell you why," he said. "I have always seen you—I didn't let you know it, but I have— on the evening of that day grow very sad. I have seen you cry when Grip and I were most glad; and look frightened with no reason; and I have touched your hand, and felt that it was cold—as it is now. Once, mother (on a birthday that was, also), Grip and I thought of this after we went up-stairs to bed, and when it was midnight, striking one o'clock, we came down to your door to see if you were well. You were on your knees. I forget what it was you said. Grip, what was it we heard her say that night?"

"I'm a devil!" rejoined the raven promptly.

"No, no," said Barnaby. "But you said something in a prayer; and when you rose and walked about, you looked (as you have done ever since, mother, towards night on my birthday) just as you do now. I have found that out, you see, though I am silly. So I say you're wrong; and this must be my birthday—my birthday, Grip!"

179

The bird received this information with a crow of such duration as a cock, gifted with intelligence beyond all others of his kind, might usher in the longest day with. Then, as if he had well considered the sentiment, and regarded it as apposite to birthdays, he cried, " Never say die ! " a great many times, and flapped his wings for emphasis.

The widow tried to make light of Barnaby's remark, and endeavoured to divert his attention to some new subject; too easy a task at all times, as she knew. His supper done, Barnaby, regardless of her entreaties, stretched himself on the mat before the fire; Grip perched upon his leg, and divided his time between dozing in the grateful warmth, and endeavouring (as it presently appeared) to recall a new accomplishment he had been studying all day.

A long and profound silence ensued, broken only by some change of position on the part of Barnaby, whose eyes were still wide open and intently fixed upon the fire; or by an effort of recollection on the part of Grip, who would cry in a low voice from time to time, " Polly put the ket— " and there stop short, forgetting the remainder, and go off in a doze again.

After a long interval, Barnaby's breathing grew more deep and regular, and his eyes were closed. But even then the unquiet spirit of the raven interposed. " Polly put the ket— " cried Grip, and his master was broad awake again.

At length Barnaby slept soundly, and the bird with his bill sunk upon his breast, his breast itself puffed out into a comfortable alderman-like form, and his bright eye growing smaller and smaller, really seemed to be subsiding into a state of repose. Now and then he muttered in a sepulchral voice, " Polly put the ket— " but very drowsily, and more like a drunken man than a reflecting raven.

The widow, scarcely venturing to breathe, rose from her seat. The man glided from the closet, and extinguished the candle.

" —tle on," cried Grip, suddenly struck with an idea and very much excited. " —tle on. Hurrah! Polly put the ket-tle on, we'll all have tea; Polly put the ket-tle on, we'll all have tea. Hurrah, hurrah, hurrah! I'm a devil, I'm a devil, I'm a ket-tle on, Keep up your spirits, Never say die, Bow, wow, wow, I'm a devil, I'm a ket-tle, I'm a—Polly put the ket-tle on, we'll all have tea."

They stood rooted to the ground, as though it had been a voice from the grave.

But even this failed to awaken the sleeper. He turned over towards the fire, his arm fell to the ground, and his head drooped heavily upon it. The widow and her un-welcome visitor gazed at him and at each other for a moment, and then she motioned him towards the door.

"Stay," he whispered. "You teach your son well."

"I have taught him nothing that you heard to-night. Depart instantly, or I will rouse him."

"You are free to do so. Shall *I* rouse him?"

"You dare not do that."

"I dare do anything, I have told you. He knows me well, it seems. At least I will know him."

"Would you kill him in his sleep?" cried the widow, throwing herself between them.

"Woman," he returned between his teeth, as he motioned her aside, "I would see him nearer, and I will. If you want one of us to kill the other, wake him."

With that he advanced, and bending down over the prostrate form, softly turned back the head and looked into the face. The light of the fire was upon it, and its every lineament was revealed distinctly. He contemplated it for a brief space, and hastily uprose.

"Observe," he whispered in the widow's ear: "In him, of whose existence I was ignorant until to-night, I have you in my power. Be careful how you use me. Be careful how you use me. I am destitute and starving, and a wanderer upon the earth. I may take a sure and slow revenge."

"There is some dreadful meaning in your words. I do not fathom it."

"There is a meaning in them, and I see you fathom it to its very depth. You have anticipated it for years; you have told me as much. I leave you to digest it. Do not forget my warning."

He pointed, as he left her, to the slumbering form, and stealthily withdrawing, made his way into the street. She fell on her knees beside the sleeper, and remained like one stricken into stone, until the tears which fear had frozen so long, came tenderly to her relief.

"Oh Thou," she cried, "who hast taught me such deep love for this one remnant of tl promise of a happy life, out of whose affliction, even perhaps the comfort springs that he is ever a relying, loving child to me—never growing old or cold at heart, but needing my care and duty in his manly strength as in his cradle-time—help him, in his darkened walk through this sad world, or he is doomed, and my poor heart is broken!"

CHAPTER XVIII

GLIDING along the silent streets, and holding his course where they were darkest and most gloomy, the man who had left the widow's house crossed London Bridge, and arriving in the City, plunged into the backways, lanes, and courts, between Cornhill and Smithfield; with no more fixedness of purpose than to lose himself among their windings, and baffle pursuit, if any one were dogging his steps.

It was the dead time of the night, and all was quiet. Now and then a drowsy watchman's footsteps sounded on the pavement, or the lamp-lighter on his rounds went flashing past, leaving behind a little track of smoke mingled with glowing morsels of his red hot link. He hid himself even from these partakers of his lonely walk, and, shrinking in some arch or doorway while they passed, issued forth again when they were gone and so pursued his solitary way.

To be shelterless and alone in the open country, hearing the wind moan and watching for day through the whole long weary night; to listen to the falling rain, and crouch for warmth beneath the lee of some old barn or rick, or in the hollow of a tree; are dismal things—but not so dismal as the wandering up and down where shelter is, and beds and sleepers are by thousands; a houseless rejected creature. To pace the echoing stones from hour to hour, counting the dull chimes of the clocks; to watch the lights twinkling in chamber windows, to think what happy forgetfulness each

183

house shuts in; that here are children coiled together in their beds, here youth, here age, here poverty, here wealth, all equal in their sleep, and all at rest; to have nothing in common with the slumbering world around, not even sleep, Heaven's gift to all its creatures, and be akin to nothing but despair; to feel, by the wretched contrast with everything on every hand, more utterly alone and cast away than in a trackless desert; this is a kind of suffering, on which the rivers of great cities close full many a time, and which the solitude in crowds alone awakens.

The miserable man paced up and down the streets—so long, so wearisome, so like each other—and often cast a wistful look towards the east, hoping to see the first faint streaks of day. But obdurate night had yet possession of the sky, and his disturbed and restless walk found no relief.

One house in a back street was bright with the cheerful glare of lights; there was the sound of music in it too, and the tread of dancers, and there were cheerful voices, and many a burst of laughter. To this place—to be near something that was awake and glad—he returned again and again; and more than one of those who left it when the merriment was at its height, felt it a check upon their mirthful mood to see him flitting to and fro like an uneasy ghost. At last the guests departed, one and all; and then the house was close shut up, and became as dull and silent as the rest.

His wanderings brought him at one time to the city jail. Instead of hastening from it as a place of ill omen, and one he had cause to shun, he sat down on some steps hard by, and resting his chin upon his hand, gazed upon its rough and frowning walls as though even they became a refuge in his jaded eyes. He paced it round and round, came back to the same spot, and sat down again. He did this often, and once, with a hasty movement, crossed to where some men were watching in the prison lodge, and had his foot upon the steps as though determined to accost them. But looking round, he saw that the day began to break, and failing in his purpose, turned and fled.

He was soon in the quarter he had lately traversed, and pacing to and fro again as he had done before. He was passing down a mean street, when from an alley close at hand some shouts of revelry arose, and there came straggling forth a dozen madcaps, whooping and calling to each other, who, parting noisily, took different ways and dispersed in smaller groups.

Hoping that some low place of entertainment which would afford him a safe refuge might be near at hand, he turned into this court when they were all gone, and looked about for a half-opened door, or lighted window, or other indication of the place whence they had come. It was so profoundly dark, however, and so ill-favoured, that he concluded they had but turned up there, missing their way, and were pouring out again when he observed them. With this impression, and finding there was no outlet but that by which he had entered, he was about to turn, when from a grating near his feet a sudden stream of light appeared, and the sound of talking came. He retreated into a doorway to see who these talkers were, and to listen to them.

The light came to the level of the pavement as he did this, and a man ascended, bearing in his hand a torch. This figure unlocked and held open the grating as for the passage of another, who presently appeared, in the form of a young man of small stature and uncommon self-importance, dressed in an obsolete and very gaudy fashion.

" Good night, noble captain," said he with the torch. "Farewell, commander. Good luck, illustrious general ! "

In return to these compliments the other bade him hold his tongue, and keep his noise to himself; and laid upon him many similar injunctions, with great fluency of speech and sternness of manner.

" Commend me, captain, to the stricken Miggs," returned the torch-bearer in a lower voice. " My captain flies at higher game than Miggses. Ha, ha, ha! My captain is an eagle, both as respects his eye and soaring wings. My captain breaketh hearts as other bachelors break eggs at breakfast."

"What a fool you are, Stagg!" said Mr. Tappertit, stepping on the pavement of the court, and brushing from his legs the dust he had contracted in his passage upward.

" His precious limbs ! " cried Stagg, clasping one of his ankles. " Shall a Miggs aspire to these proportions ! No, no, my captain. We will inveigle ladies fair, and wed them in our secret cavern. We will unite ourselves with blooming beauties, captain."

" I'll tell you what, my buck," said Mr. Tappertit, releasing his leg ; " I'll trouble you not to take liberties, and not to broach certain questions unless certain questions are broached to you. Speak when you're spoke to on particular subjects, and not otherways. Hold the torch up till I've got to the end of the court, and then kennel yourself, do you hear ? "

" I hear you, noble captain."

" Obey then," said Mr. Tappertit haughtily. " Gentlemen, lead on ! " With which word of command (addressed to an imaginary staff or retinue) he folded his arms, and walked with surpassing dignity down the court.

His obsequious follower stood holding the torch above his head, and then the observer saw for the first time, from his place of concealment, that he was blind. Some involuntary motion on his part caught the quick ear of the blind man, before he was conscious of having moved an inch towards him, for he turned suddenly and cried, " Who's there ? "

" A man," said the other, advancing. " A friend."

" A stranger ! " rejoined the blind man. " Strangers are not my friends. What do you do there ? "

" I saw your company come out, and waited here till they were gone. I want a lodging."

" A lodging at this time ! " returned Stagg, pointing towards the dawn as though he saw it. " Do you know the day is breaking ? "

" I know it," rejoined the other, " to my cost. I have been traversing this iron-hearted town all night."

" You had better traverse it again," said the blind man, preparing to descend, " till you find some lodgings suitable to your taste. I don't let any."

" Stay ! " cried the other, holding him by the arm.

187

"I'll beat this light about that hangdog face of yours (for hangdog it is, if it answers to your voice), and rouse the neighbourhood besides, if you detain me," said the blind man. "Let me go. Do you hear?"

"Do *you* hear!" returned the other, chinking a few shillings together, and hurriedly pressing them into his hand. "I beg nothing of you. I will pay for the shelter you give me. Death! Is it much to ask of such as you! I have come from the country, and desire to rest where there are none to question me. I am faint, exhausted, worn out, almost dead. Let me lie down, like a dog, before your fire. I ask no more than that. If you would be rid of me, I will depart to-morrow."

"If a gentleman has been unfortunate on the road," muttered Stagg, yielding to the other, who, pressing on him, had already gained a footing on the steps—"and can pay for his accommodation—"

"I will pay you with all I have. I am just now past the want of food, God knows, and wish but to purchase shelter. What companion have you below?"

"None."

"Then fasten your grate there, and show me the way. Quick!"

The blind man complied after a moment's hesitation, and they descended together. The dialogue had passed as hurriedly as the words could be spoken, and they stood in his wretched room before he had had time to recover from his first surprise.

"May I see where that door leads to, and what is beyond?" said the man, glancing keenly round. "You will not mind that?"

"I will show you myself. Follow me, or go before. Take your choice."

He bade him lead the way, and, by the light of the torch which his conductor held up for the purpose, inspected all three cellars narrowly. Assured that the blind man had

188

spoken truth, and that he lived there alone, the visitor returned with him to the first, in which a fire was burning, and flung himself with a deep groan upon the ground before it.

His host pursued his usual occupation without seeming to heed him any further. But directly he fell asleep—and he noted his falling into a slumber, as readily as the keenest-sighted man could have done—he knelt down beside him, and passed his hand lightly but carefully over his face and person.

His sleep was checkered with starts and moans, and sometimes with a muttered word or two. His hands were clenched, his brow bent, and his mouth firmly set. All this, the blind man accurately marked; and as if his curiosity were strongly awakened, and he had already some inkling of his mystery, he sat watching him, if the expression may be used, and listening, until it was broad day.

CHAPTER XIX

DOLLY VARDEN's pretty little head was yet bewildered by various recollections of the party, and her bright eyes were yet dazzled by a crowd of images, dancing before them like motes in the sunbeams, among which the effigy of one partner in particular did especially figure, the same being a young coachmaker (a master in his own right) who had given her to understand, when he handed her into the chair at parting, that it was his fixed resolve to neglect his business from that time, and die slowly for the love of her—Dolly's head, and eyes, and thoughts, and seven senses, were all in a state of flutter and confusion for which the party was accountable, although it was now three days old, when, as she was sitting listlessly at breakfast, reading all manner of fortunes (that is to say, of married and flourishing fortunes) in the grounds of her tea-cup, a step was heard in the workshop, and Mr. Edward Chester was descried through the glass door, standing among the rusty locks and keys, like love among the roses— for which apt comparison the historian may by no means take any credit to himself, the same being the invention, in a sentimental mood, of the chaste and modest Miggs, who, beholding him from the doorsteps she was then cleaning, did, in her maiden meditation, give utterance to the simile.

The locksmith, who happened at the moment to have his eyes thrown upward and his head backward, in an intense communing with Toby, did not see his visitor, until Mrs.

Varden, more watchful than the rest, had desired Sim
Tappertit to open the glass door and give him admission—
from which untoward circumstance the good lady argued (for
she could deduce a precious moral from the most trifling
event) that to take a draught of small ale in the morning
was to observe a pernicious, irreligious, and Pagan custom,
the relish whereof should be left to swine, and Satan, or
at least to Popish persons, and should be shunned by the
righteous as a work of sin and evil. She would no doubt
have pursued her admonition much further, and would have
founded on it a long list of precious precepts of inestimable
value, but that the young gentleman standing by in a somewhat uncomfortable and discomfited manner while she read
her spouse this lecture, occasioned her to bring it to a
premature conclusion.

"I'm sure you'll excuse me, sir," said Mrs. Varden, rising
and curtseying. "Varden is so very thoughtless, and needs
so much reminding—Sim, bring a chair here."

Mr. Tappertit obeyed, with a flourish implying that he
did so, under protest.

"And you can go, Sim," said the locksmith.

Mr. Tappertit obeyed again, still under protest; and be-
taking himself to the workshop, began seriously to fear that
he might find it necessary to poison his master, before his
time was out.

In the meantime, Edward returned suitable replies to Mrs.
Varden's courtesies, and that lady brightened up very much;
so that when he accepted a dish of tea from the fair hands
of Dolly, she was perfectly agreeable.

"I am sure if there's anything we can do,—Varden, or I,
or Dolly either,—to serve you, sir, at any time, you have
only to say it, and it shall be done," said Mrs. V.

"I am much obliged to you, I am sure," returned Edward.
"You encourage me to say that I have come here now, to
beg your good offices."

Mrs. Varden was delighted beyond measure.

191

"It occurred to me that probably your fair daughter might be going to the Warren, either to-day or to-morrow," said Edward, glancing at Dolly; "and if so, and you will allow her to take charge of this letter, ma'am, you will oblige me more than I can tell you. The truth is, that while I am very anxious it should reach its destination, I have particular reasons for not trusting it to any other conveyance; so that without your help, I am wholly at a loss."

"She was not going that way, sir, either to-day, or to-morrow, nor indeed all next week," the lady graciously rejoined, "but we shall be very glad to put ourselves out of the way on your account, and if you wish it, you may depend upon its going to-day. You might suppose," said Mrs. Varden, frowning at her husband, "from Varden's sitting there so glum and silent, that he objected to this arrangement; but you must not mind that, sir, if you please. It's his way at home. Out of doors, he can be cheerful and talkative enough."

Now, the fact was, that the unfortunate locksmith, blessing his stars to find his helpmate in such good humour, had been sitting with a beaming face, hearing this discourse with a joy past all expression. Wherefore this sudden attack quite took him by surprise.

"My dear Martha—" he said.

"Oh yes, I dare say," interrupted Mrs. Varden, with a smile of mingled scorn and pleasantry. "Very dear! We all know that."

"No, but, my good soul," said Gabriel, "you are quite mistaken. You are indeed. I was delighted to find you so kind and ready. I waited, my dear, anxiously, I assure you, to hear what you would say."

"You waited anxiously," repeated Mrs. V. "Yes! Thank you, Varden. You waited, as you always do, that I might bear the blame, if any came of it. But I am used to it," said the lady with a kind of solemn titter, "and that's my comfort!"

"I give you my word, Martha——" said Gabriel.

"Let me give you *my* word, my dear," interposed his wife with a Christian smile, "that such discussions as these between married people, are much better left alone. Therefore, if you please, Varden, we'll drop the subject. I have no wish to pursue it. I could. I might say a great deal. But I would rather not. Pray don't say any more."

"I don't want to say any more," rejoined the goaded locksmith.

"Well then, don't," said Mrs. Varden.

"Nor did I begin it, Martha," added the locksmith, good humouredly, "I must say that."

"You did not begin it, Varden!" exclaimed his wife, opening her eyes very wide and looking round upon the company, as though she would say, You hear this man! "You did not begin it, Varden! But you shall not say I was out of temper. No, you did not begin it, oh dear no, not you, my dear!"

"Well, well," said the locksmith. "That's settled then."

"Oh yes," rejoined his wife, "quite. If you like to say Dolly began it, my dear, I shall not contradict you. I know my duty. I need know it, I am sure. I am often obliged to bear it in mind, when my inclination perhaps would be for the moment to forget it. Thank you, Varden." And so, with a mighty show of humility and forgiveness, she folded her hands, and looked round again, with a smile which plainly said, "If you desire to see the first and foremost among female martyrs, here she is, on view!"

This little incident, illustrative though it was of Mrs. Varden's extraordinary sweetness and amiability, had so strong a tendency to check the conversation and to disconcert all parties but that excellent lady, that only a few monosyllables were uttered until Edward withdrew; which he presently did, thanking the lady of the house a great many times for her condescension, and whispering in Dolly's ear that he would call on the morrow, in case there should happen to be an answer to the note—which, indeed, she knew without his telling, as Barnaby and his friend Grip had dropped in on the previous night to prepare her for the visit which was then terminating.

Gabriel, who had attended Edward to the door, came back with his hands in his pockets; and, after fidgeting about the room in a very uneasy manner, and casting a great many sidelong looks at Mrs. Varden (who with the calmest countenance in the world was five fathoms deep in the Protestant Manual), inquired of Dolly how she meant to go. Dolly supposed by the stage-coach, and looked at her lady mother, who finding herself silently appealed to, dived down at least another fathom into the Manual, and became unconscious of all earthly things.

"Martha—" said the locksmith.

"I hear you, Varden," said his wife, without rising to the surface.

"I am sorry, my dear, you have such an objection to the Maypole and old John, for otherways as it's a very fine morning, and Saturday's not a busy day with us, we might have all three gone to Chigwell in the chaise, and had quite a happy day of it."

Mrs. Varden immediately closed the Manual, and bursting into tears, requested to be led up-stairs.

"What is the matter now, Martha?" inquired the locksmith.

To which Martha rejoined, "Oh! don't speak to me," and protested in agony that if anybody had told her so, she wouldn't have believed it.

"But, Martha," said Gabriel, putting himself in the way as she was moving off with the aid of Dolly's shoulder, "wouldn't have believed what? Tell me what's wrong now. Do tell me. Upon my soul I don't know. Do *you* know, child? Damme!" cried the locksmith, plucking at his wig in a kind of frenzy, "nobody does know, I verily believe, but Miggs!"

A SPASMODIC ATTACK

"Miggs," said Mrs. Varden faintly, and with symptoms of approaching incoherence, "is attached to me, and that is sufficient to draw down hatred upon her in this house. She is a comfort to me, whatever she may be to others."

"She's no comfort to me," cried Gabriel, made bold by despair. "She's the misery of my life. She's all the plagues of Egypt in one."

"She's considered so, I have no doubt," said Mrs. Varden. "I was prepared for that; it's natural; it's of a piece with the rest. When you taunt me as you do to my face, how can I wonder that you taunt her behind her back!" And here the incoherence coming on very strong, Mrs. Varden wept, and laughed, and sobbed, and shivered, and hiccoughed, and choked; and said she knew it was very foolish but she couldn't help it; and that when she was dead and gone, perhaps they would be sorry for it—which really under the circumstances did not appear quite so probable as she seemed to think—with a great deal more to the same effect. In a word, she passed with great decency through all the ceremonies incidental to such occasions; and being supported up-stairs, was deposited in a highly spasmodic state on her own bed, where Miss Miggs shortly afterwards flung herself upon the body.

The philosophy of all this was, that Mrs. Varden wanted to go to Chigwell; that she did not want to make any concession or explanation; that she would only go on being implored and entreated so to do; and that she would accept no other terms. Accordingly, after a vast amount of moaning and crying up-stairs, and much damping of foreheads, and vinegaring of temples, and hartshorning of noses, and so forth; and after most pathetic adjurations from Miggs, assisted by warm brandy-and-water not over-weak, and divers other cordials, also of a stimulating quality, administered at first in teaspoonfuls and afterwards in increasing doses, and of which Miss Miggs herself partook as a preventive measure (for fainting is infectious); after all these remedies, and many more too numerous to mention, but not to take, had been applied; and many verbal consolations, moral, religious, and miscellaneous, had been superadded thereto; the locksmith humbled himself, and the end was gained.

"If it's only for the sake of peace and quietness, father," said Dolly, urging him to go up-stairs.

"Oh, Doll, Doll," said her good-natured father. "If you ever have a husband of your own—"

Dolly glanced at the glass.

"—Well, *when* you have," said the locksmith, "never faint, my darling. More domestic unhappiness has come of easy fainting, Doll, than from all the greater passions put together. Remember that, my dear, if you would be really happy, which you never can be, if your husband isn't. And a word in your ear, my precious. Never have a Miggs about you!"

With this advice he kissed his blooming daughter on the cheek, and slowly repaired to Mrs. Varden's room; where that lady, lying all pale and languid on her couch, was refreshing herself with a sight of her last new bonnet, which Miggs, as a means of calming her scattered spirits, displayed to the best advantage at her bedside.

"Here's master, mim," said Miggs. "Oh, what a happiness it is when man and wife come round again! Oh gracious, to think that him and her should ever have a word together!" In the energy of these sentiments, which were uttered as an apostrophe to the Heavens in general, Miss Miggs perched the bonnet on the top of her own head, and folding her hands, turned on her tears.

"I can't help it," cried Miggs. "I couldn't, if I was to be drownded in 'em. She has such a forgiving spirit! She'll forget all that has passed, and go along with you, sir—Oh, if it was to the world's end, she'd go along with you."

Mrs. Varden with a faint smile gently reproved her attendant for this enthusiasm, and reminded her at the same time that she was far too unwell to venture out that day.

SUCH A FORGIVING SPIRIT!

"Oh no, you're not, mim, indeed you're not," said Miggs; "I repeal to master; master knows you're not, mim. The hair, and motion of the shay, will do you good, mim, and you must not give way, you must not raly. She must keep up, mustn't she, sir, for all our sakes? I was a telling her that, just now. She must remember us, even if she forgets herself. Master will persuade you, mim, I'm sure. There's Miss Dolly's a-going you know, and master, and you, and all so happy and so comfortable. Oh!" cried Miggs, turning on the tears again, previous to quitting the room in great emotion, "I never see such a blessed one as she is for the forgiveness of her spirit, I never, never, never did. Nor more did master neither; no, nor no one—never!"

For five minutes or thereabouts, Mrs. Varden remained mildly opposed to all her husband's prayers that she would oblige him by taking a day's pleasure, but relenting at length, she suffered herself to be persuaded, and granting him her free forgiveness (the merit whereof, she meekly said, rested with the Manual and not with her), desired that Miggs might come and help her dress. The handmaid attended promptly, and it is but justice to their joint exertions to record that, when the good lady came down-stairs in course of time, completely decked out for the journey, she really looked as if nothing had happened, and appeared in the very best health imaginable.

As to Dolly, there she was again, the very pink and pattern of good looks, in a smart little cherry-coloured mantle, with a hood of the same drawn over her head, and upon the top of that hood, a little straw hat trimmed with cherry-coloured ribbons, and worn the merest trifle on one side—just enough in short to make it the wickedest and most provoking head-dress that ever malicious milliner devised. And not to speak of the manner in which these cherry-coloured decorations brightened her eyes, or vied with her lips, or shed a new bloom on her face, she wore such a cruel little muff, and such a heart-rending pair of shoes, and was so surrounded

197

and hemmed in, as it were, by aggravations of all kinds, that when Mr. Tappertit, holding the horse's head, saw her come out of the house alone, such impulses came over him to decoy her into the chaise and drive off like mad, that he would unquestionably have done it, but for certain uneasy doubts besetting him as to the shortest way to Gretna Green; whether it was up the street or down, or up the right-hand turning or the left; and whether, supposing all the turnpikes to be carried by storm, the blacksmith in the end would marry them on credit; which by reason of his clerical office appeared, even to his excited imagination, so unlikely, that he hesitated. And while he stood hesitating, and looking post-chaises-and-six at Dolly, out came his master and his mistress, and the constant Miggs, and the opportunity was gone for ever. For now the chaise creaked upon its springs, and Mrs. Varden was inside; and now it creaked again, and more than ever, and the locksmith was inside; and now it bounded once, as if its heart beat lightly, and Dolly was inside; and now it was gone and its place was empty, and he and that dreary Miggs were standing in the street together.

The hearty locksmith was in as good a humour as if nothing had occurred for the last twelve months to put him out of his way, Dolly was all smiles and graces, and Mrs. Varden was agreeable beyond all precedent. As they jogged through the streets talking of this thing and of that, who should be descried upon the pavement but that very coach-maker, looking so genteel that nobody would have believed he had ever had anything to do with a coach but riding in it, and bowing like any nobleman. To be sure Dolly was confused when she bowed again, and to be sure the cherry-coloured ribbons trembled a little when she met his mournful eye, which seemed to say, "I have kept my word, I have begun, the business is going to the devil, and you're the cause of it." There he stood, rooted to the ground: as Dolly said, like a statue; and as Mrs. Varden said, like a pump;

till they turned the corner: and when her father thought it was like his impudence, and her mother wondered what he meant by it, Dolly blushed again till her very hood was pale.

But on they went, not the less merrily for this, and there was the locksmith in the incautious fulness of his heart "pulling-up" at all manner of places, and evincing a most intimate acquaintance with all the taverns on the road, and all the landlords and all the landladies, with whom, indeed, the little horse was on equally friendly terms, for he kept on stopping of his own accord. Never were people so glad to see other people as these landlords and landladies were to behold Mr. Varden and Mrs. Varden and Miss Varden; and wouldn't they get out, said one; and they really must walk up-stairs, said another; and she would take it ill and be quite certain they were proud if they wouldn't have a little taste of something, said a third; and so on, that it was really quite a Progress rather than a ride, and one continued scene of hospitality from beginning to end. It was pleasant enough to be held in such esteem, not to mention the refreshments; so Mrs. Varden said nothing at the time, and was all affability and delight—but such a body of evidence as she collected against the unfortunate locksmith that day, to be used thereafter as occasion might require, never was got together for matrimonial purposes.

In course of time—and in course of a pretty long time too, for these agreeable interruptions delayed them not a little,—they arrived upon the skirts of the Forest, and riding pleasantly on among the trees, came at last to the Maypole, where the locksmith's cheerful "Yoho!" speedily brought to the porch old John, and after him young Joe, both of whom were so transfixed at sight of the ladies, that for a moment they were perfectly unable to give them any welcome, and could do nothing but stare.

It was only for a moment, however, that Joe forgot himself, for speedily reviving he thrust his drowsy father aside—to Mr. Willet's mighty and inexpressible indignation

—and darting out, stood ready to help them to alight. It
was necessary for Dolly to get out first. Joe had her in his
arms;—yes, though for a space of time no longer than you
could count one in, Joe had her in his arms. Here was a
glimpse of happiness!

It would be difficult to describe what a flat and common-
place affair the helping Mrs. Varden out afterwards was, but
Joe did it, and did it too with the best grace in the world.
Then old John, who, entertaining a dull and foggy sort of
idea that Mrs. Varden wasn't fond of him, had been in
some doubt whether she might not have come for purposes
of assault and battery, took courage, hoped she was well, and
offered to conduct her into the house. This tender being
amicably received, they marched in together; Joe and Dolly
followed, arm-in-arm, (happiness again!) and Varden brought
up the rear.

Old John would have it that they must sit in the bar,
and nobody objecting, into the bar they went. All bars
are snug places, but the Maypole's was the very snuggest,
cosiest, and completest bar, that ever the wit of man devised.
Such amazing bottles in old oaken pigeon-holes; such
gleaming tankards dangling from pegs at about the same
inclination as thirsty men would hold them to their lips;
such sturdy little Dutch kegs ranged in rows on shelves;
so many lemons hanging in separate nets, and forming the
fragrant grove already mentioned in this chronicle, suggestive,
with goodly loaves of snowy sugar stowed away hard by, of
punch, idealised beyond all mortal knowledge; such closets,
such presses, such drawers full of pipes, such places for
putting things away in hollow window-seats, all crammed
to the throat with eatables, drinkables, or savoury condi-
ments; lastly, and to crown all, as typical of the immense
resources of the establishment, and its defiances to all visitors
to cut and come again, such a stupendous cheese!

It is a poor heart that never rejoices—it must have been
the poorest, weakest, and most watery heart that ever beat,

which would not have warmed towards the Maypole bar. Mrs. Varden's did directly. She could no more have reproached John Willet among those household gods, the kegs and bottles, lemons, pipes, and cheese, than she could have stabbed him with his own bright carving-knife. The order for dinner too—it might have soothed a savage. "A bit of fish," said John to the cook, "and some lamb chops (breaded, with plenty of ketchup), and a good salad, and a roast spring chicken, with a dish of sausages and mashed potatoes, or something of that sort." Something of that sort! The resources of these inns! To talk carelessly about dishes, which in themselves were a first-rate holiday kind of dinner, suitable to one's wedding-day, as something of that sort: meaning, if you can't get a spring chicken, any other trifle in the way of poultry will do—such as a peacock, perhaps! The kitchen too, with its great broad cavernous chimney; the kitchen, where nothing in the way of cookery seemed impossible; where you could believe in anything to eat, they chose to tell you of. Mrs. Varden returned from the contemplation of these wonders to the bar again, with a head quite dizzy and bewildered. Her housekeeping capacity was not large enough to comprehend them. She was obliged to go to sleep. Waking was pain, in the midst of such immensity.

Dolly in the meanwhile, whose gay heart and head ran upon other matters, passed out at the garden door, and glancing back now and then (but of course not wondering whether Joe saw her), tripped away by a path across the fields with which she was well acquainted, to discharge her mission at the Warren; and this deponent hath been informed and verily believes, that you might have seen many less pleasant objects than the cherry-coloured mantle and ribbons as they went fluttering along the green meadows in the bright light of the day, like giddy things as they were.

CHAPTER XX

The proud consciousness of her trust, and the great importance she derived from it, might have advertised it to all the house if she had had to run the gauntlet of its inhabitants; but as Dolly had played in every dull room and passage many and many a time, when a child, and had ever since been the humble friend of Miss Haredale, whose foster-sister she was, she was as free of the building as the young lady herself. So, using no greater precaution than holding her breath and walking on tiptoe as she passed the library door, she went straight to Emma's room as a privileged visitor.

It was the liveliest room in the building. The chamber was sombre like the rest for the matter of that, but the presence of youth and beauty would make a prison cheerful (saving alas! that confinement withers them), and lend some charms of their own to the gloomiest scene. Birds, flowers, books, drawing, music, and a hundred such graceful tokens of feminine loves and cares, filled it with more of life and human sympathy than the whole house besides seemed made to hold. There was heart in the room; and who that has a heart, ever fails to recognise the silent presence of another!

Dolly had one undoubtedly, and it was not a tough one either, though there was a little mist of coquettishness about it, such as sometimes surrounds that sun of life in its morning, and slightly dims its lustre. Thus, when Emma rose to greet her, and kissing her affectionately on the cheek, told her, in her quiet way, that she had been very unhappy, the tears stood in Dolly's eyes, and she felt more sorry than she could tell; but next moment she happened to raise them to the glass, and really there was something there so exceedingly agreeable, that as she sighed, she smiled, and felt surprisingly consoled.

"I have heard about it, Miss," said Dolly, "and it's very sad indeed, but when things are at the worst they are sure to mend."

"But are you sure they are at the worst?" asked Emma with a smile.

"Why, I don't see how they can very well be more un-promising than they are; I really don't," said Dolly. "And I bring something to begin with."

"Not from Edward?"

Dolly nodded and smiled, and feeling in her pockets (there were pockets in those days) with an affectation of not being able to find what she wanted, which greatly enhanced her importance, at length produced the letter. As Emma hastily broke the seal and became absorbed in its contents, Dolly's eyes, by one of those strange accidents for which there is no accounting, wandered to the glass again. She could not help wondering whether the coachmaker suffered very much, and quite pitied the poor man.

It was a long letter—a very long letter, written close on all four sides of the sheet of paper, and crossed afterwards; but it was not a consolatory letter, for as Emma read it she stopped from time to time to put her handkerchief to her eyes. To be sure Dolly marvelled greatly to see her in so much distress, for to her thinking a love affair ought to be one of the best jokes, and the slyest, merriest kind of thing in life. But she set it down in her own mind that all this came from Miss Haredale's being so constant, and that if she would only take on with some other young gentleman—just in the most innocent way possible, to keep her first lover up to the mark—she would find herself inexpressibly comforted.

"I am sure that's what I should do if it was me," thought Dolly. "To make one's sweetheart miserable is well enough and quite right, but to be made miserable one's self is a little too much!"

However it wouldn't do to say so, and therefore she sat looking on in silence. She needed a pretty considerable stretch of patience, for when the long letter had been read once all through it was read again, and when it had been read twice all through it was read again. During this tedious process, Dolly beguiled the time in the most improving manner that occurred to her, by curling her hair on her fingers, with the aid of the looking-glass before mentioned, and giving it some killing twists.

Everything has an end. Even young ladies in love cannot read their letters for ever. In course of time the packet was folded up, and it only remained to write the answer.

But as this promised to be a work of time likewise, Emma said she would put it off until after dinner, and that Dolly must dine with her. As Dolly had made up her mind to do so beforehand, she required very little pressing; and when they had settled this point, they went to walk in the garden.

They strolled up and down the terrace walks, talking incessantly—at least, Dolly never left off once—and making that quarter of the sad and mournful house quite gay. Not that they talked loudly or laughed much, but they were both so very handsome, and it was such a breezy day, and their light dresses and dark curls appeared so free and joyous in their abandonment, and Emma was so fair, and Dolly so rosy, and Emma so delicately shaped, and Dolly so plump, and—in short, there are no flowers for any garden like such flowers, let horticulturists say what they may, and both house and garden seemed to know it, and to brighten up sensibly.

After this, came the dinner and the letter writing, and some more talking, in the course of which Miss Haredale took occasion to charge upon Dolly certain flirtish and inconstant propensities, which accusations Dolly seemed to think very complimentary indeed, and to be mightily amused with. Finding her quite incorrigible in this respect, Emma suffered her to depart; but not before she had confided to her that important and never-sufficiently-to-be-taken-care-of answer, and endowed her moreover with a pretty little bracelet as a keepsake. Having clasped it on her arm, and again advised her half in jest and half in earnest to amend her roguish ways, for she knew she was fond of Joe at heart (which Dolly stoutly denied, with a great many haughty protestations that she hoped she could do better than that indeed! and so forth), she bade her farewell; and after calling her back to give her more supplementary messages for Edward, than anybody with tenfold the gravity of Dolly Varden could be reasonably expected to remember, at length dismissed her.

Dolly bade her good-bye, and tripping lightly down the stairs arrived at the dreaded library door, and was about to pass it again on tiptoe, when it opened, and behold! there stood Mr. Haredale. Now, Dolly had from her childhood associated with this gentleman the idea of something grim and ghostly, and being at the moment conscience-stricken besides, the sight of him threw her into such a flurry that she could neither acknowledge his presence nor run away, so she gave a great start, and then with downcast eyes stood still and trembled.

"Come here, girl," said Mr. Haredale, taking her by the hand. "I want to speak to you."

"If you please, sir, I'm in a hurry," faltered Dolly, "and— you have frightened me by coming so suddenly upon me, sir— I would rather go, sir, if you'll be so good as to let me."

"Immediately," said Mr. Haredale, who had by this time led her into the room and closed the door. "You shall go directly. You have just left Emma?"

"Yes, sir, just this minute.—Father's waiting for me, sir, if you'll please to have the goodness—"

"I know. I know," said Mr. Haredale. "Answer me a question. What did you bring here to-day?"

"Bring here, sir?" faltered Dolly.

"You will tell me the truth, I am sure. Yes."

Dolly hesitated for a little while, and somewhat emboldened by his manner, said at last, "Well then, sir. It was a letter."

"From Mr. Edward Chester, of course. And you are the bearer of the answer?"

Dolly hesitated again, and not being able to decide upon any other course of action, burst into tears.

"You alarm yourself without cause," said Mr. Haredale. "Why are you so foolish? Surely you can answer me. You know that I have but to put the question to Emma and learn the truth directly. Have you the answer with you?"

Dolly had what is popularly called a spirit of her own, and being now fairly at bay, made the best of it.

"Yes, sir," she rejoined, trembling and frightened as she was. "Yes, sir, I have. You may kill me if you please, sir, but I won't give it up. I'm very sorry,—but I won't. There, sir."

"I commend your firmness and your plain-speaking," said Mr. Haredale. "Rest assured that I have as little desire to take your letter as your life. You are a very discreet messenger and a good girl."

Not feeling quite certain, as she afterwards said, whether he might not be "coming over her" with these compliments, Dolly kept as far from him as she could, cried again, and resolved to defend her pocket (for the letter was there) to the last extremity.

"I have some design," said Mr. Haredale after a short silence, during which a smile, as he regarded her, had struggled through the gloom and melancholy that was natural to his face, "of providing a companion for my niece; for her life is a very lonely one. Would you like the office? You are the oldest friend she has, and the best entitled to it."

"I don't know, sir," answered Dolly, not sure but he was bantering her; "I can't say. I don't know what they might wish at home. I couldn't give an opinion, sir."

"If your friends had no objection, would you have any?" said Mr. Haredale. "Come. There's a plain question; and easy to answer."

"None at all that I know of, sir," replied Dolly. "I should be very glad to be near Miss Emma of course, and always am."

"That's well," said Mr. Haredale. "That is all I had to say. You are anxious to go. Don't let me detain you."

Dolly didn't let him, nor did she wait for him to try, for the words had no sooner passed his lips than she was out of the room, out of the house, and in the fields again.

The first thing to be done, of course, when she came to herself, and considered what a flurry she had been in, was to cry afresh; and the next thing, when she reflected how well she had got over it, was to laugh heartily. The tears once banished gave place to the smiles, and at last Dolly laughed so much that she was fain to lean against a tree, and give vent to her exultation. When she could laugh no longer, and was quite tired, she put her head-dress to rights, dried her eyes, looked back very merrily and triumphantly at the Warren chimneys, which were just visible, and resumed her walk.

The twilight had come on, and it was quickly growing dusk, but the path was so familiar to her from frequent traversing that she hardly thought of this, and certainly felt no uneasiness at being left alone. Moreover, there was the bracelet to admire; and when she had given it a good rub, and held it out at arm's length, it sparkled and glittered so beautifully on her wrist, that to look at it in every point of view and with every possible turn of the arm, was quite an absorbing business. There was the letter too, and it looked so mysterious and knowing, when she took it out of her pocket, and it held, as she knew, so much inside, that to turn it over and over, and think about it, and wonder how it began, and how it ended, and what it said all through, was another matter of constant occupation. Between the bracelet and the letter, there was quite enough to do without thinking of anything else; and admiring each by turns, Dolly went on gaily.

As she passed through a wicket-gate to where the path was narrow, and lay between two hedges garnished here and there with trees, she heard a rustling close at hand, which brought her to a sudden stop. She listened. All was very quiet, and she went on again—not absolutely frightened, but a little quicker than before perhaps, and possibly not quite so much at her ease, for a check of that kind is startling.

She had no sooner moved on again, than she was conscious of the same sound, which was like that of a person tramping stealthily among bushes and brushwood. Looking towards the spot whence it appeared to come, she almost fancied she could make out a crouching figure. She stopped again. All was quiet as before. On she went once more—decidedly faster now—and tried to sing softly to herself. It must be the wind.

But how came the wind to blow only when she walked, and cease when she stood still? She stopped involuntarily as she made the reflection, and the rustling noise stopped likewise. She was really frightened now, and was yet hesitating what to do, when the bushes crackled and snapped, and a man came plunging through them, close before her.

CHAPTER XXI

It was for the moment an inexpressible relief to Dolly, to recognise in the person who forced himself into the path so abruptly, and now stood directly in her way, Hugh of the Maypole, whose name she uttered in a tone of delighted surprise that came from her heart.

"Was it you?" she said. "How glad I am to see you! and how could you terrify me so!"

In answer to which, he said nothing at all, but stood quite still, looking at her.

"Did you come to meet me?" asked Dolly.

Hugh nodded, and muttered something to the effect that he had been waiting for her, and had expected her sooner.

"I thought it likely they would send," said Dolly, greatly reassured by this.

"Nobody sent me," was his sullen answer. "I came of my own accord."

The rough bearing of this fellow, and his wild, uncouth appearance, had often filled the girl with a vague apprehension even when other people were by, and had occasioned her to shrink from him involuntarily. The having him for an unbidden companion in so solitary a place, with the darkness fast gathering about them, renewed and even increased the alarm she had felt at first.

If his manner had been merely dogged and passively fierce,

as usual, she would have had no greater dislike to his company than she always felt—perhaps, indeed, would have been
rather glad to have had him at hand. But there was some-

thing of coarse bold admiration in his look, which terrified
her very much. She glanced timidly towards him, uncertain
whether to go forward or retreat, and he stood gazing at her
like a handsome satyr ; and so they remained for some short

time without stirring or breaking silence. At length Dolly took courage, shot past him, and hurried on.

"Why do you spend so much breath in avoiding me?" said Hugh, accommodating his pace to hers, and keeping close at her side.

"I wish to get back as quickly as I can, and you walk too near me," answered Dolly.

"Too near!" said Hugh, stooping over her so that she could feel his breath upon her forehead. "Why too near? You're always proud to *me*, mistress."

"I am proud to no one. You mistake me," answered Dolly. "Fall back, if you please, or go on."

"Nay, mistress," he rejoined, endeavouring to draw her arm through his, "I'll walk with you."

She released herself, and clenching her little hand, struck him with right good will. At this, Maypole Hugh burst into a roar of laughter, and passing his arm about her waist, held her in his strong grasp as easily as if she had been a bird.

"Ha ha ha! Well done, mistress! Strike again. You shall beat my face, and tear my hair, and pluck my beard up by the roots, and welcome, for the sake of your bright eyes. Strike again, mistress. Do. Ha ha ha! I like it."

"Let me go," she cried, endeavouring with both her hands to push him off. "Let me go this moment."

"You had as good be kinder to me, Sweetlips," said Hugh. "You had, indeed? Come. Tell me now. Why are you always so proud? I don't quarrel with you for it. I love you when you're proud. Ha ha ha! You can't hide your beauty from a poor fellow; that's a comfort!"

She gave him no answer, but as he had not yet checked her progress, continued to press forward as rapidly as she could. At length, between the hurry she had made, her terror, and the tightness of his embrace, her strength failed her, and she could go no further.

"Hugh," cried the panting girl, "good Hugh; if you will

212

leave me I will give you anything—everything I have—and never tell one word of this to any living creature."

"You had best not," he answered. "Harkye, little dove, ye had best not. All about here know me, and what I dare do if I have a mind. If ever you are going to tell, stop when the words are on your lips, and think of the mischief you'll bring, if you do, upon some innocent heads that you wouldn't wish to hurt a hair of. Bring trouble on me, and I'll bring trouble and something more on them in return. I care no more for them than for so many dogs; not so much—why should I? I'd sooner kill a man than a dog any day. I've never been sorry for a man's death in all my life, and I have for a dog's."

There was something so thoroughly savage in the manner of these expressions, and the looks and gestures by which they were accompanied, that her great fear of him gave her new strength, and enabled her by a sudden effort to extricate herself and run fleetly from him. But Hugh was as nimble, strong, and swift of foot, as any man in broad England, and it was but a fruitless expenditure of energy, for he had her in his encircling arms again before she had gone a hundred yards.

"Softly, darling—gently—would you fly from rough Hugh, that loves you as well as any drawing-room gallant?"

"I would," she answered, struggling to free herself again. "I will. Help!'

"A fine for crying out," said Hugh. "Ha ha ha! A fine, pretty one, from your lips. I pay myself! Ha ha ha!"

"Help! help! help!" As she shrieked with the utmost violence she could exert, a shout was heard in answer, and another, and another.

"Thank Heaven!" cried the girl in an ecstasy. "Joe, dear Joe, this way. Help!"

Her assailant paused, and stood irresolute for a moment, but the shouts drawing nearer and coming quick upon them, forced him to a speedy decision. He released her, whispered

213

with a menacing look, "Tell *him:* and see what follows!" and leaping the hedge, was gone in an instant. Dolly darted off, and fairly ran into Joe Willet's open arms.

"What is the matter? are you hurt? what was it? who was it? where is he? what was he like?" with a great many encouraging expressions and assurances of safety, were the first words Joe poured forth. But poor little Dolly was so breathless and terrified that for some time she was quite unable to answer him, and hung upon his shoulder, sobbing and crying as if her heart would break.

Joe had not the smallest objection to have her hanging on his shoulder; no, not the least, though it crushed the cherry-coloured ribbons sadly, and put the smart little hat out of all shape. But he couldn't bear to see her cry; it went to his very heart. He tried to console her, bent over her, whispered to her—some say kissed her, but that's a fable. At any rate he said all the kind and tender things he could think of, and Dolly let him go on and didn't interrupt him once, and it was a good ten minutes before she was able to raise her head and thank him.

"What was it that frightened you?" said Joe.

A man whose person was unknown to her had followed her, she answered; he began by begging, and went on to threats of robbery, which he was on the point of carrying into execution, and would have executed, but for Joe's timely aid. The hesitation and confusion with which she said this, Joe attributed to the fright she had sustained, and no suspicion of the truth occurred to him for a moment.

"Stop when the words are on your lips." A hundred times that night, and very often afterwards, when the disclosure was rising to her tongue, Dolly thought of that, and repressed it. A deeply rooted dread of the man; the conviction that his ferocious nature, once roused, would stop at nothing; and the strong assurance that if she impeached him, the full measure of his wrath and vengeance would be wreaked on Joe, who had preserved her; these were considerations she had not the courage to overcome, and inducements to secrecy too powerful for her to surmount.

Joe, for his part, was a great deal too happy to inquire very curiously into the matter; and Dolly being yet too tremulous to walk without assistance, they went forward very slowly, and in his mind very pleasantly, until the Maypole lights were near at hand, twinkling their cheerful welcome, when Dolly stopped suddenly and with a half scream exclaimed,

" The letter ! "

" What letter ? " cried Joe.

" That I was carrying—I had it in my hand. My bracelet too," she said, clasping her wrist. " I have lost them both."

" Do you mean just now ? " said Joe.

" Either I dropped them then, or they were taken from me," answered Dolly, vainly searching her pocket and rustling her dress. " They are gone, both gone. What an unhappy girl I am ! " With these words poor Dolly, who to do her justice was quite as sorry for the loss of the letter as for her bracelet, fell a crying again, and bemoaned her fate most movingly.

Joe tried to comfort her with the assurance that directly he had housed her in the Maypole, he would return to the spot with a lantern (for it was now quite dark) and make strict search for the missing articles, which there was great probability of his finding, as it was not likely that anybody had passed that way since, and she was not conscious that they had been forcibly taken from her. Dolly thanked him very heartily for this offer, though with no great hope of his quest being successful ; and so with many lamentations on her side, and many hopeful words on his, and much weakness on the part of Dolly and much tender supporting on the part of Joe, they reached the Maypole bar at last, where the locksmith and his wife and old John were yet keeping high festival.

Mr. Willet received the intelligence of Dolly's trouble with that surprising presence of mind and readiness of speech for

215

which he was so eminently distinguished above all other men. Mrs. Varden expressed her sympathy for her daughter's distress by scolding her roundly for being so late; and the honest locksmith divided himself between condoling with and kissing Dolly, and shaking hands heartily with Joe, whom he could not sufficiently praise or thank.

In reference to this latter point, old John was far from agreeing with his friend; for besides that he by no means approved of an adventurous spirit in the abstract, it occurred to him that if his son and heir had been seriously damaged in a scuffle, the consequences would assuredly have been expensive and inconvenient, and might perhaps have proved detrimental to the Maypole business. Wherefore, and because he looked with no favourable eye upon young girls, but rather considered that they and the whole female sex were a kind of nonsensical mistake on the part of Nature, he took occasion to retire and shake his head in private at the boiler; inspired by which silent oracle, he was moved to give Joe various stealthy nudges with his elbow, as a parental reproof and gentle admonition to mind his own business and not make a fool of himself.

Joe, however, took down the lantern and lighted it; and arming himself with a stout stick, asked whether Hugh was in the stable.

"He's lying asleep before the kitchen fire, sir," said Mr. Willet. "What do you want him for?"

"I want him to come with me to look after this bracelet and letter," answered Joe. "Halloa there! Hugh!"

Dolly turned pale as death, and felt as if she must faint forthwith. After a few moments, Hugh came staggering in, stretching himself and yawning according to custom, and presenting every appearance of having been roused from a sound nap.

"Here, sleepy-head," said Joe, giving him the lantern. "Carry this, and bring the dog, and that small cudgel of yours. And woe betide the fellow if we come upon him."

216

"What fellow?" growled Hugh, rubbing his eyes and shaking himself.

"What fellow?" returned Joe, who was in a state of great valour and bustle; "a fellow you ought to know of, and be more alive about. It's well for the like of you, lazy giant that you are, to be snoring your time away in chimney-corners, when honest men's daughters can't cross even our quiet meadows at nightfall without being set upon by footpads, and frightened out of their precious lives."

"They never rob me," cried Hugh with a laugh. "I have got nothing to lose. But I'd as lief knock them at head as any other men. How many are there?"

"Only one," said Dolly faintly, for everybody looked at her.

"And what was he like, mistress?" said Hugh with a glance at young Willet, so slight and momentary that the scowl it conveyed was lost on all but her. "About my height?"

"Not—not so tall," Dolly replied, scarce knowing what she said.

"His dress," said Hugh, looking at her keenly, "like—like any of ours now? I know all the people hereabouts, and maybe could give a guess at the man, if I had anything to guide me."

Dolly faltered and turned paler yet; then answered that he was wrapped in a loose coat and had his face hidden by a handkerchief, and that she could give no other description of him.

"You wouldn't know him if you saw him then, belike?" said Hugh with a malicious grin.

"I should not," answered Dolly, bursting into tears again. "I don't wish to see him. I can't bear to think of him. I can't talk about him any more. Don't go to look for these things, Mr. Joe, pray don't. I entreat you not to go with that man."

"Not to go with me!" cried Hugh. "I'm too rough for them all. They're all afraid of me. Why, bless you, mistress,

I've the tenderest heart alive. I love all the ladies, ma'am," said Hugh, turning to the locksmith's wife.

Mrs. Varden opined that if he did, he ought to be ashamed of himself; such sentiments being more consistent (so she argued) with a benighted Mussulman or wild Islander than with a staunch Protestant. Arguing from this imperfect state of his morals, Mrs. Varden further opined that he had never studied the Manual. Hugh admitting that he never had, and moreover that he couldn't read, Mrs. Varden declared with much severity, that he ought to be even more ashamed of himself than before, and strongly recommended him to save up his pocket-money for the purchase of one, and further to teach himself the contents with all convenient diligence. She was still pursuing this train of discourse, when Hugh, somewhat unceremoniously and irreverently, followed his young master out, and left her to edify the rest of the company. This she proceeded to do, and finding that Mr. Willet's eyes were fixed upon her with an appearance of deep attention, gradually addressed the whole of her discourse to him, whom she entertained with a moral and theological lecture of considerable length, in the conviction that great workings were taking place in his spirit. The simple truth was, however, that Mr. Willet, although his eyes were wide open and he saw a woman before him whose head by long and steady looking at seemed to grow bigger and bigger until it filled the whole bar, was to all other intents and purposes fast asleep; and so sat leaning back in his chair with his hands in his pockets until his son's return caused him to wake up with a deep sigh, and a faint impression that he had been dreaming about pickled pork and greens—a vision of his slumbers which was no doubt referable to the circumstance of Mrs. Varden's having frequently pronounced the word "Grace" with much emphasis; which word, entering the portals of Mr. Willet's brain as they stood ajar, and coupling itself with the words "before meat," which were there ranging about, did in time suggest a particular kind of meat together with that description of vegetable which is usually its companion.

The search was wholly unsuccessful. Joe had groped along the path a dozen times, and among the grass, and in the dry ditch, and in the hedge, but all in vain. Dolly, who was quite inconsolable for her loss, wrote a note to Miss Haredale giving her the same account of it that she had given at the Maypole, which Joe undertook to deliver as soon as the family were stirring next day. That done, they sat down to tea in the bar, where there was an uncommon display of buttered toast, and—in order that they might not grow faint for want of sustenance, and might have a decent halting-place or half-way house between dinner and supper—a few savoury trifles in the shape of great rashers of broiled ham, which being well cured, done to a turn, and smoking hot, sent forth a tempting and delicious fragrance.

Mrs. Varden was seldom very Protestant at meals, unless it happened that they were under-done, or over-done, or indeed that anything occurred to put her out of humour. Her spirits rose considerably on beholding these goodly preparations, and from the nothingness of good works, she passed to the somethingness of ham and toast with great cheerfulness. Nay, under the influence of these wholesome stimulants, she sharply reproved her daughter for being low and despondent (which she considered an unacceptable frame of mind), and remarked, as she held her own plate for a fresh supply, that it would be well for Dolly, who pined over the loss of a toy and a sheet of paper, if she would reflect upon the voluntary sacrifices of the missionaries in foreign parts who lived chiefly on salads.

The proceedings of such a day occasion various fluctuations in the human thermometer, and especially in instruments so sensitively and delicately constructed as Mrs. Varden. Thus, at dinner Mrs. V. stood at summer heat; genial, smiling, and delightful. After dinner, in the sunshine of the wine, she went up at least half-a-dozen degrees, and was perfectly enchanting. As its effect subsided, she fell rapidly, went to sleep for an hour or so at temperate, and woke at something below freezing. Now she was at summer heat again, in the shade; and when tea was over, and old John, producing a bottle of cordial from one of the oaken cases, insisted on her sipping two glasses thereof in slow succession, she stood steadily at ninety for one hour and a quarter. Profiting by experience, the locksmith took advantage of this genial weather to smoke his pipe in the porch, and in consequence of this prudent management, he was fully prepared, when the glass went down again, to start homewards directly.

The horse was accordingly put in, and the chaise brought round to the door. Joe, who would on no account be dissuaded from escorting them until they had passed the most dreary and solitary part of the road, led out the grey mare at the same time; and having helped Dolly into her seat (more happiness!) sprung gaily into the saddle. Then, after many good nights, and admonitions to wrap up, and glancing of lights, and handing in of cloaks and shawls, the chaise rolled away, and Joe trotted beside it—on Dolly's side, no doubt, and pretty close to the wheel too.

CHAPTER XXII

It was a fine bright night, and for all her lowness of spirits Dolly kept looking up at the stars in a manner so bewitching (and *she* knew it!) that Joe was clean out of his senses, and plainly showed that if ever a man were—not to say over head and ears, but over the Monument and the top of Saint Paul's in love, that man was himself. The road was a very good one; not at all a jolting road, or an uneven one; and yet Dolly held the side of the chaise with one little hand, all the way. If there had been an executioner behind him with an uplifted axe ready to chop off his head if he touched that hand, Joe couldn't have helped doing it. From putting his own hand upon it as if by chance, and taking it away again after a minute or so, he got to riding along without taking it off at all; as if he, the escort, were bound to do that as an important part of his duty, and had come out for the purpose. The most curious circumstance about this little incident was, that Dolly didn't seem to know of it. She looked so innocent and unconscious when she turned her eyes on Joe, that it was quite provoking.

She talked though; talked about her fright, and about Joe's coming up to rescue her, and about her gratitude, and about her fear that she might not have thanked him enough, and about their always being friends from that time forth— and about all that sort of thing. And when Joe said, not friends he hoped, Dolly was quite surprised, and said not enemies she hoped; and when Joe said, couldn't they be something much better than either, Dolly all of a sudden found out a star which was brighter than all the other stars, and begged to call his attention to the same, and was ten thousand times more innocent and unconscious than ever.

In this manner they travelled along, talking very little above a whisper, and wishing the road could be stretched out to some dozen times its natural length—at least that was Joe's desire—when, as they were getting clear of the forest and emerging on the more frequented road, they heard behind them the sound of a horse's feet at a round trot, which growing rapidly louder as it drew nearer, elicited a scream from Mrs. Varden, and the cry "A friend!" from the rider, who now came panting up, and checked his horse beside them.

"This man again!" cried Dolly, shuddering.

"Hugh!" said Joe. "What errand are you upon?"

"I come to ride back with you," he answered, glancing covertly at the locksmith's daughter. "He sent me."

"My father!" said poor Joe; adding under his breath, with a very unfilial apostrophe, "Will he never think me man enough to take care of myself!"

"Aye!" returned Hugh to the first part of the inquiry. "The roads are not safe just now, he says, and you'd better have a companion."

"Ride on then," said Joe. "I'm not going to turn yet."

Hugh complied, and they went on again. It was his whim or humour to ride immediately before the chaise, and from this position he constantly turned his head, and looked back. Dolly felt that he looked at her, but she averted her eyes and feared to raise them once, so great was the dread with which he had inspired her.

This interruption, and the consequent wakefulness of Mrs. Varden, who had been nodding in her sleep up to this point, except for a minute or two at a time, when she roused herself to scold the locksmith for audaciously taking hold of her to prevent her nodding herself out of the chaise, put a restraint upon the whispered conversation, and made it difficult of resumption. Indeed, before they had gone another mile, Gabriel stopped at his wife's desire, and that good lady protested she would not hear of Joe's going a step further on any account whatever. It was in vain for Joe to protest on the other hand that he was by no means tired, and would turn back presently, and would see them safely past such a point, and so forth. Mrs. Varden was obdurate, and being so was not to be overcome by mortal agency.

"Good night—if I must say it," said Joe, sorrowfully.

"Good night," said Dolly. She would have added, "Take care of that man, and pray don't trust him," but he had turned his horse's head, and was standing close to them. She had therefore nothing for it but to suffer Joe to give her hand a gentle squeeze, and when the chaise had gone on for some distance, to look back and wave it, as he still lingered on the spot where they had parted, with the tall dark figure of Hugh beside him.

What she thought about, going home; and whether the coachmaker held as favourable a place in her meditations as he had occupied in the morning, is unknown. They reached home at last—at last, for it was a long way, made none the shorter by Mrs. Varden's grumbling. Miggs hearing the sound of wheels was at the door immediately.

"Here they are, Simmun! Here they are!" cried Miggs, clapping her hands, and issuing forth to help her mistress to alight. "Bring a chair, Simmun. Now, an't you the better for it, mim? Don't you feel more yourself than you would have done if you'd have stopped at home? Oh, gracious! how cold you are! Goodness me, sir, she's a perfect heap of ice."

"I can't help it, my good girl. You had better take her in to the fire," said the locksmith.

"Master sounds unfeeling, mim," said Miggs, in a tone of commiseration, "but such is not his intentions, I'm sure. After what he has seen of you this day, I never will believe

but that he has a deal more affection in his heart than to
speak unkind. Come in and sit yourself down by the fire;
there's a good dear—do."

Mrs. Varden complied. The locksmith followed with his
hands in his pockets, and Mr. Tappertit trundled off with
the chaise to a neighbouring stable.

"Martha, my dear," said the locksmith, when they reached
the parlour, "if you'll look to Dolly yourself, or let somebody else do it, perhaps it will be only kind and reasonable.
She has been frightened, you know, and is not at all well
to-night."

In fact, Dolly had thrown herself upon the sofa, quite
regardless of all the little finery of which she had been so
proud in the morning, and with her face buried in her hands
was crying very much.

At first sight of this phenomenon (for Dolly was by no
means accustomed to displays of this sort, rather learning
from her mother's example to avoid them as much as possible)
Mrs. Varden expressed her belief that never was any woman
so beset as she; that her life was a continued scene of trial;
that whenever she was disposed to be well and cheerful, so
sure were the people around her to throw, by some means or
other, a damp upon her spirits; and that, as she had enjoyed
herself that day, and Heaven knew it was very seldom she
did enjoy herself, so she was now to pay the penalty. To all
such propositions Miggs assented freely. Poor Dolly, however, grew none the better for these restoratives, but rather
worse, indeed; and seeing that she was really ill, both Mrs.
Varden and Miggs were moved to compassion, and tended
her in earnest.

But even then, their very kindness shaped itself into their
usual course of policy, and though Dolly was in a swoon, it
was rendered clear to the meanest capacity, that Mrs. Varden
was the sufferer. Thus when Dolly began to get a little
better, and passed into that stage in which matrons hold
that remonstrance and argument may be successfully applied,

her mother represented to her, with tears in her eyes, that if
she had been flurried and worried that day, she must remember
it was the common lot of humanity, and in especial of woman-
kind, who through the whole of their existence must expect
no less, and were bound to make up their minds to meek
endurance and patient resignation. Mrs. Varden entreated
her to remember that one of these days she would, in all
probability, have to do violence to her feelings so far as to
be married; and that marriage, as she might see every day
of her life (and truly she did) was a state requiring great
fortitude and forbearance. She represented to her in lively
colours, that if she (Mrs. V.) had not, in steering her course
through this vale of tears, been supported by a strong
principle of duty which alone upheld and prevented her from
drooping, she must have been in her grave many years ago;
in which case she desired to know what would have become
of that errant spirit (meaning the locksmith), of whose eye
she was the very apple, and in whose path she was, as it
were, a shining light and guiding star?

Miss Miggs also put in her word to the same effect. She
said that indeed and indeed Miss Dolly might take pattern
by her blessed mother, who, she always had said, and always
would say, though she were to be hanged, drawn, and
quartered for it next minute, was the mildest, amiablest,
forgivingest-spirited, longest-sufferingest female as ever she
could have believed; the mere narration of whose excellencies
had worked such a wholesome change in the mind of her
own sister-in-law, that, whereas, before, she and her husband
lived like cat and dog, and were in the habit of exchanging
brass candlesticks, pot-lids, flat-irons, and other such strong
resentments, they were now the happiest and affectionatest
couple upon earth; as could be proved any day on application
at Golden Lion Court, number twenty-sivin, second bell-
handle on the right-hand door-post. After glancing at herself
as a comparatively worthless vessel, but still as one of some
desert, she besought her to bear in mind that her aforesaid

dear and only mother was of a weakly constitution and excitable temperament, who had constantly to sustain afflictions in domestic life, compared with which thieves and robbers were as nothing, and yet never sunk down or gave way to despair or wrath, but, in prize-fighting phraseology, always came up to time with a cheerful countenance, and went in to win as if nothing had happened. When Miggs finished her solo, her mistress struck in again, and the two together performed a duet to the same purpose; the burden being, that Mrs. Varden was persecuted perfection, and Mr. Varden, as the representative of mankind in that apartment, a creature of vicious and brutal habits, utterly insensible to the blessings he enjoyed. Of so refined a character, indeed, was their talent of assault under the mask of sympathy, that when Dolly, recovering, embraced her father tenderly, as in vindication of his goodness, Mrs. Varden expressed her solemn hope that this would be a lesson to him for the remainder of his life, and that he would do some little justice to a woman's nature ever afterwards—in which aspiration Miss Miggs, by divers sniffs and coughs, more significant than the longest oration, expressed her entire concurrence.

But the great joy of Miggs's heart was, that she not only picked up a full account of what had happened, but had the exquisite delight of conveying it to Mr. Tappertit for his jealousy and torture. For that gentleman, on account of Dolly's indisposition, had been requested to take his supper in the workshop, and it was conveyed thither by Miss Miggs's own fair hands.

"Oh, Simmun!" said the young lady, "such goings on to-day! Oh, gracious me, Simmun!"

Mr. Tappertit, who was not in the best of humours, and who disliked Miss Miggs more when she laid her hand on her heart and panted for breath than at any other time, as her deficiency of outline was most apparent under such circumstances, eyed her over in his loftiest style, and deigned to express no curiosity whatever.

"I never heard the like, nor nobody else," pursued Miggs. "The idea of interfering with *her*. What people can see in her to make it worth their while to do so, that's the joke—he he he!"

Finding there was a lady in the case, Mr. Tappertit haughtily requested his fair friend to be more explicit, and demanded to know what she meant by "her."

"Why, that Dolly," said Miggs, with an extremely sharp emphasis on the name. "But, oh upon my word and honour, young Joseph Willet is a brave one; and he do deserve her, that he do."

"Woman!" said Mr. Tappertit, jumping off the counter on which he was seated; "beware!"

"My stars, Simmun!" cried Miggs, in affected astonishment. "You frighten me to death! What's the matter?"

"There are strings," said Mr. Tappertit, flourishing his bread-and-cheese knife in the air, "in the human heart that had better not be wibrated. That's what's the matter."

"Oh, very well—if you're in a huff," cried Miggs, turning away.

"Huff or no huff," said Mr. Tappertit, detaining her by the wrist. "What do you mean, Jezebel? What were you going to say? Answer me!"

Notwithstanding this uncivil exhortation, Miggs gladly did as she was required; and told him how that their young mistress, being alone in the meadows after dark, had been attacked by three or four tall men, who would have certainly borne her away and perhaps murdered her, but for the timely arrival of Joseph Willet, who with his own single hand put them all to flight, and rescued her; to the lasting admiration of his fellow-creatures generally, and to the eternal love and gratitude of Dolly Varden.

"Very good," said Mr. Tappertit, fetching a long breath when the tale was told, and rubbing his hair up till it stood stiff and straight on end all over his head. "His days are numbered."

"Oh, Simmun!"

"I tell you," said the 'prentice, "his days are numbered. Leave me. Get along with you."

Miggs departed at his bidding, but less because of his

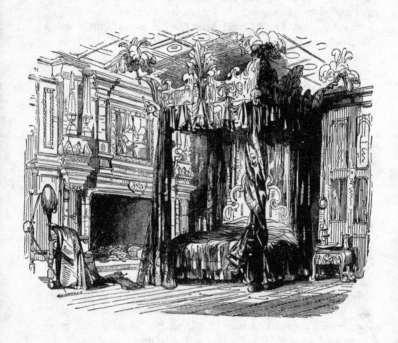

bidding than because she desired to chuckle in secret. When she had given vent to her satisfaction, she returned to the parlour; where the locksmith, stimulated by quietness and

228

A CHECK TO CHEERFULNESS

Toby, had become talkative, and was disposed to take a
cheerful review of the occurrences of the day. But Mrs.
Varden, whose practical religion (as is not uncommon) was
usually of the retrospective order, cut him short by declaiming
on the sinfulness of such junketings, and holding that it was
high time to go to bed. To bed therefore she withdrew,
with an aspect as grim and gloomy as that of the Maypole's
own state couch; and to bed the rest of the establishment
soon afterwards repaired.

CHAPTER XXIII

TWILIGHT had given place to night some hours, and it was
high noon in those quarters of the town in which "the world"
condescended to dwell—the world being then, as now, of
very limited dimensions and easily lodged—when Mr. Chester
reclined upon a sofa in his dressing-room in the Temple,
entertaining himself with a book.

He was dressing, as it seemed, by easy stages, and having
performed half the journey was taking a long rest. Completely attired as to his legs and feet in the trimmest
fashion of the day, he had yet the remainder of his toilet to
perform. The coat was stretched, like a refined scarecrow,
on its separate horse; the waistcoat was displayed to the
best advantage; the various ornamental articles of dress were
severally set out in most alluring order; and yet he lay
dangling his legs between the sofa and the ground, as intent
upon his book as if there were nothing but bed before him.

"Upon my honour," he said, at length raising his eyes to

the ceiling with the air of a man who was reflecting seriously on what he had read; "upon my honour, the most masterly composition, the most delicate thoughts, the finest code of morality, and the most gentlemanly sentiments in the universe! Ah, Ned, Ned, if you would but form your mind by such precepts, we should have but one common feeling on every subject that could possibly arise between us!"

This apostrophe was addressed, like the rest of his remarks, to empty air: for Edward was not present, and the father was quite alone.

"My Lord Chesterfield," he said, pressing his hand tenderly upon the book as he laid it down, "if I could but have profited by your genius soon enough to have formed my son on the model you have left to all wise fathers, both he and I would have been rich men. Shakspeare was undoubtedly very fine in his way; Milton good, though prosy; Lord Bacon deep, and decidedly knowing; but the writer who should be his country's pride, is my Lord Chesterfield."

He became thoughtful again, and the toothpick was in requisition.

"I thought I was tolerably accomplished as a man of the world," he continued, "I flattered myself that I was pretty well versed in all those little arts and graces which distinguish men of the world from boors and peasants, and separate their character from those intensely vulgar sentiments which are called the national character. Apart from any natural prepossession in my own favour, I believed I was. Still, in every page of this enlightened writer, I find some captivating hypocrisy which has never occurred to me before, or some superlative piece of selfishness to which I was utterly a stranger. I should quite blush for myself before this stupendous creature, if, remembering his precepts, one might blush at anything. An amazing man! a nobleman indeed! any King or Queen may make a Lord, but only the Devil himself—and the Graces—can make a Chesterfield."

Men who are thoroughly false and hollow, seldom try to

hide those vices from themselves; and yet in the very act of avowing them, they lay claim to the virtues they feign most to despise. "For," say they, "this is honesty, this is truth. All mankind are like us, but they have not the candour to avow it." The more they affect to deny the existence of any sincerity in the world, the more they would be thought to possess it in its boldest shape; and this is an unconscious compliment to Truth on the part of these philosophers, which will turn the laugh against them to the Day of Judgment.

Mr. Chester, having extolled his favourite author, as above recited, took up the book again in the excess of his admiration and was composing himself for a further perusal of its sublime morality, when he was disturbed by a noise at the outer door; occasioned as it seemed by the endeavours of his servant to obstruct the entrance of some unwelcome visitor.

"A late hour for an importunate creditor," he said, raising his eyebrows with as indolent an expression of wonder as if the noise were in the street, and one with which he had not the smallest possible concern. "Much after their accustomed time. The usual pretence I suppose. No doubt a heavy payment to make up to-morrow. Poor fellow, he loses time, and time is money as the good proverb says—I never found it out though. Well. What now? You know I am not at home."

"A man, sir," replied the servant, who was to the full as cool and negligent in his way as his master, "has brought home the riding-whip you lost the other day. I told him you were out, but he said he was to wait while I brought it in, and wouldn't go till I did."

"He was quite right," returned his master, "and you're a blockhead, possessing no judgment or discretion whatever. Tell him to come in, and see that he rubs his shoes for exactly five minutes first."

The man laid the whip on a chair, and withdrew. The master, who had only heard his foot upon the ground and had not taken the trouble to turn round and look at him,

232

shut his book, and pursued the train of ideas his entrance had disturbed.

"If time were money," he said, handling his snuff-box, "I would compound with my creditors, and give them—let me see —how much a day? There's my nap after dinner—an hour— they're extremely welcome to that, and to make the most of it. In the morning, between my breakfast and the paper, I could spare them another hour; in the evening before dinner say another. Three hours a day. They might pay themselves in calls, with interest, in twelve months. I think I shall propose it to them. Ah, my centaur, are you there?"

"Here I am," replied Hugh, striding in, followed by a dog, as rough and sullen as himself; "and trouble enough I've had to get here. What do you ask me to come for, and keep me out when I *do* come?"

"My good fellow," returned the other, raising his head a little from the cushion and carelessly surveying him from top to toe, "I am delighted to see you, and to have, in your being here, the very best proof that you are not kept out. How are you?"

"I'm well enough," said Hugh impatiently.

"You look a perfect marvel of health. Sit down."

"I'd rather stand," said Hugh.

"Please yourself, my good fellow," returned Mr. Chester rising, slowly pulling off the loose robe he wore, and sitting down before the dressing-glass. "Please yourself by all means."

Having said this in the politest and blandest tone possible, he went on dressing, and took no further notice of his guest, who stood in the same spot as uncertain what to do next, eyeing him sulkily from time to time.

"Are you going to speak to me, master?" he said, after a long silence.

"My worthy creature," returned Mr. Chester, "you are a little ruffled and out of humour. I'll wait till you're quite yourself again. I am in no hurry."

This behaviour had its intended effect. It humbled and

233

abashed the man, and made him still more irresolute and uncertain. Hard words he could have returned, violence he would have repaid with interest; but this cool, complacent, contemptuous, self-possessed reception, caused him to feel his inferiority more completely than the most elaborate arguments. Everything contributed to this effect. His own rough speech, contrasted with the soft persuasive accents of the other; his rude bearing, and Mr. Chester's polished manner; the disorder and negligence of his ragged dress, and the elegant attire he saw before him; with all the unaccustomed luxuries and comforts of the room, and the silence that gave him leisure to observe these things, and feel how ill at ease they made him; all these influences, which have too often some effect on tutored minds and become of almost resistless power when brought to bear on such a mind as his, quelled Hugh completely. He moved by little and little nearer to Mr. Chester's chair, and glancing over his shoulder at the reflection of his face in the glass, as if seeking for some encouragement in its expression, said at length, with a rough attempt at conciliation,

"*Are* you going to speak to me, master, or am I to go away?"

"Speak you," said Mr. Chester, "speak you, good fellow. I have spoken, have I not? I am waiting for you."

"Why, look'ee, sir," returned Hugh with increased embarrassment, "am I the man that you privately left your whip with before you rode away from the Maypole, and told to bring it back whenever he might want to see you on a certain subject?"

"No doubt the same, or you have a twin brother," said Mr. Chester, glancing at the reflection of his anxious face; "which is not probable, I should say."

"Then I have come, sir," said Hugh, "and I have brought it back, and something else along with it. A letter, sir, it is, that I took from the person who had charge of it." As he spoke, he laid upon the dressing-table, Dolly's lost epistle. The very letter that had cost her so much trouble.

"Did you obtain this by force, my good fellow?" said Mr. Chester, casting his eye upon it without the least perceptible surprise or pleasure.

"Not quite," said Hugh. "Partly."

"Who was the messenger from whom you took it?"

"A woman. One Varden's daughter."

"Oh indeed!" said Mr. Chester gaily. "What else did you take from her?"

"What else?"

"Yes," said the other, in a drawling manner, for he was fixing a very small patch of sticking plaster on a very small pimple near the corner of his mouth. "What else?"

"Well—a kiss," replied Hugh, after some hesitation.

"And what else?"

"Nothing."

"I think," said Mr. Chester, in the same easy tone, and smiling twice or thrice to try if the patch adhered—"I think there was something else. I have heard a trifle of jewellery spoken of—a mere trifle—a thing of such little value, indeed, that you may have forgotten it. Do you remember anything of the kind—such as a bracelet now, for instance?"

Hugh with a muttered oath thrust his hand into his breast, and drawing the bracelet forth, wrapped in a scrap of hay, was about to lay it on the table likewise, when his patron stopped his hand and bade him put it up again.

"You took that for yourself, my excellent friend," he said, "and may keep it. I am neither a thief, nor a receiver. Don't show it to me. You had better hide it again, and lose no time. Don't let me see where you put it either," he added, turning away his head.

"You're not a receiver!" said Hugh bluntly, despite the increasing awe in which he held him. "What do you call *that*, master?" striking the letter with his heavy hand.

"I call that quite another thing," said Mr. Chester coolly. "I shall prove it presently, as you will see. You are thirsty, I suppose?"

Hugh drew his sleeve across his lips, and gruffly answered yes.

"Step to that closet and bring me a bottle you will see there, and a glass."

He obeyed. His patron followed him with his eyes, and when his back was turned, smiled as he had never done when he stood beside the mirror. On his return he filled the glass, and bade him drink. That dram despatched, he poured him out another, and another.

"How many can you bear?" he said, filling the glass again.

"As many as you like to give me. Pour on. Fill high. A bumper with a bead in the middle! Give me enough of this," he added, as he tossed it down his hairy throat, "and I'll do murder if you ask me!'

"As I don't mean to ask you, and you might possibly do it without being invited if you went on much further," said Mr. Chester with great composure, "we will stop, if agreeable to you, my good friend, at the next glass. You were drinking before you came here."

"I always am when I can get it," cried Hugh boisterously, waving the empty glass above his head, and throwing himself into a rude dancing attitude. "I always am. Why not? Ha ha ha! What's so good to me as this? What ever has been? What else has kept away the cold on bitter nights, and driven hunger off in starving times? What else has given me the strength and courage of a man, when men would have left me to die, a puny child? I should never have had a man's heart but for this. I should have died in a ditch. Where's he who when I was a weak and sickly wretch, with trembling legs and fading sight, bade me cheer up, as this did? I never knew him; not I. I drink to the drink, master. Ha ha ha!"

"You are an exceedingly cheerful young man," said Mr. Chester, putting on his cravat with great deliberation, and slightly moving his head from side to side to settle his chin in its proper place. "Quite a boon companion."

"Do you see this hand, master," said Hugh, "and this

arm?" baring the brawny limb to the elbow. "It was once mere skin and bone, and would have been dust in some poor churchyard by this time, but for the drink."

"You may cover it," said Mr. Chester, "it's sufficiently real in your sleeve."

"I should never have been spirited up to take a kiss from the proud little beauty, master, but for the drink," cried Hugh. "Ha ha ha! It was a good one. As sweet as honey-suckle I warrant you. I thank the drink for it. I'll drink to the drink again, master. Fill me one more. Come. One more!"

"You are such a promising fellow," said his patron, putting on his waistcoat with great nicety, and taking no heed of this request, "that I must caution you against having too many impulses from the drink, and getting hung before your time. What's your age?"

"I don't know."

"At any rate," said Mr. Chester, "you are young enough to escape what I may call a natural death for some years to come. How can you trust yourself in my hands on so short an acquaintance, with a halter round your neck? What a confiding nature yours must be!"

Hugh fell back a pace or two and surveyed him with a look of mingled terror, indignation, and surprise. Regarding himself in the glass with the same complacency as before, and speaking as smoothly as if he were discussing some pleasant chit-chat of the town, his patron went on:

"Robbery on the king's highway, my young friend, is a very dangerous and ticklish occupation. It is pleasant, I have no doubt, while it lasts; but like many other pleasures in this transitory world, it seldom lasts long. And really if, in the ingenuousness of youth, you open your heart so readily on the subject, I am afraid your career will be an extremely short one."

"How's this?" said Hugh. "What do you talk of, master? Who was it set me on?"

"Who?" said Mr. Chester, wheeling sharply round, and looking full at him for the first time. "I didn't hear you. Who was it?"

Hugh faltered, and muttered something which was not audible.

"Who was it? I am curious to know," said Mr. Chester, with surpassing affability. "Some rustic beauty perhaps? But be cautious, my good friend. They are not always to be trusted. Do take my advice now, and be careful of yourself." With these words he turned to the glass again, and went on with his toilet.

Hugh would have answered him that he, the questioner himself, had set him on, but the words stuck in his throat. The consummate art with which his patron had led him to this point, and managed the whole conversation, perfectly baffled him. He did not doubt that if he had made the retort which was on his lips when Mr. Chester turned round and questioned him so keenly, he would straightway have given him into custody and had him dragged before a justice with the stolen property upon him; in which case it was as certain he would have been hung as it was that he had been born. The ascendency which it was the purpose of the man of the world to establish over this savage instrument, was gained from that time. Hugh's submission was complete. He dreaded him beyond description; and felt that accident and artifice had spun a web about him, which at a touch from such a master-hand as his, would bind him to the gallows.

With these thoughts passing through his mind, and yet wondering at the very same time how he who came there rioting in the confidence of this man (as he thought), should be so soon and so thoroughly subdued, Hugh stood cowering before him, regarding him uneasily from time to time, while he finished dressing. When he had done so, he took up the letter, broke the seal, and throwing himself back in his chair, read it leisurely through.

"Very neatly worded upon my life! Quite a woman's

238

letter, full of what people call tenderness, and disinterested-
ness, and heart, and all that sort of thing!"

As he spoke, he twisted it up, and glancing lazily round
at Hugh as though he would say "You see this?" held it in
the flame of the candle. When it was in a full blaze, he
tossed it into the grate, and there it smouldered away.

"It was directed to my son," he said, turning to Hugh,
"and you did quite right to bring it here. I opened it on
my own responsibility, and you see what I have done with
it. Take this, for your trouble."

Hugh stepped forward to receive the piece of money he
held out to him. As he put it in his hand, he added:

"If you should happen to find anything else of this sort,
or to pick up any kind of information you may think I
would like to have, bring it here, will you, my good fellow?"

This was said with a smile which implied—or Hugh
thought it did—"fail to do so at your peril!" He answered
that he would.

"And don't," said his patron, with an air of the very
kindest patronage, "don't be at all downcast or uneasy respecting that little rashness we have been speaking of. Your
neck is as safe in my hands, my good fellow, as though a
baby's fingers clasped it, I assure you.—Take another glass.
You are quieter now."

Hugh accepted it from his hand, and looking stealthily at
his smiling face, drank the contents in silence.

"Don't you—ha, ha!—don't you drink to the drink any
more?" said Mr. Chester, in his most winning manner.

"To you, sir," was the sullen answer, with something
approaching to a bow. "I drink to you."

"Thank you. God bless you. By the bye, what is your
name, my good soul? You are called Hugh, I know, of
course—your other name?"

"I have no other name."

"A very strange fellow! Do you mean that you never
knew one, or that you don't choose to tell it? Which?"

239

"I'd tell it if I could," said Hugh, quickly. "I can't. I have been always called Hugh; nothing more. I never knew, nor saw, nor thought about a father; and I was a boy of six —that's not very old—when they hung my mother up at Tyburn for a couple of thousand men to stare at. They might have let her live. She was poor enough."

"How very sad!" exclaimed his patron, with a condescending smile. "I have no doubt she was an exceedingly fine woman."

"You see that dog of mine?" said Hugh, abruptly.

"Faithful, I dare say?" rejoined his patron, looking at him through his glass; "and immensely clever? Virtuous and gifted animals, whether man or beast, always are so very hideous."

"Such a dog as that, and one of the same breed, was the only living thing except me that howled that day," said Hugh. "Out of the two thousand odd—there was a larger crowd for its being a woman—the dog and I alone had any pity. If he'd have been a man, he'd have been glad to be quit of her, for she had been forced to keep him lean and half-starved; but being a dog, and not having a man's sense, he was sorry."

"It was dull of the brute, certainly," said Mr. Chester, "and very like a brute."

Hugh made no rejoinder, but whistling to his dog, who sprung up at the sound and came jumping and sporting about him, bade his sympathising friend good night.

"Good night," he returned. "Remember; you're safe with me—quite safe. So long as you deserve it, my good fellow, as I hope you always will, you have a friend in me, on whose silence you may rely. Now do be careful of yourself, pray do, and consider what jeopardy you might have stood in. Good night! bless you."

Hugh truckled before the hidden meaning of these words as much as such a being could, and crept out of the door so submissively and subserviently—with an air, in short, so different from that with which he had entered—that his patron on being left alone, smiled more than ever.

"And yet," he said, as he took a pinch of snuff, "I do not like their having hanged his mother. The fellow has a fine eye, and I am sure she was handsome. But very probably she was coarse—red-nosed perhaps, and had clumsy feet. Aye, it was all for the best, no doubt."

With this comforting reflection, he put on his coat, took a farewell glance at the glass, and summoned his man, who promptly attended, followed by a chair and its two bearers.

"Foh!" said Mr. Chester. "The very atmosphere that centaur has breathed, seems tainted with the cart and ladder. Here, Peak. Bring some scent and sprinkle the floor; and take away the chair he sat upon, and air it; and dash a little of that mixture upon me. I am stifled!"

The man obeyed; and the room and its master being both purified, nothing remained for Mr. Chester but to demand his hat, to fold it jauntily under his arm, to take his seat in the chair and be carried off; humming a fashionable tune.

CHAPTER XXIV

How the accomplished gentleman spent the evening in the midst of a dazzling and brilliant circle; how he enchanted all those with whom he mingled by the grace of his deportment, the politeness of his manner, the vivacity of his conversation, and the sweetness of his voice; how it was observed in every corner, that Chester was a man of that happy disposition that nothing ruffled him, that he was one on whom the world's cares and errors sat lightly as his dress, and in whose smiling face a calm and tranquil mind was constantly reflected; how honest men, who by instinct knew him better, bowed down before him nevertheless, deferred to his every word, and courted his favourable notice; how people, who really had good in them, went with the stream, and fawned and flattered, and approved, and despised themselves while they did so, and yet had not the courage to resist; how, in short, he was one of those who are received and cherished in society (as the phrase is) by scores who individually would shrink from and be repelled by the object of their lavish regard; are things of course, which will suggest themselves. Matter so common-place needs but a passing glance, and there an end.

The despisers of mankind—apart from the mere fools and mimics, of that creed—are of two sorts. They who believe their merit neglected and unappreciated, make up one class; they who receive adulation and flattery, knowing their own worthlessness, compose the other. Be sure that the coldest-hearted misanthropes are ever of this last order.

Mr. Chester sat up in bed next morning, sipping his coffee, and remembering with a kind of contemptuous satisfaction how he had shone last night, and how he had been caressed and courted, when his servant brought in a very small scrap of dirty paper, tightly sealed in two places, on the inside whereof was inscribed in pretty large text these words. "A friend. Desiring of a conference. Immediate. Private. Burn it when you've read it."

"Where in the name of the Gunpowder Plot did you pick up this?" said his master.

It was given him by a person then waiting at the door, the man replied.

"With a cloak and dagger?" said Mr. Chester.

With nothing more threatening about him, it appeared, than a leather apron and a dirty face. "Let him come in." In he came—Mr. Tappertit; with his hair still on end, and a great lock in his hand, which he put down on the floor in the middle of the chamber as if he were about to go through some performances in which it was a necessary agent.

"Sir," said Mr. Tappertit with a low bow, "I thank you for this condescension, and am glad to see you. Pardon the menial office in which I am engaged, sir, and extend your sympathies to one, who, humble as his appearance is, has inn'ard workings far above his station."

Mr. Chester held the bed-curtain farther back, and looked at him with a vague impression that he was some maniac, who had not only broken open the door of his place of confinement, but had brought away the lock. Mr. Tappertit bowed again, and displayed his legs to the best advantage.

"You have heard, sir," said Mr. Tappertit, laying his hand upon his breast, "of G. Varden Locksmith and bell-hanger and repairs neatly executed in town and country, Clerkenwell, London?"

"What then?" asked Mr. Chester.

"I'm his 'prentice, sir."

"What *then?*"

"Ahem!" said Mr. Tappertit. "Would you permit me to shut the door, sir, and will you further, sir, give me your honour bright, that what passes between us is in the strictest confidence?"

Mr. Chester laid himself calmly down in bed again, and turning a perfectly undisturbed face towards the strange apparition, which had by this time closed the door, begged him to speak out, and to be as rational as he could, without putting himself to any very great personal inconvenience.

"In the first place, sir," said Mr. Tappertit, producing a small pocket-handkerchief, and shaking it out of the folds, "as I have not a card about me (for the envy of masters debases us below that level) allow me to offer the best substitute that circumstances will admit of. If you will take that in your own hand, sir, and cast your eye on the right-hand corner," said Mr. Tappertit, offering it with a graceful air, "you will meet with my credentials."

"Thank you," answered Mr. Chester, politely accepting, and turning to some blood-red characters at one end. "'Four. Simon Tappertit. One.' Is that the——"

"Without the numbers, sir, that is my name," replied the 'prentice. "They are merely intended as directions to the washerwoman, and have no connection with myself or family. *Your* name, sir," said Mr. Tappertit, looking very hard at his nightcap, "is Chester, I suppose? You needn't pull it off, sir, thank you. I observe E. C. from here. We will take the rest for granted."

"Pray, Mr. Tappertit," said Mr. Chester, "has that complicated piece of ironmongery which you have done me the favour to bring with you, any immediate connection with the business we are to discuss?"

"It has not, sir," rejoined the 'prentice. "It's going to be fitted on a ware'us-door in Thames-street."

'Perhaps, as that is the case," said Mr. Chester, "and as

244

it has a stronger flavour of oil than I usually refresh my bedroom with, you will oblige me so far as to put it outside the door?"

"By all means, sir," said Mr. Tappertit, suiting the action to the word.

"You'll excuse my mentioning it, I hope?"

"Don't apologise, sir, I beg. And now, if you please, to business."

During the whole of this dialogue, Mr. Chester had suffered nothing but his smile of unvarying serenity and politeness to appear upon his face. Sim Tappertit, who had far too good an opinion of himself to suspect that anybody could be playing upon him, thought within himself that this was something like the respect to which he was entitled, and drew a comparison from this courteous demeanour of a stranger, by no means favourable to the worthy locksmith.

"From what passes in our house," said Mr. Tappertit, "I am aware, sir, that your son keeps company with a young lady against your inclinations. Sir, your son has not used me well."

"Mr. Tappertit," said the other, "you grieve me beyond description."

"Thank you, sir," replied the 'prentice. "I'm glad to hear you say so. He's very proud, sir, is your son; very haughty."

"I am afraid he *is* haughty," said Mr. Chester. "Do you know I was really afraid of that before; and you confirm me?"

"To recount the menial offices I've had to do for your son, sir," said Mr. Tappertit; "the chairs I've had to hand him, the coaches I've had to call for him, the numerous degrading duties, wholly unconnected with my indenters, that I've had to do for him, would fill a family Bible. Besides which, sir, he is but a young man himself, and I do not consider 'thank'ee, Sim,' a proper form of address on those occasions."

"Mr. Tappertit, your wisdom is beyond your years. Pray go on."

"I thank you for your good opinion, sir," said Sim, much gratified, "and will endeavour so to do. Now, sir, on this account (and perhaps for another reason or two which I needn't go into) I am on your side. And what I tell you is this—that as long as our people go backwards and forwards, to and fro, up and down, to that there jolly old Maypole, lettering, and messaging, and fetching and carrying, you couldn't help your son keeping company with that young lady by deputy,—not if he was minded night and day by all the Horse Guards, and every man of 'em in the very fullest uniform."

Mr. Tappertit stopped to take breath after this, and then started fresh again.

"Now, sir, I am a coming to the point. You will inquire of me, 'how is this to be prevented?' I'll tell you how. If an honest, civil, smiling gentleman like you—"

"Mr. Tappertit—really—"

"No, no, I'm serious," rejoined the 'prentice, "I am, upon my soul. If an honest, civil, smiling gentleman like you, was to talk but ten minutes to our old woman—that's Mrs. Varden—and flatter her up a bit, you'd gain her over for ever. Then there's this point got—that her daughter Dolly," —here a flush came over Mr. Tappertit's face—"wouldn't be allowed to be a go-between from that time forward; and till that point's got, there's nothing ever will prevent her. Mind that."

"Mr. Tappertit, your knowledge of human nature—"

"Wait a minute," said Sim, folding his arms with a dreadful calmness. "Now I come to THE point. Sir, there is a villain at that Maypole, a monster in human shape, a vagabond of the deepest dye, that unless you get rid of, and have kidnapped and carried off at the very least—nothing less will do—will marry your son to that young woman, as certainly and as surely as if he was the Archbishop of

246

DOWN WITH JOSEPH WILLET!

Canterbury himself. He will, sir, for the hatred and malice
that he bears to you; let alone the pleasure of doing a bad
action, which to him is its own reward. If you knew how
this chap, this Joseph Willet—that's his name—comes backwards and forwards to our house, libelling, and denouncing,
and threatening you, and how I shudder when I hear him,
you'd hate him worse than I do,—worse than I do, sir," said
Mr. Tappertit wildly, putting his hair up straighter, and
making a crunching noise with his teeth; "if such a thing
is possible."

"A little private vengeance in this, Mr. Tappertit?"

"Private vengeance, sir, or public sentiment, or both combined—destroy him," said Mr. Tappertit. "Miggs says so
too. Miggs and me both say so. We can't bear the plotting
and undermining that takes place. Our souls recoil from it.
Barnaby Rudge and Mrs. Rudge are in it likewise; but the
villain, Joseph Willet, is the ringleader. Their plottings and
schemes are known to me and Miggs. If you want information
of 'em, apply to us. Put Joseph Willet down, sir. Destroy
him. Crush him. And be happy."

With these words, Mr. Tappertit, who seemed to expect
no reply, and to hold it as a necessary consequence of his
eloquence that his hearer should be utterly stunned, dumb-
foundered, and overwhelmed, folded his arms so that the
palm of each hand rested on the opposite shoulder, and
disappeared after the manner of those mysterious warners of
whom he had read in cheap story-books.

"That fellow," said Mr. Chester, relaxing his face when
he was fairly gone, "is good practice. I *have* some command
of my features, beyond all doubt. He fully confirms what I
suspected, though; and blunt tools are sometimes found of
use, where sharper instruments would fail. I fear I may be
obliged to make great havoc among these worthy people. A
troublesome necessity! I quite feel for them."

With that he fell into a quiet slumber:—subsided into such
a gentle, pleasant sleep, that it was quite infantine.

247

CHAPTER XXV

Leaving the favoured, and well-received, and flattered of the world; him of the world most worldly, who never compromised himself by an ungentlemanly action, and never was guilty of a manly one; to lie smilingly asleep—for even sleep, working but little change in his dissembling face, became with him a piece of cold, conventional hypocrisy—we follow in the steps of two slow travellers on foot, making towards Chigwell.

Barnaby and his mother. Grip in their company, of course.

The widow, to whom each painful mile seemed longer than the last, toiled wearily along; while Barnaby, yielding to every inconstant impulse, fluttered here and there, now leaving her far behind, now lingering far behind himself, now darting into some by-lane or path and leaving her to pursue her way alone, until he stealthily emerged again and came upon her with a wild shout of merriment, as his wayward and capricious nature prompted. Now he would call to her from the topmost branch of some high tree by the roadside; now using his tall staff as a leaping-pole, come flying over ditch or hedge or five-barred gate; now run with surprising swiftness for a mile or more on the straight road, and halting, sport upon a patch of grass with Grip till she came up. These were his delights; and when his patient mother heard his merry voice, or looked into his flushed and healthy face, she would not have abated them by one sad word or murmur, though each had been to her a source of suffering in the same degree as it was to him of pleasure.

It is something to look upon enjoyment, so that it be free and wild and in the face of nature, though it is but the enjoyment of an idiot. It is something to know that Heaven has left the capacity of gladness in such a creature's breast; it is something to be assured that, however lightly men may crush that faculty in their fellows, the Great Creator of mankind imparts it even to his despised and slighted work. Who would not rather see a poor idiot happy in the sunlight, than a wise man pining in a darkened jail!

Ye men of gloom and austerity, who paint the face of Infinite Benevolence with an eternal frown; read in the Everlasting Book, wide open to your view, the lesson it would teach. Its pictures are not in black and sombre hues, but bright and glowing tints; its music—save when ye drown it—is not in sighs and groans, but songs and cheerful sounds. Listen to the million voices in the summer air, and find one dismal as your own. Remember, if ye can, the sense of hope and pleasure which every glad return of day awakens in the breast of all your kind who have not changed their nature; and learn some wisdom even from the witless, when their hearts are lifted up they know not why, by all the mirth and happiness it brings.

The widow's breast was full of care, was laden heavily with secret dread and sorrow; but her boy's gaiety of heart gladdened her, and beguiled the long journey. Sometimes he would bid her lean upon his arm, and would keep beside her steadily for a short distance; but it was more his nature to be rambling to and fro, and she better liked to see him free and happy, even than to have him near her, because she loved him better than herself.

She had quitted the place to which they were travelling, directly after the event which had changed her whole existence; and for two-and-twenty years had never had courage to revisit it. It was her native village. How many recollections crowded on her mind when it appeared in sight!

Two-and-twenty years. Her boy's whole life and history. The last time she looked back upon those roofs among the trees, she carried him in her arms, an infant. How often since that time had she sat beside him night and day, watching for the dawn of mind that never came; how had she feared, and doubted, and yet hoped, long after conviction forced itself upon her! The little stratagems she had devised to try him, the little tokens he had given in his childish way—not of dulness but of something infinitely worse, so ghastly and unchild-like in its cunning—came back as vividly as if but yesterday had intervened. The room in which they used to be; the spot in which his cradle stood; he, old and elfin-like in face, but ever dear to her, gazing at her with a wild and vacant eye, and crooning some uncouth song as she sat by and rocked him; every circumstance of his infancy came thronging back, and the most trivial, perhaps, the most distinctly.

His older childhood, too; the strange imaginings he had; his terror of certain senseless things—familiar objects he endowed with life; the slow and gradual breaking out of that one horror, in which, before his birth, his darkened intellect began; how, in the midst of all, she had found some hope and comfort in his being unlike another child, and had gone on almost believing in the slow development of his mind until he grew a man, and then his childhood was complete and lasting; one after another, all these old thoughts sprung up within her, strong after their long slumber and bitterer than ever.

She took his arm and they hurried through the village street. It was the same as it was wont to be in old times, yet different too, and wore another air. The change was in herself, not it; but she never thought of that, and wondered at its alteration, and where it lay, and what it was.

The people all knew Barnaby, and the children of the

place came flocking round him—as she remembered to have done with their fathers and mothers round some silly beggarman, when a child herself. None of them knew her; they passed each well-remembered house, and yard, and homestead; and striking into the fields, were soon alone again.

The Warren was the end of their journey. Mr. Haredale was walking in the garden, and seeing them as they passed the iron gate, unlocked it, and bade them enter that way.

"At length you have mustered heart to visit the old place," he said to the widow. "I am glad you have."

"For the first time, and the last, sir," she replied.

"The first for many years, but not the last?"

"The very last.

"You mean," said Mr. Haredale, regarding her with some surprise, "that having made this effort, you are resolved not to persevere and are determined to relapse? This is unworthy of you. I have often told you, you should return here. You would be happier here than elsewhere, I know. As to Barnaby, it's quite his home."

"And Grip's," said Barnaby, holding the basket open. The raven hopped gravely out, and perching on his shoulder and addressing himself to Mr. Haredale, cried—as a hint, perhaps, that some temperate refreshment would be acceptable —"Polly put the ket-tle on, we'll all have tea!"

"Hear me, Mary," said Mr. Haredale kindly, as he motioned her to walk with him towards the house. "Your life has been an example of patience and fortitude, except in this one particular which has often given me great pain. It is enough to know that you were cruelly involved in the calamity which deprived me of an only brother, and Emma of her father, without being obliged to suppose (as I sometimes am) that you associate us with the author of our joint misfortunes."

"Associate *you* with him, sir!" she cried.

"Indeed," said Mr. Haredale, "I think you do. I almost believe that because your husband was bound by so many

251

ties to our relation, and died in his service and defence, you have come in some sort to connect us with his murder."

"Alas!" she answered. "You little know my heart, sir. You little know the truth!"

"It is natural you should do so; it is very probable you may, without being conscious of it," said Mr. Haredale, speaking more to himself than her. "We are a fallen house. Money, dispensed with the most lavish hand, would be a poor recompense for sufferings like yours; and thinly scattered by hands so pinched and tied as ours, it becomes a miserable mockery. I feel it so, God knows," he added, hastily. "Why should I wonder if she does!"

"You do me wrong, dear sir, indeed," she rejoined with great earnestness; "and yet when you come to hear what I desire your leave to say——"

"I shall find my doubts confirmed?" he said, observing that she faltered and became confused. "Well!"

He quickened his pace for a few steps, but fell back again to her side, and said:

"And have you come all this way at last, solely to speak to me?"

She answered, "Yes."

"A curse," he muttered, "upon the wretched state of us proud beggars, from whom the poor and rich are equally at a distance; the one being forced to treat us with a show of cold respect; the other condescending to us in their every deed and word, and keeping more aloof, the nearer they approach us.—Why, if it were pain to you (as it must have been) to break for this slight purpose the chain of habit forged through two-and-twenty years, could you not let me know your wish, and beg me to come to you?"

"There was not time, sir," she rejoined. "I took my resolution but last night, and taking it, felt that I must not lose a day—a day! an hour—in having speech with you."

They had by this time reached the house. Mr. Haredale paused for a moment and looked at her as if surprised by

252

the energy of her manner. Observing, however, that she took no heed of him, but glanced up, shuddering, at the old walls with which such horrors were connected in her mind, he led her by a private stair into his library, where Emma was seated in a window, reading.

The young lady, seeing who approached, hastily rose and laid aside her book, and with many kind words, and not without tears, gave her a warm and earnest welcome. But the widow shrunk from her embrace as though she feared her, and sunk down trembling on a chair.

"It is the return to this place after so long an absence," said Emma gently. "Pray ring, dear uncle—or stay— Barnaby will run himself and ask for wine—"

"Not for the world," she cried. "It would have another taste—I could not touch it. I want but a minute's rest. Nothing but that."

Miss Haredale stood beside her chair, regarding her with silent pity. She remained for a little time quite still; then rose and turned to Mr. Haredale, who had sat down in his easy chair, and was contemplating her with fixed attention.

The tale connected with the mansion borne in mind, it seemed, as has been already said, the chosen theatre for such a deed as it had known. The room in which this group were now assembled—hard by the very chamber where the act was done—dull, dark, and sombre; heavy with worm-eaten books; deadened and shut in by faded hangings, muffling every sound; shadowed mournfully by trees whose rustling boughs gave ever and anon a spectral knocking at the glass; wore, beyond all others in the house, a ghostly, gloomy air. Nor were the group assembled there, unfitting tenants of the spot. The widow, with her marked and startling face and downcast eyes; Mr. Haredale stern and despondent ever; his niece beside him, like, yet most unlike, the picture of her father, which gazed reproachfully down upon them from the blackened wall; Barnaby, with his vacant look and restless eye; were all in keeping with the place, and actors in the

legend. Nay, the very raven, who had hopped upon the
table and with the air of some old necromancer appeared to
be profoundly studying a great folio volume that lay open

on a desk, was strictly in unison with the rest, and looked
like the embodied spirit of evil biding his time of mischief.

"I scarcely know," said the widow, breaking silence, "how
to begin. You will think my mind disordered."

"The whole tenor of your quiet and reproachless life since you were last here," returned Mr. Haredale, mildly, "shall bear witness for you. Why do you fear to awaken such a suspicion? You do not speak to strangers. You have not to claim our interest or consideration for the first time. Be more yourself. Take heart. Any advice or assistance that I can give you, you know is yours of right, and freely yours."

"What if I came, sir," she rejoined, "I who have but one other friend on earth, to reject your aid from this moment, and to say that henceforth I launch myself upon the world, alone and unassisted, to sink or swim as Heaven may decree!"

"You would have, if you came to me for such a purpose," said Mr. Haredale calmly, "some reason to assign for conduct so extraordinary, which—if one may entertain the possibility of anything so wild and strange—would have its weight, of course."

"That, sir," she answered, "is the misery of my distress. I can give no reason whatever. My own bare word is all that I can offer. It is my duty, my imperative and bounden duty. If I did not discharge it, I should be a base and guilty wretch. Having said that, my lips are sealed, and I can say no more."

As though she felt relieved at having said so much, and had nerved herself to the remainder of her task, she spoke from this time with a firmer voice and heightened courage.

"Heaven is my witness, as my own heart is—and yours, dear young lady, will speak for me, I know—that I have lived, since that time we all have bitter reason to remember, in unchanging devotion and gratitude to this family. Heaven is my witness that go where I may, I shall preserve those feelings unimpaired. And it is my witness, too, that they alone impel me to the course I must take, and from which nothing now shall turn me, as I hope for mercy."

"These are strange riddles," said Mr. Haredale.

"In this world, sir," she replied, "they may, perhaps, never be explained. In another, the Truth will be discovered in its own good time. And may that time," she added in a low voice, "be far distant!"

"Let me be sure," said Mr. Haredale, "that I understand you, for I am doubtful of my own senses. Do you mean that you are resolved voluntarily to deprive yourself of those means of support you have received from us so long—that you are determined to resign the annuity we settled on you twenty years ago—to leave house, and home, and goods, and begin life anew—and this, for some secret reason or monstrous fancy which is incapable of explanation, which only now exists, and has been dormant all this time? In the name of God, under what delusion are you labouring?"

"As I am deeply thankful," she made answer, "for the kindness of those, alive and dead, who have owned this house; and as I would not have its roof fall down and crush me, or its very walls drip blood, my name being spoken in their hearing; I never will again subsist upon their bounty, or let it help me to subsistence. You do not know," she added, suddenly, "to what uses it may be applied; into what hands it may pass. I do, and I renounce it."

"Surely," said Mr. Haredale, "its uses rest with you."

"They did. They rest with me no longer. It may be—it *is*—devoted to purposes that mock the dead in their graves. It never can prosper with me. It will bring some other heavy judgment on the head of my dear son, whose innocence will suffer for his mother's guilt."

"What words are these!" cried Mr. Haredale, regarding her with wonder. "Among what associates have you fallen? Into what guilt have you ever been betrayed?"

"I am guilty, and yet innocent; wrong, yet right; good in intention, though constrained to shield and aid the bad. Ask me no more questions, sir; but believe that I am rather to be pitied than condemned. I must leave my house to-morrow, for while I stay there, it is haunted. My future dwelling, if I am to live in peace, must be a secret. If my poor boy should ever stray this way, do not tempt him to

256

disclose it or have him watched when he returns; for if we are hunted, we must fly again. And now this load is off my mind I beseech you—and you, dear Miss Haredale, too—to trust me if you can, and think of me kindly as you have been used to do. If I die and cannot tell my secret even then (for that may come to pass), it will sit the lighter on my breast in that hour for this day's work; and on that day, and every day until it comes, I will pray for and thank you both, and trouble you no more."

With that, she would have left them, but they detained her, and with many soothing words and kind entreaties, besought her to consider what she did, and above all to repose more freely upon them, and say what weighed so sorely on her mind. Finding her deaf to their persuasions, Mr. Haredale suggested, as a last resource, that she should confide in Emma, of whom, as a young person and one of her own sex, she might stand in less dread than of himself. From this proposal, however, she recoiled with the same indescribable repugnance she had manifested when they met. The utmost that could be wrung from her was, a promise that she would receive Mr. Haredale at her own house next evening, and in the mean time reconsider her determination and their dissuasions—though any change on her part, as she told them, was quite hopeless. This condition made at last, they reluctantly suffered her to depart, since she would neither eat nor drink within the house; and she, and Barnaby, and Grip, accordingly went out as they had come, by the private stair and garden-gate; seeing and being seen of no one by the way.

It was remarkable in the raven that during the whole interview he had kept his eye on his book with exactly the air of a very sly human rascal, who, under the mask of pretending to read hard, was listening to everything. He still appeared to have the conversation very strongly in his mind, for although, when they were alone again, he issued orders for the instant preparation of innumerable kettles for purposes of tea, he was thoughtful, and rather seemed to do so from an abstract sense of duty, than with any regard to making himself agreeable, or being what is commonly called good company.

They were to return by the coach. As there was an interval of full two hours before it started, and they needed rest and some refreshment, Barnaby begged hard for a visit to the Maypole. But his mother, who had no wish to be recognised by any of those who had known her long ago, and who feared besides that Mr. Haredale might, on second thoughts, despatch some messenger to that place of entertainment in quest of her, proposed to wait in the churchyard instead. As it was easy for Barnaby to buy and carry thither such humble viands as they required, he cheerfully assented, and in the churchyard they sat down to take their frugal dinner.

Here again, the raven was in a highly reflective state; walking up and down when he had dined, with an air of elderly complacency which was strongly suggestive of his having his hands under his coat-tails; and appearing to read the tombstones with a very critical taste. Sometimes, after a long inspection of an epitaph, he would strop his beak upon the grave to which it referred, and cry in his hoarse tones, "I'm a devil, I'm a devil, I'm a devil!" but whether he addressed his observations to any supposed person below, or merely threw them off as a general remark, is matter of uncertainty.

It was a quiet pretty spot, but a sad one for Barnaby's mother; for Mr. Reuben Haredale lay there, and near the vault in which his ashes rested, was a stone to the memory of her own husband, with a brief inscription recording how and when he had lost his life. She sat here, thoughtful and apart, until their time was out, and the distant horn told that the coach was coming.

Barnaby, who had been sleeping on the grass, sprung up quickly at the sound; and Grip, who appeared to understand it equally well, walked into his basket straightway, entreating society in general (as though he intended a kind of satire upon them in connection with churchyards) never to say die on any terms. They were soon on the coach-top and rolling along the road.

It went round by the Maypole, and stopped at the door. Joe was from home, and Hugh came sluggishly out to hand up the parcel that it called for. There was no fear of old

John coming out. They could see him from the coach-roof fast asleep in his cosy bar. It was a part of John's character. He made a point of going to sleep at the coach's time. He despised gadding about; he looked upon coaches as things that ought to be indicted; as disturbers of the peace of mankind; as restless, bustling, busy, horn-blowing contrivances, quite beneath the dignity of men, and only suited to giddy girls that did nothing but chatter and go a-shopping. "We know nothing about coaches here, sir," John would say, if any unlucky stranger made inquiry touching the offensive vehicles; "we don't book for 'em; we'd rather not; they're more trouble than they're worth, with their noise and rattle. If you like to wait for 'em you can; but we don't know anything about 'em; they may call and they may not—there's a carrier—he was looked upon as quite good enough for us, when *I* was a boy."

She dropped her veil as Hugh climbed up, and while he hung behind, and talked to Barnaby in whispers. But neither he nor any other person spoke to her, or noticed her, or had any curiosity about her; and so, an alien, she visited and left the village where she had been born, and had lived a merry child, a comely girl, a happy wife—where she had known all her enjoyment of life, and had entered on its hardest sorrows.

CHAPTER XXVI

"AND you're not surprised to hear this, Varden?" said Mr. Haredale. "Well! You and she have always been the best friends, and you should understand her if anybody does."

"I ask your pardon, sir," rejoined the locksmith. "I didn't say I understood her. I wouldn't have the presumption to say that of any woman. It's not so easily done. But I am not so much surprised, sir, as you expected me to be, certainly."

"May I ask why not, my good friend?"

"I have seen, sir," returned the locksmith with evident reluctance, "I have seen in connection with her, something that has filled me with distrust and uneasiness. She has made bad friends, how, or when, I don't know; but that her house is a refuge for one robber and cut-throat at least, I am certain. There, sir! Now it's out."

"Varden!"

"My own eyes, sir, are my witnesses, and for her sake I would be willingly half-blind, if I could but have the pleasure of mistrusting 'em. I have kept the secret till now, and it will go no further than yourself, I know; but I tell you that with my own eyes—broad awake—I saw, in the passage of her house one evening after dark, the highwayman who robbed and wounded Mr. Edward Chester, and on the same night threatened me."

"And you made no effort to detain him?" said Mr. Haredale quickly.

"Sir," returned the locksmith, "she herself prevented me —held me, with all her strength, and hung about me until he had got clear off." And having gone so far, he related circumstantially all that had passed upon the night in question.

This dialogue was held in a low tone in the locksmith's little parlour, into which honest Gabriel had shown his visitor on his arrival. Mr. Haredale had called upon him to entreat his company to the widow's, that he might have the assistance of his persuasion and influence; and out of this circumstance the conversation had arisen.

"I forbore," said Gabriel, "from repeating one word of this to anybody, as it could do her no good and might do her great harm. I thought and hoped, to say the truth, that she would come to me, and talk to me about it, and tell me how it was; but though I have purposely put myself in her way more than once or twice, she has never touched upon the subject—except by a look. And indeed," said the good-natured locksmith, "there was a good deal in the look, more than could have been put into a great many words. It said among other matters 'Don't ask me anything' so imploringly, that I didn't ask her anything. You'll think me an old fool, I know, sir. If it's any relief to call me one, pray do."

"I am greatly disturbed by what you tell me," said Mr. Haredale, after a silence. "What meaning do you attach to it?"

The locksmith shook his head, and looked doubtfully out of window at the failing light.

"She cannot have married again," said Mr. Haredale.

"Not without our knowledge surely, sir."

"She may have done so, in the fear that it would lead, if known, to some objection or estrangement. Suppose she married incautiously—it is not improbable, for her existence has been a lonely and monotonous one for many years—and the man turned out a ruffian, she would be anxious to screen him, and yet would revolt from his crimes. This might be. It bears strongly on the whole drift of her discourse yesterday, and would quite explain her conduct. Do you suppose Barnaby is privy to these circumstances?"

"Quite impossible to say, sir," returned the locksmith, shaking his head again: "and next to impossible to find out from him. If what you suppose is really the case, I tremble for the lad—a notable person, sir, to put to bad uses—"

"It is not possible, Varden," said Mr. Haredale, in a still lower tone of voice than he had spoken yet, "that we have been blinded and deceived by this woman from the beginning? It is not possible that this connection was formed in her husband's lifetime, and led to his and my brother's—"

"Good God, sir," cried Gabriel, interrupting him, "don't entertain such dark thoughts for a moment. Five-and-twenty years ago, where was there a girl like her? A gay, handsome, laughing, bright-eyed damsel! Think what she was, sir. It makes my heart ache now, even now, though I'm an old man, with a woman for a daughter, to think what she was and what she is. We all change, but that's with Time; Time does his work honestly, and I don't mind him. A fig for Time, sir. Use him well, and he's a hearty fellow, and scorns to have you at a disadvantage. But care and suffering (and those have changed her) are devils, sir—secret, stealthy, undermining devils—who tread down the brightest flowers in Eden, and do more havoc in a month than Time does in a year. Picture to yourself for one minute what Mary was before they went to work with her fresh heart and face—do her that justice—and say whether such a thing is possible."

"You're a good fellow, Varden," said Mr. Haredale, "and are quite right. I have brooded on that subject so long, that every breath of suspicion carries me back to it. You are quite right."

"It isn't, sir," cried the locksmith with brightened eyes, and sturdy honest voice; "it isn't because I courted her before Rudge, and failed, that I say she was too good for him. She would have been as much too good for me. But she *was* too good for him; he wasn't free and frank enough for her. I don't reproach his memory with it, poor fellow; I only want to put her before you as she really was. For myself, I'll keep her old picture in my mind; and thinking of that, and what has altered her, I'll stand her friend, and try to win her back to peace. And damme, sir," cried Gabriel, "with your pardon for the word, I'd do the same if she had married fifty highwaymen in a twelvemonth; and think it in the Protestant Manual too, though Martha said it wasn't, tooth and nail, till doomsday!"

If the dark little parlour had been filled with a dense fog, which, clearing away in an instant, left it all radiance and brightness, it could not have been more suddenly cheered than by this outbreak on the part of the hearty locksmith. In a voice nearly as full and round as his own, Mr. Haredale cried "Well said!" and bade him come away without more parley. The locksmith complied right willingly; and both getting into a hackney coach which was waiting at the door, drove off straightway.

They alighted at the street corner, and dismissing their conveyance, walked to the house. To their first knock at the door there was no response. A second met with the like result. But in answer to the third, which was of a more vigorous kind, the parlour window-sash was gently raised, and a musical voice cried:

"Haredale, my dear fellow, I am extremely glad to see you. How very much you have improved in your appearance since our last meeting! I never saw you looking better. *How* do you do?"

Mr. Haredale turned his eyes towards the casement whence the voice proceeded, though there was no need to do so, to recognise the speaker, and Mr. Chester waved his hand, and smiled a courteous welcome.

"The door will be opened immediately," he said. "There

is nobody but a very dilapidated female to perform such offices. You will excuse her infirmities? If she were in a more elevated station of society, she would be gouty. Being but a hewer of wood and drawer of water, she is rheumatic. My dear Haredale, these are natural class distinctions, depend upon it."

Mr. Haredale, whose face resumed its lowering and distrustful look the moment he heard the voice, inclined his head stiffly, and turned his back upon the speaker.

"Not opened yet," said Mr. Chester. "Dear me! I hope the aged soul has not caught her foot in some unlucky cobweb by the way. She is there at last! Come in, I beg!"

Mr. Haredale entered, followed by the locksmith. Turning with a look of great astonishment to the old woman who had opened the door, he inquired for Mrs. Rudge—for Barnaby. They were both gone, she replied, wagging her ancient head, for good. There was a gentleman in the parlour, who perhaps could tell them more. That was all *she* knew.

"Pray, sir," said Mr. Haredale, presenting himself before this new tenant, "where is the person whom I came here to see?"

"My dear friend," he returned, "I have not the least idea."

"Your trifling is ill-timed," retorted the other in a suppressed tone and voice, "and its subject ill-chosen. Reserve it for those who are your friends, and do not expend it on me. I lay no claim to the distinction, and have the self-denial to reject it."

"My dear, good sir," said Mr. Chester, "you are heated with walking. Sit down, I beg. Our friend is—"

"Is but a plain honest man," returned Mr. Haredale, "and quite unworthy of your notice."

"Gabriel Varden by name, sir," said the locksmith bluntly.

"A worthy English yeoman!" said Mr. Chester. "A most worthy yeoman, of whom I have frequently heard my son Ned—darling fellow—speak, and have often wished to see.

Varden, my good friend, I am glad to know you. You wonder now," he said, turning languidly to Mr. Haredale, "to see me here. Now, I am sure you do."

Mr. Haredale glanced at him—not fondly or admiringly—smiled, and held his peace.

"The mystery is solved in a moment," said Mr. Chester; "in a moment. Will you step aside with me one instant? You remember our little compact in reference to Ned, and your dear niece, Haredale? You remember the list of assistants in their innocent intrigue? You remember these two people being among them? My dear fellow, congratulate yourself, and me. I have bought them off."

"You have done what?" said Mr. Haredale.

"Bought them off," returned his smiling friend. "I have found it necessary to take some active steps towards setting this boy and girl attachment quite at rest, and have begun by removing these two agents. You are surprised? Who *can* withstand the influence of a little money! They wanted it, and have been bought off. We have nothing more to fear from them. They are gone."

"Gone!" echoed Mr. Haredale. "Where?"

"My dear fellow—and you must permit me to say again, that you never looked so young; so positively boyish as you do to-night—the Lord knows where; I believe Columbus himself wouldn't find them. Between you and me they have their hidden reasons, but upon that point I have pledged myself to secrecy. She appointed to see you here to-night I know, but found it inconvenient, and couldn't wait. Here is the key of the door. I am afraid you'll find it inconveniently large; but as the tenement is yours, your good-nature will excuse that, Haredale, I am certain!"

CHAPTER XXVII

Mr. Haredale stood in the widow's parlour with the door-key in his hand, gazing by turns at Mr. Chester and at Gabriel Varden, and occasionally glancing downward at the key as in the hope that of its own accord it would unlock the mystery; until Mr. Chester, putting on his hat and gloves, and sweetly inquiring whether they were walking in the same direction, recalled him to himself.

"No," he said. "Our roads diverge—widely, as you know. For the present, I shall remain here."

"You will be hipped, Haredale; you will be miserable, melancholy, utterly wretched," returned the other. "It's a place of the very last description for a man of your temper. I know it will make you very miserable."

"Let it," said Mr. Haredale, sitting down; "and thrive upon the thought. Good night!"

Feigning to be wholly unconscious of the abrupt wave of the hand which rendered this farewell tantamount to a dismissal, Mr. Chester retorted with a bland and heartfelt benediction, and inquired of Gabriel in what direction *he* was going.

"Yours, sir, would be too much honour for the like of me," replied the locksmith, hesitating.

"I wish you to remain here a little while, Varden," said Mr. Haredale, without looking towards them. "I have a word or two to say to you."

"I will not intrude upon your conference another moment," said Mr. Chester with inconceivable politeness. "May it be satisfactory to you both! God bless you!" So saying, and bestowing upon the locksmith a most refulgent smile, he left them.

"A deplorably constituted creature, that rugged person," he said, as he walked along the street; "he is an atrocity that carries its own punishment along with it—a bear that gnaws himself. And here is one of the inestimable advantages of having a perfect command over one's inclinations. I have been tempted in these two short interviews, to draw upon that fellow, fifty times. Five men in six would have yielded to the impulse. By suppressing mine, I wound him deeper and more keenly than if I were the best swordsman in all Europe, and he the worst. You are the wise man's very last resource," he said, tapping the hilt of his weapon; "we can but appeal to you when all else is said and done. To come to you before, and thereby spare our adversaries so much, is a barbarian mode of warfare, quite unworthy of any man with the remotest pretensions to delicacy of feeling, or refinement."

He smiled so very pleasantly as he communed with himself after this manner, that a beggar was emboldened to follow for alms, and to dog his footsteps for some distance. He was gratified by the circumstance, feeling it complimentary to his power of feature, and as a reward suffered the man to follow him until he called a chair, when he graciously dismissed him with a fervent blessing.

"Which is as easy as cursing," he wisely added, as he took his seat, "and more becoming to the face.—To Clerkenwell, my good creatures, if you please!" The chairmen were rendered quite vivacious by having such a courteous burden, and to Clerkenwell they went at a fair round trot.

Alighting at a certain point he had indicated to them upon the road, and paying them something less than they expected from a fare of such gentle speech, he turned into the street in which the locksmith dwelt, and presently stood beneath the shadow of the Golden Key. Mr. Tappertit, who was hard at work by lamp-light, in a corner of the work-shop, remained unconscious of his presence until a hand upon his shoulder made him start and turn his head.

"Industry," said Mr. Chester, "is the soul of business, and the key-stone of prosperity. Mr. Tappertit, I shall expect you to invite me to dinner when you are Lord Mayor of London."

"Sir," returned the 'prentice, laying down his hammer, and rubbing his nose on the back of a very sooty hand, "I scorn the Lord Mayor and everything that belongs to him. We must have another state of society, sir, before you catch me being Lord Mayor. How de do, sir?"

"The better, Mr. Tappertit, for looking into your ingenuous face once more. I hope you are well."

"I am as well, sir," said Sim, standing up to get nearer to his ear, and whispering hoarsely, "as any man can be under the aggrawations to which I am exposed. My life's a burden to me. If it wasn't for wengeance, I'd play at pitch and toss with it on the losing hazard."

"Is Mrs. Varden at home?" said Mr. Chester.

"Sir," returned Sim, eyeing him over with a look of con-centrated expression—"she is. Did you wish to see her?"

Mr. Chester nodded.

"Then come this way, sir," said Sim, wiping his face upon his apron. "Follow me, sir.—Would you permit me to whisper in your ear, one half a second?"

"By all means."

Mr. Tappertit raised himself on tiptoe, applied his lips to Mr. Chester's ear, drew back his head without saying anything, looked hard at him, applied them to his ear again, again drew back, and finally whispered—"The name is Joseph Willet. Hush! I say no more."

Having said that much, he beckoned the visitor with a mysterious aspect to follow him to the parlour door, where he announced him in the voice of a gentleman usher. "Mr. Chester."

"And not Mr. Ed'dard, mind," said Sim, looking into the door again, and adding this by way of postscript in his own person; "it's his father."

"But do not let his father," said Mr. Chester, advancing hat in hand, as he observed the effect of this last explanatory announcement, "do not let his father be any check or restraint on your domestic occupations, Miss Varden."

"Oh! Now! There! An't I always a-saying it!" exclaimed Miggs, clapping her hands. "If he an't been and took Missis for her own daughter. Well, she *do* look like it, that she do. Only think of that, mim!"

"Is it possible," said Mr. Chester in his softest tones, "that this is Mrs. Varden! I am amazed. That is not your daughter, Mrs. Varden? No, no. Your sister."

"My daughter, indeed, sir," returned Mrs. V., blushing with great juvenility.

"Ah, Mrs. Varden!" cried the visitor. "Ah, ma'am—humanity is indeed a happy lot, when we can repeat ourselves in others, and still be young as they. You must allow me to salute you—the custom of the country, my dear madam—your daughter too."

Dolly showed some reluctance to perform this ceremony, but was sharply reproved by Mrs. Varden, who insisted on her undergoing it that minute. For pride, she said with great severity, was one of the seven deadly sins, and humility and lowliness of heart were virtues. Wherefore she desired that Dolly would be kissed immediately, on pain of her just displeasure; at the same time giving her to understand that whatever she saw her mother do, she might safely do herself, without being at the trouble of any reasoning or reflection on the subject—which, indeed, was offensive and undutiful, and in direct contravention of the church catechism.

Thus admonished, Dolly complied, though by no means willingly; for there was a broad, bold look of admiration

in Mr. Chester's face, refined and polished though it sought
to be, which distressed her very much. As she stood with
downcast eyes, not liking to look up and meet his, he gazed
upon her with an approving air, and then turned to her
mother.

"My friend Gabriel (whose acquaintance I only made this
very evening) should be a happy man, Mrs. Varden."

"Ah!" sighed Mrs. V., shaking her head.

"Ah!" echoed Miggs.

"Is that the case?" said Mr. Chester, compassionately.
"Dear me!"

"Master has no intentions, sir," murmured Miggs as she
sidled up to him, "but to be as grateful as his natur will
let him, for everythink he owns which it is in his powers to
appreciate. But we never, sir"—said Miggs, looking sideways
at Mrs. Varden, and interlarding her discourse with a sigh
—"we never know the full value of *some* wines and fig-trees
till we lose 'em. So much the worse, sir, for them as has
the slighting of 'em on their consciences when they're gone
to be in full blow elsewhere." And Miss Miggs cast up her
eyes to signify where that might be.

As Mrs. Varden distinctly heard, and was intended to
hear, all that Miggs said, and as these words appeared to
convey in metaphorical terms a presage or foreboding that
she would at some early period droop beneath her trials and
take an easy flight towards the stars, she immediately began
to languish, and taking a volume of the Manual from a neighbouring table, leant her arm upon it as though she were Hope
and that her Anchor. Mr. Chester perceiving this, and seeing
how the volume was lettered on the back, took it gently from
her hand, and turned the fluttering leaves.

"My favourite book, dear madam. How often, how very
often in his early life—before he can remember"—(this
clause was strictly true)—"have I deduced little easy moral
lessons from its pages, for my dear son Ned! You know
Ned?"

Mrs. Varden had that honour, and a fine affable young gentleman he was.

"You're a mother, Mrs. Varden," said Mr. Chester, taking a pinch of snuff, "and you know what I, as a father, feel, when he is praised. He gives me some uneasiness—much uneasiness—he's of a roving nature, ma'am—from flower to flower—from sweet to sweet—but his is the butterfly time of life, and we must not be hard upon such trifling."

He glanced at Dolly. She was attending evidently to what he said. Just what he desired!

"The only thing I object to in this little trait of Ned's, is," said Mr. Chester, "—and the mention of his name reminds me, by the way, that I am about to beg the favour of a minute's talk with you alone—the only thing I object to in it, is, that it *does* partake of insincerity. Now, however I may attempt to disguise the fact from myself in my affection for Ned, still I always revert to this—that if we are not sincere, we are nothing. Nothing upon earth. Let us be sincere, my dear madam—"

"—and Protestant," murmured Mrs. Varden.

"—and Protestant above all things. Let us be sincere and Protestant, strictly moral, strictly just (though always with a leaning towards mercy), strictly honest, and strictly true, and we gain—it is a slight point, certainly, but still it is something tangible; we throw up a groundwork and foundation, so to speak, of goodness, on which we may afterwards erect some worthy superstructure."

Now, to be sure, Mrs. Varden thought, here is a perfect character. Here is a meek, righteous, thoroughgoing Christian, who, having mastered all these qualities, so difficult of attainment; who, having dropped a pinch of salt on the tails of all the cardinal virtues, and caught them every one; makes light of their possession, and pants for more morality. For the good woman never doubted (as many good men and women never do), that this slighting kind of profession, this setting so little store by great matters, this seeming to say,

"I am not proud, I am what you hear, but I consider myself no better than other people; let us change the subject,
pray"—was perfectly genuine and true. He so contrived it,

and said it in that way that it appeared to have been forced
from him, and its effect was marvellous.

Aware of the impression he had made—few men were
quicker than he at such discoveries—Mr. Chester followed up

the blow by propounding certain virtuous maxims, somewhat vague and general in their nature, doubtless, and occasionally partaking of the character of truisms, worn a little out at elbow, but delivered in so charming a voice and with such uncommon serenity and peace of mind, that they answered as well as the best. Nor is this to be wondered at; for as hollow vessels produce a far more musical sound in falling than those which are substantial, so it will oftentimes be found that sentiments which have nothing in them make the loudest ringing in the world, and are the most relished.

Mr. Chester, with the volume gently extended in one hand, and with the other planted lightly on his breast, talked to them in the most delicious manner possible; and quite enchanted all his hearers, notwithstanding their conflicting interests and thoughts. Even Dolly, who, between his keen regards and her eyeing over by Mr. Tappertit, was put quite out of countenance, could not help owning within herself that he was the sweetest-spoken gentleman she had ever seen. Even Miss Miggs, who was divided between admiration of Mr. Chester and a mortal jealousy of her young mistress, had sufficient leisure to be propitiated. Even Mr. Tappertit, though occupied as we have seen in gazing at his heart's delight, could not wholly divert his thoughts from the voice of the other charmer. Mrs. Varden, to her own private thinking, had never been so improved in all her life; and when Mr. Chester, rising and craving permission to speak with her apart, took her by the hand and led her at arm's length up-stairs to the best sitting-room, she almost deemed him something more than human.

"Dear madam," he said, pressing her hand delicately to his lips; "be seated."

Mrs. Varden called up quite a courtly air, and became seated.

"You guess my object?" said Mr. Chester, drawing a chair towards her. "You divine my purpose? I am an affectionate parent, my dear Mrs. Varden."

"That I am sure you are, sir," said Mrs. V.

"Thank you," returned Mr. Chester, tapping his snuff-box lid. "Heavy moral responsibilities rest with parents, Mrs. Varden."

Mrs. Varden slightly raised her hands, shook her head, and looked at the ground as though she saw straight through the globe, out at the other end, and into the immensity of space beyond.

"I may confide in you," said Mr. Chester, "without reserve. I love my son, ma'am, dearly; and loving him as I do, I would save him from working certain misery. You know of his attachment to Miss Haredale. You have abetted him in it, and very kind of you it was to do so. I am deeply obliged to you—most deeply obliged to you—for your interest in his behalf; but, my dear ma'am, it is a mistaken one, I do assure you."

Mrs. Varden stammered that she was sorry—

"Sorry, my dear ma'am," he interposed. "Never be sorry for what is so very amiable, so very good in intention, so perfectly like yourself. But there are grave and weighty reasons, pressing family considerations, and apart even from these, points of religious difference, which interpose themselves, and render their union impossible; utterly im-possible. I should have mentioned these circumstances to your husband; but he has—you will excuse my saying this so freely—he has *not* your quickness of apprehension or depth of moral sense. What an extremely airy house this is, and how beautifully kept! For one like myself—a widower so long—these tokens of female care and superintendence have inexpressible charms."

Mrs. Varden began to think (she scarcely knew why) that the young Mr. Chester must be in the wrong and the old Mr. Chester must be in the right.

"My son Ned," resumed her tempter with his utmost winning air, "has had, I am told, your lovely daughter's aid, and your open-hearted husband's."

"—Much more than mine, sir," said Mrs. Varden; "a great deal more. I have often had my doubts. It's a—"

"A bad example," suggested Mr. Chester. "It is. No doubt it is. Your daughter is at that age when to set before her an encouragement for young persons to rebel against their parents on this most important point, is particularly injudicious. You are quite right. I ought to have thought of that myself, but it escaped me, I confess—so far superior are your sex to ours, dear madam, in point of penetration and sagacity."

Mrs. Varden looked as wise as if she had really said something to deserve this compliment—firmly believed she had, in short—and her faith in her own shrewdness increased considerably.

"My dear ma'am," said Mr. Chester, "you embolden me to be plain with you. My son and I are at variance on this point. The young lady and her natural guardian differ upon it, also. And the closing point is, that my son is bound by his duty to me, by his honour, by every solemn tie and obligation, to marry some one else."

"Engaged to marry another lady!" quoth Mrs. Varden, holding up her hands.

"My dear madam, brought up, educated, and trained, expressly for that purpose. Expressly for that purpose.— Miss Haredale, I am told, is a very charming creature."

"I am her foster-mother, and should know—the best young lady in the world," said Mrs. Varden.

"I have not the smallest doubt of it. I am sure she is. And you, who have stood in that tender relation towards her, are bound to consult her happiness. Now, can I—as I have said to Haredale, who quite agrees—can I possibly stand by, and suffer her to throw herself away (although she *is* of a Catholic family) upon a young fellow who, as yet, has no heart at all? It is no imputation upon him to say he has not, because young men who have plunged deeply into the frivolities and conventionalities of society, very

276

seldom have. Their hearts never grow, my dear ma'am, till after thirty. I don't believe, no, I do *not* believe, that I had any heart myself when I was Ned's age."

"Oh, sir," said Mrs. Varden, "I think you must have had. It's impossible that you, who have so much now, can ever have been without any."

"I hope," he answered, shrugging his shoulders meekly, "I have a little; I hope, a very little—Heaven knows! But to return to Ned; I have no doubt you thought, and therefore interfered benevolently in his behalf, that I objected to Miss Haredale. How very natural! My dear madam, I object to him—to him—emphatically to Ned himself."

Mrs. Varden was perfectly aghast at the disclosure.

"He has, if he honourably fulfils this solemn obligation of which I have told you—and he must be honourable, dear Mrs. Varden, or he is no son of mine—a fortune within his reach. He is of most expensive, ruinously expensive habits; and if, in a moment of caprice and wilfulness, he were to marry this young lady, and so deprive himself of the means of gratifying the tastes to which he had been so long accustomed, he would—my dear madam, he would break the gentle creature's heart. Mrs. Varden, my good lady, my dear soul, I put it to you—is such a sacrifice to be endured? Is the female heart a thing to be trifled with in this way? Ask your own, my dear madam. Ask your own, I beseech you."

"Truly," thought Mrs. Varden, "this gentleman is a saint. But," she added aloud, and not unnaturally, "if you take Miss Emma's lover away, sir, what becomes of the poor thing's heart then?"

"The very point," said Mr. Chester, not at all abashed, "to which I wished to lead you. A marriage with my son, whom I should be compelled to disown, would be followed by years of misery; they would be separated, my dear madam, in a twelvemonth. To break off this attachment, which is more fancied than real, as you and I know very well, will cost the dear girl but a few tears, and she is happy again. Take the case of your own daughter, the young lady down-stairs, who is your breathing image"— Mrs. Varden coughed and simpered—" there is a young man, (I am sorry to say, a dissolute fellow, of very indifferent character,) of whom I have heard Ned speak—Bullet was it—Pullet—Mullet—"

"There is a young man of the name of Joseph Willet, sir," said Mrs. Varden, folding her hands loftily.

"That's he," cried Mr. Chester. "Suppose this Joseph Willet now, were to aspire to the affections of your charming daughter, and were to engage them."

"It would be like his impudence," interposed Mrs. Varden, bridling, " to dare to think of such a thing!"

"My dear madam, that's the whole case. I know it would be like his impudence. It is like Ned's impudence to do as he has done; but you would not on that account, or because of a few tears from your beautiful daughter, refrain from checking their inclinations in their birth. I meant to have reasoned thus with your husband when I saw him at Mrs. Rudge's this evening—"

"My husband," said Mrs. Varden, interposing with emotion, "would be a great deal better at home than going to Mrs. Rudge's so often. I don't know what he does there. I don't see what occasion he has to busy himself in her affairs at all, sir."

"If I don't appear to express my concurrence in those last sentiments of yours," returned Mr. Chester, "quite so strongly as you might desire, it is because his being there, my dear madam, and not proving conversational, led me hither, and procured me the happiness of this interview with one, in whom the whole management, conduct, and prosperity of her family are centred, I perceive."

With that he took Mrs. Varden's hand again, and having pressed it to his lips with the high-flown gallantry of the day—a little burlesqued to render it the more striking in the good lady's unaccustomed eyes—proceeded in the same

278

strain of mingled sophistry, cajolery, and flattery, to entreat that her utmost influence might be exerted to restrain her husband and daughter from any further promotion of Edward's suit to Miss Haredale, and from aiding or abetting either party in any way. Mrs. Varden was but a woman, and had her share of vanity, obstinacy, and love of power. She entered into a secret treaty of alliance, offensive and defensive, with her insinuating visitor; and really did believe, as many others would have done who saw and heard him, that in so doing she furthered the ends of truth, justice, and morality, in a very uncommon degree.

Overjoyed by the success of his negotiation, and mightily amused within himself, Mr. Chester conducted her down-stairs in the same state as before ; and having repeated the previous ceremony of salutation, which also as before comprehended Dolly, took his leave ; first completing the conquest of Miss Miggs's heart, by inquiring if "this young lady" would light him to the door.

"Oh, mim," said Miggs, returning with the candle. "Oh gracious me, mim, there's a gentleman! Was there ever such an angel to talk as he is—and such a sweet-looking man! So upright and noble, that he seems to despise the very ground he walks on! and yet so mild and condescending, that he seems to say 'but I will take notice on it too.' And to think of his taking you for Miss Dolly, and Miss Dolly for your sister—Oh, my goodness me, if I was master wouldn't I be jealous of him!"

Mrs. Varden reproved her handmaid for this vain-speaking; but very gently and mildly—quite smilingly indeed—remarking that she was a foolish, giddy, light-headed girl, whose spirits carried her beyond all bounds, and who didn't mean half she said, or she would be quite angry with her.

"For my part," said Dolly, in a thoughtful manner, "I half believe Mr. Chester is something like Miggs in that respect. For all his politeness and pleasant speaking, I am pretty sure he was making game of us, more than once."

"If you venture to say such a thing again, and to speak ill of people behind their backs in my presence, Miss," said Mrs. Varden, "I shall insist upon your taking a candle and going to bed directly. How dare you, Dolly? I'm astonished at you. The rudeness of your whole behaviour this evening has been disgraceful. Did anybody ever hear," cried the enraged matron, bursting into tears, "of a daughter telling her own mother she has been made game of!"

What a very uncertain temper Mrs. Varden's was!

CHAPTER XXVIII

REPAIRING to a noted coffee-house in Covent Garden when he left the locksmith's, Mr. Chester sat long over a late dinner, entertaining himself exceedingly with the whimsical recollection of his recent proceedings, and congratulating himself very much on his great cleverness. Influenced by these thoughts, his face wore an expression so benign and tranquil, that the waiter in immediate attendance upon him felt he could almost have died in his defence, and settled in his own mind (until the receipt of the bill, and a very small fee for very great trouble disabused it of the idea) that such an apostolic customer was worth half-a-dozen of the ordinary run of visitors, at least.

A visit to the gaming-table—not as a heated, anxious venturer, but one whom it was quite a treat to see staking his two or three pieces in deference to the follies of society, and smiling with equal benevolence on winners and losers—made it late before he reached home. It was his custom to bid his servant go to bed at his own time unless he had orders to the contrary, and to leave a candle on the common stair. There was a lamp on the landing by which he could always light it when he came home late, and having a key of the door about him he could enter and go to bed at his pleasure.

He opened the glass of the dull lamp, whose wick, burnt up and swollen like a drunkard's nose, came flying off in little carbuncles at the candle's touch, and scattering hot sparks about, rendered it matter of some difficulty to kindle the lazy taper; when a noise, as of a man snoring deeply some steps higher up, caused him to pause and listen. It was the heavy breathing of a sleeper, close at hand. Some fellow had lain down on the open staircase, and was slumbering soundly. Having lighted the candle at length and opened his own door, he softly ascended, holding the taper high above his head, and peering cautiously about; curious to see what kind of man had chosen so comfortless a shelter for his lodging.

With his head upon the landing and his great limbs flung over half-a-dozen stairs, as careless as though he were a dead man whom drunken bearers had thrown down by chance, there lay Hugh, face uppermost, his long hair drooping like some wild weed upon his wooden pillow, and his huge chest heaving with the sounds which so unwontedly disturbed the place and hour.

He who came upon him so unexpectedly was about to break his rest by thrusting him with his foot, when, glancing at his upturned face, he arrested himself in the very action, and stooping down and shading the candle with his hand, examined his features closely. Close as his first inspection was, it did not suffice, for he passed the light, still carefully shaded as before, across and across his face, and yet observed him with a searching eye.

While he was thus engaged, the sleeper, without any starting or turning round, awoke. There was a kind of fascination in meeting his steady gaze so suddenly, which took from the other the presence of mind to withdraw his eyes, and forced him, as it were, to meet his look. So they remained staring at each other, until Mr. Chester at last broke silence, and asked him in a low voice, why he lay sleeping there.

"I thought," said Hugh, struggling into a sitting posture and gazing at him intently still, "that you were a part of my dream. It was a curious one. I hope it may never come true, master."

" What makes you shiver ?"

"The—the cold, I suppose," he growled, as he shook himself and rose. "I hardly know where I am yet."

" Do you know me ?" said Mr. Chester.

"Ay, I know you," he answered. "I was dreaming of you—we're not where I thought we were. That's a comfort."

He looked round him as he spoke, and in particular looked above his head, as though he half expected to be standing under some object which had had existence in his dream. Then he rubbed his eyes and shook himself again, and followed his conductor into his own rooms.

Mr. Chester lighted the candles which stood upon his dressing-table, and wheeling an easy-chair towards the fire, which was yet burning, stirred up a cheerful blaze, sat down before it, and bade his uncouth visitor " Come here," and draw his boots off.

"You have been drinking again, my fine fellow," he said, as Hugh went down on one knee, and did as he was told.

"As I'm alive, master, I've walked the twelve long miles, and waited here I don't know how long, and had no drink between my lips since dinner-time at noon."

"And can you do nothing better, my pleasant friend, than fall asleep, and shake the very building with your snores ?" said Mr. Chester. "Can't you dream in your straw at home, dull dog as you are, that you need come here to do it ?— Reach me those slippers, and tread softly."

Hugh obeyed in silence.

"And harkee, my dear young gentleman," said Mr. Chester, as he put them on, "the next time you dream, don't let it be of me, but of some dog or horse with whom you are better acquainted. Fill the glass once—you'll find it and the bottle in the same place—and empty it to keep yourself awake."

Hugh obeyed again—even more zealously—and having done so, presented himself before his patron.

"Now," said Mr. Chester, "what do you want with me?"

"There was news to-day," returned Hugh. "Your son was at our house—came down on horseback. He tried to see the young woman, but couldn't get sight of her. He left some letter or some message which our Joe had charge of, but he and the old one quarrelled about it when your son had gone, and the old one wouldn't let it be delivered. He says (that's the old one does) that none of his people shall interfere and get him into trouble. He's a landlord, he says, and lives on everybody's custom."

"He's a jewel," smiled Mr. Chester, "and the better for being a dull one.—Well?"

"Varden's daughter—that's the girl I kissed—"

"—and stole the bracelet from upon the king's highway," said Mr. Chester, composedly. "Yes; what of her?"

"She wrote a note at our house to the young woman, saying she lost the letter I brought to you, and you burnt. Our Joe was to carry it, but the old one kept him at home all next day, on purpose that he shouldn't. Next morning he gave it to me to take; and here it is."

"You didn't deliver it then, my good friend?" said Mr. Chester, twirling Dolly's note between his finger and thumb, and feigning to be surprised.

"I supposed you'd want to have it," retorted Hugh. "Burn one, burn all, I thought."

"My devil-may-care acquaintance," said Mr. Chester— "really if you do not draw some nicer distinctions, your career will be cut short with most surprising suddenness. Don't you know that the letter you brought to me, was directed to my son who resides in this very place? And can you descry no difference between his letters and those addressed to other people?"

"If you don't want it," said Hugh, disconcerted by this reproof, for he had expected high praise, "give it me back, and I'll deliver it. I don't know how to please you, master."

"I shall deliver it," returned his patron, putting it away

after a moment's consideration, "myself. Does the young lady walk out, on fine mornings?"

"Mostly—about noon is her usual time."

"Alone?"

"Yes, alone."

"Where?"

"In the grounds before the house.—Them that the footpath crosses."

"If the weather should be fine, I may throw myself in her way to-morrow, perhaps," said Mr. Chester, as coolly as if she were one of his ordinary acquaintance. "Mr. Hugh, if I should ride up to the Maypole door, you will do me the favour only to have seen me once. You must suppress your gratitude, and endeavour to forget my forbearance in the matter of the bracelet. It is natural it should break out, and it does you honour; but when other folks are by, you must, for your own sake and safety, be as like your usual self as though you owed me no obligation whatever, and had never stood within these walls. You comprehend me?"

Hugh understood him perfectly. After a pause he muttered that he hoped his patron would involve him in no trouble about this last letter; for he had kept it back solely with the view of pleasing him. He was continuing in this strain, when Mr. Chester with a most beneficent and patronising air cut him short by saying:

"My good fellow, you have my promise, my word, my sealed bond (for a verbal pledge with me is quite as good), that I will always protect you so long as you deserve it. Now, do set your mind at rest. Keep it at ease, I beg of you. When a man puts himself in my power so thoroughly as you have done, I really feel as though he had a kind of claim upon me. I am more disposed to mercy and forbearance under such circumstances than I can tell you, Hugh. Do look upon me as your protector, and rest assured, I entreat you, that on the subject of that indiscretion, you may preserve, as long as you and I are friends, the lightest heart that ever beat within a human breast. Fill that glass once more to cheer you on your road homewards—I am really quite ashamed to think how far you have to go—and then God bless you for the night."

"They think," said Hugh, when he had tossed the liquor down, "that I am sleeping soundly in the stable. Ha ha ha! The stable door is shut, but the steed's gone, master."

"You are a most convivial fellow," returned his friend, "and I love your humour of all things. Good night! Take the greatest possible care of yourself, for my sake!"

It was remarkable that during the whole interview, each had endeavoured to catch stolen glances of the other's face, and had never looked full at it. They interchanged one brief and hasty glance as Hugh went out, averted their eyes directly, and so separated. Hugh closed the double doors behind him, carefully and without noise; and Mr. Chester remained in his easy-chair, with his gaze intently fixed upon the fire.

"Well!" he said, after meditating for a long time—and said with a deep sigh and an uneasy shifting of his attitude, as though he dismissed some other subject from his thoughts, and returned to that which had held possession of them all the day—"the plot thickens; I have thrown the shell; it will explode, I think, in eight-and-forty hours, and should scatter these good folks amazingly. We shall see!"

He went to bed and fell asleep, but had not slept long when he started up and thought that Hugh was at the outer door, calling in a strange voice, very different from his own, to be admitted. The delusion was so strong upon him, and was so full of that vague terror of the night in which such visions have their being, that he rose, and taking his sheathed sword in his hand, opened the door, and looked out upon the staircase, and towards the spot where Hugh had lain asleep; and even spoke to him by name. But all was dark and quiet, and creeping back to bed again, he fell, after an hour's uneasy watching, into a second sleep, and woke no more till morning.

CHAPTER XXIX

THE thoughts of worldly men are for ever regulated by a moral law of gravitation, which, like the physical one, holds them down to earth. The bright glory of day, and the silent wonders of a starlit night, appeal to their minds in vain. There are no signs in the sun, or in the moon, or in the stars, for their reading. They are like some wise men, who, learning to know each planet by its Latin name, have quite forgotten such small heavenly constellations as Charity, Forbearance, Universal Love, and Mercy, although they shine by night and day so brightly that the blind may see them; and who, looking upward at the spangled sky, see nothing there but the reflection of their own great wisdom and book-learning.

It is curious to imagine these people of the world, busy in thought, turning their eyes towards the countless spheres that shine above us, and making them reflect the only images their minds contain. The man who lives but in the breath of princes, has nothing in his sight but stars for courtiers' breasts. The envious man beholds his neighbours' honours even in the sky; to the money-hoarder, and the mass of worldly folk, the whole great universe above glitters with sterling coin—fresh from the mint—stamped with the sovereign's head coming always between them and heaven, turn where they may. So do the shadows of our own desires stand between us and our better angels, and thus their brightness is eclipsed.

Everything was fresh and gay, as though the world were

but that morning made, when Mr. Chester rode at a tranquil pace along the Forest road. Though early in the season, it was warm and genial weather; the trees were budding into leaf, the hedges and the grass were green, the air was musical with songs of birds, and high above them all the lark poured out her richest melody. In shady spots, the morning dew sparkled on each young leaf and blade of grass; and where the sun was shining, some diamond drops yet glistened brightly, as in unwillingness to leave so fair a world, and have such brief existence. Even the light wind, whose rustling was as gentle to the ear as softly-falling water, had its hope and promise; and, leaving a pleasant fragrance in its track as it went fluttering by, whispered of its intercourse with Summer, and of his happy coming.

The solitary rider went glancing on among the trees, from sunlight into shade and back again, at the same even pace—looking about him, certainly, from time to time, but with no greater thought of the day or the scene through which he moved, than that he was fortunate (being choicely dressed) to have such favourable weather. He smiled very complacently at such times, but rather as if he were satisfied with himself than with anything else: and so went riding on, upon his chestnut cob, as pleasant to look upon as his own horse, and probably far less sensitive to the many cheerful influences by which he was surrounded.

In the course of time, the Maypole's massive chimneys rose upon his view: but he quickened not his pace one jot, and with the same cool gravity rode up to the tavern porch. John Willet, who was toasting his red face before a great fire in the bar, and who, with surpassing foresight and quickness of apprehension, had been thinking, as he looked at the blue sky, that if that state of things lasted much longer, it might ultimately become necessary to leave off fires and throw the windows open, issued forth to hold his stirrup; calling lustily for Hugh.

" Oh, you're here, are you, sir?" said John, rather surprised by the quickness with which he appeared. " Take this here valuable animal into the stable, and have more than particular care of him if you want to keep your place. A mortal lazy fellow, sir; he needs a deal of looking after."

"But you have a son," returned Mr. Chester, giving his bridle to Hugh as he dismounted, and acknowledging his salute by a careless motion of his hand towards his hat. " Why don't you make *him* useful ? "

"Why, the truth is, sir," replied John with great importance, "that my son — what, you're a-listening are you, villain ? "

" Who's listening ? " returned Hugh angrily. " A treat, indeed, to hear *you* speak ! Would you have me take him in till he's cool ? "

" Walk him up and down further off then, sir," cried old John, " and when you see me and a noble gentleman entertaining ourselves with talk, keep your distance. If you don't know your distance, sir," added Mr. Willet, after an enormously long pause, during which he fixed his great dull eyes on Hugh, and waited with exemplary patience for any little property in the way of ideas that might come to him, " we'll find a way to teach you, pretty soon."

Hugh shrugged his shoulders scornfully, and in his reckless swaggering way, crossed to the other side of the little green, and there, with the bridle slung loosely over his shoulder, led the horse to and fro, glancing at his master every now and then from under his bushy eyebrows, with as sinister an aspect as one would desire to see.

Mr. Chester, who, without appearing to do so, had eyed him attentively during this brief dispute, stepped into the porch, and turning abruptly to Mr. Willet, said,

" You keep strange servants, John."

" Strange enough to look at, sir, certainly," answered the host; " but out of doors; for horses, dogs, and the likes of that; there an't a better man in England than is that Maypole Hugh yonder. He an't fit for in-doors," added Mr.

BARNABY RUDGE

Willet, with the confidential air of a man who felt his own superior nature. "*I* do that; but if that chap had only a little imagination, sir—"

"He's an active fellow now, I dare swear," said Mr. Chester, in a musing tone, which seemed to suggest that he would have said the same had there been nobody to hear him.

"Active, sir!" retorted John, with quite an expression in his face; "that chap! Hallo there! You, sir! Bring that horse here, and go and hang my wig on the weathercock, to show this gentleman whether you're one of the lively sort or not."

Hugh made no answer, but throwing the bridle to his master, and snatching his wig from his head, in a manner so unceremonious and hasty that the action discomposed Mr. Willet not a little, though performed at his own special desire, climbed nimbly to the very summit of the maypole before the house, and hanging the wig upon the weathercock, sent it twirling round like a roasting jack. Having achieved this performance, he cast it on the ground, and sliding down the pole with inconceivable rapidity, alighted on his feet almost as soon as it had touched the earth.

"There, sir," said John, relapsing into his usual stolid state, "you won't see that at many houses, besides the Maypole, where there's good accommodation for man and beast—nor that neither, though that with him is nothing."

This last remark bore reference to his vaulting on horse-back, as upon Mr. Chester's first visit, and quickly disappearing by the stable gate.

"That with him is nothing," repeated Mr. Willet, brushing his wig with his wrist, and inwardly resolving to distribute a small charge for dust and damage to that article of dress, through the various items of his guest's bill; "he'll get out of a'most any winder in the house. There never was such a chap for flinging himself about and never hurting his bones. It's my opinion, sir, that it's pretty nearly all owing to his not having any imagination; and if that imagination could

290

be (which it can't) knocked into him, he'd never be able to do it any more. But we was a-talking, sir, about my son."

"True, Willet, true," said his visitor, turning again towards the landlord with that serenity of face. "My good friend, what about him?"

It has been reported that Mr. Willet, previously to making answer, winked. But as he was never known to be guilty of such lightness of conduct either before or afterwards, this may be looked upon as a malicious invention of his enemies— founded, perhaps, upon the undisputed circumstance of his taking his guest by the third breast button of his coat, counting downwards from the chin, and pouring his reply into his ear:

"Sir," whispered John, with dignity, "I know my duty. We want no love-making here, sir, unbeknown to parents. I respect a certain young gentleman, taking him in the light of a young gentleman; I respect a certain young lady, taking her in the light of a young lady; but of the two as a couple, I have no knowledge, sir, none whatever. My son, sir, is upon his patrole."

"I thought I saw him looking through the corner window but this moment," said Mr. Chester, who naturally thought that being on patrole, implied walking about somewhere.

"No doubt you did, sir," returned John. "He is upon his patrole of honour, sir, not to leave the premises. Me and some friends of mine that use the Maypole of an evening, sir, considered what was best to be done with him, to prevent his doing anything unpleasant in opposing your desires; and we've put him on his patrole. And what's more, sir, he won't be off his patrole for a pretty long time to come, I can tell you that."

When he had communicated this bright idea, which had its origin in the perusal by the village cronies of a newspaper, containing among other matters, an account of how some officer pending the sentence of some court-martial had been enlarged on parole, Mr. Willet drew back from his guest's ear, and without any visible alteration of feature, chuckled thrice audibly. This nearest approach to a laugh in which he ever indulged (and that but seldom and only on extreme occasions), never even curled his lip or effected the smallest change in—no, not so much as a slight wagging of—his great, fat, double chin, which at these times, as at all others, remained a perfect desert in the broad map of his face; one changeless, dull, tremendous blank.

Lest it should be matter of surprise to any, that Mr. Willet adopted this bold course in opposition to one whom he had often entertained, and who had always paid his way at the Maypole gallantly, it may be remarked that it was his very penetration and sagacity in this respect, which occasioned him to indulge in those unusual demonstrations of jocularity, just now recorded. For Mr. Willet, after carefully balancing father and son in his mental scales, had arrived at the distinct conclusion that the old gentleman was a better sort of a customer than the young one. Throwing his landlord into the same scale, which was already turned by this consideration, and heaping upon him, again, his strong desires to run counter to the unfortunate Joe, and his opposition as a general principle to all matters of love and matrimony, it went down to the very ground straightway, and sent the light cause of the younger gentleman flying upwards to the ceiling. Mr. Chester was not the kind of man to be by any means dim-sighted to Mr. Willet's motives, but he thanked him as graciously as if he had been one of the most disinterested martyrs that ever shone on earth; and leaving him, with many complimentary reliances on his great taste and judgment, to prepare whatever dinner he might deem most fitting the occasion, bent his steps towards the Warren.

Dressed with more than his usual elegance; assuming a gracefulness of manner, which, though it was the result of long study, sat easily upon him and became him well; composing his features into their most serene and prepossessing expression; and setting in short that guard upon himself,

at every point, which denoted that he attached no slight
importance to the impression he was about to make; he
entered the bounds of Miss Haredale's usual walk. He had

not gone far, or looked about him long, when he descried
coming towards him, a female figure. A glimpse of the
form and dress as she crossed a little wooden bridge which

lay between them, satisfied him that he had found her whom he desired to see. He threw himself in her way, and a very few paces brought them close together.

He raised his hat from his head, and yielding the path, suffered her to pass him. Then, as if the idea had but that moment occurred to him, he turned hastily back and said in an agitated voice:

"I beg pardon—do I address Miss Haredale?"

She stopped in some confusion at being so unexpectedly accosted by a stranger; and answered "Yes."

"Something told me," he said, *looking* a compliment to her beauty, "that it could be no other. Miss Haredale, I bear a name which is not unknown to you—which it is a pride, and yet a pain to me to know, sounds pleasantly in your ears. I am a man advanced in life, as you see. I am the father of him whom you honour and distinguish above all other men. May I for weighty reasons which fill me with distress, beg but a minute's conversation with you here?"

Who that was inexperienced in deceit, and had a frank and youthful heart, could doubt the speaker's truth—could doubt it too, when the voice that spoke, was like the faint echo of one she knew so well, and so much loved to hear? She inclined her head, and stopping, cast her eyes upon the ground.

"A little more apart—among these trees. It is an old man's hand, Miss Haredale; an honest one, believe me."

She put hers in it as he said these words, and suffered him to lead her to a neighbouring seat.

"You alarm me, sir," she said in a low voice. "You are not the bearer of any ill news, I hope?"

"Of none that you anticipate," he answered, sitting down beside her. "Edward is well—quite well. It is of him I wish to speak, certainly; but I have no misfortune to communicate."

She bowed her head again, and made as though she would have begged him to proceed; but said nothing.

" I am sensible that I speak to you at a disadvantage, dear Miss Haredale. Believe me that I am not so forgetful of the feelings of my younger days as not to know that you are little disposed to view me with favour. You have heard me described as cold-hearted, calculating, selfish—"

" I have never, sir,"—she interposed with an altered manner and a firmer voice; " I have never heard you spoken of in harsh or disrespectful terms. You do a great wrong to Edward's nature if you believe him capable of any mean or base proceeding."

" Pardon me, my sweet young lady, but your uncle—"

" Nor is it my uncle's nature either," she replied, with a heightened colour in her cheek. " It is not his nature to stab in the dark, nor is it mine to love such deeds."

She rose as she spoke, and would have left him; but he detained her with a gentle hand, and besought her in such persuasive accents to hear him but another minute, that she was easily prevailed upon to comply, and so sat down again.

" And it is," said Mr. Chester, looking upward, and apostrophising the air; " it is this frank, ingenuous, noble nature, Ned, that you can wound so lightly. Shame—shame upon you, boy ! "

She turned towards him quickly, and with a scornful look and flashing eyes. There were tears in Mr. Chester's eyes, but he dashed them hurriedly away, as though unwilling that his weakness should be known, and regarded her with mingled admiration and compassion.

" I never until now," he said, " believed, that the frivolous actions of a young man could move me like these of my own son. I never knew till now, the worth of a woman's heart, which boys so lightly win, and lightly fling away. Trust me, dear young lady, that I never until now did know your worth ; and though an abhorrence of deceit and falsehood has impelled me to seek you out, and would have done so had you been the poorest and least gifted of your sex, I should have lacked the fortitude to sustain this interview could I have pictured you to my imagination as you really are."

Oh! If Mrs. Varden could have seen the virtuous gentleman as he said these words, with indignation sparkling from his eyes—if she could have heard his broken, quavering voice—if she could have beheld him as he stood bareheaded in the sunlight, and with unwonted energy poured forth his eloquence!

With a haughty face, but pale and trembling too, Emma regarded him in silence. She neither spoke nor moved, but gazed upon him as though she would look into his heart.

"I throw off," said Mr. Chester, "the restraint which natural affection would impose on some men, and reject all bonds but those of truth and duty. Miss Haredale, you are deceived; you are deceived by your unworthy lover, and my unworthy son."

Still she looked at him steadily, and still said not one word.

"I have ever opposed his professions of love for you; you will do me the justice, dear Miss Haredale, to remember that. Your uncle and myself were enemies in early life, and if I had sought retaliation, I might have found it here. But as we grow older, we grow wiser—better, I would fain hope—and from the first, I have opposed him in this attempt. I foresaw the end, and would have spared you, if I could."

"Speak plainly, sir," she faltered. " You deceive me, or are deceived yourself. I do not believe you—I cannot—I should not."

"First," said Mr. Chester, soothingly, "for there may be in your mind some latent angry feeling to which I would not appeal, pray take this letter. It reached my hand by chance, and by mistake, and should have accounted to you (as I am told) for my son's not answering some other note of yours. God forbid, Miss Haredale," said the good gentleman, with great emotion, "that there should be in your gentle breast one causeless ground of quarrel with him. You should know, and you will see, that he was in no fault here."

There appeared something so very candid, so scrupulously

honourable, so very truthful and just in this course—something which rendered the upright person who resorted to it, so worthy of belief—that Emma's heart, for the first time, sunk within her. She turned away and burst into tears.

"I would," said Mr. Chester, leaning over her, and speaking in mild and quite venerable accents; "I would, dear girl, it were my task to banish, not increase, those tokens of your grief. My son, my erring son,—I will not call him deliberately criminal in this, for men so young, who have been inconstant twice or thrice before, act without reflection, almost without a knowledge of the wrong they do,—will break his plighted faith to you; has broken it even now. Shall I stop here, and having given you this warning, leave it to be fulfilled; or shall I go on?"

"You will go on, sir," she answered, "and speak more plainly yet, in justice both to him and me."

"My dear girl," said Mr. Chester, bending over her more affectionately still; "whom I would call my daughter, but the Fates forbid, Edward seeks to break with you upon a false and most unwarrantable pretence. I have it on his own showing; in his own hand. Forgive me, if I have had a watch upon his conduct; I am his father; I had a regard for your peace and his honour, and no better resource was left me. There lies on his desk at this present moment, ready for transmission to you, a letter, in which he tells you that our poverty—our poverty; his and mine, Miss Haredale— forbids him to pursue his claim upon your hand; in which he offers, involuntarily proposes, to free you from your pledge; and talks magnanimously (men do so, very commonly, in such cases) of being in time more worthy of your regard—and so forth. A letter, to be plain, in which he not only jilts you —pardon the word; I would summon to your aid your pride and dignity—not only jilts you, I fear, in favour of the object whose slighting treatment first inspired his brief passion for yourself and gave it birth in wounded vanity, but affects to make a merit and a virtue of the act."

297

She glanced proudly at him once more, as by an involuntary impulse, and with a swelling breast rejoined, " If what you say be true, he takes much needless trouble, sir, to compass his design. He is very tender of my peace of mind. I quite thank him."

" The truth of what I tell you, dear young lady," he replied, " you will test by the receipt or non-receipt of the letter of which I speak.—Haredale, my dear fellow, I am delighted to see you, although we meet under singular circumstances, and upon a melancholy occasion. I hope you are very well."

At these words the young lady raised her eyes, which were filled with tears; and seeing that her uncle indeed stood before them, and being quite unequal to the trial of hearing or of speaking one word more, hurriedly withdrew, and left them. They stood looking at each other, and at her retreating figure, and for a long time neither of them spoke.

" What does this mean? Explain it," said Mr. Haredale at length. " Why are you here, and why with her?"

" My dear friend," rejoined the other, resuming his accustomed manner with infinite readiness, and throwing himself upon the bench with a weary air, " you told me not very long ago, at that delightful old tavern of which you are the esteemed proprietor (and a most charming establishment it is for persons of rural pursuits and in robust health, who are not liable to take cold), that I had the head and heart of an evil spirit in all matters of deception. I thought at the time; I really did think; you flattered me. But now I begin to wonder at your discernment, and vanity apart, do honestly believe you spoke the truth. Did you ever counterfeit extreme ingenuousness and honest indignation? My dear fellow, you have no conception, if you never did, how faint the effort makes one."

Mr. Haredale surveyed him with a look of cold contempt. " You may evade an explanation, I know," he said, folding his arms. " But I must have it. I can wait."

" Not at all. Not at all, my good fellow. You shall not

wait a moment," returned his friend, as he lazily crossed his legs. "The simplest thing in the world. It lies in a nutshell. Ned has written her a letter—a boyish, honest, sentimental composition, which remains as yet in his desk, because he hasn't had the heart to send it. I have taken a liberty, for which my parental affection and anxiety are a sufficient excuse, and possessed myself of the contents. I have described them to your niece (a most enchanting person, Haredale; quite an angelic creature), with a little colouring and description adapted to our purpose. It's done. You may be quite easy. It's all over. Deprived of their adherents and mediators; her pride and jealousy roused to the utmost; with nobody to undeceive her, and you to confirm me; you will find that their intercourse will close with her answer. If she receives Ned's letter by to-morrow noon, you may date their parting from to-morrow night. No thanks, I beg; you owe me none. I have acted for myself; and if I have forwarded our compact with all the ardour even you could have desired, I have done so selfishly, indeed."

"I curse the compact, as you call it, with my whole heart and soul," returned the other. "It was made in an evil hour. I have bound myself to a lie; I have leagued myself with you; and though I did so with a righteous motive, and though it cost me such an effort as haply few men know, I hate and despise myself for the deed."

"You are very warm," said Mr. Chester with a languid smile.

"I *am* warm. I am maddened by your coldness. 'Death, Chester, if your blood ran warmer in your veins, and there were no restraints upon me, such as those that hold and drag me back—well; it is done; you tell me so, and on such a point I may believe you. When I am most remorseful for this treachery, I will think of you and your marriage, and try to justify myself in such remembrances, for having torn asunder Emma and your son, at any cost. Our bond is cancelled now, and we may part."

Mr. Chester kissed his hand gracefully; and with the same tranquil face he had preserved throughout—even when he had seen his companion so tortured and transported by his passion that his whole frame was shaken—lay in his lounging posture on the seat and watched him as he walked away.

"My scape-goat and my drudge at school," he said, raising his head to look after him; "my friend of later days, who could not keep his mistress when he had won her, and threw me in her way to carry off the prize; I triumph in the present and the past. Bark on, ill-favoured, ill-conditioned cur; fortune has ever been with me—I like to hear you."

The spot where they had met, was in an avenue of trees. Mr. Haredale not passing out on either hand, had walked straight on. He chanced to turn his head when at some considerable distance, and seeing that his late companion had by that time risen and was looking after him, stood still as though he half expected him to follow and waited for his coming up.

"It *may* come to that one day, but not yet," said Mr. Chester, waving his hand, as though they were the best of friends, and turning away. "Not yet, Haredale. Life is pleasant enough to me; dull and full of heaviness to you. No. To cross swords with such a man—to indulge his humour unless upon extremity—would be weak indeed."

For all that, he drew his sword as he walked along, and in an absent humour ran his eye from hilt to point full twenty times. But thoughtfulness begets wrinkles; remembering this, he soon put it up, smoothed his contracted brow, hummed a gay tune with greater gaiety of manner, and was his unruffled self again.

CHAPTER XXX

A HOMELY proverb recognises the existence of a troublesome class of persons who, having an inch conceded them, will take an ell. Not to quote the illustrious examples of those heroic scourges of mankind, whose amiable path in life has been from birth to death through blood, and fire, and ruin, and who would seem to have existed for no better purpose than to teach mankind that as the absence of pain is pleasure, so the earth, purged of their presence, may be deemed a blessed place—not to quote such mighty instances, it will be sufficient to refer to old John Willet.

Old John having long encroached a good standard inch, full measure, on the liberty of Joe, and having snipped off a Flemish ell in the matter of the parole, grew so despotic and so great, that his thirst for conquest knew no bounds. The more young Joe submitted, the more absolute old John became. The ell soon faded into nothing. Yards, furlongs, miles arose; and on went old John in the pleasantest manner possible, trimming off an exuberance in this place, shearing away some liberty of speech or action in that, and conducting himself in his small way with as much high mightiness and majesty, as the most glorious tyrant that ever had his statue reared in the public ways, of ancient or of modern times.

As great men are urged on to the abuse of power (when they need urging, which is not often), by their flatterers and dependents, so old John was impelled to these exercises of authority by the applause and admiration of his Maypole cronies, who, in the intervals of their nightly pipes and pots, would shake their heads and say that Mr. Willet was a father of the good old English sort; that there were no new-fangled notions or modern ways in him; that he put them in mind of what their fathers were when they were boys; that there was no mistake about him; that it would be well for the country if there were more like him, and more was the pity that there were not; with many other original remarks of that nature. Then they would condescendingly give Joe to understand that it was all for his good, and he would be thankful for it one day; and in particular, Mr. Cobb would acquaint him, that when he was his age, his father thought no more of giving him a parental kick, or a box on the ears, or a cuff on the head, or some little admonition of that sort, than he did of any other ordinary duty of life; and he would further remark, with looks of great significance, that but for this judicious bringing up, he might have never been the man he was at that present speaking; which was probable enough, as he was, beyond all question, the dullest dog of the party. In short, between old John and old John's friends, there never was an unfortunate young fellow so bullied, badgered, worried, fretted, and brow-beaten; so constantly beset, or made so tired of his life, as poor Joe Willet.

This had come to be the recognised and established state of things; but as John was very anxious to flourish his supremacy before the eyes of Mr. Chester, he did that day exceed himself, and did so goad and chafe his son and heir, that but for Joe's having made a solemn vow to keep his hands in his pockets when they were not otherwise engaged, it is impossible to say what he might have done with them. But the longest day has an end, and at length Mr. Chester came down-stairs to mount his horse, which was ready at the door.

As old John was not in the way at the moment, Joe, who was sitting in the bar ruminating on his dismal fate and the

manifold perfections of Dolly Varden, ran out to hold the
guest's stirrup and assist him to mount. Mr. Chester was
scarcely in the saddle, and Joe was in the very act of making

him a graceful bow, when old John came diving out of the
porch, and collared him.

"None of that, sir," said John, "none of that, sir. No
breaking of patroles. How dare you come out of the door,

sir, without leave? You're trying to get away, sir, are you, and to make a traitor of yourself again? What do you mean, sir?"

"Let me go, father," said Joe, imploringly, as he marked the smile upon their visitor's face, and observed the pleasure his disgrace afforded him. "This is too bad. Who wants to get away?"

"Who wants to get away!" cried John, shaking him. "Why you do, sir, you do. You're the boy, sir," added John, collaring with one hand, and aiding the effect of a farewell bow to the visitor with the other, "that wants to sneak into houses, and stir up differences between noble gentlemen and their sons, are you, eh? Hold your tongue, sir."

Joe made no effort to reply. It was the crowning circumstance of his degradation. He extricated himself from his father's grasp, darted an angry look at the departing guest, and returned into the house.

"But for her," thought Joe, as he threw his arms upon a table in the common room, and laid his head upon them, "but for Dolly, who I couldn't bear should think me the rascal they would make me out to be if I ran away, this house and I should part to-night."

It being evening by this time, Solomon Daisy, Tom Cobb, and Long Parkes, were all in the common room too, and had from the window been witnesses of what had just occurred. Mr. Willet joining them soon afterwards, received the compliments of the company with great composure, and lighting his pipe, sat down among them.

"We'll see, gentlemen," said John, after a long pause, "who's the master of this house, and who isn't. We'll see whether boys are to govern men, or men are to govern boys."

"And quite right too," assented Solomon Daisy with some approving nods; "quite right, Johnny. Very good, Johnny. Well said, Mr. Willet. Brayvo, sir."

John slowly brought his eyes to bear upon him, looked at him for a long time, and finally made answer, to the unspeakable consternation of his hearers, "When I want encouragement from you, sir, I'll ask you for it. You let me alone, sir. I can get on without you, I hope. Don't you tackle me, sir, if you please."

"Don't take it ill, Johnny; I didn't mean any harm," pleaded the little man.

"Very good, sir," said John, more than usually obstinate after his late success. "Never mind, sir. I can stand pretty firm of myself, sir, I believe, without being shored up by you." And having given utterance to this retort, Mr. Willet fixed his eyes upon the boiler, and fell into a kind of tobacco-trance.

The spirits of the company being somewhat damped by this embarrassing line of conduct on the part of their host, nothing more was said for a long time; but at length Mr. Cobb took upon himself to remark, as he rose to knock the ashes out of his pipe, that he hoped Joe would thenceforth learn to obey his father in all things; that he had found, that day, he was not one of the sort of men who were to be trifled with; and that he would recommend him, poetically speaking, to mind his eye for the future.

"I'd recommend you, in return," said Joe, looking up with a flushed face, "not to talk to me."

"Hold your tongue, sir," cried Mr. Willet, suddenly rousing himself, and turning round.

"I won't, father," cried Joe, smiting the table with his fist, so that the jugs and glasses rung again; "these things are hard enough to bear from you; from anybody else I never will endure them any more. Therefore I say, Mr. Cobb, don't talk to me."

"Why, who are you," said Mr. Cobb, sneeringly, "that you're not to be talked to, eh, Joe?"

To which Joe returned no answer, but with a very ominous shake of the head, resumed his old position, which he would have peacefully preserved until the house shut up at night, but that Mr. Cobb, stimulated by the wonder of the company at the young man's presumption, retorted with sundry taunts, which proved too much for flesh and blood to bear. Crowding into one moment the vexation and the wrath of years, Joe started up, overturned the table, fell upon his long enemy, pummelled him with all his might and main, and finished by driving him with surprising swiftness against a heap of spittoons in one corner; plunging into which, head foremost, with a tremendous crash, he lay at full length among the ruins, stunned and motionless. Then, without waiting to receive the compliments of the bystanders on the victory he had won, he retreated to his own bed-chamber, and considering himself in a state of siege, piled all the portable furniture against the door by way of barricade.

"I have done it now," said Joe, as he sat down upon his bedstead and wiped his heated face. "I knew it would come at last. The Maypole and I must part company. I'm a roving vagabond—she hates me for evermore—it's all over!"

CHAPTER XXXI

PONDERING on his unhappy lot, Joe sat and listened for a
long time, expecting every moment to hear their creaking
footsteps on the stairs, or to be greeted by his worthy father
with a summons to capitulate unconditionally, and deliver
himself up straightway. But neither voice nor footstep came;
and though some distant echoes, as of closing doors and
people hurrying in and out of rooms, resounding from time
to time through the great passages, and penetrating to his
remote seclusion, gave note of unusual commotion down-stairs,
no nearer sound disturbed his place of retreat, which seemed
the quieter for these far-off noises, and was as dull and full
of gloom as any hermit's cell.

It came on darker and darker. The old-fashioned furniture
of the chamber, which was a kind of hospital for all the
invalided movables in the house, grew indistinct and shadowy

in its many shapes; chairs and tables, which by day were as honest cripples as need be, assumed a doubtful and mysterious character; and one old leprous screen of faded India leather and gold binding, which had kept out many a cold breath of air in days of yore and shut in many a jolly face, frowned on him with a spectral aspect, and stood at full height in its allotted corner, like some gaunt ghost who waited to be questioned. A portrait opposite the window—a queer, old grey-eyed general, in an oval frame—seemed to wink and doze as the light decayed, and at length, when the last faint glimmering speck of day went out, to shut its eyes in good earnest, and fall sound asleep. There was such a hush and mystery about everything, that Joe could not help following its example; and so went off into a slumber likewise, and dreamed of Dolly, till the clock of Chigwell church struck two.

Still nobody came. The distant noises in the house had ceased, and out of doors all was quiet too; save for the occasional barking of some deep-mouthed dog, and the shaking of the branches by the night wind. He gazed mournfully out of window at each well-known object as it lay sleeping in the dim light of the moon; and creeping back to his former seat, thought about the late uproar, until, with long thinking of, it seemed to have occurred a month ago. Thus, between dozing, and thinking, and walking to the window and looking out, the night wore away; the grim old screen, and the kindred chairs and tables, began slowly to reveal themselves in their accustomed forms; the grey-eyed general seemed to wink and yawn and rouse himself; and at last he was broad awake again, and very uncomfortable and cold and haggard he looked, in the dull grey light of morning.

The sun had begun to peep above the forest trees, and already flung across the curling mist bright bars of gold, when Joe dropped from his window on the ground below, a little bundle and his trusty stick, and prepared to descend himself.

THE BLACK LION

It was not a very difficult task; for there were so many projections and gable ends in the way, that they formed a series of clumsy steps, with no greater obstacle than a jump of some few feet at last. Joe, with his stick and bundle on his shoulder, quickly stood on the firm earth, and looked up at the old Maypole, it might be for the last time.

He didn't apostrophise it, for he was no great scholar. He didn't curse it, for he had little ill-will to give to anything on earth. He felt more affectionate and kind to it than ever he had done in all his life before, so said with all his heart, "God bless you!" as a parting wish, and turned away.

He walked along at a brisk pace, big with great thoughts of going for a soldier and dying in some foreign country where it was very hot and sandy, and leaving God knows what unheard-of wealth in prize-money to Dolly, who would be very much affected when she came to know of it; and full of such youthful visions, which were sometimes sanguine and sometimes melancholy, but always had her for their main point and centre, pushed on vigorously until the noise of London sounded in his ears, and the Black Lion hove in sight.

It was only eight o'clock then, and very much astonished the Black Lion was, to see him come walking in with dust upon his feet at that early hour, with no grey mare to bear him company. But as he ordered breakfast to be got ready with all speed, and on its being set before him gave indisputable tokens of a hearty appetite, the Lion received him, as usual, with a hospitable welcome; and treated him with those marks of distinction, which, as a regular customer, and one within the freemasonry of the trade, he had a right to claim.

This Lion or landlord,—for he was called both man and beast, by reason of his having instructed the artist who painted his sign, to convey into the features of the lordly brute whose effigy it bore, as near a counterpart of his own face as his skill could compass and devise,—was a gentleman almost as quick of apprehension, and of almost as subtle a wit, as the mighty John himself. But the difference between them lay in this; that whereas Mr. Willet's extreme sagacity and acuteness were the efforts of unassisted nature, the Lion stood indebted, in no small amount, to beer; of which he swigged such copious draughts, that most of his faculties were utterly drowned and washed away, except the one great faculty of sleep, which he retained in surprising perfection. The creaking Lion over the house-door was, therefore, to say the truth, rather a drowsy, tame, and feeble lion; and as these social representatives of a savage class are usually of a conventional character (being depicted, for the most part, in impossible attitudes and of unearthly colours), he was frequently supposed by the more ignorant and uninformed among the neighbours, to be the veritable portrait of the host as he appeared on the occasion of some great funeral ceremony or public mourning.

"What noisy fellow is that in the next room?" said Joe, when he had disposed of his breakfast, and had washed and brushed himself.

"A recruiting serjeant," replied the Lion.

Joe started involuntarily. Here was the very thing he had been dreaming of, all the way along.

"And I wish," said the Lion, "he was anywhere else but here. The party make noise enough, but don't call for much. There's great cry there, Mr. Willet, but very little wool. Your father wouldn't like 'em, *I* know."

Perhaps not much under any circumstances. Perhaps if he could have known what was passing at that moment in Joe's mind, he would have liked them still less.

"Is he recruiting for a—for a fine regiment?" said Joe, glancing at a little round mirror that hung in the bar.

"I believe he is," replied the host. "It's much the same thing, whatever regiment he's recruiting for. I'm told there an't a deal of difference between a fine man and another one, when they're shot through and through."

"They're not all shot," said Joe.

"No," the Lion answered, "not all. Those that are—supposing it's done easy—are the best off in my opinion."

"Ah!" retorted Joe, "but you don't care for glory."

"For what?" said the Lion.

"Glory."

"No," returned the Lion, with supreme indifference. "I don't. You're right in that, Mr. Willet. When Glory comes here, and calls for anything to drink and changes a guinea to pay for it, I'll give it him for nothing. It's my belief, sir, that the Glory's arms wouldn't do a very strong business."

These remarks were not at all comforting. Joe walked out, stopped at the door of the next room, and listened. The serjeant was describing a military life. It was all drinking, he said, except that there were frequent intervals of eating and love-making. A battle was the finest thing in the world —when your side won it—and Englishmen always did that. "Supposing you should be killed, sir?" said a timid voice in one corner. "Well, sir, supposing you should be," said the serjeant, "what then? Your country loves you, sir; his Majesty King George the Third loves you; your memory is honoured, revered, respected; everybody's fond of you, and grateful to you; your name's wrote down at full length in a book in the War-office. Damme, gentlemen, we must all die some time, or another, eh?"

The voice coughed, and said no more.

Joe walked into the room. A group of half-a-dozen fellows had gathered together in the tap-room, and were listening with greedy ears. One of them, a carter in a smock frock, seemed wavering and disposed to enlist. The rest, who were by no means disposed, strongly urged him to do so (according to the custom of mankind), backed the serjeant's arguments, and grinned among themselves. "I say nothing, boys," said the serjeant, who sat a little apart, drinking his liquor. "For lads of spirit"—here he cast an eye on Joe—"this is the time. I don't want to inveigle you. The king's not

311

come to that, I hope. Brisk young blood is what we want; not milk and water. We won't take five men out of six. We want top-sawyers, we do. I'm not a-going to tell tales out of school, but, damme, if every gentleman's son that carries arms in our corps, through being under a cloud and having little differences with his relations, was counted up"—here his eye fell on Joe again, and so good-naturedly, that Joe beckoned him out. He came directly.

"You're a gentleman, by G—!" was his first remark, as he slapped him on the back. "You're a gentleman in disguise. So am I. Let's swear a friendship."

Joe didn't exactly do that, but he shook hands with him, and thanked him for his good opinion.

"You want to serve," said his new friend. "You shall. You were made for it. You're one of us by nature. What'll you take to drink?"

"Nothing just now," replied Joe, smiling faintly. "I haven't quite made up my mind."

"A mettlesome fellow like you, and not made up his mind!" cried the serjeant. "Here—let me give the bell a pull, and you'll make up your mind in half a minute, I know."

"You're right so far"—answered Joe, "for if you pull the bell here, where I'm known, there'll be an end of my soldiering inclinations in no time. Look in my face. You see me, do you?"

"I do," replied the serjeant with an oath, "and a finer young fellow or one better qualified to serve his king and country I never set my"—he used an adjective in this place—"eyes on."

"Thank you," said Joe, "I didn't ask you for want of a compliment, but thank you all the same. Do I look like a sneaking fellow or a liar?"

The serjeant rejoined with many choice asseverations that he didn't; and that if his (the serjeant's) own father were to say he did, he would run the old gentleman through the body cheerfully, and consider it a meritorious action.

Joe expressed his obligations, and continued, "You can trust me then, and credit what I say. I believe I shall enlist in your regiment to-night. The reason I don't do so now is because I don't want until to-night, to do what I can't recall. Where shall I find you, this evening?"

His friend replied with some unwillingness, and after much ineffectual entreaty having for its object the immediate settlement of the business, that his quarters would be at the Crooked Billet in Tower-street; where he would be found waking until midnight, and sleeping until breakfast time to-morrow.

"And if I do come—which it's a million to one, I shall—when will you take me out of London?" demanded Joe.

"To-morrow morning, at half after eight o'clock," replied the serjeant. "You'll go abroad—a country where it's all sunshine and plunder—the finest climate in the world."

"To go abroad," said Joe, shaking hands with him, "is the very thing I want. You may expect me."

"You're the kind of lad for us," cried the serjeant, holding Joe's hand in his, in the excess of his admiration. "You're the boy to push your fortune. I don't say it because I bear you any envy, or would take away from the credit of the rise you'll make, but if I had been bred and taught like you, I'd have been a colonel by this time."

"Tush, man!" said Joe, "I'm not so young as that. Needs must when the devil drives; and the devil that drives me is an empty pocket and an unhappy home. For the present, good-bye."

"For king and country!" cried the serjeant, flourishing his cap.

"For bread and meat!" cried Joe, snapping his fingers. And so they parted.

He had very little money in his pocket; so little, indeed, that after paying for his breakfast (which he was too honest and perhaps too proud to score up to his father's charge) he had but a penny left. He had courage, notwithstanding, to

313

resist all the affectionate importunities of the serjeant, who
waylaid him at the door with many protestations of eternal
friendship, and did in particular request that he would do
him the favour to accept of only one shilling as a temporary
accommodation. Rejecting his offers both of cash and credit,
Joe walked away with stick and bundle as before, bent upon
getting through the day as he best could, and going down
to the locksmith's in the dusk of the evening; for it should
go hard, he had resolved, but he would have a parting word
with charming Dolly Varden.

He went out by Islington and so on to Highgate, and sat
on many stones and gates, but there were no voices in the
bells to bid him turn. Since the time of noble Whittington,
fair flower of merchants, bells have come to have less
sympathy with humankind. They only ring for money and
on state occasions. Wanderers have increased in number;
ships leave the Thames for distant regions, carrying from
stem to stern no other cargo; the bells are silent; they ring
out no entreaties or regrets; they are used to it and have
grown worldly.

Joe bought a roll, and reduced his purse to the condition
(with a difference) of that celebrated purse of Fortunatus,
which, whatever were its favoured owner's necessities, had
one unvarying amount in it. In these real times, when all
the Fairies are dead and buried, there are still a great many
purses which possess that quality. The sum-total they
contain is expressed in arithmetic by a circle, and whether
it be added to or multiplied by its own amount, the result
of the problem is more easily stated than any known in
figures.

Evening drew on at last. With the desolate and solitary
feeling of one who had no home or shelter, and was alone
utterly in the world for the first time, he bent his steps
towards the locksmith's house. He had delayed till now,
knowing that Mrs. Varden sometimes went out alone, or
with Miggs for her sole attendant, to lectures in the evening;

and devoutly hoping that this might be one of her nights of moral culture.

He had walked up and down before the house, on the opposite side of the way, two or three times, when as he returned to it again, he caught a glimpse of a fluttering skirt at the door. It was Dolly's—to whom else could it belong? no dress but hers had such a flow as that. He plucked up his spirits, and followed it into the workshop of the Golden Key.

His darkening the door caused her to look round. Oh that face! "If it hadn't been for that," thought Joe, "I should never have walked into poor Tom Cobb. She's twenty times handsomer than ever. She might marry a Lord!"

He didn't say this. He only thought it—perhaps looked it also. Dolly was glad to see him, and was *so* sorry her father and mother were away from home. Joe begged she wouldn't mention it on any account.

Dolly hesitated to lead the way into the parlour, for there it was nearly dark; at the same time she hesitated to stand talking in the workshop, which was yet light and open to the street. They had got by some means, too, before the little forge; and Joe having her hand in his (which he had no right to have, for Dolly only gave it him to shake), it was so like standing before some homely altar being married, that it was the most embarrassing state of things in the world.

"I have come," said Joe, "to say good-bye—to say good-bye for I don't know how many years; perhaps for ever. I am going abroad."

Now this was exactly what he should not have said. Here he was, talking like a gentleman at large who was free to come and go and roam about the world at pleasure, when that gallant coachmaker had vowed but the night before that Miss Varden held him bound in adamantine chains; and had positively stated in so many words that she was killing him by inches, and that in a fortnight more or thereabouts he expected to make a decent end and leave the business to his mother.

Dolly released her hand and said "Indeed!" She remarked in the same breath that it was a fine night, and in short, betrayed no more emotion than the forge itself.

"I couldn't go," said Joe, "without coming to see you. I hadn't the heart to."

Dolly was more sorry than she could tell, that he should have taken so much trouble. It was such a long way, and he must have such a deal to do. And how *was* Mr. Willet —that dear old gentleman—"

"Is this all you say!" cried Joe.

All! Good gracious, what did the man expect! She was obliged to take her apron in her hand and run her eyes along the hem from corner to corner, to keep herself from laughing in his face;—not because his gaze confused her— not at all.

Joe had small experience in love affairs, and had no notion how different young ladies are at different times; he had expected to take Dolly up again at the very point where he had left her after that delicious evening ride, and was no more prepared for such an alteration than to see the sun and moon change places. He had buoyed himself up all day with an indistinct idea that she would certainly say "Don't go," or "Don't leave us," or "Why do you go?" or "Why do you leave us?" or would give him some little encouragement of that sort; he had even entertained the possibility of her bursting into tears, of her throwing herself into his arms, of her falling down in a fainting fit without previous word or sign; but any approach to such a line of conduct as this, had been so far from his thoughts that he could only look at her in silent wonder.

Dolly in the meanwhile, turned to the corners of her apron, and measured the sides, and smoothed out the wrinkles, and was as silent as he. At last after a long pause, Joe said good-bye. "Good-bye"—said Dolly—with as pleasant a smile as if he were going into the next street, and were coming back to supper; "good-bye."

"Come," said Joe, putting out both hands, "Dolly, dear Dolly, don't let us part like this. I love you dearly, with all my heart and soul; with as much truth and earnestness as ever man loved woman in this world, I do believe. I am a poor fellow, as you know—poorer now than ever, for I have fled from home, not being able to bear it any longer, and must fight my own way without help. You are beautiful, admired, are loved by everybody, are well off and happy; and may you ever be so! Heaven forbid I should ever make you otherwise; but give me a word of comfort. Say something kind to me. I have no right to expect it of you, I know, but I ask it because I love you, and shall treasure the slightest word from you all through my life. Dolly, dearest, have you nothing to say to me?"

No. Nothing. Dolly was a coquette by nature, and a spoilt child. She had no notion of being carried by storm in this way. The coachmaker would have been dissolved in tears, and would have knelt down, and called himself names, and clasped his hands, and beat his breast, and tugged wildly at his cravat, and done all kinds of poetry. Joe had no business to be going abroad. He had no right to be able to do it. If he was in adamantine chains, he couldn't.

"I have said good-bye," said Dolly, "twice. Take your arm away directly, Mr. Joseph, or I'll call Miggs."

"I'll not reproach you," answered Joe, "it's my fault, no doubt. I have thought sometimes that you didn't quite despise me, but I was a fool to think so. Every one must, who has seen the life I have led—you most of all. God bless you!"

He was gone, actually gone. Dolly waited a little while, thinking he would return, peeped out at the door, looked up the street and down as well as the increasing darkness would allow, came in again, waited a little longer, went up-stairs humming a tune, bolted herself in, laid her head down on her

317

bed, and cried as if her heart would break. And yet such natures are made up of so many contradictions, that if Joe Willet had come back that night, next day, next week, next month, the odds are a hundred to one she would have treated him in the very same manner, and have wept for it afterwards with the very same distress.

She had no sooner left the workshop than there cautiously peered out from behind the chimney of the forge, a face which had already emerged from the same concealment twice or thrice, unseen, and which, after satisfying itself that it was now alone, was followed by a leg, a shoulder, and so on by degrees, until the form of Mr. Tappertit stood confessed, with a brown-paper cap stuck negligently on one side of its head, and its arms very much akimbo.

"Have my ears deceived me," said the 'prentice, "or do I dream! am I to thank thee, Fortun', or to cus thee—which?"

He gravely descended from his elevation, took down his piece of looking-glass, planted it against the wall upon the usual bench, twisted his head round, and looked closely at his legs.

"If they're a dream," said Sim, "let sculptures have such wisions, and chisel 'em out when they wake. This is reality. Sleep has no such limbs as them. Tremble, Willet, and despair. She's mine! She's mine!"

With these triumphant expressions, he seized a hammer and dealt a heavy blow at a vice, which in his mind's eye represented the sconce or head of Joseph Willet. That done, he burst into a peal of laughter which startled Miss Miggs even in her distant kitchen, and dipping his head into a bowl of water, had recourse to a jack-towel inside the closet door, which served the double purpose of smothering his feelings and drying his face.

Joe, disconsolate and down-hearted, but full of courage too, on leaving the locksmith's house made the best of his way to the Crooked Billet, and there inquired for his friend the serjeant, who, expecting no man less, received him with open arms. In the course of five minutes after his arrival at that house of entertainment, he was enrolled among the gallant defenders of his native land; and within half an hour, was regaled with a steaming supper of boiled tripe and onions, prepared, as his friend assured him more than once, at the express command of his most Sacred Majesty the King. To this meal, which tasted very savoury after his long fasting, he did ample justice; and when he had followed it up, or down, with a variety of loyal and patriotic toasts, he was conducted to a straw mattress in a loft over the stable, and locked in there for the night.

The next morning, he found that the obliging care of his martial friend had decorated his hat with sundry parti-coloured streamers, which made a very lively appearance; and in company with that officer, and three other military gentlemen newly enrolled, who were under a cloud so dense that it only left three shoes, a boot, and a coat and a half visible among them, repaired to the river-side. Here they were joined by a corporal and four more heroes, of whom two were drunk and daring, and two sober and penitent, but each of whom, like Joe, had his dusty stick and bundle. The party embarked in a passage-boat bound for Gravesend, whence they were to proceed on foot to Chatham; the wind was in their favour, and they soon left London behind them, a mere dark mist—a giant phantom in the air.

CHAPTER XXXII

MISFORTUNES, saith the adage, never come singly. There is little doubt that troubles are exceedingly gregarious in their nature, and flying in flocks, are apt to perch capriciously; crowding on the heads of some poor wights until there is not an inch of room left on their unlucky crowns, and taking no more notice of others who offer as good resting-places for the soles of their feet, than if they had no existence. It may have happened that a flight of troubles brooding over London, and looking out for Joseph Willet, whom they couldn't find, darted down haphazard on the first young man that caught their fancy, and settled on him instead. However this may be, certain it is that on the very day of Joe's departure they swarmed about the ears of Edward Chester, and did so buzz and flap their wings, and persecute him, that he was most profoundly wretched.

It was evening, and just eight o'clock, when he and his father, having wine and dessert set before them, were left to themselves for the first time that day. They had dined together, but a third person had been present during the meal, and until they met at table they had not seen each other since the previous night.

Edward was reserved and silent, Mr. Chester was more than usually gay; but not caring, as it seemed, to open a conversation with one whose humour was so different, he vented the lightness of his spirit in smiles and sparkling looks, and made no effort to awaken his attention. So they remained for some time: the father lying on a sofa with his accustomed air of negligence ; the son seated opposite to him with downcast eyes, busied, it was plain, with painful and uneasy thoughts.

"My dear Edward," said Mr. Chester at length, with a most engaging laugh, "do not extend your drowsy influence to the decanter. Suffer *that* to circulate, let your spirits be never so stagnant."

Edward begged his pardon, passed it, and relapsed into his former state.

"You do wrong not to fill your glass," said Mr. Chester, holding up his own before the light. "Wine in moderation —not in excess, for that makes men ugly—has a thousand pleasant influences. It brightens the eye, improves the voice, imparts a new vivacity to one's thoughts and conversation : you should try it, Ned."

"Ah, father !" cried his son, "if— "

"My good fellow," interposed the parent hastily, as he set down his glass, and raised his eyebrows with a startled and horrified expression, "for Heaven's sake don't call me by that obsolete and ancient name. Have some regard for delicacy. Am I grey, or wrinkled, do I go on crutches, have I lost my teeth, that you adopt such a mode of address ? Good God, how very coarse ! "

"I was about to speak to you from my heart, sir," returned Edward, "in the confidence which should subsist between us ; and you check me in the outset."

"Now *do*, Ned, *do* not," said Mr. Chester, raising his delicate hand imploringly, "talk in that monstrous manner. About to speak from your heart. Don't you know that the heart is an ingenious part of our formation—the centre of the blood-vessels and all that sort of thing—which has no more to do with what you say or think, than your knees have ? How can you be so very vulgar and absurd ? These anatomical allusions should be left to gentlemen of the medical profession. They are really not agreeable in society. You quite surprise me, Ned."

"Well! there are no such things to wound, or heal, or have regard for. I know your creed, sir, and will say no more," returned his son.

"There again," said Mr. Chester, sipping his wine, "you are wrong. I distinctly say there are such things. We know there are. The hearts of animals—of bullocks, sheep, and so forth—are cooked and devoured, as I am told, by the lower classes, with a vast deal of relish. Men are sometimes stabbed to the heart, shot to the heart; but as to speaking from the heart, or to the heart, or being warm-hearted, or cold-hearted, or broken-hearted, or being all heart, or having no heart— pah! these things are nonsense, Ned."

"No doubt, sir," returned his son, seeing that he paused for him to speak. "No doubt."

"There's Haredale's niece, your late flame," said Mr. Chester, as a careless illustration of his meaning. "No doubt in your mind she was all heart once. Now she has none at all. Yet she is the same person, Ned, exactly."

"She is a changed person, sir," cried Edward, reddening; "and changed by vile means, I believe."

"You have had a cool dismissal, have you?" said his father. "Poor Ned! I told you last night what would happen.—May I ask you for the nut-crackers?"

"She has been tampered with, and most treacherously deceived," cried Edward, rising from his seat. "I never will believe that the knowledge of my real position, given her by myself, has worked this change. I know she is beset and tortured. But though our contract is at an end, and broken past all redemption; though I charge upon her want of firmness and want of truth, both to herself and me; I do not now, and never will believe, that any sordid motive, or her own unbiassed will, has led her to this course—never!"

"You make me blush," returned his father gaily, "for the folly of your nature, in which—but we never know ourselves

—I devoutly hope there is no reflection of my own. With regard to the young lady herself, she has done what is very natural and proper, my dear fellow; what you yourself

proposed, as I learn from Haredale; and what I predicted —with no great exercise of sagacity—she would do. She supposed you to be rich, or at least quite rich enough; and found you poor. Marriage is a civil contract; people marry to better their worldly condition and improve appearances; it is an affair of house and furniture, of liveries, servants, equipage, and so forth. The lady being poor and you poor also, there is an end of the matter. You cannot enter upon these considerations, and have no manner of business with the ceremony. I drink her health in this glass, and respect and honour her for her extreme good sense. It is a lesson to you. Fill yours, Ned."

"It is a lesson," returned his son, "by which I hope I may never profit, and if years and experience impress it on—"

"Don't say on the heart," interposed his father.

"On men whom the world and its hypocrisy have spoiled," said Edward warmly; "Heaven keep me from its knowledge."

"Come, sir," returned his father, raising himself a little on the sofa, and looking straight towards him; "we have had enough of this. Remember, if you please, your interest, your duty, your moral obligations, your filial affections, and all that sort of thing which it is so very delightful and charming to reflect upon; or you will repent it."

"I shall never repent the preservation of my self-respect, sir," said Edward. "Forgive me if I say that I will not sacrifice it at your bidding, and that I will not pursue the track which you would have me take, and to which the secret share you have had in this late separation tends."

His father rose a little higher still, and looking at him as though curious to know if he were quite resolved and earnest, dropped gently down again, and said in the calmest voice— eating his nuts meanwhile,

"Edward, my father had a son, who being a fool like you, and, like you, entertaining low and disobedient sentiments, he disinherited and cursed one morning after breakfast. The circumstance occurs to me with a singular clearness of recollection this evening. I remember eating muffins at the time, with marmalade. He led a miserable life (the son, I mean) and died early; it was a happy release on all accounts; he degraded the family very much. It is a sad circumstance,

324

Edward, when a father finds it necessary to resort to such strong measures."

"It is," replied Edward, "and it is sad when a son, proffering him his love and duty in their best and truest sense, finds himself repelled at every turn, and forced to disobey. Dear father," he added, more earnestly though in a gentler tone, "I have reflected many times on what occurred between us when we first discussed this subject. Let there be a confidence between us; not in terms, but truth. Hear what I have to say."

"As I anticipate what it is, and cannot fail to do so, Edward," returned his father coldly, "I decline. I couldn't possibly. I am sure it would put me out of temper, which is a state of mind I can't endure. If you intend to mar my plans for your establishment in life, and the preservation of that gentility and becoming pride, which our family have so long sustained—if, in short, you are resolved to take your own course, you must take it, and my curse with it. I am very sorry, but there's really no alternative."

"The curse may pass your lips," said Edward, "but it will be but empty breath. I do not believe that any man on earth has greater power to call one down upon his fellow— least of all, upon his own child—than he has to make one drop of rain or flake of snow fall from the clouds above us at his impious bidding. Beware, sir, what you do."

"You are so very irreligious, so exceedingly undutiful, so horribly profane," rejoined his father, turning his face lazily towards him, and cracking another nut, "that I positively must interrupt you here. It is quite impossible we can continue to go on, upon such terms as these. If you will do me the favour to ring the bell, the servant will show you to the door. Return to this roof no more, I beg you. Go, sir, since you have no moral sense remaining; and go to the Devil, at my express desire. Good day."

Edward left the room without another word or look, and turned his back upon the house for ever.

The father's face was slightly flushed and heated, but his manner was quite unchanged, as he rang the bell again, and addressed the servant on his entrance.

"Peak—if that gentleman who has just gone out—"

"I beg your pardon, sir, Mr. Edward?"

"Were there more than one, dolt, that you ask the question? —If that gentleman should send here for his wardrobe, let him have it, do you hear? If he should call himself at any time, I'm not at home. You'll tell him so, and shut the door."

So, it soon got whispered about, that Mr. Chester was very unfortunate in his son, who had occasioned him great grief and sorrow. And the good people who heard this and told it again, marvelled the more at his equanimity and even temper, and said what an amiable nature that man must have, who, having undergone so much, could be so placid and so calm. And when Edward's name was spoken, Society shook its head, and laid its finger on its lip, and sighed, and looked very grave; and those who had sons about his age, waxed wrathful and indignant, and hoped, for Virtue's sake, that he was dead. And the world went on turning round, as usual, for five years, concerning which this Narrative is silent.

CHAPTER XXXIII

ONE wintry evening, early in the year of our Lord one
thousand seven hundred and eighty, a keen north wind arose
as it grew dark, and night came on with black and dismal
looks. A bitter storm of sleet, sharp, dense, and icy-cold,
swept the wet streets, and rattled on the trembling windows.
Sign-boards, shaken past endurance in their creaking frames,
fell crashing on the pavement; old tottering chimneys reeled
and staggered in the blast; and many a steeple rocked again
that night, as though the earth were troubled.

It was not a time for those who could by any means get
light and warmth, to brave the fury of the weather. In
coffee-houses of the better sort, guests crowded round the fire,
forgot to be political, and told each other with a secret gladness that the blast grew fiercer every minute. Each humble
tavern by the water-side, had its group of uncouth figures

327

round the hearth, who talked of vessels foundering at sea, and all hands lost; related many a dismal tale of shipwreck and drowned men, and hoped that some they knew were safe, and shook their heads in doubt. In private dwellings, children clustered near the blaze; listening with timid pleasure to tales of ghosts and goblins, and tall figures clad in white standing by bedsides, and people who had gone to sleep in old churches and being over-looked had found themselves alone there at the dead hour of the night: until they shuddered at the thought of the dark rooms up-stairs, yet loved to hear the wind moan too, and hoped it would continue bravely. From time to time these happy in-door people stopped to listen, or one held up his finger and cried "Hark!" and then above the rumbling in the chimney, and the fast pattering on the glass, was heard a wailing, rushing sound, which shook the walls as though a giant's hand were on them; then a hoarse roar as if the sea had risen; then such a whirl and tumult that the air seemed mad; and then, with a lengthened howl, the waves of wind swept on, and left a moment's interval of rest.

Cheerily, though there were none abroad to see it, shone the Maypole light that evening. Blessings on the red—deep, ruby, glowing red—old curtain of the window; blending into one rich stream of brightness, fire and candle, meat, drink, and company, and gleaming like a jovial eye upon the bleak waste out of doors! Within, what carpet like its crunching sand, what music merry as its crackling logs, what perfume like its kitchen's dainty breath, what weather genial as its hearty warmth! Blessings on the old house, how sturdily it stood! How did the vexed wind chafe and roar about its stalwart roof; how did it pant and strive with its wide chimneys, which still poured forth from their hospitable throats, great clouds of smoke, and puffed defiance in its face; how, above all, did it drive and rattle at the casement, emulous to extinguish that cheerful glow, which would not be put down and seemed the brighter for the conflict!

The profusion too, the rich and lavish bounty, of that goodly tavern! It was not enough that one fire roared and sparkled on its spacious hearth; in the tiles which paved and compassed it, five hundred flickering fires burnt brightly also. It was not enough that one red curtain shut the wild night out, and shed its cheerful influence on the room. In every saucepan lid, and candlestick, and vessel of copper, brass, or tin that hung upon the walls, were countless ruddy hangings, flashing and gleaming with every motion of the blaze, and offering, let the eye wander where it might, interminable vistas of the same rich colour. The old oak wainscoting, the beams, the chairs, the seats, reflected it in a deep dull glimmer. There were fires and red curtains in the very eyes of the drinkers, in their buttons, in their liquor, in the pipes they smoked.

Mr. Willet sat in what had been his accustomed place five years before, with his eyes on the eternal boiler; and had sat there since the clock struck eight, giving no other signs of life than breathing with a loud and constant snore (though he was wide awake), and from time to time putting his glass to his lips, or knocking the ashes out of his pipe, and filling it anew. It was now half-past ten. Mr. Cobb and long Phil Parkes were his companions, as of old, and for two mortal hours and a half, none of the company had pronounced one word.

Whether people, by dint of sitting together in the same place and the same relative positions, and doing exactly the same things for a great many years, acquire a sixth sense, or some unknown power of influencing each other which serves them in its stead, is a question for philosophy to settle. But certain it is that old John Willet, Mr. Parkes, and Mr. Cobb, were one and all firmly of opinion that they were very jolly companions—rather choice spirits than otherwise; that they looked at each other every now and then as if there were a perpetual interchange of ideas going on among them; that no man considered himself or his neighbour by any means silent; and that each of them nodded occasionally when he caught the eye of another, as if he would say "You have expressed yourself extremely well, sir, in relation to that sentiment, and I quite agree with you."

The room was so very warm, the tobacco so very good, and the fire so very soothing, that Mr. Willet by degrees began to doze; but as he had perfectly acquired, by dint of long habit, the art of smoking in his sleep, and as his breathing was pretty much the same, awake or asleep, saving that in the latter case he sometimes experienced a slight difficulty in respiration (such as a carpenter meets with when he is planing and comes to a knot), neither of his companions was aware of the circumstance, until he met with one of these impediments and was obliged to try again.

"Johnny's dropped off," said Mr. Parkes in a whisper.

"Fast as a top," said Mr. Cobb.

Neither of them said any more until Mr. Willet came to another knot—one of surpassing obduracy—which bade fair to throw him into convulsions, but which he got over at last without waking, by an effort quite superhuman.

"He sleeps uncommon hard," said Mr. Cobb.

Mr. Parkes, who was possibly a hard sleeper himself, replied with some disdain "Not a bit on it;" and directed his eyes towards a handbill pasted over the chimney-piece, which was decorated at the top with a woodcut representing a youth of tender years running away very fast, with a bundle over his shoulder at the end of a stick, and—to carry out the idea —a finger-post and a mile-stone beside him. Mr. Cobb like-wise turned his eyes in the same direction, and surveyed the placard as if that were the first time he had ever beheld it. Now, this was a document which Mr. Willet had himself indited on the disappearance of his son Joseph, acquainting the nobility and gentry and the public in general with the circumstances of his having left his home; describing his dress and appearance; and offering a reward of five pounds to any person or persons who would pack him up and return him safely to the Maypole at Chigwell, or lodge him in any of his Majesty's jails until such time as his father should come and claim him. In this advertisement Mr. Willet had obstinately persisted, despite the advice and entreaties of his friends, in describing his son as a "young boy;" and furthermore as being from eighteen inches to a couple of feet shorter than he really was; two circumstances which perhaps acounted, in some degree, for its never having been productive of any other effect than the transmission to Chigwell at various times and at a vast expense, of some five-and-forty runaways varying from six years old to twelve.

Mr. Cobb and Mr. Parkes looked mysteriously at this composition, at each other, and at old John. From the time he had pasted it up with his own hands, Mr. Willet had never by word or sign alluded to the subject, or encouraged any one else to do so. Nobody had the least notion what his thoughts or opinions were, connected with it; whether he remembered it or forgot it; whether he had any idea that such an event had ever taken place. Therefore, even while he slept, no one ventured to refer to it in his presence; and for such sufficient reasons, these his chosen friends were silent now.

Mr. Willet had got by this time into such a complication of knots, that it was perfectly clear he must wake or die. He chose the former alternative, and opened his eyes.

"If he don't come in five minutes," said John, "I shall have supper without him."

The antecedent of this pronoun had been mentioned for the last time at eight o'clock. Messrs. Parkes and Cobb being used to this style of conversation, replied without difficulty that to be sure Solomon was very late, and they wondered what had happened to detain him.

"He an't blown away, I suppose," said Parkes. "It's enough to carry a man of his figure off his legs, and easy too. Do you hear it? It blows great guns, indeed. There'll be many a crash in the Forest to-night, I reckon, and many a broken branch upon the ground to-morrow."

"It won't break anything in the Maypole, I take it, sir," returned old John. "Let it try. I give it leave—what's that?"

"The wind," cried Parkes. "It's howling like a Christian, and has been all night long."

"Did you ever, sir," asked John, after a minute's contemplation, "hear the wind say 'Maypole?'"

"Why, what man ever did?" said Parkes.

"Nor 'ahoy,' perhaps?" added John.

"No. Nor that either."

"Very good, sir," said Mr. Willet, perfectly unmoved; "then if that was the wind just now, and you'll wait a little time without speaking, you'll hear it say both words very plain."

Mr. Willet was right. After listening for a few moments, they could clearly hear, above the roar and tumult out of doors, this shout repeated; and that with a shrillness and energy, which denoted that it came from some person in great distress or terror. They looked at each other, turned pale, and held their breath. No man stirred.

It was in this emergency that Mr. Willet displayed something of that strength of mind and plenitude of mental resource, which rendered him the admiration of all his friends and neighbours. After looking at Messrs. Parkes and Cobb for some time in silence, he clapped his two hands to his cheeks, and sent forth a roar which made the glasses dance and rafters ring—a long-sustained, discordant bellow, that rolled onward with the wind, and startling every echo, made the night a hundred times more boisterous—a deep, loud, dismal bray, that sounded like a human gong. Then, with every vein in his head and face swoln with the great exertion, and his countenance suffused with a lively purple, he drew a little nearer to the fire, and turning his back upon it, said with dignity:

"If that's any comfort to anybody, they're welcome to it. If it an't, I'm sorry for 'em. If either of you two gentlemen likes to go out and see what's the matter, you can. I'm not curious, myself."

While he spoke the cry drew nearer and nearer, footsteps passed the window, the latch of the door was raised, it opened, was violently shut again, and Solomon Daisy, with a lighted lantern in his hand, and the rain streaming from his disordered dress, dashed into the room.

A more complete picture of terror than the little man presented, it would be difficult to imagine. The perspiration stood in beads upon his face, his knees knocked together, his every limb trembled, the power of articulation was quite gone; and there he stood, panting for breath, gazing on them with such livid ashy looks, that they were infected with his fear, though ignorant of its occasion, and, reflecting his dismayed and horror-stricken visage, stared back again without venturing to question him; until old John Willet, in a fit of temporary insanity, made a dive at his cravat, and, seizing him by that portion of his dress, shook him to and fro until his very teeth appeared to rattle in his head.

"Tell us what's the matter, sir," said John, "or I'll kill you. Tell us what's the matter, sir, or in another second I'll have your head under the biler. How dare you look like that? Is anybody a-following of you? What do you mean? Say something, or I'll be the death of you, I will."

Mr. Willet, in his frenzy, was so near keeping his word to the very letter (Solomon Daisy's eyes already beginning to roll in an alarming manner, and certain guttural sounds, as of a choking man, to issue from his throat), that the two bystanders, recovering in some degree, plucked him off his victim by main force, and placed the little clerk of Chigwell in a chair. Directing a fearful gaze all round the room, he implored them in a faint voice to give him some drink; and above all to lock the house-door and close and bar the shutters of the room, without a moment's loss of time. The latter request did not tend to reassure his hearers, or to fill them with the most comfortable sensations; they complied with it, however, with the greatest expedition; and having handed him a bumper of brandy-and-water, nearly boiling hot, waited to hear what he might have to tell them.

"Oh, Johnny," said Solomon, shaking him by the hand. "Oh, Parkes. Oh, Tommy Cobb. Why did I leave this house to-night! On the nineteenth of March—of all nights in the year, on the nineteenth of March!"

They all drew closer to the fire. Parkes, who was nearest to the door, started and looked over his shoulder. Mr. Willet, with great indignation, inquired what the devil he meant by that — and then said, "God forgive me," and glanced over his own shoulder, and came a little nearer.

"When I left here to-night," said Solomon Daisy, "I little thought what day of the month it was. I have never gone alone into the church after dark on this day, for seven-and-twenty years. I have heard it said that as we keep our birthdays when we are alive, so the ghosts of dead people, who are not easy in their graves, keep the day they died upon. —How the wind roars!"

Nobody spoke. All eyes were fastened on Solomon.

"I might have known," he said, "what night it was, by the foul weather. There's no such night in the whole year round as this is, always. I never sleep quietly in my bed on the nineteenth of March."

"Go on," said Tom Cobb, in a low voice. "Nor I neither."

Solomon Daisy raised his glass to his lips; put it down upon the floor with such a trembling hand that the spoon tinkled in it like a little bell; and continued thus:

"Have I ever said that we are always brought back to this subject in some strange way, when the nineteenth of this month comes round? Do you suppose it was by accident, I forgot to wind up the church-clock? I never forgot it at any other time, though it's such a clumsy thing that it has to be wound up every day. Why should it escape my memory on this day of all others?

"I made as much haste down there as I could when I went

from here, but I had to go home first for the keys; and the wind and rain being dead against me all the way, it was pretty well as much as I could do at times to keep my legs. I got there at last, opened the church-door, and went in. I had not met a soul all the way, and you may judge whether it was dull or not. Neither of you would bear me company. If you could have known what was to come, you'd have been in the right.

"The wind was so strong, that it was as much as I could do to shut the church-door by putting my whole weight against it; and even as it was, it burst wide open twice, with such strength that any of you would have sworn, if you had been leaning against it, as I was, that somebody was pushing on the other side. However, I got the key turned, went into the belfry, and wound up the clock—which was very near run down, and would have stood stock-still in half an hour.

"As I took up my lantern again to leave the church, it came upon me all at once that this was the nineteenth of March. It came upon me with a kind of shock, as if a hand had struck the thought upon my forehead; at the very same moment, I heard a voice outside the tower—rising from among the graves."

Here old John precipitately interrupted the speaker, and begged that if Mr. Parkes (who was seated opposite to him and was staring directly over his head) saw anything, he would have the goodness to mention it. Mr. Parkes apologised, and remarked that he was only listening; to which Mr. Willet angrily retorted, that his listening with that kind of expression in his face was not agreeable, and that if he couldn't look like other people, he had better put his pocket-handkerchief over his head. Mr. Parkes with great submission pledged himself to do so, if again required, and John Willet turning to Solomon desired him to proceed. After waiting until a violent gust of wind and rain, which seemed to shake even that sturdy house to its foundation, had passed away, the little man complied:

"Never tell me that it was my fancy, or that it was any other sound which I mistook for that I tell you of. I heard the wind whistle through the arches of the church. I heard the steeple strain and creak. I heard the rain as it came driving against the walls. I felt the bells shake. I saw the ropes sway to and fro. And I heard that voice."

"What did it say?" asked Tom Cobb.

"I don't know what; I don't know that it spoke. It gave a kind of cry, as any one of us might do, if something dreadful followed us in a dream, and came upon us unawares; and then it died off: seeming to pass quite round the church."

"I don't see much in that," said John, drawing a long breath, and looking round him like a man who felt relieved.

"Perhaps not," returned his friend, "but that's not'all."

"What more do you mean to say, sir, is to come?" asked John, pausing in the act of wiping his face upon his apron. "What are you a-going to tell us of next?"

"What I saw."

"Saw!" echoed all three, bending forward.

"When I opened the church-door to come out," said the little man, with an expression of face which bore ample testimony to the sincerity of his conviction, "when I opened the church-door to come out, which I did suddenly, for I wanted to get it shut again before another gust of wind came up, there crossed me—so close, that by stretching out my finger I could have touched it—something in the likeness of a man. It was bareheaded to the storm. It turned its face without stopping, and fixed its eyes on mine. It was a ghost—a spirit."

"Whose?" they all three cried together.

In the excess of his emotion (for he fell back trembling in his chair, and waved his hand as if entreating them to question him no further), his answer was lost on all but old John Willet, who happened to be seated close beside him.

"Who!" cried Parkes and Tom Cobb, looking eagerly by turns at Solomon Daisy and at Mr. Willet. "Who was it?"

THE STORY TO BE KEPT SECRET

" Gentlemen," said Mr. Willet after a long pause, " you needn't ask. The likeness of a murdered man. This is the nineteenth of March."

A profound silence ensued.

" If you'll take my advice," said John, " we had better, one and all, keep this a secret. Such tales would not be liked at the Warren. Let us keep it to ourselves for the present time at all events, or we may get into trouble, and Solomon may lose his place. Whether it was really as he says, or whether it wasn't, is no matter. Right or wrong, nobody would believe him. As to the probabilities, I don't myself think," said Mr. Willet, eyeing the corners of the room in a manner which showed that, like some other philosophers, he was not quite easy in his theory, " that a ghost as had been a man of sense in his lifetime, would be out a-walking in such weather—I only know that *I* wouldn't, if I was one."

But this heretical doctrine was strongly opposed by the other three, who quoted a great many precedents to show that bad weather was the very time for such appearances ; and Mr. Parkes (who had had a ghost in his family, by the mother's side) argued the matter with so much ingenuity and force of illustration, that John was only saved from having to retract his opinion by the opportune appearance of supper, to which they applied themselves with a dreadful relish. Even Solomon Daisy himself, by dint of the elevating influences of fire, lights, brandy, and good company, so far recovered as to handle his knife and fork in a highly creditable manner, and to display a capacity both of eating and drinking, such as banished all fear of his having sustained any lasting injury from his fright.

Supper done, they crowded round the fire again, and, as is common on such occasions, propounded all manner of leading questions calculated to surround the story with new horrors and surprises. But Solomon Daisy, notwithstanding these temptations, adhered so steadily to his original account, and repeated it so often, with such slight variations, and with such solemn asseverations of its truth and reality, that his hearers were (with good reason) more astonished than at first. As he took John Willet's view of the matter in regard to the propriety of not bruiting the tale abroad, unless the spirit should appear to him again, in which case it would be necessary to take immediate counsel with the clergyman, it was solemnly resolved that it should be hushed up and kept quiet. And as most men like to have a secret to tell which may exalt their own importance, they arrived at this conclusion with perfect unanimity.

As it was by this time growing late, and was long past their usual hour of separating, the cronies parted for the night. Solomon Daisy, with a fresh candle in his lantern, repaired homewards under the escort of long Phil Parkes and Mr. Cobb, who were rather more nervous than himself. Mr. Willet, after seeing them to the door, returned to collect his thoughts with the assistance of the boiler, and to listen to the storm of wind and rain, which had not yet abated one jot of its fury.

CHAPTER XXXIV

BEFORE old John had looked at the boiler quite twenty minutes, he got his ideas into a focus, and brought them to bear upon Solomon Daisy's story. The more he thought of it the more impressed he became with a sense of his own wisdom, and a desire that Mr. Haredale should be impressed with it likewise. At length, to the end that he might sustain a principal and important character in the affair; and might have the start of Solomon and his two friends, through whose means he knew the adventure, with a variety of exaggerations, would be known to at least a score of people, and most likely to Mr. Haredale himself, by breakfast-time to-morrow; he determined to repair to the Warren before going to bed.

"He's my landlord," thought John, as he took a candle in his hand, and setting it down in a corner out of the wind's way, opened a casement in the rear of the house, looking towards the stables. "We haven't met of late years so often as we used to do—changes are taking place in the family— it's desirable that I should stand as well with them, in point of dignity, as possible—the whispering about of this here tale will anger him—it's good to have confidences with a gentleman of his natur', and set one's-self right besides. Halloa there! Hugh—Hugh. Hal-loa!"

When he had repeated this shout a dozen times, and started every pigeon from its slumbers, a door in one of the ruinous old buildings opened, and a rough voice demanded what was amiss now, that a man couldn't even have his sleep in quiet.

"What! Haven't you sleep enough, growler, that you're not to be knocked up for once?" said John.

"No," replied the voice, as the speaker yawned and shook himself. "Not half enough."

"I don't know how you *can* sleep, with the wind a bellowsing and roaring about you, making the tiles fly like a pack of cards," said John; "but no matter for that. Wrap yourself up in something or another, and come here, for you must go as far as the Warren with me. And look sharp about it."

Hugh, with much low growling and muttering, went back into his lair; and presently reappeared, carrying a lantern and a cudgel, and enveloped from head to foot in an old, frowzy, slouching horse-cloth. Mr. Willet received this figure at the back-door, and ushered him into the bar, while he wrapped himself in sundry great-coats and capes, and so tied and knotted his face in shawls and handkerchiefs, that how he breathed was a mystery.

"You don't take a man out of doors at near midnight in such weather, without putting some heart into him, do you, master?" said Hugh.

"Yes I do, sir," returned Mr. Willet. "I put the heart (as you call it) into him when he has brought me safe home again, and his standing steady on his legs an't of so much consequence. So hold that light up, if you please, and go on a step or two before, to show the way."

Hugh obeyed with a very indifferent grace, and a longing glance at the bottles. Old John, laying strict injunctions on his cook to keep the doors locked in his absence, and to open to nobody but himself on pain of dismissal, followed him into the blustering darkness out of doors.

The way was wet and dismal, and the night so black, that if Mr. Willet had been his own pilot, he would have walked into a deep horse-pond within a few hundred yards of his own house, and would certainly have terminated his career in that ignoble sphere of action. But Hugh, who had a sight as keen as any hawk's, and, apart from that endowment, could have found his way blindfold to any place within a dozen miles, dragged old John along, quite deaf to his remonstrances, and took his own course without the slightest reference to, or notice of, his master. So they made head against the wind as they best could; Hugh crushing the wet grass beneath his heavy tread, and stalking on after his ordinary savage fashion; John Willet following at arm's length, picking his steps, and looking about him, now for bogs and ditches, and now for such stray ghosts as might be wandering abroad, with looks of as much dismay and uneasiness as his immovable face was capable of expressing.

At length they stood upon the broad gravel-walk before the Warren-house. The building was profoundly dark, and none were moving near it save themselves. From one solitary turret-chamber, however, there shone a ray of light; and towards this speck of comfort in the cold, cheerless, silent scene, Mr. Willet bade his pilot lead him.

"The old room," said John, looking timidly upward; "Mr. Reuben's own apartment, God be with us! I wonder his brother likes to sit there, so late at night—on this night too."

"Why, where else should he sit?" asked Hugh, holding the lantern to his breast, to keep the candle from the wind, while he trimmed it with his fingers. "It's snug enough, an't it?"

"Snug!" said John indignantly. "You have a comfortable idea of snugness, you have, sir. Do you know what was done in that room, you ruffian?"

"Why, what is it the worse for that!" cried Hugh, looking into John's fat face. "Does it keep out the rain, and snow, and wind, the less for that? Is it less warm or dry, because a man was killed there? Ha, ha, ha! Never believe it, master. One man's no such matter as that comes to."

Mr. Willet fixed his dull eyes on his follower, and began —by a species of inspiration—to think it just barely possible that he was something of a dangerous character, and that it might be advisable to get rid of him one of these days. He was too prudent to say anything, with the journey home before him; and therefore turned to the iron gate before which this brief dialogue had passed, and pulled the handle of the bell that hung beside it. The turret at which the light appeared being at one corner of the building, and only divided from the path by one of the garden-walks, upon which this gate opened, Mr. Haredale threw up the window directly, and demanded who was there.

"Begging pardon, sir," said John, "I knew you sat up late, and made bold to come round, having a word to say to you."

"Willet—is it not?"

"Of the Maypole—at your service, sir."

Mr. Haredale closed the window, and withdrew. He presently appeared at a door in the bottom of the turret, and coming across the garden-walk, unlocked the gate and let them in.

"You are a late visitor, Willet. What is the matter?"

"Nothing to speak of, sir," said John; "an idle tale, I thought you ought to know of; nothing more."

"Let your man go forward with the lantern, and give me your hand. The stairs are crooked and narrow. Gently with your light, friend. You swing it like a censer."

Hugh, who had already reached the turret, held it more steadily, and ascended first, turning round from time to time to shed his light downward on the steps. Mr. Haredale following next, eyed his lowering face with no great favour; and Hugh, looking down on him, returned his glances with interest, as they climbed the winding stairs.

It terminated in a little ante-room adjoining that from which they had seen the light. Mr. Haredale entered first, and led the way through it into the latter chamber, where he seated himself at a writing-table from which he had risen when they had rung the bell.

"Come in," he said, beckoning to old John, who remained bowing at the door. "Not you, friend," he added hastily to Hugh, who entered also. "Willet, why do you bring that fellow here?"

"Why, sir," returned John, elevating his eyebrows, and lowering his voice to the tone in which the question had been asked him, "he's a good guard, you see."

"Don't be too sure of that," said Mr. Haredale, looking towards him as he spoke. "I doubt it. He has an evil eye."

"There's no imagination in his eye," returned Mr. Willet, glancing over his shoulder at the organ in question, "certainly."

"There is no good there, be assured," said Mr. Haredale. "Wait in that little room, friend, and close the door between us."

Hugh shrugged his shoulders, and with a disdainful look, which showed, either that he had overheard, or that he guessed the purport of their whispering, did as he was told. When he was shut out, Mr. Haredale turned to John, and bade him go on with what he had to say, but not to speak too loud, for there were quick ears yonder.

Thus cautioned, Mr. Willet, in an oily whisper, recited all that he had heard and said that night; laying particular stress upon his own sagacity, upon his great regard for the family, and upon his solicitude for their peace of mind and happiness. The story moved his auditor much more than he had expected. Mr. Haredale often changed his attitude, rose and paced the room, returned again, desired him to repeat, as nearly as he could, the very words that Solomon had used, and gave so many other signs of being disturbed and ill at ease, that even Mr. Willet was surprised.

"You did quite right," he said, at the end of a long conversation, "to bid them keep this story secret. It is a foolish fancy on the part of this weak-brained man, bred in his fears and superstition. But Miss Haredale, though she would know it to be so, would be disturbed by it if it reached her ears; it is too nearly connected with a subject very painful to us all, to be heard with indifference. You were most prudent, and have laid me under a great obligation. I thank you very much."

This was equal to John's most sanguine expectations; but he would have preferred Mr. Haredale's looking at him when he spoke, as if he really did thank him, to his walking up and down, speaking by fits and starts, often stopping with his eyes fixed on the ground, moving hurriedly on again, like one distracted, and seeming almost unconscious of what he said or did.

This, however, was his manner; and it was so embarrassing to John that he sat quite passive for a long time, not knowing what to do. At length he rose. Mr. Haredale stared at him for a moment as though he had quite forgotten his being present, then shook hands with him, and opened the door. Hugh, who was, or feigned to be, fast asleep on the ante-chamber floor, sprang up on their entrance, and throwing his cloak about him, grasped his stick and lantern, and prepared to descend the stairs.

"Stay," said Mr. Haredale. "Will this man drink?"

"Drink! He'd drink the Thames up, if it was strong enough, sir," replied John Willet. "He'll have something when he gets home. He's better without it, now, sir."

"Nay. Half the distance is done," said Hugh. "What a hard master you are! I shall go home the better for one glassful, half-way. Come!"

As John made no reply, Mr. Haredale brought out a glass of liquor, and gave it to Hugh, who, as he took it in his hand, threw part of it upon the floor.

"What do you mean by splashing your drink about a gentleman's house, sir?" said John.

"I'm drinking a toast," Hugh rejoined, holding the glass above his head, and fixing his eyes on Mr. Haredale's face; "a toast to this house and its master." With that he muttered something to himself, and drank the rest, and setting down the glass, preceded them without another word.

John was a good deal scandalised by this observance, but seeing that Mr. Haredale took little heed of what Hugh said or did, and that his thoughts were otherwise employed, he offered no apology, and went in silence down the stairs, across the walk, and through the garden-gate. They stopped upon the outer side for Hugh to hold the light while Mr

Haredale locked it on the inner; and then John saw with wonder (as he often afterwards related), that he was very pale, and that his face had changed so much and grown so haggard since their entrance, that he almost seemed another man.

They were in the open road again, and John Willet was walking on behind his escort, as he had come, thinking very steadily of what he had just now seen, when Hugh drew him suddenly aside, and almost at the same instant three horsemen swept past—the nearest brushed his shoulder even then—who, checking their steeds as suddenly as they could, stood still, and waited for their coming up.

CHAPTER XXXV

WHEN John Willet saw that the horsemen wheeled smartly round, and drew up three abreast in the narrow road, waiting for him and his man to join them, it occurred to him with unusual precipitation that they must be highwaymen; and had Hugh been armed with a blunderbuss, in place of his stout cudgel, he would certainly have ordered him to fire it off at a venture, and would, while the word of command was obeyed, have consulted his own personal safety in immediate flight. Under the circumstances of disadvantage, however, in which he and his guard were placed, he deemed it prudent to adopt a different style of generalship, and therefore whispered his attendant to address them in the most peaceable and courteous terms. By way of acting up to the spirit and letter of this instruction, Hugh stepped forward, and flourishing his staff before the very eyes of the rider nearest to him, demanded roughly what he and his fellows meant by so nearly galloping over them, and why they scoured the king's highway at that late hour of night.

The man whom he addressed was beginning an angry reply in the same strain, when he was checked by the horseman in the centre, who, interposing with an air of authority, inquired in a somewhat loud but not harsh or unpleasant voice:

"Pray, is this the London road?"

"If you follow it right, it is," replied Hugh roughly.

"Nay, brother," said the same person, "you're but a

347

BARNABY RUDGE

churlish Englishman, if Englishman you be—which I should much doubt but for your tongue. Your companion, I am sure, will answer me more civilly. How say you, friend?"

"I say it *is* the London road, sir," answered John. "And I wish," he added in a subdued voice, as he turned to Hugh, "that you was in any other road, you vagabond. Are you tired of your life, sir, that you go a-trying to provoke three great neck-or-nothing chaps, that could keep on running over us, back'ards and for'ards, till we was dead, and then take our bodies up behind 'em, and drown us ten miles off?"

"How far is it to London?" inquired the same speaker.

"Why, from here, sir," answered John, persuasively, "it's thirteen very easy mile."

The adjective was thrown in, as an inducement to the travellers to ride away with all speed; but instead of having the desired effect, it elicited from the same person, the remark, "Thirteen miles! That's a long distance!" which was followed by a short pause of indecision.

"Pray," said the gentleman, "are there any inns hereabouts?"

At the word "inns," John plucked up his spirit in a surprising manner; his fears rolled off like smoke; all the landlord stirred within him.

"There are no inns," rejoined Mr. Willet, with a strong emphasis on the plural number; "but there's a Inn—one Inn—the Maypole Inn. That's a Inn indeed. You won't see the like of that Inn often."

"You keep it, perhaps?" said the horseman, smiling.

"I do, sir," replied John, greatly wondering how he had found this out.

"And how far is the Maypole from here?"

"About a mile"—John was going to add that it was the easiest mile in all the world, when the third rider, who had hitherto kept a little in the rear, suddenly interposed:

"And have you one excellent bed, landlord? Hem! A bed that you can recommend—a bed that you are sure is

348

well aired—a bed that has been slept in by some perfectly respectable and unexceptionable person?"

"We don't take in no tagrag and bobtail at our house, sir," answered John. "And as to the bed itself—"

"Say, as to three beds," interposed the gentleman who had spoken before; "for we shall want three if we stay, though my friend only speaks of one."

"No, no, my lord; you are too good, you are too kind; but your life is of far too much importance to the nation in these portentous times, to be placed upon a level with one so useless and so poor as mine. A great cause, my lord, a mighty cause, depends on you. You are its leader and its champion, its advanced guard and its van. It is the cause of our altars and our homes, our country and our faith. Let *me* sleep on a chair—the carpet—anywhere. No one will repine if *I* take cold or fever. Let John Grueby pass the night beneath the open sky—no one will pine for *him*. But forty thousand men of this our island in the wave (exclusive of women and children) rivet their eyes and thoughts on Lord George Gordon; and every day, from the rising up of the sun to the going down of the same, pray for his health and vigour. My lord," said the speaker, rising in his stirrups, "it is a glorious cause, and must not be forgotten. My lord, it is a mighty cause, and must not be endangered. My lord, it is a holy cause, and must not be deserted."

"It *is* a holy cause," exclaimed his lordship, lifting up his hat with great solemnity. "Amen."

"John Grueby," said the long-winded gentleman, in a tone of mild reproof, "his lordship said Amen."

"I heard my lord, sir," said the man, sitting like a statue on his horse.

"And do not *you* say Amen, likewise?"

To which John Grueby made no reply at all, but sat looking straight before him.

"You surprise me, Grueby," said the gentleman. "At a crisis like the present, when Queen Elizabeth, that maiden monarch, weeps within her tomb, and Bloody Mary, with a brow of gloom and shadow, stalks triumphant—"

"Oh, sir," cried the man, gruffly, "where's the use of talking of Bloody Mary, under such circumstances as the present, when my lord's wet through, and tired with hard riding? Let's either go on to London, sir, or put up at once; or that unfort'nate Bloody Mary will have more to answer for—and she's done a deal more harm in her grave than she ever did in her lifetime, I believe."

By this time Mr. Willet, who had never heard so many words spoken together at one time, or delivered with such volubility and emphasis as by the long-winded gentleman; and whose brain, being wholly unable to sustain or compass them, had quite given itself up for lost; recovered so far as to observe that there was ample accommodation at the May-pole for all the party: good beds; neat wines; excellent entertainment for man and beast; private rooms for large and small parties; dinners dressed upon the shortest notice; choice stabling, and a lock-up coach-house; and, in short, to run over such recommendatory scraps of language as were painted up on various portions of the building, and which in the course of some forty years he had learnt to repeat with tolerable correctness. He was considering whether it was at all possible to insert any novel sentences to the same purpose, when the gentleman who had spoken first, turning to him of the long wind, exclaimed, "What say you, Gashford? Shall we tarry at this house he speaks of, or press forward? You shall decide."

"I would submit, my lord, then," returned the person he appealed to, in a silky tone, "that your health and spirits—so important, under Providence, to our great cause, our pure and truthful cause"—here his lordship pulled off his hat again, though it was raining hard—"require refreshment and repose."

"Go on before, landlord, and show the way," said Lord George Gordon; "we will follow at a footpace."

"If you'll give me leave, my lord," said John Grueby, in a low voice, "I'll change ᴛ proper place, and ride before you. The looks of the landlord's friend are not over honest, and it may be as well to be cautious with him."

"John Grueby is quite right," interposed Mr. Gashford, falling back hastily. "My lord, a life so precious as yours must not be put in peril. Go forward, John, by all means. If you have any reason to suspect the fellow, blow his brains out."

John made no answer, but looking straight before him, as his custom seemed to be when the secretary spoke, bade Hugh push on, and followed close behind him. Then came his lordship, with Mr. Willet at his bridle rein; and, last of all, his lordship's secretary—for that, it seemed, was Gashford's office.

Hugh strode briskly on, often looking back at the servant, whose horse was close upon his heels, and glancing with a leer at his holster case of pistols, by which he seemed to set great store. He was a square-built, strong-made, bull-necked fellow, of the true English breed; and as Hugh measured him with his eye, he measured Hugh, regarding him meanwhile with a look of bluff disdain. He was much older than the Maypole man, being to all appearance five-and-forty; but was one of those self-possessed, hard-headed, imperturbable fellows, who, if they are ever beaten at fisticuffs, or other kind of warfare, never know it, and go on coolly till they win.

"If I led you wrong now," said Hugh, tauntingly, "you'd —ha ha ha!—you'd shoot me through the head, I suppose."

John Grueby took no more notice of this remark than if he had been deaf and Hugh dumb; but kept riding on quite comfortably, with his eyes fixed on the horizon.

"Did you ever try a fall with a man when you were young, master?" said Hugh. "Can you make any play at single-stick?"

John Grueby looked at him sideways with the same contented air, but deigned not a word in answer.

" —Like this?" said Hugh, giving his cudgel one of those skilful flourishes, in which the rustic of that time delighted. "Whoop!"

" —Or that," returned John Grueby, beating down his guard with his whip, and striking him on the head with its butt end. "Yes, I played a little once. You wear your hair too long; I should have cracked your crown if it had been a little shorter."

It was a pretty smart, loud-sounding rap, as it was, and evidently astonished Hugh; who, for the moment, seemed disposed to drag his new acquaintance from his saddle. But his face betokening neither malice, triumph, rage, nor any lingering idea that he had given him offence; his eyes gazing steadily in the old direction, and his manner being as careless and composed as if he had merely brushed away a fly; Hugh was so puzzled, and so disposed to look upon him as a customer of almost supernatural toughness, that he merely laughed, and cried "Well done!" then, sheering off a little, led the way in silence.

Before the lapse of many minutes the party halted at the Maypole door. Lord George and his secretary quickly dismounting, gave their horses to their servant, who, under the guidance of Hugh, repaired to the stables. Right glad to escape from the inclemency of the night, they followed Mr. Willet into the common room, and stood warming themselves and drying their clothes before the cheerful fire, while he busied himself with such orders and preparations as his guest's high quality required.

As he bustled in and out of the room intent on these arrangements, he had an opportunity of observing the two travellers, of whom, as yet, he knew nothing but the voice. The lord, the great personage who did the Maypole so much honour, was about the middle height, of a slender make, and sallow complexion, with an aquiline nose, and long hair of a reddish brown, combed perfectly straight and smooth about his ears, and slightly powdered, but without the faintest vestige of a curl. He was attired, under his great-coat, in a full suit of black, quite free from any ornament, and of the most precise and sober cut. The gravity of his dress, together with a certain lankness of cheek and stiffness of deportment, added nearly ten years to his age, but his figure was that of one not yet past thirty. As he stood musing in the red glow of the fire, it was striking to observe his very bright large eye, which betrayed a restlessness of thought and purpose, singularly at variance with the studied composure and sobriety of his mien, and with his quaint and sad apparel. It had nothing harsh or cruel in its expression; neither had his face, which was thin and mild, and wore an air of melancholy; but it was suggestive of an air of indefinable uneasiness, which infected those who looked upon him, and filled them with a kind of pity for the man: though why it did so, they would have had some trouble to explain.

Gashford, the secretary, was taller, angularly made, high-shouldered, bony, and ungraceful. His dress, in imitation of his superior, was demure and staid in the extreme; his manner, formal and constrained. This gentleman had an overhanging brow, great hands and feet and ears, and a pair of eyes that seemed to have made an unnatural retreat into his head, and to have dug themselves a cave to hide in. His manner was smooth and humble, but very sly and slinking. He wore the aspect of a man who was always lying in wait for something that *wouldn't* come to pass; but he looked patient—very patient—and fawned like a spaniel dog. Even now, while he warmed and rubbed his hands before the blaze, he had the air of one who only presumed to enjoy it in his degree as a commoner; and though he knew his lord was not regarding him, he looked into his face from time to time, and with a meek and deferential manner, smiled as if for practice.

Such were the guests whom old John Willet, with a fixed and leaden eye, surveyed a hundred times, and to whom he now advanced with a state candlestick in each hand, beseeching them to follow him into a worthier chamber. "For my lord," said John—it is odd enough, but certain people seem to have as great a pleasure in pronouncing titles as their owners

have in wearing them—"this room, my lord, isn't at all the sort of place for your lordship, and I have to beg your lordship's pardon for keeping you here, my lord, one minute."

With this address, John ushered them up-stairs into the

state apartment, which, like many other things of state, was cold and comfortless. Their own footsteps, reverberating through the spacious room, struck upon their hearing with a hollow sound; and its damp and chilly atmosphere was rendered doubly cheerless by contrast with the homely warmth they had deserted.

It was of no use, however, to propose a return to the place they had quitted, for the preparations went on so briskly that there was no time to stop them. John, with the tall candlesticks in his hands, bowed them up to the fire-place; Hugh, striding in with a lighted brand and pile of fire-wood, cast it down upon the hearth, and set it in a blaze; John Grueby (who had a great blue cockade in his hat, which he appeared to despise mightily) brought in the portmanteau he had carried on his horse, and placed it on the floor; and presently all three were busily engaged in drawing out the screen, laying the cloth, inspecting the beds, lighting fires in the bedrooms, expediting the supper, and making everything as cosy and as snug as might be, on so short a notice. In less than an hour's time, supper had been served, and ate, and cleared away; and Lord George and his secretary, with slippered feet, and legs stretched out before the fire, sat over some hot mulled wine together.

"So ends, my lord," said Gashford, filling his glass with great complacency, "the blessed work of a most blessed day."

"And of a blessed yesterday," said his lordship, raising his head.

"Ah!"—and here the secretary clasped his hands—"a blessed yesterday indeed! The Protestants of Suffolk are godly men and true. Though others of our countrymen have lost their way in darkness, even as we, my lord, did lose our road to-night, theirs is the light and glory."

"Did I move them, Gashford?" said Lord George.

"Move them, my lord! Move them! They cried to be led on against the Papists, they vowed a dreadful vengeance on their heads, they roared like men possessed—"

"But not by devils," said his lord.

"By devils! my lord! By angels."

"Yes—oh surely—by angels, no doubt," said Lord George, thrusting his hands into his pockets, taking them out again to bite his nails, and looking uncomfortably at the fire. "Of course by angels—eh, Gashford?"

"You do not doubt it, my lord?" said the secretary.

"No—no," returned his lord. "No. Why should I? I suppose it would be decidedly irreligious to doubt it—wouldn't it, Gashford? Though there certainly were," he added, without waiting for an answer, "some plaguy ill-looking characters among them."

"When you warmed," said the secretary, looking sharply at the other's downcast eyes, which brightened slowly as he spoke; "when you warmed into that noble outbreak; when you told them that you were never of the lukewarm or the timid tribe, and bade them take heed that they were prepared to follow one who would lead them on, though to the very death; when you spoke of a hundred and twenty thousand men across the Scottish border who would take their own redress at any time, if it were not conceded; when you cried 'Perish the Pope and all his base adherents; the penal laws against them shall never be repealed while Englishmen have hearts and hands'—and waved your own and touched your sword; and when they cried 'No Popery!' and you cried 'No; not even if we wade in blood,' and they threw up their hats and cried 'Hurrah! not even if we wade in blood; No Popery! Lord George! Down with the Papists —Vengeance on their heads:' when this was said and done, and a word from you, my lord, could raise or still the tumult—ah! then I felt what greatness was indeed, and thought, When was there ever power like this of Lord George Gordon's!"

"It's a great power. You're right. It is a great power!" he cried with sparkling eyes. "But—dear Gashford—did I really say all that?"

"And how much more!" cried the secretary, looking upwards. "Ah! how much more!"

"And I told them what you say, about the one hundred and forty thousand men in Scotland, did I!" he asked with evident delight. "That was bold."

"Our cause is boldness. Truth is always bold."

"Certainly. So is religion. She's bold, Gashford?"

"The true religion is, my lord."

"And that's ours," he rejoined, moving uneasily in his seat, and biting his nails as though he would pare them to the quick. "There can be no doubt of ours being the true one. You feel as certain of that as I do, Gashford, don't you?"

"Does my lord ask *me*," whined Gashford, drawing his chair nearer with an injured air, and laying his broad flat hand upon the table; "*me*," he repeated, bending the dark hollows of his eyes upon him with an unwholesome smile, "who, stricken by the magic of his eloquence in Scotland but a year ago, abjured the errors of the Romish church, and clung to him as one whose timely hand had plucked me from a pit?"

"True. No—no. I—I didn't mean it," replied the other, shaking him by the hand, rising from his seat, and pacing restlessly about the room. "It's a proud thing to lead the people, Gashford," he added as he made a sudden halt.

"By force of reason too," returned the pliant secretary.

"Ay, to be sure. They may cough and jeer, and groan in Parliament, and call me fool and madman, but which of them can raise this human sea and make it swell and roar at pleasure? Not one."

"Not one," repeated Gashford.

"Which of them can say for his honesty, what I can say for mine; which of them has refused a minister's bribe of one thousand pounds a year, to resign his seat in favour of another? Not one."

"Not one," repeated Gashford again—taking the lion's share of the mulled wine between whiles.

"And as we are honest, true, and in a sacred cause,

Gashford," said Lord George with a heightened colour and in a louder voice, as he laid his fevered hand upon his shoulder, "and are the only men who regard the mass of people out of doors, or are regarded by them, we will uphold them to the last; and will raise a cry against these un-English Papists which shall re-echo through the country, and roll with a noise like thunder. I will be worthy of the motto on my coat of arms, 'Called and chosen and faithful.'"

"Called," said the secretary, " by Heaven."

"I am."

"Chosen by the people."

"Yes."

"Faithful to both."

"To the block!"

It would be difficult to convey an adequate idea of the excited manner in which he gave these answers to the secretary's promptings; of the rapidity of his utterance, or the violence of his tone and gesture in which, struggling through his Puritan's demeanour, was something wild and ungovernable which broke through all restraint. For some minutes he walked rapidly up and down the room, then stopping suddenly, exclaimed,

"Gashford—*You* moved them yesterday too. Oh yes! You did."

"I shone with a reflected light, my lord," replied the humble secretary, laying his hand upon his heart. "I did my best."

"You did well," said his master, "and are a great and worthy instrument. If you will ring for John Grueby to carry the portmanteau into my room, and will wait here while I undress, we will dispose of business as usual, if you're not too tired."

"Too tired, my lord!—But this is his consideration! Christian from head to foot." With which soliloquy, the secretary tilted the jug, and looked very hard into the mulled wine, to see how much remained.

John Willet and John Grueby appeared together. The one bearing the great candlesticks, and the other the portmanteau, showed the deluded lord into his chamber; and left the secretary alone, to yawn and shake himself, and finally to fall asleep before the fire.

"Now, Mr. Gashford sir," said John Grueby in his ear, after what appeared to him a moment of unconsciousness; "my lord's abed."

"Oh. Very good, John," was his mild reply. "Thank you, John. Nobody need sit up. I know my room."

"I hope you're not a-going to trouble your head to-night, or my lord's head neither, with anything more about Bloody Mary," said John. "I wish the blessed old creetur had never been born."

"I said you might go to bed, John," returned the secretary. "You didn't hear me, I think."

"Between Bloody Marys, and blue cockades, and glorious Queen Besses, and no Poperys, and Protestant associations, and making of speeches," pursued John Grueby, looking, as usual, a long way off, and taking no notice of this hint, "my lord's half off his head. When we go out o' doors, such a set of ragamuffins comes a-shouting after us, 'Gordon for ever!' that I'm ashamed of myself and don't know where to look. When we're in-doors they come a-roaring and screaming about the house like so many devils; and my lord instead of ordering them to be drove away, goes out into the balcony and demeans himself by making speeches to 'em, and calls 'em 'Men of England,' and 'Fellow-countrymen,' as if he was fond of 'em and thanked 'em for coming. I can't make it out, but they're all mixed up somehow or another with that unfort'nate Bloody Mary, and call her name out till they're hoarse. They're all Protestants too—every man and boy among 'em: and Protestants are very fond of spoons I find, and silver-plate in general, whenever area-gates is left open accidentally. I wish that was the worst of it, and that no more harm might be to come; but if you don't stop these ugly customers in time, Mr. Gashford (and I know you; you're the man that blows the fire), you'll find 'em grow a little bit too strong for you. One of these evenings, when the weather gets warmer and Protestants are thirsty, they'll be pulling London down,—and I never heard that Bloody Mary went as far as *that*."

Gashford had vanished long ago, and these remarks had been bestowed on empty air. Not at all discomposed by the discovery, John Grueby fixed his hat on, wrong side foremost that he might be unconscious of the shadow of the obnoxious cockade, and withdrew to bed; shaking his head in a very gloomy and pathetic manner until he reached his chamber.

CHAPTER XXXVI

GASHFORD, with a smiling face, but still with looks of profound deference and humility, betook himself towards his
master's room, smoothing his hair down as he went, and humming a psalm tune. As he approached Lord George's door,
he cleared his throat and hummed more vigorously.

There was a remarkable contrast between this man's occupation at the moment, and the expression of his countenance,
which was singularly repulsive and malicious. His beetling
brow almost obscured his eyes; his lip was curled contemptuously; his very shoulders seemed to sneer in stealthy whisper-
ings with his great flapped ears.

"Hush!" he muttered softly, as he peeped in at the
chamber-door. "He seems to be asleep. Pray Heaven he
is! Too much watching, too much care, too much thought—
ah! Lord preserve him for a martyr! He is a saint, if ever
saint drew breath on this bad earth."

Placing his light upon a table, he walked on tiptoe to
the fire, and sitting in a chair before it with his back towards
the bed, went on communing with himself like one who
thought aloud:

"The saviour of his country and his country's religion, the
friend of his poor countrymen, the enemy of the proud and
harsh; beloved of the rejected and oppressed, adored by forty
thousand bold and loyal English hearts—what happy slumbers
his should be!" And here he sighed, and warmed his hands,

and shook his head as men do when their hearts are full, and heaved another sigh, and warmed his hands again.

"Why, Gashford?" said Lord George, who was lying broad awake, upon his side, and had been staring at him from his entrance.

"My—my lord," said Gashford, starting and looking round as though in great surprise. "I have disturbed you!"

"I have not been sleeping."

"Not sleeping!" he repeated, with assumed confusion. "What can I say for having in your presence given utterance to thoughts—but they were sincere—they were sincere!" exclaimed the secretary, drawing his sleeve in a hasty way across his eyes; "and why should I regret your having heard them?"

"Gashford," said the poor lord, stretching out his hand with manifest emotion. "Do not regret it. You love me well, I know—too well. I don't deserve such homage."

Gashford made no reply, but grasped the hand and pressed it to his lips. Then rising, and taking from the trunk a little desk, he placed it on the table near the fire, unlocked it with a key he carried in his pocket, sat down before it, took out a pen, and, before dipping it in the inkstand, sucked it—to compose the fashion of his mouth perhaps, on which a smile was hovering yet.

"How do our numbers stand since last enrolling-night?" inquired Lord George. "Are we really forty thousand strong, or do we still speak in round numbers when we take the Association at that amount?"

"Our total now exceeds that number by a score and three," Gashford replied, casting his eyes upon his papers.

"The funds?"

"Not *very* improving; but there is some manna in the wilderness, my lord. Hem! On Friday night the widows' mites dropped in. 'Forty scavengers, three and fourpence. An aged pew-opener of St. Martin's parish, sixpence. A bell-ringer of the established church, sixpence. A Protestant infant, newly born, one halfpenny. The United Link Boys, three shillings—one bad. The anti-popish prisoners in New-gate, five and fourpence. A friend in Bedlam, half-a-crown. Dennis the hangman, one shilling.'"

"That Dennis," said his lordship, "is an earnest man. I marked him in the crowd in Welbeck-street, last Friday."

"A good man," rejoined the secretary, "a staunch, sincere, and truly zealous man."

"...ould be encouraged," said Lord George. "Make a note of Dennis. I'll talk with him."

Gashford obeyed, and went on reading from his list:

"'The Friends of Reason, half-a-guinea. The Friends of Liberty, half-a-guinea. The Friends of Peace, half-a-guinea. The Friends of Charity, half-a-guinea. The Friends of Mercy, half-a-guinea. The Associated Rememberers of Bloody Mary, half-a-guinea. The United Bull-dogs, half-a-guinea.'"

"The United Bull-dogs," said Lord George, biting his nails most horribly, "are a new society, are they not?"

"Formerly the 'Prentice Knights, my lord. The indentures of the old members expiring by degrees, they changed their name, it seems, though they still have 'prentices among them, as well as workmen."

"What is their president's name?" inquired Lord George.

"President," said Gashford, reading, "Mr. Simon Tappertit."

"I remember him. The little man, who sometimes brings an elderly sister to our meetings, and sometimes another female too, who is conscientious, I have no doubt, but not well-favoured?"

"The very same, my lord."

"Tappertit is an earnest man," said Lord George, thought-fully. "Eh, Gashford?"

"One of the foremost among them all, my lord. He snuffs the battle from afar, like the war-horse. He throws his hat up in the street as if he were inspired, and makes most stirring speeches from the shoulders of his friends."

"Make a note of Tappertit," said Lord George Gordon. "We may advance him to a place of trust."

"That," rejoined the secretary, doing as he was told, "is all—except Mrs. Varden's box (fourteenth time of opening), seven shillings and sixpence in silver and copper, and half-a guinea in gold; and Miggs (being the saving of a quarter's wages), one-and-threepence."

"Miggs," said Lord George. "Is that a man?"

"The name is entered on the list as a woman," replied the secretary. "I think she is the tall spare female of whom you spoke just now, my lord, as not being well-favoured, who sometimes comes to hear the speeches—along with Tappertit and Mrs. Varden."

"Mrs. Varden is the elderly lady then, is she?"

The secretary nodded, and rubbed the bridge of his nose with the feather of his pen.

"She is a zealous sister," said Lord George. "Her collection goes on prosperously, and is pursued with fervour. Has her husband joined?"

"A malignant," returned the secretary, folding up his papers. "Unworthy such a wife. He remains in outer darkness and steadily refuses."

"The consequences be upon his own head!—Gashford!"

"My lord!"

"You don't think," he turned restlessly in his bed as he spoke, "these people will desert me, when the hour arrives? I have spoken boldly for them, ventured much, suppressed nothing. They'll not fall off, will they?"

"No fear of that, my lord," said Gashford, with a meaning look, which was rather the involuntary expression of his own thoughts than intended as any confirmation of his words, for the other's face was turned away. "Be sure there is no fear of that."

"Nor," he said with a more restless motion than before, "of their—but they *can* sustain no harm from leaguing for this purpose. Right is on our side, though Might may be against us. You feel as sure of that as I—honestly, you do?"

CALLED, CHOSEN, AND FAITHFUL

The secretary was beginning with "You do not doubt," when the other interrupted him, and impatiently rejoined:

"Doubt. No. Who says I doubt? If I doubted should I cast away relatives, friends, everything, for this unhappy country's sake; this unhappy country," he cried, springing up in bed, after repeating the phrase "unhappy country's sake" to himself, at least a dozen times, "forsaken of God and man, delivered over to a dangerous confederacy of Popish powers; the prey of corruption, idolatry, and despotism! Who says I doubt? Am I called, and chosen, and faithful? Tell me. Am I, or am I not?"

"To God, the country, and yourself," cried Gashford.

"I am. I will be. I say again, I will be: to the block. Who says as much! Do you? Does any man alive?"

The secretary drooped his head with an expression of perfect acquiescence in anything that had been said or might be; and Lord George gradually sinking down upon his pillow, fell asleep.

Although there was something very ludicrous in his vehement manner, taken in conjunction with his meagre aspect and ungraceful presence, it would scarcely have provoked a smile in any man of kindly feeling; or even if it had, he would have felt sorry and almost angry with himself next moment, for yielding to the impulse. This lord was sincere in his violence and in his wavering. A nature prone to false enthusiasm, and the vanity of being a leader, were the worst qualities apparent in his composition. All the rest was weakness—sheer weakness; and it is the unhappy lot of thoroughly weak men, that their very sympathies, affections, confidences—all the qualities which in better constituted minds are virtues—dwindle into foibles, or turn into downright vices.

Gashford, with many a sly look towards the bed, sat chuckling at his master's folly, until his deep and heavy breathing warned him that he might retire. Locking his desk, and replacing it within the trunk (but not before he had taken from a secret lining two printed handbills), he cautiously withdrew; looking back, as he went, at the pale face of the slumbering man, above whose head the dusty plumes that crowned the Maypole couch, waved drearily and sadly as though it were a bier.

Stopping on the staircase to listen that all was quiet, and to take off his shoes lest his footsteps should alarm any light sleeper who might be near at hand, he descended to the ground floor, and thrust one of his bills beneath the great door of the house. That done, he crept softly back to his own chamber, and from the window let another fall—carefully wrapt round a stone to save it from the wind—into the yard below.

They were addressed on the back "To every Protestant into whose hands this shall come," and bore within what follows:

"Men and Brethren. Whoever shall find this letter, will take it as a warning to join, without delay, the friends of Lord George Gordon. There are great events at hand; and the times are dangerous and troubled. Read this carefully, keep it clean, and drop it somewhere else. For King and Country. Union."

"More seed, more seed," said Gashford as he closed the window. "When will the harvest come!"

CHAPTER XXXVII

To surround anything, however monstrous or ridiculous, with an air of mystery, is to invest it with a secret charm, and power of attraction which to the crowd is irresistible. False priests, false prophets, false doctors, false patriots, false prodigies of every kind, veiling their proceedings in mystery, have always addressed themselves at an immense advantage to the popular credulity, and have been, perhaps, more indebted to that resource in gaining and keeping for a time the upper hand of Truth and Common Sense, than to any half-dozen items in the whole catalogue of imposture. Curiosity is, and has been from the creation of the world, a master-passion. To awaken it, to gratify it by slight degrees, and yet leave something always in suspense, is to establish the surest hold that can be had, in wrong, on the unthinking portion of mankind.

If a man had stood on London Bridge, calling till he was hoarse, upon the passers-by, to join with Lord George Gordon, although for an object which no man understood, and which in that very incident had a charm of its own,—the probability is, that he might have influenced a score of people in a month. If all zealous Protestants had been publicly urged to join an association for the avowed purpose of singing a hymn or two occasionally, and hearing some indifferent speeches made, and ultimately of petitioning Parliament not

to pass an act for abolishing the penal laws against Roman
Catholic priests, the penalty of perpetual imprisonment
denounced against those who educated children in that persuasion, and the disqualification of all members of the Romish
church to inherit real property in the United Kingdom by
right of purchase or descent,—matters so far removed from
the business and bosoms of the mass, might perhaps have
called together a hundred people. But when vague rumours
got abroad, that in this Protestant association a secret power
was mustering against the government for undefined and
mighty purposes; when the air was filled with whispers of a
confederacy among the Popish powers to degrade and enslave
England, establish an inquisition in London, and turn the
pens of Smithfield market into stakes and cauldrons; when
terrors and alarms which no man understood were perpetually
broached, both in and out of Parliament, by one enthusiast
who did not understand himself, and bygone bugbears which
had lain quietly in their graves for centuries, were raised again
to haunt the ignorant and credulous; when all this was done,
as it were, in the dark, and secret invitations to join the
Great Protestant Association in defence of religion, life, and
liberty, were dropped in the public ways, thrust under the
house-doors, tossed in at windows, and pressed into the hands
of those who trod the streets by night; when they glared
from every wall, and shone on every post and pillar, so that
stocks and stones appeared infected with the common fear,
urging all men to join together blindfold in resistance of they
knew not what, they knew not why;—then the mania spread
indeed, and the body, still increasing every day, grew forty
thousand strong.

So said, at least, in this month of March, 1780, Lord
George Gordon, the Association's president. Whether it
was the fact or otherwise, few men knew or cared to ascertain.
It had never made any public demonstration; had scarcely
ever been heard of, save through him; had never been seen;
and was supposed by many to be the mere creature of his

disordered brain. He was accustomed to talk largely about numbers of men—stimulated, as it was inferred, by certain successful disturbances, arising out of the same subject, which had occurred in Scotland in the previous year; was looked upon as a cracked-brained member of the lower house, who attacked all parties and sided with none, and was very little regarded. It was known that there was discontent abroad— there always is; he had been accustomed to address the people by placard, speech, and pamphlet, upon other questions; nothing had come, in England, of his past exertions, and nothing was apprehended from his present. Just as he has come upon the reader, he had come, from time to time, upon the public, and been forgotten in a day; as suddenly as he appears in these pages, after a blank of five long years, did he and his proceedings begin to force themselves, about this period, upon the notice of thousands of people, who had mingled in active life during the whole interval, and who, without being deaf or blind to passing events, had scarcely ever thought of him before.

" My lord," said Gashford in his ear, as he drew the curtains of his bed betimes; " my lord ! "

" Yes—who's that ?   What is it ? "

" The clock has struck nine," returned the secretary, with meekly folded hands. " You have slept well ?   I hope you have slept well?   If my prayers are heard, you are refreshed indeed."

" To say the truth, I have slept so soundly," said Lord George, rubbing his eyes and looking round the room, " that I don't remember quite—what place is this ? "

" My lord ! " cried Gashford, with a smile.

" Oh ! " returned his superior. " Yes.   You're not a Jew then ? "

" A Jew ! " exclaimed the pious secretary, recoiling.

" I dreamed that we were Jews, Gashford. You and I— both of us—Jews with long beards."

" Heaven forbid, my lord !   We might as well be Papists."

"I suppose we might," returned the other, very quickly.
"Eh? You really think so, Gashford?"

"Surely I do," the secretary cried, with looks of great
surprise.

"Humph!" he muttered. "Yes, that seems reasonable."

"I hope, my lord—" the secretary began.

"Hope!" he echoed, interrupting him. "Why do you
say, you hope? There's no harm in thinking of such things."

"Not in dreams," returned the secretary.

"In dreams! No, nor waking either."

—"'Called, and chosen, and faithful,'" said Gashford,
taking up Lord George's watch which lay upon a chair, and
seeming to read the inscription on the seal, abstractedly.

It was the slightest action possible, not obtruded on his
notice, and apparently the result of a moment's absence of
mind, not worth remark. But as the words were uttered,
Lord George, who had been going on impetuously, stopped
short, reddened, and was silent. Apparently quite unconscious
of this change in his demeanour, the wily secretary stepped
a little apart, under pretence of pulling up the window-blind,
and returning when the other had had time to recover, said:

"The holy cause goes bravely on, my lord. I was not
idle, even last night. I dropped two of the handbills before
I went to bed, and both are gone this morning. Nobody in
the house has mentioned the circumstance of finding them,
though I have been down-stairs full half-an-hour. One or
two recruits will be their first fruit, I predict; and who shall
say how many more, with Heaven's blessing on your inspired
exertions!"

"It was a famous device in the beginning," replied Lord
George; "an excellent device, and did good service in
Scotland. It was quite worthy of you. You remind me not
to be a sluggard, Gashford, when the vineyard is menaced
with destruction, and may be trodden down by Papist feet.
Let the horses be saddled in half-an-hour. We must be up
and doing!"

He said this with a heightened colour, and in a tone of such enthusiasm, that the secretary deemed all further prompting needless, and withdrew.

" —Dreamed he was a Jew," he said thoughtfully, as he closed the bedroom door. "He may come to that before he dies. It's like enough. Well! After a time, and provided I lost nothing by it, I don't see why that religion shouldn't suit me as well as any other. There are rich men among the Jews; shaving is very troublesome ;—yes, it would suit me well enough. For the present, though, we must be Christian to the core. Our prophetic motto will suit all creeds in their turn, that's a comfort." Reflecting on this source of consolation, he reached the sitting-room, and rang the bell for breakfast.

Lord George was quickly dressed (for his plain toilet was easily made), and as he was no less frugal in his repasts than in his Puritan attire, his share of the meal was soon dispatched. The secretary, however, more devoted to the good things of this world, or more intent on sustaining his strength and spirits for the sake of the Protestant cause, ate and drank to the last minute, and required indeed some three or four reminders from John Grueby, before he could resolve to tear himself away from Mr. Willet's plentiful providing.

At length he came down-stairs, wiping his greasy mouth, and having paid John Willet's bill, climbed into his saddle. Lord George, who had been walking up and down before the house talking to himself with earnest gestures, mounted his horse ; and returning old John Willet's stately bow, as well as the parting salutation of a dozen idlers whom the rumour of a live lord being about to leave the Maypole had gathered round the porch, they rode away, with stout John Grueby in the rear.

If Lord George Gordon had appeared in the eyes of Mr. Willet, overnight, a nobleman of somewhat quaint and odd exterior, the impression was confirmed this morning, and increased a hundred-fold. Sitting bolt upright upon his bony

371

steed, with his long, straight hair, dangling about his face and fluttering in the wind; his limbs all angular and rigid, his elbows stuck out on either side ungracefully, and his whole frame jogged and shaken at every motion of his horse's feet; a more grotesque or more ungainly figure can hardly be conceived. In lieu of whip, he carried in his hand a great gold-headed cane, as large as any footman carries in these days; and his various modes of holding this unwieldy weapon—now upright before his face like the sabre of a horse-soldier, now over his shoulder like a musket, now between his finger and thumb, but always in some uncouth and awkward fashion—contributed in no small degree to the absurdity of his appearance. Stiff, lank, and solemn, dressed in an unusual manner, and ostentatiously exhibiting—whether by design or accident—all his peculiarities of carriage, gesture, and conduct, all the qualities, natural and artificial, in which he differed from other men; he might have moved the sternest looker-on to laughter, and fully provoked the smiles and whispered jests which greeted his departure from the May-pole inn.

Quite unconscious, however, of the effect he produced, he trotted on beside his secretary, talking to himself nearly all the way, until they came within a mile or two of London, when now and then some passenger went by who knew him by sight, and pointed him out to some one else, and perhaps stood looking after him, or cried in jest or earnest as it might be, "Hurrah, Geordie! No Popery!" At which he would gravely pull off his hat, and bow. When they reached the town and rode along the streets, these notices became more frequent; some laughed, some hissed, some turned their heads and smiled, some wondered who he was, some ran along the pavement by his side and cheered. When this happened in a crush of carts and chairs and coaches, he would make a dead stop, and pulling off his hat, cry, "Gentlemen, No Popery!" to which the gentlemen would respond with lusty voices, and with three times three; and then, on he would go again with a score or so of the raggedest, following at his horse's heels, and shouting till their throats were parched.

The old ladies too—there were a great many old ladies in the streets, and these all knew him. Some of them—not those of the highest rank, but such as sold fruit from baskets and carried burdens—clapped their shrivelled hands, and raised a weazen, piping, shrill " Hurrah, my lord." Others waved their hands or handkerchiefs, or shook their fans or parasols, or threw up windows and called in haste to those within, to come and see. All these marks of popular esteem, he received with profound gravity and respect; bowing very low, and so frequently that his hat was more off his head than on; and looking up at the houses as he passed along, with the air of one who was making a public entry, and yet was not puffed up or proud.

So they rode (to the deep and unspeakable disgust of John Grueby) the whole length of Whitechapel, Leadenhall-street, and Cheapside, and into St. Paul's Churchyard. Arriving close to the cathedral, he halted; spoke to Gashford; and looking upward at its lofty dome, shook his head, as though he said " The Church in Danger!" Then to be sure, the bystanders stretched their throats indeed; and he went on again with mighty acclamations from the mob, and lower bows than ever.

So along the Strand, up Swallow-street, into the Oxford-road, and thence to his house in Welbeck-street, near Cavendish-square, whither he was attended by a few dozen idlers; of whom he took leave on the steps with this brief parting, " Gentlemen, No Popery. Good day. God bless you." This being rather a shorter address than they expected, was received with some displeasure, and cries of " A speech! a speech!" which might have been complied with, but that John Grueby, making a mad charge upon them with all three horses, on his way to the stables, caused them to disperse into the adjoining fields, where they presently fell to pitch and toss, chuck-farthing, odd or even, dog-fighting, and other Protestant recreations.

In the afternoon Lord George came forth again, dressed in a black velvet coat, and trousers and waistcoat of the Gordon plaid, all of the same Quaker cut; and in this costume, which made him look a dozen times more strange and singular than before, went down on foot to Westminster. Gashford, meanwhile, bestirred himself in business matters; with which he was still engaged when, shortly after dusk, John Grueby entered and announced a visitor.

"Let him come in," said Gashford.

"Here! come in!" growled John to somebody without. "You're a Protestant, an't you?"

"*I* should think so," replied a deep gruff voice.

"You've the looks of it," said John Grueby. "I'd have known you for one, anywhere." With which remark he gave the visitor admission, retired, and shut the door.

The man who now confronted Gashford, was a squat, thickset personage, with a low, retreating forehead, a coarse shock head of hair, and eyes so small and near together, that his broken nose alone seemed to prevent their meeting and fusing into one of the usual size. A dingy handkerchief twisted like a cord about his neck, left its great veins exposed to view, and they were swoln and starting, as though with gulping down strong passions, malice, and ill-will. His dress was of threadbare velveteen—a faded, rusty, whitened black, like the ashes of a pipe or a coal fire after a day's extinction; discoloured with the soils of many a stale debauch, and reeking yet with pot-house odours. In lieu of buckles at his knees, he wore unequal loops of packthread; and in his grimy hands he held a knotted stick, the knob of which was carved into a rough likeness of his own vile face. Such was the visitor who doffed his three-cornered hat in Gashford's presence, and waited, leering, for his notice.

"Ah! Dennis!" cried the secretary. "Sit down."

"I see my lord down yonder—" cried the man, with a jerk

of his thumb towards the quarter that he spoke of, "and he says to me, says my lord, 'If you've nothing to do, Dennis, go up to my house and talk with Muster Gashford.' Of course I'd nothing to do, you know. These an't my working hours. Ha ha! I was a-taking the air when I see my lord, that's what I was doing. I takes the air by night, as the howls does, Muster Gashford."

"And sometimes in the day-time, eh?" said the secretary —"when you go out in state you know."

"Ha ha!" roared the fellow, smiting his leg; "for a gentleman as 'ull say a pleasant thing in a pleasant way, give me Muster Gashford agin' all London and Westminster! My lord an't a bad 'un at that, but he's a fool to you. Ah to be sure,—when I go out in state."

"And have your carriage," said the secretary; "and your chaplain, eh? and all the rest of it?"

"You'll be the death of me," cried Dennis, with another roar, "you will. But what's in the wind now, Muster Gashford," he asked hoarsely, "eh? Are we to be under orders to pull down one of them Popish chapels—or what?"

"Hush!" said the secretary, suffering the faintest smile to play upon his face. "Hush! God bless me, Dennis! We associate, you know, for strictly peaceable and lawful purposes."

"*I* know, bless you," returned the man, thrusting his tongue into his cheek; "I entered a' purpose, didn't I!"

"No doubt," said Gashford, smiling as before. And when he said so, Dennis roared again, and smote his leg still harder, and falling into fits of laughter, wiped his eyes with the corner of his neckerchief, and cried "Muster Gashford agin' all England hollow!"

"Lord George and I were talking of you last night," said Gashford, after a pause. "He says you are a very earnest fellow."

"So I am," returned the hangman.

"And that you truly hate the Papists."

"So I do," and he confirmed it with a good round oath. "Lookye here, Muster Gashford," said the fellow, laying his hat and stick upon the floor, and slowly beating the palm of one hand with the fingers of the other; "Ob-serve. I'm a constitutional officer that works for my living, and does my work creditable. Do I, or do I not?"

"Unquestionably."

"Very good. Stop a minute. My work is sound, Protestant, constitutional, English work. Is it, or is it not?"

"No man alive can doubt it."

"Nor dead neither. Parliament says this here—says Parliament, 'If any man, woman, or child, does anything which goes again a certain number of our acts'—how many hanging laws may there be at this present time, Muster Gashford? Fifty?"

"I don't exactly know how many," replied Gashford, leaning back in his chair and yawning; "a great number though."

"Well, say fifty. Parliament says 'If any man, woman, or child, does anything again any one of them fifty acts, that man, woman, or child, shall be worked off by Dennis.' George the Third steps in when they number very strong at the end of a sessions, and says 'These are too many for Dennis. I'll have half for *my*self and Dennis shall have half for *him*self;' and sometimes he throws me in one over that I don't expect, as he did three year ago, when I got Mary Jones, a young woman of nineteen who come up to Tyburn with a infant at her breast, and was worked off for taking a piece of cloth off the counter of a shop in Ludgate-hill, and putting it down again when the shopman see her; and who had never done any harm before, and only tried to do that, in consequence of her husband having been pressed three weeks previous, and she being left to beg, with two young children—as was proved upon the trial. Ha ha!—Well! That being the law and the practice of England, is the glory of England, an't it, Muster Gashford?"

"Certainly," said the secretary.

"And in times to come," pursued the hangman, "if our grandsons should think of their grandfathers' times, and find these things altered, they'll say 'Those were days indeed, and we've been going down hill ever since.'—Won't they, Muster Gashford?"

"I have no doubt they will," said the secretary.

"Well then, look here," said the hangman. "If these Papists gets into power, and begins to boil and roast instead of hang, what becomes of my work! If they touch my work that's a part of so many laws, what becomes of the laws in general, what becomes of the religion, what becomes of the country!—Did you ever go to church, Muster Gashford?"

"Ever!" repeated the secretary with some indignation; "of course."

"Well," said the ruffian, "I've been once—twice, counting the time I was christened—and when I heard the Parliament prayed for, and thought how many new hanging laws they made every sessions, I considered that *I* was prayed for. Now mind, Muster Gashford," said the fellow, taking up his stick and shaking it with a ferocious air, "I mustn't have my Protestant work touched, nor this here Protestant state of things altered in no degree, if I can help it; I mustn't have no Papists interfering with me, unless they come to be worked off in course of law; I mustn't have no biling, no roasting, no frying—nothing but hanging. My lord may well call me an earnest fellow. In support of the great Protestant principle of having plenty of that, I'll," and here he beat his club upon the ground, "burn, fight, kill—do anything you bid me, so that it's bold and devilish—though the end of it was, that I got hung myself.—There, Muster Gashford!"

He appropriately followed up this frequent prostitution of a noble word to the vilest purposes, by pouring out in a kind of ecstasy at least a score of most tremendous oaths; then wiped his heated face upon his neckerchief, and cried, "No Popery! I'm a religious man, by G—!"

Gashford had leant back in his chair, regarded him with eyes so sunken, and so shadowed by his heavy brows, that for aught the hangman saw of them, he might have been stone blind. He remained smiling in silence for a short time longer, and then said, slowly and distinctly:

"You are indeed an earnest fellow, Dennis—a most valuable fellow—the staunchest man I know of in our ranks. But you must calm yourself; you must be peaceful, lawful, mild as any lamb. I am sure you will be though."

"Ay, ay, we shall see, Muster Gashford, we shall see. You won't have to complain of me," returned the other, shaking his head.

"I am sure I shall not," said the secretary in the same mild tone, and with the same emphasis. "We shall have, we think, about next month, or May, when this Papist relief bill comes before the house, to convene our whole body for the first time. My lord has thoughts of our walking in procession through the streets—just as an innocent display of strength—and accompanying our petition down to the door of the House of Commons."

"The sooner the better," said Dennis, with another oath.

"We shall have to draw up in divisions, our numbers being so large; and, I believe I may venture to say," resumed Gashford, affecting not to hear the interruption, "though I have no direct instructions to that effect—that Lord George has thought of you as an excellent leader for one of these parties. I have no doubt you would be an admirable one."

"Try me," said the fellow, with an ugly wink.

"You would be cool, I know," pursued the secretary, still smiling, and still managing his eyes so that he could watch him closely, and really not be seen in turn, "obedient to orders, and perfectly temperate. You would lead your party into no danger, I am certain."

"I'd lead them, Muster Gashford,"—the hangman was

beginning in a reckless way, when Gashford started forward, laid his finger on his lips, and feigned to write, just as the door was opened by John Grueby.

"Oh!" said John, looking in; "here's another Protestant."

"Some other room, John," cried Gashford in his blandest voice. "I am engaged just now."

But John had brought this new visitor to the door, and he walked in unbidden, as the words were uttered; giving to view the form and features, rough attire, and reckless air, of Hugh.

CHAPTER XXXVIII

THE secretary put his hand before his eyes to shade them from the glare of the lamp, and for some moments looked at Hugh with a frowning brow, as if he remembered to have seen him lately, but could not call to mind where, or on what occasion. His uncertainty was very brief, for before Hugh had spoken a word, he said, as his countenance cleared up:

"Ay, ay, I recollect. It's quite right, John, you needn't wait. Don't go, Dennis."

"Your servant, master," said Hugh, as Grueby disappeared.

"Yours, friend," returned the secretary in his smoothest manner. "What brings *you* here? We left nothing behind us, I hope?"

Hugh gave a short laugh, and thrusting his hand into his breast, produced one of the handbills, soiled and dirty from lying out of doors all night, which he laid upon the secretary's desk after flattening it upon his knee, and smoothing out the wrinkles with his heavy palm.

"Nothing but that, master. It fell into good hands, you see."

"What is this!" said Gashford, turning it over with an air of perfectly natural surprise. "Where did you get it from, my good fellow; what does it mean? I don't understand this at all."

A little disconcerted by this reception, Hugh looked from

the secretary to Dennis, who had risen and was standing at the table too, observing the stranger by stealth, and seeming to derive the utmost satisfaction from his manners and appearance. Considering himself silently appealed to by this action, Mr. Dennis shook his head thrice, as if to say of Gashford, "No. He don't know anything at all about it. I know he don't. I'll take my oath he don't ;" and hiding his profile from Hugh with one long end of his frowzy neckerchief, nodded and chuckled behind this screen in extreme approval of the secretary's proceedings.

"It tells the man that finds it, to come here, don't it?" asked Hugh. "I'm no scholar, myself, but I showed it to a friend, and he said it did."

"It certainly does," said Gashford, opening his eyes to their utmost width; "really this is the most remarkable circumstance I have ever known. How did you come by this piece of paper, my good friend?"

"Muster Gashford," wheezed the hangman under his breath, "agin' all Newgate!"

Whether Hugh heard him, or saw by his manner that he was being played upon, or perceived the secretary's drift of himself, he came in his blunt way to the point at once.

"Here!" he said, stretching out his hand and taking it back; "never mind the bill, or what it says, or what it don't say. You don't know anything about it, master,—no more do I,—no more does he," glancing at Dennis. "None of us know what it means, or where it comes from : there's an end of that. Now I want to make one against the Catholics. I'm a No-Popery man, and ready to be sworn in. That's what I've come here for."

"Put him down on the roll, Muster Gashford," said Dennis approvingly. "That's the way to go to work—right to the end at once, and no palaver."

"What's the use of shooting wide of the mark, eh, old boy!" cried Hugh.

"My sentiments all over!" rejoined the hangman. "This

is the sort of chap for my division, Muster Gashford. Down with him, sir. Put him on the roll. I'd stand godfather to him, if he was to be christened in a bonfire, made of the ruins of the Bank of England."

With these and other expressions of confidence of the like flattering kind, Mr. Dennis gave him a hearty slap on the back, which Hugh was not slow to return.

"No Popery, brother!" cried the hangman.

"No Property, brother!" responded Hugh.

"Popery, Popery," said the secretary with his usual mildness.

"It's all the same!" cried Dennis. "It's all right. Down with him, Muster Gashford. Down with everybody, down with everything! Hurrah for the Protestant religion! That's the time of day, Muster Gashford!"

The secretary regarded them both with a very favourable expression of countenance, while they gave loose to these and other demonstrations of their patriotic purpose; and was about to make some remark aloud, when Dennis, stepping up to him, and shading his mouth with his hand, said, in a hoarse whisper, as he nudged him with his elbow:

"Don't split upon a constitutional officer's profession, Muster Gashford. There are popular prejudices, you know, and he mightn't like it. Wait till he comes to be more intimate with me. He's a fine-built chap, an't he?"

"A powerful fellow indeed!"

"Did you ever, Muster Gashford," whispered Dennis, with a horrible kind of admiration, such as that with which a cannibal might regard his intimate friend, when hungry,— "did you ever"—and here he drew still closer to his ear, and fenced his mouth with both his open hands—"see such a throat as his? Do but cast your eye upon it. There's a neck for stretching, Muster Gashford!"

The secretary assented to this proposition with the best grace he could assume—it is difficult to feign a true professional relish: which is eccentric sometimes—and after asking the candidate a few unimportant questions, proceeded to enrol him a member of the Great Protestant Association of England. If anything could have exceeded Mr. Dennis's joy on the happy conclusion of this ceremony, it would have been the rapture with which he received the announcement that the new member could neither read nor write: those two arts being (as Mr. Dennis swore) the greatest possible curse a civilised community could know, and militating more against the professional emoluments and usefulness of the great constitutional office he had the honour to hold, than any adverse circumstances that could present themselves to his imagination.

The enrolment being completed, and Hugh having been informed by Gashford, in his peculiar manner, of the peaceful and strictly lawful objects contemplated by the body to which he now belonged—during which recital Mr. Dennis nudged him very much with his elbow, and made divers remarkable faces—the secretary gave them both to understand that he desired to be alone. Therefore they took their leaves without delay, and came out of the house together.

"Are you walking, brother?" said Dennis.

"Ay!" returned Hugh. "Where you will."

"That's social," said his new friend. "Which way shall we take? Shall we go and have a look at doors that we shall make a pretty good clattering at, before long—eh, brother?"

Hugh answering in the affirmative, they went slowly down to Westminster, where both houses of Parliament were then sitting. Mingling in the crowd of carriages, horses, servants, chairmen, link-boys, porters, and idlers of all kinds, they lounged about; while Hugh's new friend pointed out to him significantly the weak parts of the building, how easy it was to get into the lobby, and so to the very door of the House of Commons; and how plainly, when they marched down there in grand array, their roars and shouts would be heard by the members inside; with a great deal more to the same purpose, all of which Hugh received with manifest delight.

He told him, too, who some of the Lords and Commons were, by name, as they came in and out; whether they were friendly to the Papists or otherwise; and bade him take notice of their liveries and equipages, that he might be sure of them, in case of need. Sometimes he drew him close to the windows of a passing carriage, that he might see its master's face by the light of the lamps; and, both in respect of people and localities, he showed so much acquaintance with everything around, that it was plain he had often studied there before; as indeed, when they grew a little more confidential, he confessed he had.

Perhaps the most striking part of all this was, the number of people—never in groups of more than two or three together—who seemed to be skulking about the crowd for the same purpose. To the greater part of these, a slight nod or a look from Hugh's companion was sufficient greeting; but, now and then, some man would come and stand beside him in the throng, and, without turning his head or appearing to communicate with him, would say a word or two in a low voice, which he would answer in the same cautious manner. Then they would part, like strangers. Some of these men often reappeared again unexpectedly in the crowd close to Hugh, and, as they passed by, pressed his hand, or looked him sternly in the face; but they never spoke to him, nor he to them; no, not a word.

It was remarkable, too, that whenever they happened to stand where there was any press of people, and Hugh chanced to be looking downward, he was sure to see an arm stretched out—under his own perhaps, or perhaps across him—which thrust some paper into the hand or pocket of a bystander, and was so suddenly withdrawn that it was impossible to tell from whom it came; nor could he see in any face, on glancing quickly round, the least confusion or surprise. They often trod upon a paper like the one he carried in his breast, but his companion whispered him not to touch it or to take it up,—not even to look towards it,—so there they let them lie, and passed on.

When they had paraded the street and all the avenues of the building in this manner for near two hours, they turned away, and his friend asked him what he thought of what he had seen, and whether he was prepared for a good hot piece of work if it should come to that. " The hotter the better," said Hugh, "I'm prepared for anything."—"So am I," said his friend, " and so are many of us ; " and they shook hands upon it with a great oath, and with many terrible imprecations on the Papists.

As they were thirsty by this time, Dennis proposed that they should repair together to The Boot, where there was good company and strong liquor. Hugh yielding a ready assent, they bent their steps that way with no loss of time.

This Boot was a lone house of public entertainment, situated in the fields at the back of the Foundling Hospital ; a very solitary spot at that period, and quite deserted after dark. The tavern stood at some distance from any high road, and was approachable only by a dark and narrow lane ; so that Hugh was much surprised to find several people drinking there, and great merriment going on. He was still more surprised to find among them almost every face that had caught his attention in the crowd ; but his companion having whispered him outside the door, that it was not considered good manners at The Boot to appear at all curious about the company, he kept his own counsel, and made no show of recognition.

Before putting his lips to the liquor which was brought for them, Dennis drank in a loud voice the health of Lord George Gordon, President of the Great Protestant Association ; which toast Hugh pledged likewise, with corresponding enthusiasm. A fiddler who was present, and who appeared to act as the appointed minstrel of the company, forthwith

struck up a Scotch reel; and that in tones so invigorating,
that Hugh and his friend (who had both been drinking before)
rose from their seats as by previous concert, and, to the great
admiration of the assembled guests, performed an extempo-
raneous No-Popery Dance.

CHAPTER XXXIX

THE applause which the performance of Hugh and his new
friend elicited from the company at The Boot, had not yet
subsided, and the two dancers were still panting from their
exertions, which had been of a rather extreme and violent
character, when the party was reinforced by the arrival of
some more guests, who, being a detachment of United Bull-
dogs, were received with very flattering marks of distinction
and respect.

The leader of this small party—for, including himself, they
were but three in number—was our old acquaintance, Mr.
Tappertit, who seemed, physically speaking, to have grown
smaller with years (particularly as to his legs, which were
stupendously little), but who, in a moral point of view, in
personal dignity and self-esteem, had swelled into a giant.
Nor was it by any means difficult for the most unobservant
person to detect this state of feeling in the quondam 'prentice,
for it not only proclaimed itself impressively and beyond

mistake in his majestic walk and kindling eye, but found a striking means of revelation in his turned-up nose, which scouted all things of earth with deep disdain, and sought communion with its kindred skies.

Mr. Tappertit, as chief or captain of the Bull-dogs, was attended by his two lieutenants; one, the tall comrade of his younger life; the other, a 'Prentice Knight in days of yore —Mark Gilbert, bound in the olden time to Thomas Curzon of the Golden Fleece. These gentlemen, like himself, were now emancipated from their 'prentice thraldom, and served as journeymen; but they were, in humble emulation of his great example, bold and daring spirits, and aspired to a distinguished state in great political events. Hence their connection with the Protestant Association of England, sanctioned by the name of Lord George Gordon; and hence their present visit to The Boot.

"Gentlemen!" said Mr. Tappertit, taking off his hat as a great general might in addressing his troops. "Well met. My lord does me and you the honour to send his compliments per self."

"You've seen my lord too, have you?" asked Dennis. "*I* see him this afternoon."

"My duty called me to the Lobby when our shop shut up; and I saw him there, sir," Mr. Tappertit replied, as he and his lieutenants took their seats. "How do *you* do?"

"Lively, master, lively," said the fellow. "Here's a new brother, regularly put down in black and white by Muster Gashford; a credit to the cause; one of the stick-at-nothing sort; one arter my own heart. D'ye see him? Has he got the looks of a man that'll do, do you think?" he cried, as he slapped Hugh on the back.

"Looks or no looks," said Hugh, with a drunken flourish of his arm, "I'm the man you want. I hate the Papists, every one of 'em. They hate me and I hate them. They do me all the harm they can, and I'll do them all the harm *I* can. Hurrah!"

MR. TAPPERTIT AND HUGH

"Was there ever," said Dennis, looking round the room, when the echo of his boisterous voice had died away; "was there ever such a game boy! Why, I mean to say, brothers, that if Muster Gashford had gone a hundred mile and got together fifty men of the common run, they wouldn't have been worth this one."

The greater part of the company implicitly subscribed to this opinion, and testified their faith in Hugh by nods and looks of great significance. Mr. Tappertit sat and contemplated him for a long time in silence, as if he suspended his judgment; then drew a little nearer to him, and eyed him over more carefully; then went close up to him, and took him apart into a dark corner.

"I say," he began, with a thoughtful brow, "haven't I seen you before?"

"It's like you may," said Hugh, in his careless way. "I don't know; shouldn't wonder."

"No, but it's very easily settled," returned Sim. "Look at me. Did you ever see *me* before? You wouldn't be likely to forget it, you know, if you ever did. Look at me. Don't be afraid; I won't do you any harm. Take a good look— steady now."

The encouraging way in which Mr. Tappertit made this request, and coupled it with an assurance that he needn't be frightened, amused Hugh mightily—so much indeed, that he saw nothing at all of the small man before him, through closing his eyes in a fit of hearty laughter, which shook his great broad sides until they ached again.

"Come!" said Mr. Tappertit, growing a little impatient under this disrespectful treatment. "Do you know me, feller?"

"Not I," cried Hugh. "Ha ha ha! Not I! But I should like to."

"And yet I'd have wagered a seven-shilling piece," said Mr. Tappertit, folding his arms, and confronting him with his legs wide apart and firmly planted on the ground, "that you once were hostler at the Maypole."

Hugh opened his eyes on hearing this, and looked at him in great surprise.

"—And so you were, too," said Mr. Tappertit, pushing him away with a condescending playfulness. "When did *my* eyes ever deceive—unless it was a young woman! Don't you know me now?"

"Why it an't—" Hugh faltered.

"An't it?" said Mr. Tappertit. "Are you sure of that? You remember G. Varden, don't you?"

Certainly Hugh did, and he remembered D. Varden too; but that he didn't tell him.

"You remember coming down there, before I was out of my time, to ask after a vagabond that had bolted off, and left his disconsolate father a prey to the bitterest emotions, and all the rest of it—don't you?" said Mr. Tappertit.

"Of course I do!" cried Hugh. "And I saw you there."

"Saw me there!" said Mr. Tappertit. "Yes, I should think you did see me there. The place would be troubled to go on without me. Don't you remember my thinking you liked the vagabond, and on that account going to quarrel with you; and then finding you detested him worse than poison, going to drink with you? Don't you remember that?"

"To be sure!" cried Hugh.

"Well! and are you in the same mind now?" said Mr. Tappertit.

"Yes!" roared Hugh.

"You speak like a man," said Mr. Tappertit, "and I'll shake hands with you." With these conciliatory expressions he suited the action to the word; and Hugh meeting his advances readily, they performed the ceremony with a show of great heartiness.

"I find," said Mr. Tappertit, looking round on the assembled guests, "that brother What's-his-name and I are old acquaintance.—You never heard anything more of that rascal, I suppose, eh?"

"Not a syllable," replied Hugh. "I never want to. I don't believe I ever shall. He's dead long ago, I hope."

"It's to be hoped, for the sake of mankind in general and the happiness of society, that he is," said Mr. Tappertit, rubbing his palm upon his legs, and looking at it between whiles. "Is your other hand at all cleaner? Much the same. Well, I'll owe you another shake. We'll suppose it done, if you've no objection."

Hugh laughed again, and with such thorough abandonment to his mad humour, that his limbs seemed dislocated, and his whole frame in danger of tumbling to pieces; but Mr. Tappertit, so far from receiving this extreme merriment with any irritation, was pleased to regard it with the utmost favour, and even to join in it, so far as one of his gravity and station could, with any regard to that decency and decorum which men in high places are expected to maintain.

Mr. Tappertit did not stop here, as many public characters might have done, but calling up his brace of lieutenants, introduced Hugh to them with high commendation; declaring him to be a man who, at such times as those in which they lived, could not be too much cherished. Further, he did him the honour to remark, that he would be an acquisition of which even the United Bull-dogs might be proud; and finding, upon sounding him, that he was quite ready and willing to enter the society (for he was not at all particular, and would have leagued himself that night with anything, or anybody, for any purpose whatsoever), caused the necessary preliminaries to be gone into upon the spot. This tribute to his great merit delighted no man more than Mr. Dennis, as he himself proclaimed with several rare and surprising oaths; and indeed it gave unmingled satisfaction to the whole assembly.

"Make anything you like of me!" cried Hugh, flourishing the can he had emptied more than once. "Put me on any duty you please. I'm your man. I'll do it. Here's my captain—here's my leader. Ha ha ha! Let him give me the

word of command, and I'll fight the whole parliament House
single-handed, or set a lighted torch to the King's Throne
itself!" With that, he smote Mr. Tappertit on the back,
with such violence that his little body seemed to shrink into
a mere nothing; and roared again until the very foundlings
near at hand were startled in their beds.

In fact, a sense of something whimsical in their companionship seemed to have taken entire possession of his rude brain.
The bare fact of being patronised by a great man whom he
could have crushed with one hand, appeared in his eyes so
eccentric and humorous, that a kind of ferocious merriment
gained the mastery over him, and quite subdued his brutal
nature. He roared and roared again; toasted Mr. Tappertit
a hundred times; declared himself a Bull-dog to the core;
and vowed to be faithful to him to the last drop of blood
in his veins.

All these compliments Mr. Tappertit received as matters
of course—flattering enough in their way, but entirely attributable to his vast superiority. His dignified self-possession
only delighted Hugh the more; and in a word, this giant and
the dwarf struck up a friendship which bade fair to be of long
continuance, as the one held it to be his right to command,
and the other considered it an exquisite pleasantry to obey.
Nor was Hugh by any means a passive follower, who scrupled
to act without precise and definite orders; for when Mr.
Tappertit mounted on an empty case which stood by way
of rostrum in the room, and volunteered a speech upon the
alarming crisis then at hand, he placed himself beside the
orator, and though he grinned from ear to ear at every word
he said, threw out such expressive hints to scoffers in the
management of his cudgel, that those who were at first the
most disposed to interrupt, became remarkably attentive, and
were the loudest in their approbation.

It was not all noise and jest, however, at The Boot, nor
were the whole party listeners to the speech. There were
some men at the other end of the room (which was a long,

low-roofed chamber) in earnest conversation all the time; and when any of this group went out, fresh people were sure to come in soon afterwards and sit down in their places, as

though the others had relieved them on some watch or duty; which it was pretty clear they did, for these changes took place by the clock, at intervals of half an hour. These persons whispered very much among themselves, and kept aloof, and often looked round, as jealous of their speech being overheard; some two or three among them entered in books what seemed to be reports from the others; when they were not thus employed, one of them would turn to the newspapers which were strewn upon the table, and from the St. James's Chronicle, the Herald, Chronicle, or Public Advertiser, would read to the rest in a low voice some passage having reference to the topic in which they were all so deeply interested. But the great attraction was a pamphlet called The Thunderer, which espoused their own opinions, and was supposed at that time to emanate directly from the Association. This was always in request; and whether read aloud, to an eager knot of listeners, or by some solitary man, was certain to be followed by stormy talking and excited looks.

In the midst of all his merriment, and admiration of his captain, Hugh was made sensible by these and other tokens, of the presence of an air of mystery, akin to that which had so much impressed him out of doors. It was impossible to discard a sense that something serious was going on, and that under the noisy revel of the public-house, there lurked unseen and dangerous matter. Little affected by this, however, he was perfectly satisfied with his quarters and would have remained there till morning, but that his conductor rose soon after midnight, to go home; Mr. Tappertit following his example, left him no excuse to stay. So they all three left the house together: roaring a No-Popery song until the fields resounded with the dismal noise.

" Cheer up, captain ! " cried Hugh, when they had roared themselves out of breath. " Another stave ! "

Mr. Tappertit, nothing loath, began again; and so the three went staggering on, arm-in-arm, shouting like madmen, and defying the watch with great valour. Indeed this did not require any unusual bravery or boldness, as the watchmen of that time, being selected for the office on account of excessive age and extraordinary infirmity, had a custom of shutting themselves up tight in their boxes on the first symptoms of disturbance, and remaining there until they disappeared. In these proceedings, Mr. Dennis, who had a gruff voice and lungs of considerable power, distinguished himself very much, and acquired great credit with his two companions.

"What a queer fellow you are!" said Mr. Tappertit. "You're so precious sly and close. Why don't you ever tell what trade you're of?"

"Answer the captain instantly," cried Hugh, beating his hat down on his head; "why don't you ever tell what trade you're of?"

"I'm of as gen-teel a calling, brother, as any man in England—as light a business as any gentleman could desire."

"Was you 'prenticed to it?" asked Mr. Tappertit.

"No. Natural genius," said Mr. Dennis. "No 'prenticing. It comes by natur'. Muster Gashford knows my calling. Look at that hand of mine—many and many a job that hand has done, with a neatness and dex-terity, never known afore. When I look at that hand," said Mr. Dennis, shaking it in the air, "and remember the helegant bits of work it has turned off, I feel quite molloncholy to think it should ever grow old and feeble. But sich is life!"

He heaved a deep sigh as he indulged in these reflections, and putting his fingers with an absent air on Hugh's throat, and particularly under his left ear, as if he were studying the anatomical development of that part of his frame, shook his head in a despondent manner and actually shed tears.

"You're a kind of artist, I suppose—eh!" said Mr. Tappertit.

"Yes," rejoined Dennis; "yes—I may call myself a artist —a fancy workman—art improves natur'—that's my motto."

"And what do you call this?" said Mr. Tappertit, taking his stick out of his hand.

"That's my portrait atop," Dennis replied; "d'ye think it's like?"

"Why—it's a little too handsome," said Mr. Tappertit. "Who did it? You?"

"I!" repeated Dennis, gazing fondly on his image. "I wish I had the talent. That was carved by a friend of mine, as is now no more. The very day afore he died, he cut that with his pocket-knife from memory! 'I'll die game,' says my friend, 'and my last moments shall be dewoted to making Dennis's picter.' That's it."

"That was a queer fancy, wasn't it?" said Mr. Tappertit.

"It *was* a queer fancy," rejoined the other, breathing on his fictitious nose, and polishing it with the cuff of his coat, "but he was a queer subject altogether—a kind of gipsy—one of the finest, stand-up men, you ever see. Ah! He told me some things that would startle you a bit, did that friend of mine, on the morning when he died."

"You were with him at the time, were you?" said Mr. Tappertit.

"Yes," he answered with a curious look, "I was there. Oh! yes certainly, I was there. He wouldn't have gone off half as comfortable without me. I had been with three or four of his family under the same circumstances. They were all fine fellows."

"They must have been fond of you," remarked Mr. Tappertit, looking at him sideways.

"I don't know that they was exactly fond of me," said Dennis, with a little hesitation, "but they all had me near 'em when they departed. I come in for their wardrobes too. This very handkecher that you see round my neck, belonged to him that I've been speaking of—him as did that likeness."

Mr. Tappertit glanced at the article referred to, and appeared to think that the deceased's ideas of dress were of a peculiar and by no means an expensive kind. He made no remark upon the point, however, and suffered his mysterious companion to proceed without interruption.

"These smalls," said Dennis, rubbing his legs; "these very smalls—they belonged to a friend of mine that's left off sich incumbrances for ever: this coat too—I've often walked behind this coat, in the street, and wondered whether it would ever come to me: this pair of shoes have danced a hornpipe for another man, afore my eyes, full half-a-dozen times at least: and as to my hat," he said, taking it off, and whirling it round upon his fist—"Lord! I've seen this hat go up Holborn on the box of a hackney-coach—ah, many and many a day!"

"You don't mean to say their old wearers are *all* dead, I hope?" said Mr. Tappertit, falling a little distance from him as he spoke.

"Every one of 'em," replied Dennis. "Every man Jack!"

There was something so very ghastly in this circumstance, and it appeared to account, in such a very strange and dismal manner, for his faded dress—which, in this new aspect, seemed discoloured by the earth from graves—that Mr. Tappertit abruptly found he was going another way, and, stopping short, bade him good night with the utmost heartiness. As they happened to be near the Old Bailey, and Mr. Dennis knew there were turnkeys in the lodge with whom he could pass the night, and discuss professional subjects of common interest among them before a rousing fire, and over a social glass, he separated from his companions without any great regret, and warmly shaking hands with Hugh, and making an early appointment for their meeting at The Boot, left them to pursue their road.

"That's a strange sort of man," said Mr. Tappertit, watching the hackney-coachman's hat as it went bobbing down the street. "I don't know what to make of him. Why can't he have his smalls made to order, or wear live clothes at any rate?"

"He's a lucky man, captain," cried Hugh. "I should like to have such friends as his."

"I hope he don't get 'em to make their wills, and then knock 'em on the head," said Mr. Tappertit, musing. "But come. The United B.'s expect me. On!—What's the matter?"

"I quite forgot," said Hugh, who had started at the striking of a neighbouring clock. "I have somebody to see to-night—I must turn back directly. The drinking and singing put it out of my head. It's well I remembered it!"

Mr. Tappertit looked at him as though he were about to give utterance to some very majestic sentiments in reference to this act of desertion, but as it was clear, from Hugh's hasty manner, that the engagement was one of a pressing nature, he graciously forbore, and gave him his permission to depart immediately, which Hugh acknowledged with a roar of laughter.

"Good night, captain!" he cried. "I am yours to the death, remember!"

"Farewell!" said Mr. Tappertit, waving his hand. "Be bold and vigilant!"

"No Popery, captain!" roared Hugh.

"England in blood first!" cried his desperate leader. Whereat Hugh cheered and laughed, and ran off like a greyhound.

"That man will prove a credit to my corps," said Simon, turning thoughtfully upon his heel. "And let me see. In an altered state of society—which must ensue if we break out and are victorious—when the locksmith's child is mine, Miggs must be got rid of somehow, or she'll poison the tea-kettle one evening when I'm out. He might marry Miggs, if he was drunk enough. It shall be done. I'll make a note of it."

CHAPTER XL

LITTLE thinking of the plan for his happy settlement in life which had suggested itself to the teeming brain of his provident commander, Hugh made no pause until Saint Dunstan's giants struck the hour above him, when he worked the handle of a pump which stood hard by, with great vigour, and thrusting his head under the spout, let the water gush upon him until a little stream ran down from every uncombed hair, and he was wet to the waist. Considerably refreshed by this ablution, both in mind and body, and almost sobered for the time, he dried himself as he best could; then crossed the road, and plied the knocker of the Middle Temple gate.

The night-porter looked through a small grating in the portal with a surly eye, and cried " Halloa ! " which greeting Hugh returned in kind, and bade him open quickly.

" We don't sell beer here," cried the man ; " what else do you want ?

" To come in," Hugh replied, with a kick at the door.

" Where to go ? "

" Paper Buildings."

" Whose chambers ? "

" Sir John Chester's." Each of which answers, he emphasised with another kick.

After a little growling on the other side, the gate was opened, and he passed in : undergoing a close inspection from the porter as he did so.

" *You* wanting Sir John, at this time of night!" said the man.

"Ay!" said Hugh. "I! What of that?"

"Why, I must go with you and see that you do, for I don't believe it."

"Come along then."

Eyeing him with suspicious looks, the man, with key and lantern, walked on at his side, and attended him to Sir John Chester's door, at which Hugh gave one knock, that echoed through the dark staircase like a ghostly summons, and made the dull light tremble in the drowsy lamp.

"Do you think he wants me now?" said Hugh.

Before the man had time to answer, a footstep was heard within, a light appeared, and Sir John, in his dressing-gown and slippers, opened the door.

"I ask your pardon, Sir John," said the porter, pulling off his hat. "Here's a young man says he wants to speak to you. It's late for strangers. I thought it best to see that all was right."

"Aha!" cried Sir John, raising his eyebrows. "It's you, messenger, is it? Go in. Quite right, friend, I commend your prudence highly. Thank you. God bless you. Good night."

To be commended, thanked, God-blessed, and bade good night by one who carried " Sir " before his name, and wrote himself M.P. to boot, was something for a porter. He withdrew with much humility and reverence. Sir John followed his late visitor into the dressing-room, and sitting in his easy-chair before the fire, and moving it so that he could see him as he stood, hat in hand, beside the door, looked at him from head to foot.

The old face, calm and pleasant as ever; the complexion, quite juvenile in its bloom and clearness; the same smile; the wonted precision and elegance of dress; the white, well-ordered teeth; the delicate hands; the composed and quiet manner; everything as it used to be: no mark of age or passion, envy, hate, or discontent: all unruffled and serene, and quite delightful to behold.

He wrote himself M.P.—but how? Why, thus. It was a proud family—more proud, indeed, than wealthy. He had stood in danger of arrest; of bailiffs, and a jail—a vulgar jail, to which the common people with small incomes went. Gentlemen of ancient houses have no privilege of exemption from such cruel laws—unless they are of one great house, and then they have. A proud man of his stock and kindred had the means of sending him there. He offered—not indeed to pay his debts, but to let him sit for a close borough until his own son came of age, which, if he lived, would come to pass in twenty years. It was quite as good as an Insolvent Act, and infinitely more genteel. So Sir John Chester was a member of Parliament.

But how Sir John? Nothing so simple, or so easy. One touch with a sword of state, and the transformation was effected. John Chester, Esquire, M.P., attended court—went up with an address — headed a deputation. Such elegance of manner, so many graces of deportment, such powers of conversation, could never pass unnoticed. Mr. was too common for such merit. A man so gentlemanly should have been — but Fortune is capricious — born a Duke: just as some dukes should have been born labourers. He caught the fancy of the king, knelt down a grub, and rose a butterfly. John Chester, Esquire, was knighted and became Sir John.

"I thought when you left me this evening, my esteemed acquaintance," said Sir John after a pretty long silence, " that you intended to return with all despatch?"

"So I did, master."

"And so you have?" he retorted, glancing at his watch. " Is that what you would say?"

Instead of replying, Hugh changed the leg on which he leant, shuffled his cap from one hand to the other, looked at the ground, the wall, the ceiling, and finally at Sir John himself; before whose pleasant face he lowered his eyes again, and fixed them on the floor.

"And how have you been employing yourself in the meanwhile?" quoth Sir John, lazily crossing his legs. "Where have you been? what harm have you been doing?"

"No harm at all, master," growled Hugh, with humility. "I have only done as you ordered."

"As I *what?*" returned Sir John.

"Well then," said Hugh uneasily, "as you advised, or said I ought, or said I might, or said that you would do, if you was me. Don't be so hard upon me, master."

Something like an expression of triumph in the perfect control he had established over this rough instrument appeared in the knight's face for an instant; but it vanished directly, as he said—paring his nails while speaking:

"When you say I ordered you, my good fellow, you imply that I directed you to do something for me—something I wanted done—something for my own ends and purposes—you see? Now I am sure I needn't enlarge upon the extreme absurdity of such an idea, however unintentional; so please "— and here he turned his eyes upon him—"to be more guarded. Will you?"

"I meant to give you no offence," said Hugh. "I don't know what to say. You catch me up so very short."

"You will be caught up much shorter, my good friend—infinitely shorter—one of these days, depend upon it," replied his patron calmly. "By-the-bye, instead of wondering why you have been so long, my wonder should be why you came at all. Why did you?"

"You know, master," said Hugh, "that I couldn't read the bill I found, and that supposing it to be something particular from the way it was wrapped up, I brought it here."

"And could you ask no one else to read it, Bruin?" said Sir John.

"No one that I could trust with secrets, master. Since Barnaby Rudge was lost sight of for good and all—and that's five years ago—I haven't talked with any one but you."

" You have done me honour I am sure."

" I have come to and fro, master, all through that time, when there was anything to tell, because I knew that you'd be angry with me if I stayed away," said Hugh, blurting the words out, after an embarrassed silence; "and because I wished to please you if I could, and not to have you go against me. There. That's the true reason why I came to-night. You know that, master, I am sure."

" You are a specious fellow," returned Sir John, fixing his eyes upon him, "and carry two faces under your hood, as well as the best. Didn't you give me in this room, this evening, any other reason; no dislike of anybody who has slighted you lately, on all occasions, abused you, treated you with rudeness; acted towards you, more as if you were a mongrel dog than a man like himself?"

" To be sure I did!" cried Hugh, his passion rising, as the other meant it should; "and I say it all over now, again. I'd do anything to have some revenge on him—anything. And when you told me that he and all the Catholics would suffer from those who joined together under that handbill, I said I'd make one of 'em, if their master was the devil himself. I *am* one of 'em. See whether I am as good as my word and turn out to be among the foremost, or no. I mayn't have much head, master, but I've head enough to remember those that use me ill. You shall see, and so shall he, and so shall hundreds more, how my spirit backs me when the time comes. My bark is nothing to my bite. Some that I know had better have a wild lion among them than me, when I am fairly loose—they had!"

The knight looked at him with a smile of far deeper meaning than ordinary; and pointing to the old cupboard, followed him with his eyes while he filled and drank a glass of liquor; and smiled when his back was turned, with deeper meaning yet.

"You are in a blustering mood, my friend," he said, when Hugh confronted him again.

"Not I, master!" cried Hugh. "I don't say half I mean. I can't. I haven't got the gift. There are talkers enough among us; I'll be one of the doers."

"Oh! you have joined those fellows then?" said Sir John, with an air of most profound indifference.

"Yes. I went up to the house you told me of, and got put down upon the muster. There was another man there named Dennis—"

"Dennis, eh!" cried Sir John, laughing. "Ay, ay! a pleasant fellow, I believe?"

"A roaring dog, master—one after my own heart—hot upon the matter too—red hot."

"So I have heard," replied Sir John, carelessly. "You don't happen to know his trade, do you?"

"He wouldn't say," cried Hugh. "He keeps it secret."

"Ha ha!" laughed Sir John. "A strange fancy—a weakness with some persons—you'll know it one day, I dare swear."

"We're intimate already," said Hugh.

"Quite natural! And have been drinking together, eh?" pursued Sir John. "Did you say what place you went to in company, when you left Lord George's?"

Hugh had not said or thought of saying, but he told him; and this inquiry being followed by a long train of questions, he related all that had passed both in and out of doors, the kind of people he had seen, their numbers, state of feeling, mode of conversation, apparent expectations and intentions. His questioning was so artfully contrived, that he seemed even in his own eyes to volunteer all this information rather than to have it wrested from him; and he was brought to this state of feeling so naturally, that when Mr. Chester yawned at length and declared himself quite wearied out, he made a rough kind of excuse for having talked so much.

"There—get you gone," said Sir John, holding the door open in his hand. "You have made a pretty evening's work.

I told you not to do this. You may get into trouble. You'll have an opportunity of revenging yourself on your proud friend Haredale, though, and for that, you'd hazard anything I suppose?"

"I would," retorted Hugh, stopping in his passage out and looking back; "but what do *I* risk! What do I stand a chance of losing, master? Friends, home? A fig for 'em all; I have none; they are nothing to me. Give me a good scuffle; let me pay off old scores in a bold riot where there are men to stand by me; and then use me as you like—it don't matter much to me what the end is!"

"What have you done with that paper?" said Sir John.

"I have it here, master."

"Drop it again as you go along; it's as well not to keep such things about you."

Hugh nodded, and touching his cap with an air of as much respect as he could summon up, departed.

Sir John, fastening the doors behind him, went back to his dressing-room, and sat down once again before the fire, at which he gazed for a long time, in earnest meditation.

"This happens fortunately," he said, breaking into a smile, "and promises well. Let me see. My relative and I, who are the most Protestant fellows in the world, give our worst wishes to the Roman Catholic cause; and to Saville, who introduces their bill, I have a personal objection besides; but as each of us has himself for the first article in his creed, we cannot commit ourselves by joining with a very extravagant madman, such as this Gordon most undoubtedly is. Now really, to foment his disturbances in secret, through the medium of such a very apt instrument as my savage friend here, may further our real ends; and to express at all becoming seasons, in moderate and polite terms, a disapprobation of his proceedings, though we agree with him in principle, will certainly be to gain a character for honesty and uprightness of purpose, which cannot fail to do us infinite service, and to raise us into some importance. Good! So much for public grounds. As to private considerations, I confess that if these vagabonds *would* make some riotous demonstration (which does not appear impossible), and *would* inflict some little chastisement on Haredale as a not inactive man among his sect, it would be extremely agreeable to my feelings, and would amuse me beyond measure. Good again! Perhaps better!"

When he came to this point, he took a pinch of snuff; then beginning slowly to undress, he resumed his meditations, by saying with a smile:

"I fear, I *do* fear exceedingly, that my friend is following fast in the footsteps of his mother. His intimacy with Mr. Dennis is very ominous. But I have no doubt he must have come to that end any way. If I lend him a helping hand, the only difference is, that he may, upon the whole, possibly drink a few gallons, or puncheons, or hogsheads, less in this life than he otherwise would. It's no business of mine. It's a matter of very small importance!"

So he took another pinch of snuff, and went to bed.

CHAPTER XLI

From the workshop of the Golden Key, there issued forth a
tinkling sound, so merry and good-humoured, that it suggested
the idea of some one working blithely, and made quite pleasant
music. No man who hammered on at a dull monotonous
duty, could have brought such cheerful notes from steel and
iron; none but a chirping, healthy, honest-hearted fellow, who
made the best of everything, and felt kindly towards everybody, could have done it for an instant. He might have
been a coppersmith, and still been musical. If he had sat in
a jolting waggon, full of rods of iron, it seemed as if he
would have brought some harmony out of it.

Tink, tink, tink—clear as a silver bell, and audible at every
pause of the streets' harsher noises, as though it said, "I don't
care; nothing puts me out; I am resolved to be happy."
Women scolded, children squalled, heavy carts went rumbling
by, horrible cries proceeded from the lungs of hawkers; still
it struck in again, no higher, no lower, no louder, no softer;
not thrusting itself on people's notice a bit the more for
having been outdone by louder sounds—tink, tink, tink, tink,
tink.

It was a perfect embodiment of the still small voice, free
from all cold, hoarseness, huskiness, or unhealthiness of any
kind; foot-passengers slackened their pace, and were disposed
to linger near it; neighbours who had got up splenetic that
morning, felt good-humour stealing on them as they heard

it, and by degrees became quite sprightly; mothers danced their babies to its ringing; still the same magical tink, tink, tink, came gaily from the workshop of the Golden Key.

Who but the locksmith could have made such music! A gleam of sun shining through the unsashed window, and chequering the dark workshop with a broad patch of light, fell full upon him, as though attracted by his sunny heart. There he stood working at his anvil, his face all radiant with exercise and gladness, his sleeves turned up, his wig pushed off his shining forehead—the easiest, freest, happiest man in all the world. Beside him sat a sleek cat, purring and winking in the light, and falling every now and then into an idle dose, as from excess of comfort. Toby looked on from a tall bench hard by; one beaming smile, from his broad nut-brown face down to the slack-baked buckles in his shoes. The very locks that hung around had something jovial in their rust, and seemed like gouty gentlemen of hearty natures, disposed to joke on their infirmities. There was nothing surly or severe in the whole scene. It seemed impossible that any one of the innumerable keys could fit a churlish strong-box or a prison-door. Cellars of beer and wine, rooms where there were fires, books, gossip, and cheering laughter—these were their proper sphere of action. Places of distrust and cruelty, and restraint, they would have left quadruple-locked for ever.

Tink, tink, tink. The locksmith paused at last, and wiped his brow. The silence roused the cat, who, jumping softly down, crept to the door, and watched with tiger eyes a bird-cage in an opposite window. Gabriel lifted Toby to his mouth, and took a hearty draught.

Then, as he stood upright, with his head flung back, and his portly chest thrown out, you would have seen that Gabriel's lower man was clothed in military gear. Glancing at the wall beyond, there might have been espied, hanging on their several pegs, a cap and feather, broad-sword, sash, and coat of scarlet; which any man learned in such matters would have known from their make and pattern to be the uniform of a serjeant in the Royal East London Volunteers.

As the locksmith put his mug down empty, on the bench whence it had smiled on him before, he glanced at these articles with a laughing eye, and looking at them with his head a little on one side, as though he would get them all into a focus, said, leaning on his hammer:

"Time was, now, I remember, when I was like to run mad with the desire to wear a coat of that colour. If any one (except my father) had called me a fool for my pains, how I should have fired and fumed! But what a fool I must have been, sure-ly!"

"Ah!" sighed Mrs. Varden, who had entered unobserved. "A fool indeed. A man at your time of life, Varden, should know better now."

"Why, what a ridiculous woman you are, Martha," said the locksmith, turning round with a smile.

"Certainly," replied Mrs. V. with great demureness. "Of course I am. I know that, Varden. Thank you."

"I mean——" began the locksmith.

"Yes," said his wife, "I know what you mean. You speak quite plain enough to be understood, Varden. It's very kind of you to adapt yourself to my capacity, I am sure."

"Tut, tut, Martha," rejoined the locksmith; "don't take offence at nothing. I mean, how strange it is of you to run down volunteering, when it's done to defend you and all the other women, and our own fireside and everybody else's, in case of need."

"It's unchristian," cried Mrs. Varden, shaking her head.

"Unchristian!" said the locksmith. "Why, what the devil——"

Mrs. Varden looked at the ceiling, as in expectation that the consequence of this profanity would be the immediate descent of the four-post bedstead on the second floor, together with the best sitting-room on the first; but no visible judgment occurring, she heaved a deep sigh, and begged her husband, in a tone of resignation, to go on, and by all means to blaspheme as much as possible, because he knew she liked it.

The locksmith did for a moment seem disposed to gratify her, but he gave a great gulp, and mildly rejoined:

"I was going to say, what on earth do you call it unchristian for? Which would be most unchristian, Martha —to sit quietly down and let our houses be sacked by a foreign army, or to turn out like men and drive em off? Shouldn't I be a nice sort of a Christian, if I crept into a corner of my own chimney and looked on while a parcel of whiskered savages bore off Dolly—or you?"

When he said "or you," Mrs. Varden, despite herself, relaxed into a smile. There was something complimentary in the idea. "In such a state of things as that, indeed—" she simpered.

"As that!" repeated the locksmith. "Well, that would be the state of things directly. Even Miggs would go. Some black tambourine-player, with a great turban on, would be bearing *her* off, and, unless the tambourine-player was proof against kicking and scratching, it's my belief he'd have the worst of it. Ha ha ha! I'd forgive the tambourine-player. I wouldn't have him interfered with on any account, poor fellow." And here the locksmith laughed again so heartily, that tears came into his eyes—much to Mrs. Varden's indignation, who thought the capture of so sound a Protestant and estimable a private character as Miggs by a pagan negro, a circumstance too shocking and awful for contemplation.

The picture Gabriel had drawn, indeed, threatened serious consequences, and would indubitably have led to them, but luckily at that moment a light footstep crossed the threshold, and Dolly, running in, threw her arms round her old father's neck and hugged him tight.

"Here she is at last!" cried Gabriel. "And how well you look, Doll, and how late you are, my darling!"

How well she looked? Well? Why, if he had exhausted

every laudatory adjective in the dictionary, it wouldn't have been praise enough. When and where was there ever such a plump, roguish, comely, bright-eyed, enticing, bewitching, captivating, maddening little puss in all this world, as Dolly! What was the Dolly of five years ago, to the Dolly of that day! How many coachmakers, saddlers, cabinet-makers, and professors of other useful arts, had deserted their fathers, mothers, sisters, brothers, and, most of all, their cousins, for the love of her! How many unknown gentlemen—supposed to be of mighty fortunes, if not titles—had waited round the corner after dark, and tempted Miggs the incorruptible, with golden guineas, to deliver offers of marriage folded up in love-letters! How many disconsolate fathers and substantial tradesmen had waited on the locksmith for the same purpose, with dismal tales of how their sons had lost their appetites, and taken to shut themselves up in dark bedrooms, and wandering in desolate suburbs with pale faces, and all because of Dolly Varden's loveliness and cruelty! How many young men, in all previous times of unprecedented steadiness, had turned suddenly wild and wicked for the same reason, and, in an ecstasy of unrequited love, taken to wrench off door-knockers, and invert the boxes of rheumatic watchmen! How had she recruited the king's service, both by sea and land, through rendering desperate his loving subjects between the ages of eighteen and twenty-five! How many young ladies had publicly professed, with tears in their eyes, that for their tastes she was much too short, too tall, too bold, too cold, too stout, too thin, too fair, too dark— too everything but handsome! How many old ladies, taking counsel together, had thanked Heaven their daughters were not like her, and had hoped she might come to no harm, and had thought she would come to no good, and had wondered what people saw in her, and had arrived at the conclusion that she was "going off" in her looks, or had never come on in them, and that she was a thorough imposition and a popular mistake!

And yet here was this same Dolly Varden, so whimsical and hard to please that she was Dolly Varden still, all smiles and dimples and pleasant looks, and caring no more for the fifty or sixty young fellows who at that very moment were breaking their hearts to marry her, than if so many oysters had been crossed in love and opened afterwards.

Dolly hugged her father as has been already stated, and having hugged her mother also, accompanied both into the little parlour where the cloth was already laid for dinner, and where Miss Miggs—a trifle more rigid and bony than of yore—received her with a sort of hysterical gasp, intended for a smile. Into the hands of that young virgin, she delivered her bonnet and walking dress (all of a dreadful, artful, and designing kind), and then said with a laugh, which rivalled the locksmith's music, "How glad I always am to be at home again!"

"And how glad we always are, Doll," said her father, putting back the dark hair from her sparkling eyes, "to have you at home. Give me a kiss."

If there had been anybody of the male kind there to see her do it—but there was not—it was a mercy.

"I don't like your being at the Warren," said the locksmith, "I can't bear to have you out of my sight. And what is the news over yonder, Doll?"

"What news there is, I think you know already," replied his daughter. "I am sure you do though."

"Ay?" cried the locksmith. "What's that?"

"Come, come," said Dolly, "you know very well. I want you to tell me why Mr. Haredale—eh, how gruff he is again, to be sure!—has been away from home for some days past, and why he is travelling about (we know he *is* travelling, because of his letters) without telling his own niece why or wherefore."

"Miss Emma doesn't want to know, I'll swear," returned the locksmith.

"I don't know that," said Dolly; "but *I* do, at any rate.

Do tell me. Why is he so secret, and what is this ghost story, which nobody is to tell Miss Emma, and which seems to be mixed up with his going away? Now I see you know by your colouring so."

"What the story means, or is, or has to do with it, I know no more than you, my dear," returned the locksmith, "except that it's some foolish fear of little Solomon's—which has, indeed, no meaning in it, I suppose. As to Mr. Haredale's journey, he goes, as I believe—"

"Yes," said Dolly.

"As I believe," resumed the locksmith, pinching her cheek, "on business, Doll. What it may be, is quite another matter. Read Blue Beard, and don't be too curious, pet; it's no business of yours or mine, depend upon that; and here's dinner, which is much more to the purpose."

Dolly might have remonstrated against this summary dismissal of the subject, notwithstanding the appearance of dinner, but at the mention of Blue Beard Mrs. Varden interposed, protesting she could not find it in her conscience to sit tamely by, and hear her child recommended to peruse the adventures of a Turk and Mussulman—far less of a fabulous Turk, which she considered that potentate to be. She held that, in such stirring and tremendous times as those in which they lived, it would be much more to the purpose if Dolly became a regular subscriber to the Thunderer, where she would have an opportunity of reading Lord George Gordon's speeches word for word, which would be a greater comfort and solace to her than a hundred and fifty Blue Beards ever could impart. She appealed in support of this proposition to Miss Miggs, then in waiting, who said that indeed the peace of mind she had derived from the perusal of that paper generally, but especially of one article of the very last week as ever was, entitled "Great Britain drenched in gore," exceeded all belief; the same composition, she added, had also wrought such a comforting effect on the mind of a married sister of hers, then resident at Golden Lion Court, number twenty-sivin, second bell-handle on the right-hand door-post, that, being in a delicate state of health, and in fact expecting an addition to her family, she had been seized with fits directly after its perusal, and had raved of the Inquisition ever since; to the great improvement of her husband and friends. Miss Miggs went on to say that she would recommend all those whose hearts were hardened to hear Lord George themselves, whom she commended first, in respect of his steady Protestantism, then of his oratory, then of his eyes, then of his nose, then of his legs, and lastly of his figure generally, which she looked upon as fit for any statue, prince, or angel, to which sentiment Mrs. Varden fully subscribed.

Mrs. Varden having cut in, looked at a box upon the mantel-shelf, painted in imitation of a very red-brick dwelling-house, with a yellow roof; having at top a real chimney, down which voluntary subscribers dropped their silver, gold, or pence, into the parlour; and on the door the counterfeit presentment of a brass plate, whereon was legibly inscribed "Protestant Association:"—and looking at it, said, that it was to her a source of poignant misery to think that Varden never had, of all his substance, dropped anything into that temple, save one in secret—as she afterwards discovered—two fragments of tobacco-pipe, which she hoped would not be put down to his last account. That Dolly, she was grieved to say, was no less backward in her contributions, better loving, as it seemed, to purchase ribbons and such gauds, than to encourage the great cause, then in such heavy tribulation; and that she did entreat her (her father she much feared could not be moved) not to despise, but imitate, the bright example of Miss Miggs, who flung her wages, as it were, into the very countenance of the Pope, and bruised his features with her quarter's money.

"Oh, mim," said Miggs, "don't relude to that. I had no intentions, mim, that nobody should know. Such sacrifices as I can make, are quite a widder's mite. It's all I have," cried Miggs with a great burst of tears—for with her they never came on by degrees—"but it's made up to me in other ways; it's well made up."

This was quite true, though not perhaps in the sense that Miggs intended. As she never failed to keep her self-denial full in Mrs. Varden's view, it drew forth so many gifts of caps and gowns and other articles of dress, that upon the whole the red-brick house was perhaps the best investment for her small capital she could possibly have hit upon; returning her interest, at the rate of seven or eight per cent. in money, and fifty at least in personal repute and credit.

"You needn't cry, Miggs," said Mrs. Varden, herself in tears; "you needn't be ashamed of it, though your poor mistress *is* on the same side."

Miggs howled at this remark, in a peculiarly dismal way, and said she knowed that master hated her. That it was a dreadful thing to live in families and have dislikes, and not give satisfactions. That to make divisions was a thing she could not abear to think of, neither could her feelings let her do it. That if it was master's wishes as she and him should part, it was best they should part, and she hoped he might be the happier for it, and always wishes him well, and that he might find somebody as would meet his dispositions. It would be a hard trial, she said, to part from such a missis, but she could meet any suffering when her conscience told her she was in the rights, and therefore she was willing even to go that lengths. She did not think, she added, that she could long survive the separations, but, as she was hated and looked upon unpleasant, perhaps her dying as soon as possible would be the best endings for all parties. With this affecting conclusion, Miss Miggs shed more tears, and sobbed abundantly.

"Can you bear this, Varden?" said his wife in a solemn voice, laying down her knife and fork.

"Why, not very well, my dear," rejoined the locksmith, "but I try to keep my temper."

"Don't let there be words on my account, mim," sobbed

Miggs. "It's much the best that we should part. I wouldn't stay—oh, gracious me!—and make dissensions, not for a annual gold mine, and found in tea and sugar."

Lest the reader should be at any loss to discover the cause of Miss Miggs's deep emotion, it may be whispered apart that, happening to be listening, as her custom sometimes was, when Gabriel and his wife conversed together, she had heard the locksmith's joke relative to the foreign black who played the tambourine, and bursting with the spiteful feelings which the taunt awoke in her fair breast, exploded in the manner we have witnessed. Matters having now arrived at a crisis, the locksmith, as usual, and for the sake of peace and quietness, gave in.

"What are you crying for, girl?" he said. "What's the matter with you? What are you talking about hatred for? *I* don't hate you; I don't hate anybody. Dry your eyes and make yourself agreeable, in Heaven's name, and let us all be happy while we can."

The allied powers deeming it good generalship to consider this a sufficient apology on the part of the enemy, and confession of having been in the wrong, did dry their eyes and take it in good part. Miss Miggs observed that she bore no malice, no not to her greatest foe, whom she rather loved the more indeed, the greater persecution she sustained. Mrs. Varden approved of this meek and forgiving spirit in high terms, and incidentally declared as a closing article of agreement, that Dolly should accompany her to the Clerkenwell branch of the association, that very night. This was an extraordinary instance of her great prudence and policy; having had this end in view from the first, and entertaining a secret misgiving that the locksmith (who was bold when Dolly was in question) would object, she had backed Miss Miggs up to this point, in order that she might have him at a disadvantage. The manœuvre succeeded so well that Gabriel only made a wry face, and with the warning he had just had, fresh in his mind, did not dare to say one word.

The difference ended, therefore, in Miggs being presented with a gown by Mrs. Varden and half-a-crown by Dolly, as if she had eminently distinguished herself in the paths of morality and goodness. Mrs. V., according to custom, expressed her hope that Varden would take a lesson from what had passed and learn more generous conduct for the time to come; and the dinner being now cold and nobody's appetite very much improved by what had passed, they went on with it, as Mrs. Varden said, "like Christians."

As there was to be a grand parade of the Royal East London Volunteers that afternoon, the locksmith did no more work; but sat down comfortably with his pipe in his mouth, and his arm round his pretty daughter's waist, looking lovingly on Mrs. V., from time to time, and exhibiting from the crown of his head to the sole of his foot, one smiling surface of good humour. And to be sure, when it was time to dress him in his regimentals, and Dolly, hanging about him in all kinds of graceful winning ways, helped to button and buckle and brush him up and get him into one of the tightest coats that ever was made by mortal tailor, he was the proudest father in all England.

"What a handy jade it is!" said the locksmith to Mrs. Varden, who stood by with folded hands—rather proud of her husband too—while Miggs held his cap and sword at arm's length, as if mistrusting that the latter might run some one through the body of its own accord; "but never marry a soldier, Doll, my dear."

Dolly didn't ask why not, or say a word, indeed, but stooped her head down very low to tie his sash.

"I never wear this dress," said honest Gabriel, "but I think of poor Joe Willet. I loved Joe; he was always a favourite of mine. Poor Joe!—Dear heart, my girl, don't tie me in so tight."

Dolly laughed—not like herself at all—the strangest little laugh that could be—and held her head down lower still.

"Poor Joe!" resumed the locksmith, muttering to himself;

417

"I always wish he had come to me. I might have made it up between them, if he had. Ah! old John made a great mistake in his way of acting by that lad—a great mistake. —Have you nearly tied that sash, my dear?"

What an ill-made sash it was! There it was, loose again and trailing on the ground. Dolly was obliged to kneel down, and recommence at the beginning.

DOLLY IN TEARS

"Never mind young Willet, Varden," said his wife, frowning; "you might find some one more deserving to talk about, I think."

Miss Miggs gave a great sniff to the same effect.

"Nay, Martha," cried the locksmith, "don't let us bear too hard upon him. If the lad is dead indeed, we'll deal kindly by his memory."

"A runaway and a vagabond!" said Mrs. Varden.

Miss Miggs expressed her concurrence as before.

"A runaway, my dear, but not a vagabond," returned the locksmith in a gentle tone. "He behaved himself well, did Joe—always—and was a handsome manly fellow. Don't call him a vagabond, Martha."

Mrs. Varden coughed—and so did Miggs.

"He tried hard to gain your good opinion, Martha, I can tell you," said the locksmith smiling, and stroking his chin. "Ah! that he did. It seems but yesterday that he followed me out to the Maypole door one night, and begged me not to say how like a boy they used him—say here, at home, he meant, though at the time, I recollect, I didn't understand. 'And how's Miss Dolly, sir?' says Joe," pursued the locksmith, musing sorrowfully. "Ah! Poor Joe!"

"Well, I declare," cried Miggs. "Oh! Goodness gracious me!"

"What's the matter now?" said Gabriel, turning sharply to her.

"Why, if here an't Miss Dolly," said the handmaid, stooping down to look into her face, "a-giving way to floods of tears. Oh, mim! oh, sir. Raly it's give me such a turn," cried the susceptible damsel, pressing her hand upon her side to quell the palpitation of her heart, "that you might knock me down with a feather."

The locksmith, after glancing at Miss Miggs as if he could have wished to have a feather brought straightway, looked on with a broad stare while Dolly hurried away, followed by that sympathising young woman: then turning to his wife,

419

stammered out, "Is Dolly ill? Have *I* done anything? Is it my fault?"

"Your fault!" cried Mrs. V. reproachfully. "There—you had better make haste out."

"What have I done?" said poor Gabriel. "It was agreed that Mr. Edward's name was never to be mentioned, and I have not spoken of him, have I?"

Mrs. Varden merely replied that she had no patience with him, and bounced off after the other two. The unfortunate locksmith wound his sash about him, girded on his sword, put on his cap, and walked out.

"I am not much of a dab at my exercise," he said under his breath, "but I shall get into fewer scrapes at that work than at this. Every man came into the world for something; my department seems to be to make every woman cry without meaning it. It's rather hard!"

But he forgot it before he reached the end of the street, and went on with a shining face, nodding to the neighbours, and showering about his friendly greetings like mild spring rain.

CHAPTER XLII

THE Royal East London Volunteers made a brilliant sight that day: formed into lines, squares, circles, triangles, and what not, to the beating of drums, and the streaming of flags; and performed a vast number of complex evolutions, in all of which Serjeant Varden bore a conspicuous share. Having displayed their military prowess to the utmost in these warlike shows, they marched in glittering order to the Chelsea Bun-house, and regaled in the adjacent taverns until dark. Then at sound of drum they fell in again, and returned amidst the shouting of His Majesty's lieges to the place from whence they came.

The homeward march being somewhat tardy,—owing to the un-soldierlike behaviour of certain corporals, who, being gentlemen of sedentary pursuits in private life and excitable out of doors, broke several windows with their bayonets, and rendered it imperative on the commanding officer to deliver them over to a strong guard, with whom they fought at intervals as they came along,—it was nine o'clock when the locksmith reached home. A hackney-coach was waiting near his door; and as he passed it, Mr. Haredale looked from the window and called him by his name.

"The sight of you is good for sore eyes, sir," said the locksmith, stepping up to him. "I wish you had walked in though, rather than waited here."

"There is nobody at home, I find," Mr. Haredale answered; "besides, I desired to be as private as I could."

"Humph!" muttered the locksmith, looking round at his house. "Gone with Simon Tappertit to that precious Branch, no doubt."

Mr. Haredale invited him to come into the coach, and, if he were not tired or anxious to go home, to ride with him a little way that they might have some talk together. Gabriel cheerfully complied, and the coachman mounting his box drove off.

"Varden," said Mr. Haredale, after a minute's pause, "you will be amazed to hear what errand I am on; it will seem a very strange one."

"I have no doubt it's a reasonable one, sir, and has a meaning in it," replied the locksmith; "or it would not be yours at all. Have you just come back to town, sir?"

"But half an hour ago."

"Bringing no news of Barnaby, or his mother?" said the locksmith dubiously. "Ah! you needn't shake your head, sir. It was a wild-goose chase. I feared that, from the first. You exhausted all reasonable means of discovery when they went away. To begin again after so long a time has passed is hopeless, sir—quite hopeless."

"Why, where are they?" he returned impatiently. "Where can they be? Above ground?"

"God knows," rejoined the locksmith, "many that I knew above it five years ago, have their beds under the grass now. And the world is a wide place. It's a hopeless attempt, sir, believe me. We must leave the discovery of this mystery, like all others, to time, and accident, and Heaven's pleasure."

"Varden, my good fellow," said Mr. Haredale, "I have a deeper meaning in my present anxiety to find them out, than you can fathom. It is not a mere whim; it is not the casual revival of my old wishes and desires; but an earnest, solemn purpose. My thoughts and dreams all tend to it, and fix it in my mind. I have no rest by day or night; I have no peace or quiet; I am haunted."

His voice was so altered from its usual tones, and his

manner bespoke so much emotion, that Gabriel, in his wonder, could only sit and look towards him in the darkness, and fancy the expression of his face.

"Do not ask me," continued Mr. Haredale, "to explain myself. If I were to do so, you would think me the victim of some hideous fancy. It is enough that this is so, and that I cannot—no, I can not—lie quietly in my bed, without doing what will seem to you incomprehensible."

"Since when, sir," said the locksmith after a pause, "has this uneasy feeling been upon you?"

Mr. Haredale hesitated for some moments, and then replied: "Since the night of the storm. In short, since the last nineteenth of March."

As though he feared that Varden might express surprise, or reason with him, he hastily went on:

"You will think, I know, I labour under some delusion. Perhaps I do. But it is not a morbid one; it is a wholesome action of the mind, reasoning on actual occurrences. You know the furniture remains in Mrs. Rudge's house, and that it has been shut up, by my orders, since she went away, save once a-week or so, when an old neighbour visits it to scare away the rats. I am on my way there now."

"For what purpose?" asked the locksmith.

"To pass the night there," he replied; "and not to-night alone, but many nights. This is a secret which I trust to you in case of any unexpected emergency. You will not come, unless in case of strong necessity, to me; from dusk to broad day I shall be there. Emma, your daughter, and the rest, suppose me out of London, as I have been until within this hour. Do not undeceive them. This is the errand I am bound upon. I know I may confide it to you, and I rely upon your questioning me no more at this time."

With that, as if to change the theme, he led the astounded locksmith back to the night of the Maypole highwayman, to the robbery of Edward Chester, to the reappearance of the man at Mrs. Rudge's house, and to all the strange circumstances which afterwards occurred. He even asked him carelessly about the man's height, his face, his figure, whether he was like any one he had ever seen—like Hugh, for instance, or any man he had known at any time—and put many questions of that sort, which the locksmith, considering them as mere devices to engage his attention and prevent his expressing the astonishment he felt, answered pretty much at random.

At length, they arrived at the corner of the street in which the house stood, where Mr. Haredale, alighting, dismissed the coach. "If you desire to see me safely lodged," he said, turning to the locksmith with a gloomy smile, "you can."

Gabriel, to whom all former marvels had been nothing in comparison with this, followed him along the narrow pavement in silence. When they reached the door, Mr. Haredale softly opened it with a key he had about him, and closing it when Varden entered, they were left in thorough darkness.

They groped their way into the ground-floor room. Here Mr. Haredale struck a light, and kindled a pocket taper he had brought with him for the purpose. It was then, when the flame was full upon him, that the locksmith saw for the first time how haggard, pale, and changed he looked; how worn and thin he was; how perfectly his whole appearance coincided with all that he had said so strangely as they rode along. It was not an unnatural impulse in Gabriel, after what he had heard, to note curiously the expression of his eyes. It was perfectly collected and rational;—so much so, indeed, that he felt ashamed of his momentary suspicion, and drooped his own when Mr. Haredale looked towards him, as if he feared they would betray his thoughts.

"Will you walk through the house?" said Mr. Haredale, with a glance towards the window, the crazy shutters of which were closed and fastened. "Speak low."

There was a kind of awe about the place, which would have rendered it difficult to speak in any other manner. Gabriel whispered "Yes," and followed him up-stairs.

Everything was just as they had seen it last. There was a sense of closeness from the exclusion of fresh air, and a gloom and heaviness around, as though long imprisonment had made the very silence sad. The homely hangings of the beds and windows had begun to droop; the dust lay thick upon their dwindling folds; and damps had made their way through ceiling, wall, and floor. The boards creaked beneath their tread, as if resenting the unaccustomed intrusion; nimble spiders, paralysed by the taper's glare, checked the motion of their hundred legs upon the wall, or dropped like lifeless things upon the ground; the death-watch ticked; and the scampering feet of rats and mice rattled behind the wainscot.

As they looked about them on the decaying furniture, it was strange to find how vividly it presented those to whom it had belonged, and with whom it was once familiar. Grip seemed to perch again upon his high-backed chair; Barnaby to crouch in his old favourite corner by the fire; the mother to resume her usual seat, and watch him as of old. Even when they could separate these objects from the phantoms of the mind which they invoked, the latter only glided out of sight, but lingered near them still; for then they seemed to lurk in closets and behind the doors, ready to start out and suddenly accost them in well-remembered tones.

They went down-stairs, and again into the room they had just now left. Mr. Haredale unbuckled his sword and laid it on the table, with a pair of pocket pistols; then told the locksmith he would light him to the door.

"But this is a dull place, sir," said Gabriel, lingering; "may no one share your watch?"

He shook his head, and so plainly evinced his wish to be alone, that Gabriel could say no more. In another moment the locksmith was standing in the street, whence he could see that the light once more travelled up-stairs, and soon returning to the room below, shone brightly through the chinks of the shutters.

If ever man were sorely puzzled and perplexed, the lock-smith was, that night. Even when snugly seated by his own fireside, with Mrs. Varden opposite in a night-cap and night-jacket, and Dolly beside him (in a most distracting dishabille) curling her hair, and smiling as if she had never cried in all her life and never could—even then, with Toby at his elbow and his pipe in his mouth, and Miggs (but that perhaps was not much) falling asleep in the background, he could not quite discard his wonder and uneasiness. So in his dreams—still there was Mr. Haredale, haggard and careworn, listening in the solitary house to every sound that stirred, with the taper shining through the chinks until the day should turn it pale and end his nightly watching.

NOTES ON BARNABY RUDGE

CHAPTER I

" In the year 1775."

Objections have been made, as by Poe, to the gap of five years in
the tale, between 1775 and 1780. That " general dovetailedness " of the
Unities may be infringed, but the gap was necessary, as Joe had to
acquire glory, and lose an arm, "in the Salwanners."

CHAPTER VII

" Miggs held the male sex to be utterly contemptible."

Miss Miggs's indictment against a whole sex is much the same as that
frequently presented by lady novelists who know all about men, and
gratify the curiosity of their less learned sisters. Men must decide
whether they are all in the right, or whether they are only spiritual
counterparts of the unenticing Miggs.

CHAPTER VIII

"If I had been born a . . . brigand, gen-teel highwayman or patriot
—and they're the same thing."

This reflection of Mr. Tappertit's is borne out by Hemingford,
the chronicler of the reign of Edward I. The Scottish patriot, Sir
William Wallace, is called *publicus latro* — a highwayman — by his
English contemporary.

CHAPTER XV

" Fair Fountain Court."

The fountain is sadly elaborated for the worse since Dickens wrote,
and, in Mr. Gargery's phrase, is distinctly "too architectooralooral."

NOTES ON BARNABY RUDGE

CHAPTER XXXV

Lord George Gordon.

This erratic person (1751–1793) was a younger son of Cosmo, third Duke of Gordon. The Cocks of the North had never been famous for personal good fortune or common sense. A strain of eccentricity was in the blood, and a famous lady married into this line is said to have reassured a hesitating suitor for her daughter's hand, by confessing that the girl "had not a drop of Gordon blood." Lord Lewie Gordon—

> "Send us Lewie Gordon hame,
> And the lad I daurna name"—

had a very severe cerebral attack when in exile after 1746. Lord George left the navy, in some disgust about promotion, and contested an election in the north with General Simon Frazer, the attainted but pardoned Master of Lovat. A seat was bought for him at Ludgershall, and, in 1779, he became president of a Protestant Association for repealing the removal of certain Catholic disabilities. His conduct in the Riots, if he really pointed out opponents to the fury of the mob (as Horace Walpole says), was worse than Dickens is inclined to allow. He was tried for high treason before Lord Mansfield (February, 1781), and of course, as Horace says, "the Constitution was sure to be brought in guilty." In 1786–7, he libelled Marie Antoinette, in a defence of that "honest man," Cagliostro; and in 1788 was sentenced to five years of imprisonment. He is said to have given balls in prison, and he died there on November 1, 1793, "after singing the Ça Ira." He had adopted the Jewish religion, and grown a long beard. His vanity approached, but did not actually involve, madness, and his love of freedom and the oppressed was tempered by a love of religious persecution. Walpole feared, despised, and, when Lord George was tried for his life, pitied him. He remarks that no single person of the slightest note perished in the Riots. Their real object was drink, plunder, and anarchy, and they need Swift's *Modest Apology for the Conduct of the Rabble in all Ages.*

Gashford.

From the description of Gashford's suicide in an obscure inn, he is certainly meant for Dr. Robert Watson, the adventurer, and biographer of Lord George. Born at an uncertain date, in Elgin, Watson was a conspirator from the cradle. Beginning with the American revolt, he was in every rising, it is said, till the Greek War of Independence. He was on the English side of the Revolutionary movement, and, flying to France, became Bonaparte's head of the Scots' College there. He went to Italy to grow indigo, during the continental blockade, but in this enterprise he failed. Marrying a relation of Lord Rollo, he acquired, and published with Messrs. Longmans, the amusing memoirs of the Chevalier Johnstone, *aide-de-camp* of Prince Charles, and of Montcalm. He also obtained, for a few pounds, the vast collection of the Stuart

NOTES ON BARNABY RUDGE

Papers, which mouldered in a Roman garret after the death of Henry IX. (Cardinal York). These were partly purchased, partly wrung from him, by the British Government. At an age well over eighty, he strangled himself in an obscure inn in London, carrying with him more secrets than most men. Scars of nineteen wounds were found on his battered old body. Dickens's description of his eyes and brow is not incorrect, judging from a portrait in the Edinburgh Museum. That Watson inspired the "Sobieski Stuarts" has been conjectured ; but, in that case, they would have known more about secret history than, judging by their books, they seem to have done. Some hints on the original of Gashford may be found in Mr. F. H. Groome's novel, *Kriegsspiel*, where Watson's portrait is engraved as a frontispiece. That Watson had, on occasion, been a spy is probable enough, but not certain. He is not known to have been a Catholic, like Gashford, but his early life, indeed most of his life, is obscure.

CHAPTER XL

" A close borough."

Lord George gained his seat in the same way as Mr. Chester.

*This book
designed by William B. Taylor
is a production of
Heron Books, London*

*The introduction to this book
was originally published for the
Oxford Illustrated Dickens,
published by
the Oxford University Press*

*Printed in England by
Hazell, Watson and Viney Limited
Aylesbury, Bucks*